THE GUILD CODEX: DEMONIZED / FOUR

DELIVERING EVIL
FOR EXPERTS

ANNETTE MARIE

dark owl
fantasy

Delivering Evil for Experts
The Guild Codex: Demonized / Book Four

Copyright © 2020 by Annette Marie
www.annettemarie.ca

Dark Owl Fantasy Inc.
PO Box 88106, Rabbit Hill Post Office
Edmonton, AB, Canada T6R 0M5
www.darkowlfantasy.com

Cover Copyright © 2020 by Annette Ahner
Cover and Book Interior by Midnight Whimsy Designs
www.midnightwhimsydesigns.com

Editing by Elizabeth Darkley
arrowheadediting.wordpress.com

ISBN 978-1-988153-51-3

MORE BOOKS BY ANNETTE MARIE

STEEL & STONE UNIVERSE

Steel & Stone Series

Chase the Dark

Bind the Soul

Yield the Night

Reap the Shadows

Unleash the Storm

Steel & Stone

Spell Weaver Trilogy

The Night Realm

The Shadow Weave

The Blood Curse

OTHER WORKS

Red Winter Trilogy

Red Winter

Dark Tempest

Immortal Fire

THE GUILD CODEX

CLASSES OF MAGIC

Spiritalis

Psychica

Arcana

Demonica

Elementaria

MYTHIC

A person with magical ability

MPD / MAGIPOL

The organization that regulates mythics and their activities

ROGUE

A mythic living in violation of MPD laws

DELIVERING EVIL
FOR EXPERTS

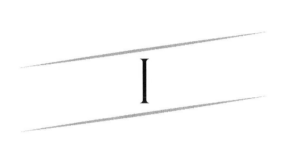

I

"THIS IS *zh'ūltis*."

I glared at Zylas. "Just be patient. All you have to do is stand still."

Positioned in front of him, I held a piece of black fabric to his shoulders, the seams glinting with pins. Behind the demon, Amalia muttered under her breath as she pinned what would become the hood of the garment to the back collar.

"Zylas!" she exclaimed. "Stop hitting me with your tail. I can't put pins in while you're whacking me."

His scowl deepened and his tail thudded to the floor, the barbed end twitching like an angry cat. Amalia rose on her tiptoes, checking the alignment of the hood piece, then nudged my fingers aside to add a few more pins.

"Okay. Gonna test it." She carefully lifted the hood and settled it on top of Zylas's head. "How's it look? Right size?"

I took a few steps back to give the demon a proper assessment. His crimson eyes glowed from beneath the hood, sharp with impatience. The garment looked like a hooded vest, but once finished, it would be a jacket—or so Amalia claimed. I was having trouble picturing it.

"Looks good to me," I said uncertainly.

She pulled the hood down to rest against his back. "I don't like how the side seam is sitting. Lift up the bottom so I can take measurements."

Zylas rumbled in the back of his throat, an exasperated half-growl that was more intimidating than it should've been.

Obediently, I slid the shirt's hem up—and my knuckles brushed against his sides, teasing across smooth, warm skin. My cheeks heated as I held the fabric halfway up his torso. Amalia looped her measuring tape around his waist, checked the number, then lowered it to his hips and pulled it tight.

"You're skinnier than I thought," she muttered. "You *look* so beefy and muscular, but you're a lightweight."

"*Ch*," was his unimpressed response.

I watched her adjust the measuring tape, ensuring it sat in the right spot just below the waistline of his dark, demonically fashionable shorts. My gaze drifted across his smooth, reddish-brown skin to his defined V line that disappeared beneath the fabric. I tried to jerk my eyes off him, but they snagged on his unfairly perfect abs.

"Move the fabric up more," Amalia instructed. "I need to measure his chest again."

"Wouldn't it be easier to take his measurements after you take this off him?" I asked, aiming to sound casual.

"Just do it."

Puffing out a breath, I slid the fabric up until it bunched under his arms. Amalia cinched the tape measure around his pectorals.

"Hmm. Zylas, take a deep breath and flex your muscles."

He grumbled—I picked up "*mailēshta*"—then inhaled, his chest expanding and muscles tightening. My blush intensified as Amalia calmly measured again. Did she even *notice* his physique? Were his flexing muscles and warm skin no different from a plastic mannequin to her?

"All right." She tossed the measuring tape into her sewing bag. "I just need to take in the side seams."

I lowered the fabric to its original position. "So the lining will be embroidered?"

"Yeah, it'll look like a normal jacket from the outside." She prodded Zylas's arm until he lifted it out of the way, then crouched beside him. "This one will be more durable than the last set I made him, and since it doesn't need to fit over his armor, I can make it look more normal."

The armor issue had originated with his shoulder plates, but they were no longer a problem. The *īnkav* had shattered them, and even if Zylas could've repaired them, we'd had neither time nor opportunity to collect the broken pieces.

"Done," Amalia declared, startling me out of my thoughts. "Help me slide this off him. Zylas, put your arms up."

He lifted his arms, and Amalia and I tugged the pin-lined garment over his head. She held the incomplete jacket up, squinting critically, then grabbed her sewing bag and headed for her bedroom.

"He's all yours, Robin," she called distractedly.

She disappeared through the door, missing the way my face had blanched at her words. I gulped, telling myself to get a grip.

"*Vayanin.*"

I turned toward Zylas, now shirtless with soft light washing over his bare skin and impossibly perfect musculature.

He peered at me, his face unreadable, and I tensed in anxious anticipation, waiting for the gavel to fall. How much of my inner dialogue had he picked up on? Had he noticed me ogling him? Was he about to—

"Where are my cookies?"

His—oh. Amalia and I had bribed him into participating in the garment fitting by promising a new type of cookie. I was supposed to feed him now.

That's what Amalia meant when she'd said he was all mine.

"Right," I squeaked, spinning on my heel. I zoomed into the kitchen where a bag of chocolate chips waited. I measured out a cup and stuck them in the microwave, then faced the counter where a dozen cookies cooled on a rack, their golden-brown tops capped with white blobs of marshmallow.

I alternated between melting the chocolate chips, which needed stirring every thirty seconds, and arranging the cookies on a piece of parchment paper. The familiar, mundane movements calmed my jitters, and I hummed as I mixed a tablespoon of shortening into the melted chocolate to smooth it out.

The aroma made my mouth water as I drizzled chocolate in zigzags across the cookie tops, then sprinkled them with crumbled walnuts. Smiling at the cute, delicious desserts, I washed out the measuring cup and tidied the counters.

When the chocolate had cooled, I stacked the cookies on a plate and ventured out of the safe kitchen.

Zylas had retreated to the far end of the sofa, his elbow propped on his knee and chin on his palm. Watching me.

All my anxiety came flooding right back.

I set the plate on the end table beside him. "These are called rocky road cookies."

"*Rocky road*? Why?" He picked up a cookie and squinted at the chocolate-drizzled marshmallow on top. "How is this a road?"

"I ... I'm not sure, actually. That's just what it's called." Now that he mentioned it, the name was kind of odd. I made a mental note to look it up later.

He gave the cookie a quick examination, then bit it in half. The sight of his white canines made my stomach drop strangely.

After a few cursory chews, he swallowed. "Part of it ... it is soft."

"That's the marshmallow." I tugged self-consciously on the sleeve of my sweater. "Do you like it?"

In answer, he tossed the rest of the cookie in his mouth. I relaxed. Why did I always worry about him liking my baking even though he'd devoured every single thing I'd ever made him?

He picked up a second cookie. His tail twitched as he studied it, then his gaze flicked to my face—or was he looking at my mouth?

Panic shot through me and I reeled backward. "I'm going to work on the grimoire!"

My feet scooted swiftly across the carpet, then I was safely in my bedroom.

Sprawled across my pillow, Socks lifted her head, her ears perked toward me. She blinked her huge green eyes as I stopped beside the bed, my heart racing uncomfortably.

Memories flitted through me. Of placing a bite of strawberry against Zylas's lips. Of his lips on my skin. Of his mouth brushing across mine. I couldn't stop thinking about it. The mere *sight* of his predatory canines had triggered a visceral recollection of what they'd felt like against my skin.

I pressed both hands to my face, breathing deep, then crouched and slid a flat metal case from beneath my bed. I whispered the incantation and flipped the lid open. The Athanas grimoire waited in its nest of brown paper with my notebook.

I lifted the latter out and flipped it to a completed translation.

> I have stood before a demon of another world and wondered that which no woman should ever wonder. I have yearned for that which no woman should ever claim. I have laid my hands upon that which no woman should ever touch.

My throat bobbed as I swallowed. Like Myrrine, my ancestor who'd added her story to the grimoire thousands of years ago, I too had stood before a demon and wondered things a woman shouldn't wonder. I'd longed for a demon. I'd touched a demon. I'd *kissed* a demon.

I could forgive myself for getting caught up in the moment. Zylas had just revealed he'd been protecting me all this time simply because he'd promised, not because our contract forced him to. I'd been emotional and overwhelmed. I hadn't been thinking straight.

That excuse no longer applied.

Myrrine had accepted her feelings for her demon, but she'd lived in a different time. I lived in a world where demons were considered brutal killers too violent for anything but enslavement as a contractor's tool. Zylas was neither a slave nor a tool nor a heartless monster—but he *was* a brutal killer.

I bit the inside of my cheek. Not only was I in a complete tailspin over our kiss, but I couldn't talk to anyone about it. Sharing my confusion with Zylas wouldn't help either of us, and confiding in Amalia was out of the question.

That had left me in the same spot for the past four days: caught in an unending spiral of doubt. Every time I convinced myself this attraction between me and Zylas was worth exploring, panic would set in that I was making a terrible mistake. But when I tried to convince myself it could never happen again, my reasons seemed so flimsy.

Exhaling, I stacked the grimoire on my pile of reference texts and headed back to the living room.

Zylas was sprawled across the sofa, eyes closed. Three of the dozen cookies remained on the plate, but he'd eaten his fill.

He opened one eye as I sank down to sit on the floor between the sofa and coffee table, my back against the cushions. His tail was draped off the seat beside me, the barbs on the end gleaming faintly. I arranged my books and pen, then opened the grimoire to the page where Anthea had begun her first experiments in Arcana Fenestram—portal magic.

Though I could feel his gaze on me, Zylas said nothing.

I squinted at the complex notation spread across the grimoire page, then flipped the aging paper until I found one of Myrrine's journal entries. Why hadn't she written more about her relationship with her demon?

The ancient sorceress lingered stubbornly in my thoughts as I mindlessly turned pages. What I wouldn't give to be able to jump back in time and speak with her. What answers could she offer about the mysterious workings of the demonic mind?

I stole a glance over my shoulder. Zylas's eyes were closed again, his breathing slow. Black hair tangled across his forehead, the small horns that marked him as a young adult in demon years poking through the messy locks.

My gaze traveled along his jawline, then down the column of his throat to the shadows of tendons that ran to the inner dip of his collarbones. His hard pectorals met those defined abdominals that I could never ignore ... and that enticing V shape.

I'd touched every inch of his back while massaging his tight muscles after an intensive healing, but his front ... somehow that was more intimate. More suggestive. More forbidden.

My hand crept upward. How deeply asleep was he? Large doses of sugar made him drowsy but he was never completely comatose.

I touched his inner forearm. The muscles beneath my fingertips tensed as he inhaled, his eyelids fluttering—and a swirl of emotion danced through my head, thoughts and feelings that weren't mine.

A vision of burnt-red sand, dotted with jagged rocks, surrounding a hidden valley among the dunes. Dwellings of chiseled stone at the valley's base. The sun's rays flaring on the horizon. A cold, teasing wind that carried a gritty scent tinged with an iron tang.

Pashir. Ahlēavah. Home.

Flickering. A twist of longing. Swirling memory, then a nightscape of dark buildings and brightly lit streets. A glowing window, beckoning. Slipping through long drapes, soft carpet underfoot. A quiet bed, covers pulled up over a sleeping body, dark hair spilling across a white pillow.

Foreign. Strange. Hh'ainun.

A slash of denial. Icy trepidation. The dark room deepened into black night. A concrete platform, glowing with lines and runes and surrounded by salty water. A ring in the center, the night sky of another world calling.

Go!

What are you waiting for?

Isn't this what you want?

The sound of my own raised voice hit me like a slap to the face and I recoiled, my fingers digging into his arm.

His eyes opened all the way, dim with drowsiness. "*Vayanin?*"

I stared at him, my lungs frozen as the fragments of his thoughts and memories slipped away—but I couldn't unhear my voice as he'd heard it. Those harsh, angry, desperate shouts ... was that what I'd sounded like when I'd told him to go through the portal?

When I merely stared at him, saying nothing, he squinted briefly, then closed his eyes again, too sleepy for the mysteries of a *hh'ainun* female.

Disquiet simmered in my chest as I robotically faced the grimoire and gazed sightlessly at the open book. I'd felt his longing and denial, but which of those memories did he long for and what was he denying?

As the question churned in my mind, the pages in front of me came into focus, the complex notation in cluttered Ancient Greek letters sinking into my distracted brain.

I leaned closer to the page. "Zylas?"

"*Var?*" he muttered unenthusiastically.

"Look at this."

He sat up and leaned forward, his face appearing beside mine, chin brushing my shoulder. He gazed down at the grimoire.

"*Hashē*," he breathed, his irritation forgotten. "You found it."

If I hadn't just revisited the array through his eidetic memory, I might not have recognized it. But the spell laid out across the ancient paper matched his recollection almost perfectly.

My hands curled into fists. "The portal spell."

2

THE PORTAL SPELL was the most dangerous Arcana array in the world. Maybe the most destructive Arcana array in history. It was the spell that had brought about the creation of Demonica—and enabled humankind's enslavement of the demon race, triggering the slow decay of their society.

"This," I said, pointing at the oversized sheet of brown paper upon which I'd traced out a large spell, "is the array Saul and his creepy twin sons used to open the portal four nights ago. Or as close as I could draw it."

I'd drawn it using Zylas's memory as my reference. It'd taken some practice to get the telepathic memory sharing thing to work, but if he focused, I could see the same thing as him.

Amalia, crouched beside me, studied the sketch.

"This," I continued, indicating a second large sheet, "is the final version of the spell from the grimoire—or I think it's the final one. It didn't have any corrections on it. Melitta wrote in her journal entry that she'd copied all the final spells into the back of the book. Claude stole those pages, but the original versions should be in the grimoire somewhere."

Amalia looked between the two arrays. "These aren't exactly the same."

I nodded. "Anthea's version is missing pieces. Saul and his sons filled in the pieces with their own Arcana, but as we know, their fix wasn't perfect."

The portal had opened, yes, but as soon as something had attempted to pass through, the magic had collapsed. I wasn't complaining, though, seeing as that "something" had been a bloodthirsty monster from the demon world that'd nearly killed Zylas.

I shivered at the memory of him lying on the helipad, his shoulder crushed and chest pierced by the *īnkav*'s horrific crisscrossing teeth.

"What does Claude want the portal for?" Amalia asked. "That's the big question here. Why does he need a direct doorway into the demon world?"

"*Ahlēavah.*"

She cast me a sideways look. "Huh?"

"*Ahlēavah.* That's what Zylas calls his home … I think." Though he'd never explained it, I'd picked up the word from his thoughts. "I'm not sure if it means a specific spot or an area or territory or what."

"*Ah-lee-ah-vah,*" Amalia sounded out. "That's … surprisingly pretty. Not what I expected."

She glanced around, probably hoping for more information, but Zylas had wandered into my bedroom for some peace and quiet after hours spent picturing the same array nonstop so I could draw it out. Too *taridis* for him. Very *mailēshta*, he'd complained.

"Anyway," Amalia continued, "Claude didn't even show up when Saul opened the portal. Does he actually care?"

"I think he was busy dealing with that 'court' thing. He planned to be waiting for someone."

"The thing Ezra got all worked up about." She nodded. "Well, you'll get answers about that in a few hours, won't you?"

Apprehension danced along my spine at the reminder. Ezra had texted me three days ago that we needed to meet ASAP to "trade," but I'd been busy preparing my report for the MPD—explaining the helipad incident without mentioning portals or monsters—and it'd taken longer than expected to schedule a rendezvous with him.

"Maybe he'll tell us, maybe not," I said. "He's not always forthcoming with information, is he? He wants answers about the Vh'alyir Amulet so he can separate from Eterran, but we don't know how it works."

"We know it's got three spells in it," Amalia clarified. "One is abjuration and is probably the 'power' Ezra described that interrupts demon contracts. One is super demonic looking. And one is Arcana Fenestram."

"Portal magic."

"Probably *the* portal magic. For opening a dimensional doorway into hell, which we'll need to send Zylas home. Won't *that* be fun?"

"Yeah," I mumbled.

She cast me a sidelong glance, then leaned closer and lowered her voice. "Are you choked up about him leaving?"

"I … I'm not …" I trailed off, ducking my head.

"Robin," she sighed. "I get that you've got a soft spot for that horned asshole … I do too, I guess … but he needs to go. Every day you're in an illegal contract puts your life at risk. You can't fake it forever."

"I know," I whispered.

"Just imagine how happy he'll be back in his world, running through demon meadows and picking fights with other demons and whatever else demons like to do."

Forcing a chuckle, I steered the conversation away from that topic. "Back to Claude, do you think he wants a portal so he can … go to the demon world?"

"If he did, he'd probably die in five minutes, which would solve a lot of our problems." She grimaced. "He can't be that stupid. He wants something else. I think he wants something *from* Demon Land."

"Like what? A demon army?"

"But how would he control demons without contracts?"

I shook my head in frustration. Why did we always have more questions than answers?

I tapped the array from the grimoire. "Well, we know a few things about this spell, at least. It needs to be built in the open air, under moonlight. And"—I arched an eyebrow—"I might know why Saul's version didn't work."

"Oh?"

I slid the grimoire over and flipped backward a few pages to one of Anthea's brief notes on an earlier iteration of the spell. "See this? She's talking about the minimum length of the central lineation of the array."

Though tempted, I didn't stop to complain about the amount of time it'd taken me to connect the Ancient Greek terminology with the modern-day Arcana jargon.

"On this page, she crossed out '*treiskaideka*,' which means thirteen, and wrote in '*oktokaideka*'—eighteen. But here ..." I flipped forward to the final iteration. "It says '*treiskaideka*' again."

"You mean it got copied wrong?"

"I think so. One of the previous scribes accidentally copied the original measurement instead of the correction. It changes the scope of the entire array."

"Then the portal on the helipad was too small?"

I nodded. "Significantly too small. That might be why it broke apart when something tried to pass through. It couldn't handle the arcane energies, like too much power in an electrical circuit."

"Well, shit. So if Claude wants to try the portal again, he'll need a location that's even larger."

"Yep."

"That'll be interesting. Maybe Ezra will spill some details on what Claude is up to. Or if we're lucky, he already killed Claude."

I didn't get my hopes up for that. If Ezra had defeated Nazhivēr, he would've told us by now.

Pushing to my feet, I scooped the papers together, collected the grimoire and my notebook, and headed into my bedroom to put everything away. The room was dark, the only light leaking in from the streetlamp outside the window. Night had fallen while Amalia and I had been reviewing the spell array.

Twin spots of crimson appeared—Zylas's glowing eyes. He was reclined across my bed, Socks lying on his stomach.

"Ready for the meeting?" I asked him as I set the grimoire in its case.

"*Hnn.* A trade with *Eterran et Dh'irath.*" His white teeth flashed, but it wasn't a smile. "He healed me."

"He did," I whispered, trying not to think about how close Zylas had come to death.

He mused in silence, then rubbed his palm over Socks's head, flattening her ears. She purred at top volume, ecstatic as always for any attention from her favorite demon.

Snapping the metal case shut on the grimoire and my notes, I slid it under the bed. "Zylas, do you trust Eterran?"

"No." His eyes gleamed. "Vh'alyir never trusts Dh'irath."

His answer didn't surprise me, but it didn't inspire confidence either. Whatever the powerful Second House *Dīnen* wanted, it would be dangerous for me and Zylas both.

WHEN EZRA had said we should meet "in private," this wasn't what I'd expected.

I nervously studied the night-swathed park where, what felt like a lifetime ago, Zylas and I had chased down Tahēsh. The surrounding streetlamps cast an orange haze across the winter grass of the park, interrupted in one corner by a dark grove of mature trees.

It unnerved me that Ezra had chosen this spot, where the First House demon had died, as the location of our meeting … and our trade.

Tugging my jacket tighter around me, I glanced from Amalia, who was squinting around suspiciously, to Zylas, who stood on my other side. He was back in his armor—chest plate over his heart, bracer on his left forearm, and greaves protecting his lower legs—but his shoulder looked oddly bare without the matching shoulder plates.

Without shifting his attention off the grove, he bared his teeth. "They are here."

I nodded. "Let's go."

The dark trees loomed as we approached. Zylas's feet were silent on the grass while Amalia and I crunched across dead leaves. I hesitated as we reached the prickly bushes, wondering how we were supposed to get through.

Zylas pointed. A few yards away, a narrow trail led into the trees.

The demon's softly glowing eyes caught mine, and a faint murmur of warning ran between us, so subtle I wasn't sure if I was hearing his silent thoughts or if it was just my imagination. Then he turned and slunk away in the opposite direction, circling the grove.

Pushing my shoulders back, I strode toward the path. Amalia followed, unusually silent and probably regretting her last-minute decision to come along. She usually left the dangerous stuff to me and Zylas.

This *shouldn't* be dangerous … but I wasn't letting my guard down.

Darkness enveloped us, the dense branches of coniferous trees dimming the glow of the streetlamps. I slowed my steps, letting my eyes adjust to the low light. A cold breeze rushed through the trees, stirring the branches, and I shivered.

The underbrush crowded in, branches scraping over the sleeves of my jacket, then the grove opened into a small, hidden clearing.

Ezra stood in the center, waiting—and he wasn't alone.

With her curly red hair tied in a ponytail and tight leather pants clinging to her long legs, Tori radiated rough, tough coolness. And on Ezra's other side, his mage friend Aaron had his arms folded, the breadth of his shoulders warning of strength. A powerful pyromage and one of the Crow and Hammer's top combat mythics, he wasn't a man to underestimate.

I clenched my jaw. When Zylas had said "they" were here, I'd thought he meant Ezra and Eterran.

You could've been clearer, I complained silently.

A flicker of amusement echoed back to me, and I knew Zylas was somewhere nearby, watching. A faint view of the clearing from a different angle reached me—somewhere high, the demon's gaze on the three mythics' backs.

"You're late," Ezra murmured.

Not for lack of trying, but it was impossible to rush Amalia.

Inching into the clearing, I gave Tori and Aaron another searching glance, wondering why they were with him. Witnesses? Backup? Part of the trade?

"Why are we meeting here?" I asked cautiously.

Ezra twitched his shoulders in a light shrug. "Some of us prefer open spaces and room to maneuver."

In other words, Eterran and Zylas might need space to do battle. And I didn't like *that* at all.

"I see." Folding my cold hands together, I locked my gaze on the demon mage. "We're ready to hear your trade."

Ezra met my intent stare without flinching, then gestured at Tori. She slid a cloth bag off her shoulder and handed it to him. I frowned as he withdrew an oversized book, the black leather cover gleaming faintly.

He weighed the book in his hand, his expression as unreadable as a stone statue. "Robin, it turns out we share an enemy ... except I know him as Xever."

My breath caught. A common enemy. That could only mean one person: Claude.

A faint sheen of red washed through Ezra's pale left iris. He stretched his arm out, offering the book.

No, not a book. A *grimoire*.

"This belongs to him."

I stepped closer, my movements slow and heart pounding. Claude's grimoire? It couldn't be ... could it? My fingers closed around the cool leather, the cover embossed with an unfamiliar symbol: a three-pointed crown inside a circle.

Gripping the book tightly, I asked, "This is what you want to trade?"

"No, not that. Tori?"

He turned expectantly toward the redhead, and her gaze darted from him to me, her brow creased. She hesitated, lips parting as though to speak, then shoved her hand into her pocket.

She lifted a fine chain out. Its length slid from her pocket, then a flat disc came free, dark metal that absorbed light more than reflected it. For an instant, I thought it was an infernus.

Then shock vibrated through me—Zylas's shock.

A sliver of light from beyond the trees caught on the swinging medallion, shining across the Vh'alyir emblem at its center.

"The amulet." The words escaped me in a breathless whisper. "Vh'alyir's Amulet."

The lost relic of Zylas's House. The artifact that held the secrets to opening a portal to hell. The key to everything.

Ezra's stare bored into me. "*That* is what we're here to trade."

3

EZRA'S WORDS took a moment to penetrate my brain. They might've taken even longer if I hadn't felt the sharp snap of Zylas's wariness.

Ezra had the amulet. He'd found it. When? How?

My first thought was that he'd acquired it as part of the urgent task he'd run off to complete a few nights ago—but then I remembered the battle that had taken place in this very park almost four months ago. Ezra, Tori, Aaron, and Kai had faced off against Tahēsh, the amulet's previous owner.

After the battle and the demon's death, the amulet had gone missing. Zylas and I had even searched the park for it.

Ezra—or one of his friends—had taken it. He'd already possessed it when he'd approached me in search of information about its magic. He'd even said, *I won't let him—or rather, us— anywhere near that amulet until I understand exactly what will happen.*

How carefully he'd skirted around lies that Zylas would have detected. He'd admitted that Tahēsh had tried to give him the amulet, and I still hadn't guessed he was already in possession of it.

I pulled myself together. "And what do you want in exchange?"

He pointed at the book I held. "I want you to use that grimoire and find a way to break the demon mage contract binding me and Eterran so he can leave my body."

Use the grimoire? Wasn't that the point of the *amulet*—to break the contract magic? How would this grimoire help?

"She *knows?*"

I started at Tori's sudden shriek. The redhead whirled on Ezra, the amulet hanging from her fist and disbelief splashed across her face.

Snorting under her breath, Amalia cocked her hip. "Well, duh."

"Since when?" Tori demanded.

With a flash of crimson across Ezra's left eye, Eterran answered, "Since you went to Enright, leaving Ezra and me to find out what she knew about the amulet."

The way Tori backpedaled from the demon's growling tones and guttural accent told me she wasn't used to Ezra and the demon swapping control. Even Aaron retreated a couple steps.

Eterran pivoted to me and Amalia. "We have made our offer. Will you accept it, or will we finally spill each other's blood, Zylas?"

I tensed. For a moment, no one moved, eerie silence descending on the grove—then Zylas's quiet laughter shivered through the night.

Tori and Aaron spun around, searching the trees for the source. Eterran turned more slowly, his gaze already angled up toward the tree branches.

Zylas's eyes glowed, two spots of crimson in the darkness. "Escaping your *hh'ainun* prison does not mean escaping the *hh'ainun* world, Eterran."

A tree branch rustled, then Zylas dropped to the ground, landing in a crouch only a few feet away from Tori. As he rose to his full height, she lurched backward. Zylas followed, smiling viciously.

Tori had seen Zylas behave like a puppet, but now she was seeing the truth—and my demon was enjoying every second of it.

She backed into Ezra, and he put a comforting hand on her waist. "Tori, Aaron, meet Zylas."

Zylas widened his grin, flashing his pointed canines. Tori didn't seem soothed by the introduction, her trembling inhalations loud in the quiet clearing. I remembered the overwhelming fear I'd felt the first time I'd realized how easily Zylas could kill me—that foolish moment when I'd first touched him through the summoning circle's barrier and he'd grabbed my hand.

As he loomed over Tori like a nightmare specter, I sighed. "Zylas, could you *try* not to terrify her?"

His irritation buzzed through me. Reluctantly, he stepped back. "No fun. When do I get to scare *hh'ainun*, *na*? Never."

I rolled my eyes. "At least you don't have to pretend to be enslaved right now."

He snapped his tail against the ground and Tori flinched. She took a couple of deep breaths, and a few paces away, Aaron slowly released the hilt of the sword jutting up from behind his shoulder.

The crimson glow in Ezra's left eye brightened. "Well? Do you accept the trade, Zylas?"

Right, the trade. *Zylas, what should we do?*

He studied Eterran with narrowed eyes.

We needed that amulet, but in exchange for it, Ezra and Eterran were asking for the impossible. Separate a demon from his demon-mage host? Save them from the madness and violent death that was their inevitable fate? How was I supposed to do that?

Assuming it was possible, we'd have to set everything else aside to focus on that task first; Ezra's clock was ticking. Finding the answer could take weeks or even months. Did we dare delay our efforts to find Claude? Did we want to involve ourselves even further with the demon mage, whose existence was more illegal than my contract with Zylas?

My attention drifted to Zylas's left side, where a layer of fabric and leather crossed his shoulder, the buckles for the armor plates empty.

Letting out a noiseless breath, I walked past the demon mage and Tori to stand beside Zylas.

I think we should accept, I told him silently, the grimoire cradled under my arm.

Amulet or no amulet, Ezra and Eterran had saved Zylas. They'd rushed back to us, fresh from their own battle, and without hesitation had expended a huge amount of magic to heal Zylas's mortal wounds.

Maybe they'd only done that because they wanted Zylas alive and able to trade, but it didn't change the outcome: they'd saved his life.

And now Ezra and Eterran were asking me to save theirs.

Zylas's attention swung back to the demon mage. "One condition, Dh'irath."

"What is that?"

"When you are free, you will bring no harm on me or my *hh'ainun*."

I blinked. The demon language didn't have plural markers as far as I could tell, so I didn't know if he meant one human or multiple humans.

Pushing Tori out of his way, Eterran stepped closer to Zylas and extended his left hand.

Magic lit up his fingers and raced up his arm in twisting veins. In response, Zylas stretched his arm out. Crimson power blazed across his hand and wrist, the red glow washing over the dark trees. The eerie scarlet haze stole all the color from Aaron's and Tori's faces, highlighting their alarm at the realization that Zylas could wield magic.

Demon and demon mage pressed their palms together, and the magic surging over their hands crackled dangerously. As the temperature around them dropped, I waited for one or both to create a spell circle.

Instead, their power tangled between their hands, twisting but not mixing.

Zylas stared into the demon mage's eyes. "*Enpedēra dīn nā.*"

"*Enpedēra dīn nā,*" Eterran rumbled in response.

The spell, whatever it was, faded and darkness closed in again. I exhaled in a rush. Tori's expression was anxious, while Aaron and Amalia observed the drama from the sidelines.

Zylas extended his hand toward the redhead. "Give it to me, *hh'ainun.*"

Clutching the amulet against her chest, she looked at Ezra for instructions.

He smiled faintly. "It's okay. You can give it to him."

"But he's …"

"It belongs to him, Tori. *Zylas et Vh'alyir*, King of the Twelfth House. The Amulet of Vh'alyir is his."

Surprise widened Tori's eyes all over again and she glanced at me, probably wondering if that's why I'd been searching for information on the amulet. Or maybe she hesitated because she knew about the amulet's power to interrupt demon contracts.

Offering Tori a small smile, I nodded my permission. She didn't need to worry. The amulet couldn't interrupt my contract with Zylas because he was immune to contract magic.

With a final glance at the etched face of the amulet, she held it out.

Zylas's fingers clamped around the metal disc.

The chain slid from her hand as he pulled the amulet away. Stepping back from her and Ezra, he balanced the medallion on his palm. We watched him carefully examine it, Tori and Aaron tense with readiness as though expecting Zylas to launch at them in a savage rage at any second.

Amalia paled slightly but otherwise didn't react. I'd told her about my discovery and why summoning the Twelfth House was forbidden, though we hadn't discussed it since. She preferred not to think about the fact that Zylas was completely unbound aside from the infernus commands.

Turning toward me, Zylas looped the chain over my head. The amulet settled on my chest, clinking against the infernus. His lips curved in a wolfish smile, then crimson light washed over him. He dissolved into light and streaked into the infernus.

Darkness returned to the grove.

"Uh." Tori blinked at me. "So ... you're going to find a way to save Ezra, then?"

"I'll do my best, but ..." I cleared my throat. "Separating a demon from a demon mage is ... well, it's considered impossible. The Vh'alyir Amulet might help, if I can figure out how to use it."

"It won't help," Ezra said quietly.

How did he know that? When we'd talked about the amulet a week ago, he hadn't known whether it would save him—but if he'd since learned it couldn't help him, that explained why they were giving it up so easily.

"Xever's grimoire should contain the ritual and the contract he used to bind me and Eterran," Ezra continued. "You need to find something in there that will allow it to be broken."

"So Claude ... Xever turned you into a demon mage?" I asked hesitantly. A common enemy indeed.

His mouth thinned. "Xever is more than a summoner. He's the leader of the Court of the Red Queen."

That must be the "court" Claude had been talking about, the reason he hadn't been present for Saul's portal attempt. "What is the Court of the Red Queen?"

"It's a cult of demon worshippers." His gaze took on that intense, viper-like quality. "The 'Red Queen' is a deified version of a female demon, and the cultists worship her as an all-powerful goddess. Some of them are fanatically obsessed."

Obsessed—like Saul, Braden, and Jaden, who were so fixated on female demons that they'd kidnapped, raped, and murdered dozens of women they'd thought resembled *payashē*.

"The abjuration sorcerers were cultists?" I asked uncomfortably.

"Most likely. If they were attached to Xever, then they were involved with the cult in one way or another." Ezra gestured at the grimoire. "You'll find details in there about the supposed power of the Red Queen and other *doctrine*."

He said "doctrine" like it was the most disgusting word he'd ever uttered.

Amalia nervously shifted her weight. "How big is this cult?"

"There's the High Court with the cult leaders, plus an unknown number of hidden sects called 'circles.' I couldn't even guess the total number of cultists, but they're dangerous."

Cold washed through me. "And Claude—Xever is their leader?"

"Yes."

I stared down at the grimoire cover—the circle with a crown inside it.

"So?" Tori prompted, watching me intently. "Can you do it?"

Claude had stolen from me and my family. He'd murdered my parents. He'd been experimenting with Demonica and contracts for who knew how long. His contract with Nazhivēr was like nothing I'd ever read about, and he'd developed a ritual to bind a demon to more than one infernus.

And now I knew he was the leader of an entire cult of demon worshippers.

Compared to defeating him, unmaking a demon mage didn't seem so impossible after all.

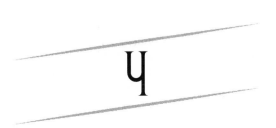

PERCHED ON A STOOL at the breakfast bar, I stared down at the black leather cover of the cult grimoire. Beside it was a new notebook, the first ten pages filled with lists, translations, and a rough table of contents for this anthology of secrets.

My enemy's secrets.

For months, what Claude wanted—what his ultimate goal was—had puzzled me. And now I had some answers ... but still so many questions.

Amalia slid onto the stool next to me. "Well?"

"So far, I've confirmed that the Court of the Red Queen and Claude are both terrifying."

"What do you mean?"

"This book is as much a religious text as a grimoire, and it talks all about the cult's beliefs. They believe in an immortal and all-powerful 'mother of magic' who created the twelve

Houses of male demons to serve her and gifted magic to humankind."

"Creative," Amalia remarked dryly.

"Right?" I shook my head. "And they believe that when they die, the Red Queen will claim her followers' souls and deliver them to an eternal afterlife in the demon world."

"You should ask Zylas if he ever ran across a river of souls on his way to the demon supermarket."

Though I doubted there were soul-filled bodies of water in his world, I would've asked his opinion if he were nearby. At the moment, he was in my bedroom with the Vh'alyir Amulet, analyzing its mysterious spells.

"The cult has a really strange view of contracted demons too," I said. "They believe that male demons are loaned out by the Red Queen and these 'Servi' willingly protect loyal worshippers, and when the contractor dies, the demon takes their soul directly to the goddess."

"Wow. Does *Claude* believe all that?"

"I don't know. My first instinct is 'no way, he's too smart.' But he has a very unusual contract with Nazhivēr."

"Their relationship does resemble that whole 'willing servant' thing." Amalia tugged on a lock of her long blond hair. "Claude is scary manipulative, though. I can see him building a cult and convincing people to worship a nonexistent god, all for his own personal gain."

"But what gain? What does he want?" I tapped the cover. "There's information in here about the twelve Houses, feeding demon blood to vampires, and other experiments with demon blood—all things Claude has been involved in. But nothing about portals."

"Well, yeah. Think about it." She propped an elbow on the table. "In real religions, you have to die before you can go to heaven or the afterlife or whatever. Same deal for the cult, because if all its followers knew you could open a portal and walk right into 'heaven,' that would become their goal instead of obeying the cult until they die."

"That makes sense," I muttered. "But what about something like the Rapture?"

"Is there anything about the end of the world in the grimoire?"

"Not that I've seen." I shifted uneasily on my stool. "If the cult's religion includes an end-time event where believers are transported directly to the goddess ... could that be the reason for Claude's portal fixation?"

"But there's no way he actually believes in the cult bullshit ... right?"

We exchanged looks of doubt and disquiet.

Amalia shook herself. "What about Ezra and the unmaking of a demon mage? Any progress?"

"I found the section on creating demon mages," I answered, opening the cult grimoire to a marked page. "I haven't done more than skim it yet."

"We can go over it together." She slid off her stool. "I just want to finish sewing the zipper on Zylas's coat first. I hate doing zippers and I need to get it done before I decide to do snaps instead."

I laughed. "He might prefer snaps."

"No one prefers snaps. Not even a demon."

She headed for her bedroom, and I focused on the grimoire. I perused the dense paragraphs of Latin on the first page of the ritual, then jumped to the opposite page, which featured a complex diagram. Yeah, I'd definitely need Amalia's help with this.

Slowly turning pages, I studied each successive diagram. Summoning wasn't simple, straightforward magic. Abjuration might have a reputation as the most difficult branch of Arcana, but most sorcerers had never tried summoning. Amalia had been studying it for years and was still a green apprentice who had yet to summon her first demon.

As Amalia's sewing machine whirred in the background, I slid my finger down an illustrated array. Interspersed through the semi-familiar Arcana were spiky runes—demon magic. How did *that* work?

Sighing, I flipped back to the first page and picked up my pencil.

"*Robin!*"

The sharp noise pinged in my brain, so unexpected that I didn't instantly react—then I leaped off my stool so fast I almost toppled it.

Zylas was yelling my name?

I sprinted into my bedroom, my heart in my throat and panic simmering.

Zylas was crouched in the middle of my room. I'd expected his shout to be related to the Vh'alyir Amulet, but he didn't have the amulet. Instead, he was leaning over Socks. The half-grown kitten squatted low to the carpet, her sides heaving and a horrible wheezing noise scraping from her throat.

His wide eyes shot from the kitten to me. "What's wrong with her?"

As I knelt beside him, Socks shook with a violent cough, made a throaty hacking sound, and swallowed a couple times.

Licking her chops, she looked up at us and blinked her large green eyes.

Zylas and I stared down at her.

"I think it was a hairball," I said after a moment.

"I do not know that word."

"Cats lick their fur to stay clean. They end up swallowing bits of fur, and sometimes they cough it up."

He looked between me and the cat, his forehead scrunched. "Coughing fur …" he muttered. "Do *hh'ainun* do this?"

I almost choked. "*No.* Not at all. It's strictly a cat thing."

"*Hnn.*"

His puzzled expression was too much for me. A giggle bubbled up my throat, and before I could stop myself, I burst into laughter. I sat back on my heels, a hand pressed to my mouth as I tried to stifle the sound.

He scowled. "Why are you laughing?"

"N-no reason," I gasped. "Sorry."

Grumbling irritably, he scooped Socks off the floor. Sitting cross-legged, he dropped her into his lap. She sprawled on her back, paws in the air, purring loudly. As he ran his fingers over her fluffy belly, faint crimson sparked over his fingertips.

My laughter died. He was checking her for unseen injuries, ensuring she was okay. He was *worried* about the kitten. Worried enough to call me over and to check her with his magic.

A strange tightness spread through my chest, and for a bizarre second, I felt like I might burst into tears.

"Socks is fine, Zylas." My voice came out in an emotional hush. "Really. It's a normal cat behavior."

"She is so small." He ruffled her fur. "Easy to break. More breakable than you."

At least he considered me *somewhat* hardier than a five-pound kitten.

He rubbed her head and she swatted at his hand, all her claws extended. Amalia and I couldn't play with her unless we used a toy; Zylas had unintentionally taught her that playtime meant claw-time. Her needlelike claws didn't bother him thanks to his tough demon skin.

He watched her half hang from his hand in an attempt to wrestle it, then let out a long, weary breath. "Keeping small things alive is hard."

Socks flopped back into his lap, rolled over, and meowed in complaint. With a jaunty flick of her tail, she waltzed off. Zylas wrinkled his nose the way he did when annoyed about a troublesome non-demon's needy ways.

"Zylas …" I began.

When his softly glowing eyes turned to me, my voice dried up. I swallowed, no idea what to say … or if I wanted to say anything.

His thoughtful stare drifted over me—then a mischievous smirk appeared. My flash of alarm had barely registered before his hands closed over my upper arms and he dragged me onto his lap.

I gasped as he pulled me against his chest and wrapped his arms around me.

"Z-Zylas!" I yanked at his wrist. "What are you doing?"

He snugged his arms tighter. "You want me to hold you like the kitten."

"What? No, I don't!"

"Yes. I heard you. *Jealous* of the kitten, *na?*"

I made a high-pitched noise, tugging harder on his arm. "I'm not *jealous* of a cat. Now let me go!"

"But you like it, *vayanin*." His face dipped close to my ear. "Don't you?"

My mouth opened, but I couldn't deny it—because he'd instantly call me out for lying. My cheeks burned.

He lifted his head, and I glimpsed his sharp grin before he pushed his fingers into my hair. Shivery gooseflesh ran down my spine.

"Do you like this too?" he crooned slyly.

"I'm not a cat," I snapped, pretending my heart wasn't slamming against my ribs. "I don't want to be *petted*."

"But you like it when I touch you."

Why had I ever admitted that to him? I grabbed his wrist, fully intending to drag his hand out of my hair with sheer force of will—until he ducked his head. The tip of his nose brushed against the side of my neck.

At the feeling of his warm breath, my stomach dropped out of my body.

He nuzzled my throat, inhaling my scent. I didn't move, my lungs locked. His nose trailed down my neck, then back up to the corner of my jaw. My skin tingled.

His mouth closed over the soft spot under my jaw, and heat plunged through my core. His tongue flicked across my skin, tasting my pulse—then the hot touch of his mouth disappeared.

I opened my eyes.

Amalia stood in my bedroom doorway.

She was frozen in place, disgusted horror twisting her features—and reality slammed through me at the sight. Her face said it all.

Disbelief.

Revulsion.

Condemnation.

The most intense shame I'd ever felt swelled through me like icy poison as she stared at me in the demon's lap. She'd seen his mouth on my neck. She'd seen me enjoying it.

I wanted to die. Just die on the spot, right now.

Amalia stood there for a moment more, then turned on her heel and strode away.

Panic burst through me. Scrambling off Zylas, I jumped up and ran out of the room.

"Amalia, wait!" I raced across the living room and through her open bedroom door. "That—that wasn't what it looked like—"

Halfway to her sewing desk, she whirled around and shouted, "*He's a demon!*"

"It—it wasn't—"

"Don't lie to me, Robin! You weren't resisting him. You were—" Repugnance contorted her face. "How far have you gone with him?"

Mortification filled my chest like hot lead. "I haven't done anything like … *that*."

Sagging with relief, she let out a huge breath, then straightened. "Look, I get that he's kind of humanish and muscular and all that, but he's a *demon*, Robin."

I cringed. "I know that. I just …"

"You just what?"

"I … got … caught up in … in the moment."

"In the moment?" Her voice rose again. "What kind of excuse is that? If you're so freakin' thirsty, we can go to any club and find you a muscular guy to throw down with."

I recoiled. "That's not why I was—"

"Then *what*? What possible reason could you have for allowing him to slobber on you like a dog? Why—"

"He's not an animal!"

Her jaw clenched at my angry retort, then she swept past me, grabbed the door, and slammed it shut, enclosing us in her bedroom. Stepping in front of me, she put her hands on my shoulders.

"Robin. Listen to me." She stared hard into my eyes. "What you're doing is wrong and you know it."

I sucked in a shaky breath, unable to reply when she was voicing my fears.

"If the fact that he's a creature—a *creature*—from another world isn't enough, this isn't a game you want to play with a *demon*." She gave me a brief shake. "Don't you realize what he can do to you? If you don't shut that shit down now, you might not get to later. He can overpower you, with or without the infernus."

My throat closed as I sensed the fear behind her revulsion.

"This isn't like roleplaying with a guy because you're into horns or something. He's from another world. His body is *part magic*. I know you believe he won't hurt you, but have you imagined what he could do to you *by accident*?"

As I bit my lower lip to hide its trembling, Amalia's expression softened.

"I don't want you to get hurt ... or worse," she whispered. "Just keep your head on straight until we can send him home, okay?"

Humiliation, remorse, uncertainty, and a sickening pain in my chest overwhelmed me, but I didn't cry. I wouldn't cry.

Tightening my hold on my emotions even more, I nodded. Keep my head on straight. Keep my heart safe.

And send Zylas home.

I STARED AT THE CEILING, the blankets pulled up to my chin. Sweet smokiness tickled my nose—Zylas's scent, clinging to the fabric from the last time he'd reclined across the blankets. Each inhalation was a reminder of his closeness, his arms around me, his mouth against my throat.

My stomach churned. Being caught like that with a guy would've been embarrassing. But with a *demon* …

It went beyond taboo. *Forbidden* didn't encompass it. Intimacy with a demon was beyond incomprehensible—to everyone but me, it seemed.

Demons were monsters. Seven-foot-tall beasts with horns, manes, scales, wings, tails, or spiny protrusions on their limbs. They were killing machines that thrived on violence. They were merciless, bloodthirsty, and brutal. To mythics, they were less than beasts. They were puppets to be used and discarded.

Zylas was more human in appearance and—after months in my company and with access to my thoughts—more human in temperament. His emotional landscape was different from a human's, but it was no less complex and nuanced.

Yet, despite that, he was far more closely related to the bestial demons of other Houses than he was to me.

Pulling my arms from under the covers, I pressed my hands to my face. I couldn't pretend I wasn't drawn to him—but what drew me? Where did my fascination end and attraction begin?

Amalia's words echoed in my head. I didn't know what to think, what to feel, but the last thing she'd said rang with truth. With finality.

I'd promised to send Zylas home.

If he was going home, if he was leaving my world and never returning, then there was no question—I needed to keep my head down and get through this. But if his desire to leave had changed …

He'd hesitated at the portal, staring into the demon world's sky as though immobilized with indecision. That glimpse I'd gotten of his drowsy thoughts taunted me—his memory of his own world … and his memory of coming home to me, but I didn't know which he longed for.

I flipped the blankets aside and climbed out of bed. My closet doors creaked faintly as I slid them open. Grabbing an oversized sweatshirt and baggy cotton pants, I pulled them on over my pajama top and shorts.

In the living room, the glow of a streetlamp through the balcony's glass door cut across Zylas where he sat beside it, a narrow slice of his face illuminated as he turned his head toward me. I padded across the carpet and stopped two long steps away.

He watched me sink into a crouch so we were on eye level.

"Zylas," I whispered. My throat tried to close and I swallowed. "Do … do you want to go home?"

His mouth shifted in a frown.

"We found the portal array in the grimoire," I added. "And we have the amulet now."

His dark pupils, dilated in the dim light, flicked side to side as he studied my face. "You promised to send me home."

My throat bobbed with another swallow. "I just wanted to check that you still want to go, since you can't be a *Dīnen* anymore."

He would return not as a king but as *Ivaknen*—"the Summoned." As he'd explained it, he would have respect but nothing else. No home, no people, no purpose.

His gaze was still roving across my features as though trying to read my thoughts. I wondered if he could hear my mind.

The way it was spinning, even if he could, he might not discern much.

Lips parting to speak, he hesitated. An uncomfortable pressure tightened my chest, a flicker of unexpected, inappropriate hope.

"I do not belong here."

The spark of hope died as quickly as it had formed. Pain followed, a swift, cutting line across my heart. He didn't belong here. Not in my world.

Not with me.

"Of—of course," I said weakly, trying to smile. "I understand. You should be in your own world."

He said nothing.

I twined my fingers together and squeezed, the dull ache cutting through the clouds of emotion in my head. "Zylas, I also wanted to say I'm sorry for earlier."

His eyes were pools of crimson mystery, giving away nothing of his thoughts.

"I don't know how to explain," I began awkwardly. "For some humans, being … uh … being really close to someone— the way we were, I mean—that's a special thing for, um, for—"

"You do not choose me."

"What?"

"A *payashē* gives a male her food when she chooses him for her bed. You gave me food. But you do not choose me."

All moisture evaporated from my mouth. I couldn't speak.

"You would like a *hh'ainun* male, *na*? A male who belongs here."

"I …" The word came out in a whisper. "I just—just don't know how to explain. It's complicated and I … don't …"

When I trailed off, he turned toward the glass and the night sky beyond. "The reason does not matter."

Because it wouldn't change anything. Because nothing could change. Because he was leaving.

The seconds ticked into a minute. He didn't turn, watching the sky the way he'd stared at the expanse of stars on the other side of the portal. My mouth opened, then closed. My fingers twisted together even harder.

Rising to my feet, I walked back to my bedroom, the silence between us thundering in my ears.

5

"SHOULDN'T THAT be south? '*Pros mesembrian*' is south."

At my correction, Amalia peered at her notes, then swore and crossed out the erroneous direction.

"*South* alignment," she grumbled. "No wonder this wasn't making any sense. Okay, then we have a directional reversal—so this array is basically a mirror image of a normal summoning."

"Except half the anterior nodes are different," I added with a sigh, tapping my pen against my notebook. "And it's paired with another array, and those are both inside *another* array."

She swore. "This is way more complicated than regular summoning. No wonder demon mages are so rare."

We were seated at the breakfast bar, the cult grimoire open in front of us. I had my laptop and reference texts beside me. Amalia had lost all her Demonica texts when her house had burned down, so she'd checked out a few books from the

Arcana Historia library and borrowed a few more sensitive ◆ tomes on Demonica from her father.

We'd been working on deciphering the demon-mage summoning ritual for an entire week now. It was so complex that, even making steady progress, we were no closer to breaking the contract than when we'd started.

"All right." Amalia pointed at the array, which featured two side-by-side circles contained within a larger ring. "This small one here is a normal summoning circle. The demon gets summoned into it. That makes sense. But this big circle is also a summoning circle. And the reversed array is *also* a summoning circle."

"Three," I muttered. "Why *three* summonings?"

She raked both hands through her hair. "Hell if I know. I'll start translating the section about the contract."

As she pulled the grimoire closer and copied out a page of Latin, I peeked behind us.

At the other end of the apartment, Zylas sat on the floor near the balcony. The Vh'alyir Amulet lay on the carpet in front of him, and faint shimmers of crimson light flickered out from it as he tapped a claw against its face.

While Amalia and I worked on the demon-mage puzzle to save Ezra, Zylas was attempting to unravel the spells in the amulet—specifically, the one that was mostly demon magic. And unlike his human roommates, who required food and sleep, he had no need for breaks—so he didn't take any, except for wandering the city at night.

He was consumed by his most important goal: unlocking the portal magic that we needed to send him home.

"This is insane," Amalia muttered, her pencil scribbling across her page. "The entire contract seems to be, 'demon agrees to bind himself to the human's soul.'"

"That's it?"

"Yeah. It's even more vague than *your* contract. How do you find a loophole in a single clause? If there were a way around it, Eterran would've figured it out by now."

"And Ezra said the Vh'alyir Amulet's contract-breaking spell doesn't work on demon mages."

"Is that because of the 'bind yourself' contract ... or because of the way the demon is sealed inside the host?"

Having no answers to offer, I turned my attention back to my notes. *Three* summoning circles. One to summon the demon. One to ... transfer the demon into the human host? And one to ... what? The demon couldn't be summoned *again*, and what other purpose did a summoning circle have?

Sighing, I tugged the grimoire away from Amalia and flipped from one page to the next. Summon the demon. Insert the demon into the host. Bind them with a contract.

If that was it, then the Vh'alyir Amulet's contract-nullifying spell should be enough to free the demon from its host. So what ...

My gaze shot back to the third, extraneous summoning circle. "Amalia, is there anything in here that resembles the ritual for binding a demon to an infernus?"

"There is no infernus," she replied distractedly. "Demon mages don't need them."

"Yes, because the demon mage *is* the infernus. That's what the ex-summoner from Odin's Eye told me."

Amalia set her pen down. We bent our heads over the grimoire and carefully flipped through each page detailing demon-mage creation.

"Nothing," she declared. "If there's nothing in this ritual that turns the host into a living infernus, then how the hell does the demon end up trapped in the human?"

"I was wondering …" I pointed at the third circle. "This one is weird, right? It's reversed, directing the magic inward."

Catching her lower lip between her teeth, she stared at the magic. "You can't be thinking … that when the demon is summoned into the human host, the human *becomes* a summoning circle?"

"It would explain why the demon can't escape the human's body, and why the Vh'alyir Amulet doesn't help. Summoning circles aren't part of a contract, and they're impenetrable to demons."

"Shit. If you're right, then Ezra might be screwed. The only way to remove a demon from a circle is to either break the circle or put the demon inside an infernus first."

I rubbed my face. "What about Claude's special ritual to bind a demon to a second infernus? Could we use that to bind Eterran to an infernus, then call him out of Ezra?"

"No. You can't call a demon into an infernus *through* a circle."

Eyes squinching, I remembered the basement where Claude had bound Zylas—and remembered the summoner thrusting his new infernus through the invisible barrier before calling Zylas into it. "Then the only way is to break the circle."

"Which would mean breaking Ezra somehow. And not just slicing his skin. Otherwise, a paper cut would mean the end for every demon mage." She snapped the grimoire closed. "We'll have to translate the rest of the ritual before we can figure out anything for sure. Let's pack this stuff up and get ready to go."

Nodding, I helped her collect everything into a pile, then we carried it into my bedroom and stashed it all under my bed beside the Athanas grimoire case.

As Amalia hurried out again to change and do her makeup, I glanced at the clock beside my bed. We had an hour before the guild meeting. It wasn't the usual monthly meeting all members were required to attend, but an emergency one Darius had scheduled. According to Tori's last text, the meeting would address the Court of the Red Queen's presence in the city.

Worry flickered through me. I stood for a moment, then squatted again.

The cold metal of the Athanas grimoire's case chilled my fingers as I slid it out. I whispered the incantation, then opened the lid. The ancient grimoire waited in its paper wrapping, but I lifted out my notebook instead.

Feeling strangely guilty, I once again read Myrrine's impassioned words.

> I offered a demon my soul, and then I offered him my heart. Madness, perhaps, but if this is madness, I will keep it.

She'd given the demon her heart without realizing he had no claim on her soul. Only after her death, and moments before his own, had the demon revealed that his banishment clause with Myrrine hadn't worked.

Had the knowledge that her life would end in two years affected Myrrine's decision? Had it made her more reckless? But how had she given everything to a demon she'd expected to kill her for her soul?

If her demon had been returning to his world instead of taking her soul, would she have chosen differently?

"Robin, what are you wearing?" Amalia's voice floated into my bedroom. "I never know what to wear to these stupid meetings."

Panicking, I shoved the grimoire case with my foot. It slid under my bed, the mattress knocking the lid shut with a clack. I tossed the notebook onto my bedside table.

"Well?" She strode through my doorway, carrying two pairs of pants. "What do you think?"

"Uh. Whatever's more casual, I'd say." The Crow and Hammer was always casual.

"Yeah, guess so. Jeans it is."

As she walked out again, I glanced at the notebook, then hastened to my closet to pick out an outfit.

FRIDAY NIGHTS at the Crow and Hammer were often busy. Members would show up for dinner or drinks to unwind after a long week and catch up on the guild gossip. I didn't usually join in since I wasn't interested in drinking or gossiping … or socializing, really. I preferred books.

Tonight, however, the atmosphere was very different.

The pub was quiet, with no one whispering or joking. Only Darius spoke, the overhead lights casting deep shadows across his salt-and-pepper hair, short beard, and somber expression.

He stood at one end of the room, facing his guildeds as he spoke. Explaining that a demon-worshipping cult had been discovered in Vancouver. That the cult included demon mages. And that our guild, and whichever other local guilds he could recruit, would be taking on this dangerous enemy.

Tori was perched on a bar stool, her red hair easy to spot. Ezra sat on one side of her and Aaron on the other, their expressions grim.

I eyed Ezra from across the room. He was a man of secrets—not that I could blame him for keeping his own counsel so diligently. When his very existence was forbidden, he couldn't be too careful.

As long as I was an illegal contractor, my life would be the same. Always hiding the truth, always wary, always holding others at arm's length.

"Tomorrow," Darius said, "I will visit Odin's Eye, the Pandora Knights, the Grand Grimoire, and the SeaDevils to speak with their GMs. Together, we will protect our city. Time is of the essence."

He paused as the gravity of the challenge before us sank in, then began a more detailed review of the Crow and Hammer's plan to expose and bring down the Court of the Red Queen.

I sat back in my chair, my chest tight. For months now, it had been me, Zylas, and Amalia against Claude. Now it was the Crow and Hammer against the cult. I didn't know how I felt about that. It was nice that we weren't completely on our own anymore, but I also didn't want to share my revenge with anyone. *I* wanted to take down the man who'd murdered my parents, stolen my family's legacy, and abused its power for his own selfish ambitions.

Me and Zylas, together. That's how it would end.

"This is gonna be a doozy."

I started, my gaze swinging toward my and Amalia's tablemate. Zora quirked her eyebrows at my surprised look.

It'd been three weeks since Nazhivēr had nearly killed the sorceress, and she'd spent over a week with a guild healer. She was back to her usual self, but the toll her injuries had taken still showed. Her cheekbones stood out sharply, her face thinner than I remembered, but that could've been because of her new hairstyle—a pixie cut that swept up into a short fauxhawk.

She braced her elbows on the table. "Darius told me that the cult kingpin is the same summoner who's been messing with you for months."

My eyes widened. Ezra must've been sharing information with Darius; that was the only way the GM could've learned that Claude and Xever were the same person. Did Darius know Ezra was a demon mage?

"Seeing as he murdered your parents," Zora continued, "I'm assuming you want to take this guy down yourself?"

I pushed my shoulders back. "Yes."

"Glad to hear it. The cult is dangerous on its own, but add in Xever and his demon? Not good. Me and a small team have been tracking suspected cultists all week, trying to get a drop on their leaders, but no sign of the boss yet."

She was tracking Claude?

"Bringing down the cult will require our entire guild— probably multiple guilds—but Xever is the head of the snake. Based on his involvement with the super-vampires and the golems, he has his fingers in a lot of pies. Are all those pies related to the cult?"

Amalia pursed her lips thoughtfully. "Claude's always seemed like a lone wolf. Is the cult just a means to an end, or is he actually a goddess-worshipping zealot?"

"He was kind of condescending toward Saul and his sons," I recalled. "I assumed that's because they were rapists, but maybe not? As for worshipping demons himself... I'm not sure. He doesn't act like the type, but he seemed to revere the Twelfth House when he talked about it being special."

"Interesting," Zora mused. "The question, then, is whether Claude—Xever—which name are we calling him?"

"Xever," I decided after a moment's thought. "It probably isn't his real name either, but his persona as Xever is closer to who he really is."

"Xever, then. The big question is whether he'll defend the cult when it comes under fire, or whether he'll see a sinking ship and bail." Zora glanced around to ensure no one was eavesdropping. "The latter makes Xever more slippery, but the former is more dangerous for the guild. Darius confided that he's very concerned about Nazhivēr."

A legitimate worry. Darius, Girard, and Alistair had taken on Nazhivēr in a brief battle and done little damage. Zylas had promised to protect the guild from Nazhivēr, but he hadn't been able to defeat the demon and Zora had nearly died as a result.

"So by the time the guild is ready to move on the cult," she concluded, "we need to be ready to take on Xever and Nazhivēr."

"We?" I repeated uncertainly.

Her expression tightened. "I know I didn't pull my weight the way I should've, but I offered to be your champion and if you still want me, I—"

"Wait, wait." I waved my hands. "Zora, you were amazing against Nazhivēr. I'm the one who let you down. Zylas and I—we screwed up and didn't pull *our* weight. We should've done better."

She looked unconvinced. "Next time, I'll be prepared."

"What do you mean?"

She smiled mysteriously. "You'll see."

Instead of being reassured, I felt more uneasy. Zylas and I were no more prepared to fight Nazhivēr than we'd been last time. The demon seemed undefeatable.

I chewed the inside of my cheek as conversation spread throughout the pub, the rising noise competing with my spinning thoughts. I glanced toward the bar where Ezra sat with Aaron and Tori, a crowd of mythics gathered around them. Ezra hadn't said much about his ties to the Court of the Red Queen, but I could guess he knew more than I did. Maybe he had inside knowledge about Nazhivēr—and ideas on how to defeat the demon.

"I'll be right back," I murmured, pushing away from the table.

Most guild members had left their tables too, forming clusters throughout the room, and I hastened through the bustle to the group around the bar. Too short to see over anyone's shoulders, I rose on my tiptoes, trying to spot the demon mage's curly brown hair.

"... balance of strengths and weaknesses for combat against contractors and demon mages."

I recognized Aaron's voice. It sounded like he was still in the same spot at the bar.

"We'll focus on defense first," he went on, "then practice the most efficient ways to kill them so we don't exhaust ourselves and our magic."

"What, you can't just incinerate demons with your unstoppable fire?" the woman in front of me asked sarcastically.

I recognized her bottle-blond hair. Cearra, an apprentice sorceress who'd mocked me for having a small demon.

"We'll want to inflict as much damage as possible," an older man replied, "and fire is a good option. We could ask the alchemists to make us firebombs."

"And some nasty-ass smoke bombs," someone else jumped in. "Blind the bastards so the demons can't spit us like damn pigs."

"But *we* need to be able to see what we're doing." That was Darren, the tall bully of a sorcerer who'd been slightly nicer to me since I'd almost drowned in the storm drains. "Bleeding them out would be better. We should be planning the easiest ways to slit some veins."

As the debate lulled, I cleared my throat. "Those tactics ..."

The people nearest to me turned, surprise on their faces when they saw me standing there.

"They probably won't work," I finished tentatively.

The dense cluster of combat mythics shifted, opening a gap to reveal Aaron, perched on his stool and blinking bright blue eyes at me. Tori sat beside him, Ezra on her opposite side. I tried to smile but couldn't manage it.

"What do *you* know?"

I started at the rough question. Darren. Of course. His guilt-fueled sympathy for the poor little contractor who'd almost drowned while on his team had run out.

"I'm a demon contractor." I straightened my glasses, annoyance flitting through me. "But I'm sure your experiences are valid too, Darren."

His jaw flexed. Before he could retort, I turned to Aaron—almost missing Tori's half-suppressed grin.

"Fire can burn legally contracted demons," I explained, "but at least one cult demon is so loosely contracted that he can wield his magic. Fire could make him stronger."

Aaron's mouth dropped open. "Stronger?"

"Demons can convert heat into magic." I tried not to think about Zylas's reaction. I was revealing demon weaknesses to the evil *hh'ainun*. He wouldn't be pleased. "To burn them, you'd have to apply heat faster than the demon can absorb it."

I paused, remembering Nazhivēr's bellow of pain when a certain volcanomage had hit him with a fistful of molten lava. "Alistair can do it, but I'm not sure about regular fire."

Everyone stared at me. Was this information that shocking?

"Cold can only kill a badly injured demon," I added. "Bleeding them out won't work very well, either. Their blood is thick and clots quickly. Even deep wounds stop bleeding within a couple minutes."

Darren folded his arms angrily. "How are we supposed to kill them, then?"

"Hmm." I debated concealing the demons' ultimate weakness, but I couldn't hide it when lives were on the line. "Vampire saliva?"

At my hesitant suggestion, the combat mythics all looked at each other like I'd proposed they kill demons with concentrated puppy cuteness.

Though it seemed obvious, I explained, "If you inject demons with a large dose of vampire saliva, they collapse."

Aaron rubbed the back of his neck. "How much is a 'large' dose?"

"Um." I pictured the syringe Nazhivēr had injected into Zylas. "About like ... a couple of tablespoons?"

Cameron—the lanky sorcerer who wasn't as nasty as Darren and would probably be a nice guy if he ditched his toxic friend—combed his fingers through his hair, oozing frustration. "Where are we supposed to get that much vampire saliva?"

"We can barely find *one* vampire lately," Darren sneered, shaking his head. "Their numbers dropped off a cliff after the December surge."

Oh. Hmm. Was that because we'd killed Vasilii? Either way, it didn't seem like a bad thing.

"We'll look into vamp spit," Aaron decided. "But as always with demons, our best bet is taking out the contractors, and that'll be our focus."

Ah yes. The classic "kill the contractor" strategy. My favorite.

"Thanks for the tips, Robin."

I blinked at Aaron, surprised by his gratitude.

As he addressed the combat mythics, movement beside me caused me to turn. Tori had slipped through the group to join me.

"Can we talk?" she asked softly.

I nodded, and she hooked her arm through mine. We started across the room, Tori assessing every mythic we passed. Her steps slowed, then stopped, and she stared around the pub with a deep crease between her brows.

Was she afraid for her guildmates, who were preparing to go up against Xever's cult, or was her apprehension rooted somewhere else?

"Tori?" I murmured.

She blinked, gaze darting toward me, then hastily pulled me into a dim corner away from everyone else and asked, "Any updates?"

"Not yet," I admitted. "We're working on it." When her worry deepened, I leaned closer. "It isn't a simple process. I know you're impatient, Tori, but as far as I can tell, unmaking a demon mage has never been done before."

"I get that." She glanced around, then lowered her voice even more. "It's just that Ezra doesn't have much time left."

The day a human became a demon mage, the clock started counting down to his end—a violent end heralded by an increasingly swift descent into madness. Though I hadn't seen any clear signs of instability from Ezra, he'd admitted his days were numbered.

"We found the demon mage ritual in the grimoire," I revealed. "It's a complex set of spells. We thought the host body acted like an infernus, but looking at the rituals, it seems more like a summoning circle. Once a demon is inside a summoning circle, the only way to get him out is to destroy the circle or move him while he's inside an infernus."

"So … what? Ezra needs to swallow an infernus?"

"Uh." Hadn't she seen the size of an infernus? They weren't small. "No, the infernus would need to breach Ezra's essence, not just his body."

She pressed her lips together. "His soul. That ex-summoner we talked to said some people believe the demon is inside the human's soul."

"And that's the problem," I agreed with a nod. "But there must be some way … I'll keep trying, and Zylas will help too."

Assuming he cooperated, which he wasn't in the mood for lately. He was focused on the Vh'alyir Amulet.

Tugging at the infernus chain around my neck, I considered what would come next—what would happen if or when we separated Ezra and Eterran. "I don't know what it will look like yet, but saving Ezra will involve some sort of ritual. We'll need a private location where we can set up a Demonica circle. Can you find one for us?"

Tori straightened. "Yeah, I can do that."

"If it has an existing circle, that would save us some time."

"Leave it to me," she said confidently.

Well, that was one less thing to worry about. I could focus on my other tasks: accomplishing the impossible by inventing a ritual that could unmake a demon mage, finding the leader of a powerful demon-worshipping cult, and defeating his unbeatable Second House demon.

No problem at all.

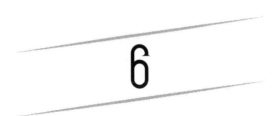

6

AMALIA DROPPED HER NOTEBOOK on the table. "I'm done. I can barely see straight."

"Yeah," I sighed. "We should go to bed."

Our work was spread across the coffee table—the cult grimoire, textbooks, notes, scribbled translations, and large copies of the demon mage rituals. We'd been working on it since getting home from the guild meeting, and the clock on Amalia's phone showed 1:10 a.m.

At my mention of bed, her gaze slid to my bedroom door. "Has Zylas left for his nightly wandering yet?"

"No, he's still attempting to dissect the amulet's magic." In my room, since our "*zh'ūltis*" arguing over translations had kept distracting him.

She grunted. "I'll stay up a bit longer, I guess."

It took my weary brain a moment to put together her motivation. "You don't have to chaperone me, Amalia. If he hasn't left by the time I'm ready to sleep, I'll kick him out of my room."

At her skeptical look, my gut twisted with shame and anger.

"Seriously," I snapped. "I explained it to him and he understands. We just got our wires crossed, okay? The whole food-sharing thing and all."

"I told you not to feed him," she muttered under her breath. "All right. I'll get ready for bed first then."

She trudged into the bathroom to brush her teeth. Desperate to think about something else, I pulled out a large sheet of brown paper and began drawing out the initial summoning spell for creating a demon mage.

The bathroom door popped open and she crossed the living room. "See you in the morning."

"Have a good sleep."

Quiet settled over the apartment as I traced out the array. The Arcana portions were familiar, if complex, but peppered throughout the spells were spiky demonic runes. Amalia had explained that summoning arrays didn't actually require a demon's magic. The runes acted as identifiers, describing the demonic aspects of the spell in the same way Arcana runes described earthly elements or effects.

I copied them out one by one, gooseflesh shivering over my arms. Anthea had created this spell; I'd seen the experimental versions in the Athanas grimoire. How had she incorporated these demonic runes? Had she learned them from a demon and added them herself? Had she somehow convinced a demon to build the summoning array with her?

Setting my pencil down, I pushed off the floor, stretched stiffly, and dropped onto the sofa. With my limbs sprawled out,

I gazed toward my bedroom, wondering when Zylas would finish so I could sleep. My eyelids drooped, heavy with fatigue.

A shadow appeared in the doorway. Zylas padded silently across the living room, the amulet's chain hanging from his fingers.

His timing was too perfect. He must've picked up on my desire to sleep. I couldn't hear much of anything from his mind, but I caught occasional whispers of his thoughts—and every time, I was surprised he hadn't blocked me out. Maybe it was harder to lock himself down now that he'd opened up to me.

He glanced over our mess on the coffee table, then tossed the amulet in my direction.

As I caught it with fumbling hands, he sank down to sit on the floor in my usual spot, his back against the sofa and his shoulder brushing my knee. A long sigh slid from him.

"I do not understand it."

Why did his husky voice in the dimly lit room make me shiver?

I uncurled my fingers, the amulet cupped between my palms. "What don't you understand?"

"There are three spells, *na*? One to break contracts. One to open a portal. One that is demon *vīsh*." He let his head fall back against the seat cushion, dark hair tangled across his forehead. "The demon *vīsh*. I do not understand it. It is not attack *vīsh*. It is not defense *vīsh*. It is not anything *vīsh*. It does not *do* anything."

"But it must do something," I muttered, tracing the Vh'alyir sigil in the medallion's center.

"I do not know what."

"Can you guess?"

"Guess? *Vīsh* is not for guessing."

I arched my eyebrows. He peered at me upside-down, then huffed and lifted his head from the seat cushion. Propping his arm on his upraised knee, he perused my and Amalia's notes.

My gaze drifted from him to the amulet, and I rubbed my thumb across the metal disc's worn edge. "It's kind of amazing, isn't it?"

He looked up from my drawing of the summoning spell. "*Ih?*"

"This amulet is thousands of years old." Quiet wonder spread through me. "My ancient ancestor made it, and it probably belonged to at least one of your ancestors too. It spent millennia in the demon world, passing from one demon to another. How many hands have touched this?"

His eyes, slowly widening, slid to the medallion.

"*Thousands* of years," I whispered, "and somehow it made it back to us—to Anthea's youngest descendent and a Vh'alyir *Dīnen.*"

Zylas turned. His warm hands touched mine, cradling them the way I cradled the amulet. He studied the medallion like he'd never seen it before, lips parted with faint astonishment.

"How long did it belong to Vh'alyir?" He canted his head. "How long before Lūsh'vēr stole it?"

"We'll probably never know."

He sighed, his hands sliding away from mine. "*Perdūsa Ahlēa valāra salith īt lidavisa ah'kan.*"

I blinked at him. "Huh?"

"It means … *Ahlēa* makes the sun fly and rain fall. It is a thing I learned … words that the wise *payapis* say." He wrinkled his nose. "It is *zh'ūltis* to fight the sun, she said."

"Wait." I leaned toward him. "Do you mean a *payapis* told you that? To your face? Aren't *payapis* the super-powerful demon matriarchs?"

His breath hitched, as though he'd said something he hadn't intended to share, then he turned back to the coffee table.

"I assumed you'd never met a matriarch," I exclaimed, alight with curiosity. "Aren't you terrified of female demons?"

His shoulders twitched in an irritated way. "I am not *terrified*," he growled. "I am *ahktallis* so I do not die."

I am smart, I silently translated. "But you said you run away from females. When did you have a conversation with a matriarch where she told you—what was it again?"

"*Ahlēa* makes the sun fly and rain fall."

"What is *Ahlēa*?"

His irritated glare swung up to me, then he jabbed a finger at my drawing of the summoning array. "*Ahlēa*."

I looked from the paper to him and back. "Huh?"

"This is *Ahlēa*." He pointed at the rune again. "It is here. In the human *vīsh*."

Confusion buzzed through me, and I slid off the sofa to sit beside him, leaving the amulet on the cushion behind us. "No one knows what those demonic runes mean. Amalia said that summoners just copy them as they appear in the spell."

His brow furrowed. "You use *vīsh* you do not understand?"

"Not me, but humans in general … I guess so." I tugged the drawing closer. "You can read these runes?"

"*Na*, of course." He pointed to one. "This is about *Ahlēavah*." He indicated a set of three. "This is about *Ahlēvīsh*."

"*Ahlēa*, *Ahlēavah*, and *Ahlēvīsh* …" I repeated slowly. "Those are connected, I'm guessing, but what do they mean?"

"*Ahlēa* is the deep *vīsh* of my world."

"You mean demon magic?"

"No." He tapped a claw against my *impello* artifact, hanging from the same chain as my infernus. "Where does the magic of this come from? Not from you, *na*?"

"It comes from the natural energies of the earth." My eyes widened. "Is *Ahlēa* the demon world's natural magic?"

"I do not know about the world, only my home. *Ahlēavah* is the land of *Ahlēa*."

Excitement shivered along my nerves. Was this knowledge any human alive possessed? "What about *Ahlēvīsh*?"

"*Hnn*." He squinted thoughtfully, then reached under the coffee table and withdrew his big book of landscape photography.

Laying it across my notes, he opened the cover and flipped past photos of mountains, rivers, islands, and cliffs before stopping on a page. Unlike the blue skies of the previous images, this one featured a colossal cave filled with massive, columnar crystals of a murky white color. They sprouted from the rocky cave floor in haphazard tangles, thirty to forty feet tall.

The caption in the bottom corner read, "Cave of Crystals, Naica, Mexico."

"*Ahlēvīsh* are like this." He traced a crystal. "The shapes are different, and some are smaller. Some are bigger. They are in many places in my world, but not in others. *Ahlēa*'s magic fills them, so we call them *Ahlēvīsh*."

I dragged my astonished stare from the photo. "So they're magical? Can you use the magic?"

"We use them, but not for magic. They are like this."

A tug on my neck. I looked down to see him holding the infernus.

"We can go inside *Ahlēvīsh* like I go inside this. It is called *kish lēvh*. Inside, we are safe. Nothing can hurt us. We can recover strength and heal from injuries."

A memory sparked: Zylas telling me that, when his father had died, he'd only known how to fight with his claws and hide in the *Ahlēvīsh*.

He pulled the infernus closer, forcing me to lean toward him. "I can feel *Ahlēvīsh* power in this. It is not the same, but ..." His crimson stare drifted across me. "Its *vīsh* tastes like *Ahlēa* and like you."

Cheeks flushing, I tugged the infernus out of his hand. "So, the demonic runes in the summoning spell invoke magic from your world. And it seems part of the infernus magic is tied to *Ahlēvīsh*."

I slid papers aside to uncover the cult grimoire, turned the page until I found the array for the second part of the demon-mage ritual, and tilted it toward Zylas.

"What about the demonic runes in this one?"

Leaning over the page, he indicated a rune in the center node. "It means 'blood.' What does this magic do?"

"The first part of the ritual summons a demon into a circle, same as you were summoned. This second part then summons the demon out of that circle and into a new summoning circle ... which has been embedded in a human. The demon is trapped forever inside the host because the circle can never be broken."

He bared his teeth, a flicker of his disgust at humankind darting from his mind through mine.

"I think," I said slowly, "that the blood rune is used to bind the summoning to the demon."

"So he is summoned instead of a new *Dīnen*."

Nodding, I gazed at the array with its two circles set inside a third. Summoned first from the demon world and into a circle. Summoned from that circle into a human body that acted like a circle. No way to link the demon to an infernus to carry him across the circle's nebulous boundary. No way to break the circle without killing the host or somehow breaching the host's soul.

Dark thoughts danced at the edge of my awareness—Zylas's swift mind speeding through his knowledge of the demonic side of this magic and what he'd learned of the Arcana.

Summoned. Called from the circle into the hh'ainun. The hh'ainun is a circle too.

Summoned twice.

Summon him again?

I gasped. My wide-eyed stare met blazing crimson eyes. "Is ... could that be it?"

He bared his teeth in a wolfish grin.

7

"WE'RE GOING TO SUMMON Eterran *out* of Ezra."

At my bold statement, Ezra, Tori, Aaron, and Kai stared at me in disbelief.

They stood on one side of Aaron's dining table, while Amalia and I stood opposite them, the surface between us spread with our notes and drawings, plus the cult grimoire. We'd just finished explaining the three stages of the demon-mage ritual and how we'd come up with an alternative to *breaking* the magic that imprisoned Eterran.

After a long, disbelieving pause, Kai fixed his dark eyes on me. I'd interacted with the electramage the least of the three mages, and his cool gaze was slightly unnerving.

"It's been a while since I studied Demonica basics," he said, "but from what I remember, summoners can call a demon of a particular type, but they can't summon an individual demon."

"Not from the demon world, no," I agreed quickly. "But making a demon mage requires summoning the already summoned demon a second time in order to insert him into the human host. We're going to do exactly that."

"There are complications," Amalia added. "The big one being blood."

"Blood?" Tori repeated worriedly.

Ezra frowned. "The second summoning required Eterran's blood. He doesn't have a body anymore. My blood isn't demon blood."

I wasn't surprised that Ezra had spotted the potential deal breaker with this plan. "No, your blood wouldn't work. But I think we can modify the spell to summon Eterran using blood from the same House."

That modification had come straight from Zylas. He'd added a sequence of runes to our new summoning array that would, if all went to plan, link the magic to Eterran—using one additional ingredient.

"Are you familiar with demon Houses?" I asked.

Aaron nodded. "Yeah. Different demon types are called Houses and there are nine or ten of them."

"Twelve," I corrected as I lifted my backpack onto the table. It landed on the wooden top with a solid *thunk*. "But yes. Their Houses are essentially lineages, so any blood from Eterran's House will be nearly identical."

"You want us to get *another* demon's blood?" Tori pressed her hands to the table. "How are we supposed to do that? We don't even know what 'House' Eterran is from!"

"Dh'irath, the Second House," I told her. "The same house as Nazhivēr."

Her face blanched at the demon's name. I could imagine what she was thinking: that I was suggesting we find Nazhivēr, defeat him in battle, and get our hands on enough of his blood to perform the summoning ritual.

A smile spread across my face. Controlling my excitement so I didn't outright laugh while they were all so tense and worried, I dragged a metal case out of my backpack. With a flourish, I flipped the lid open.

"This," I declared, displaying the five vials of dark demon blood cradled in the foam lining, "is Nazhivēr's blood."

When I'd first laid eyes on this case in Claude's apartment, I'd never imagined vials of Nazhivēr's blood would someday be useful to me. I'd only taken the case because it was evidence of Claude's crimes—and now, I was beyond grateful I'd had the foresight to grab it before police and MPD agents had swarmed the location.

Tori's disbelieving stare jumped from the case to me and back again. "Where—and *how*—did you get his blood?"

"Well, um … technically speaking, I stole it. Claude—or, rather, Xever was trading it to vampires in exchange for their saliva."

"Because vampire saliva affects demons." Tori flicked a curly lock of hair away from her face. "Is that why there are illustrations of vampires in the cult grimoire?"

"One of the reasons," I murmured. I'd seen enough of the grimoire's contents to wonder how much of Xever's experimentation had fed the cult and how much of the cult's twisted ideas had fed Xever's experimentation.

Selecting a rolled paper, I slid the elastic off. "Amalia and I put together a ritual that we think should work. We can't be sure ..." I added, the bright hope in Tori's eyes worrying me, "but this is the best we can do without any testing."

With help from Aaron, I unrolled a large sheet of drafting paper, on which Amalia and I had drawn out an altered version of the three-circle ritual array. If all went to plan, we would use this spell to summon Eterran out of Ezra's body.

Ezra studied the drawing, then reached out. As he pointed to the center of the second circle, his pale left eye flared with Eterran's power.

"This ..." A guttural accent roughened his voice. "What is this?"

"Zylas added that part," I hastily explained. "He said it's for—"

The infernus hidden under my sweater buzzed with heat, then crimson power streaked off my chest. Zylas took form beside me, red eyes narrowed on the demon mage.

"It will bind the blood to its nearest brother." He smirked. "You do not know this *vīsh*, *Dīnen et Dh'irath*?"

"I have never seen it before," Eterran replied, a sneer creeping into his voice. He either didn't notice or didn't care that Aaron and Kai had gone rigid beside him. "Is it real *vīsh*, *Dīnen et Vh'alyir*?"

"You think that if you do not know a magic, it is not real? Smart. You will live long thinking that."

"I know more *vīsh* than most *Dīnen* ever see."

"Because you are broken, so you needed greater power, *na*?" His smirk taking on a meaner edge, Zylas dragged his claw across his inner elbow. "You learned how to heal too late, Dh'irath."

I shivered, hoping that gesture didn't mean what I suspected it meant.

"You learned to fight like a coward, Vh'alyir," Eterran retorted viciously.

Zylas opened his mouth, but before he could fire back an insult, Ezra blinked the red glow out of his left eye. With an annoyed grimace, Zylas prowled away from the demon mage, his gaze sliding around the room.

Focusing on the ritual, I launched into an explanation of the changes Amalia and I—and Zylas—had made, and what the others could expect. As I spoke, Zylas ventured through a doorway into what I assumed was the kitchen.

Breaking off, I shot a worried look over my shoulder. "Don't break anything, Zylas!"

His voice drifted back to me. "*Mailēshta.*"

"Uh…" Aaron frowned in the demon's direction. "Do you mind calling him back where we can see him?"

"He'll be fine," I assured him, silently reinforcing my warning to Zylas to keep his hands to himself. "As I was saying, if the binding portion of the ritual works correctly, then the magic should link to the nearest Dh'irath demon—in this case, Eterran."

My crash course in demon-mage ritual summoning took several minutes, and when I finished, Aaron, Kai, and Ezra headed into the kitchen, following in Zylas's tracks. I was tempted to call the demon back into the infernus, but he hadn't been inside many houses. What was the harm?

Heaving a tired sigh, Tori dropped into a chair. I stepped around the table and sat beside her.

"Any luck with a location?" I asked.

"Not yet." She slumped. "I'll find something, though."

I glanced at the intricate array. "We'll need a large circle. Much larger than standard so we can fit two circles inside it."

"I'll find something," she repeated. "How long will it take to set up the ritual and stuff once we have a location?"

"A couple of days, then the Arcana will need to charge for three more days."

She mulled that over, the anxious crease in her forehead deepening. "Robin ... are you sure this will work?"

Sure? How could I be sure? This had never been done before. As far as history was concerned, no one had ever unmade a demon mage. We'd ventured from experimental Demonica into completely untested magic.

"As long as we can link the Second House blood to Eterran specifically," I said quietly, "I believe it will work. The big question is ... whether Ezra and Eterran will survive the separation."

Tori paled slightly.

Amalia folded her arms. "Not to be insensitive or anything, but they're going to die anyway. Better to try, right?"

Yeah ... that remark was absolutely insensitive.

"I never said I didn't want to try," Tori retorted coolly. "Besides, it isn't my choice. It's Ezra's—and Eterran's—and they want to try."

Amalia glanced toward the kitchen as though ensuring the demon mage in question wasn't about to walk in. "And what about after they're separated, assuming it works? It'd be just great if we freed Eterran only for him to turn around and kill us all."

Tori snorted. "You don't seem too worried about Zylas killing you."

"I worry about it every day."

I winced. Zylas didn't seem to frighten Amalia the way he used to, but she might never be completely comfortable around him.

Tugging the draft paper from under the grimoire, I rolled it up. "We don't need to worry about Eterran yet. We'll be summoning him into a circle, and he'll be trapped there until we free him."

Tori frowned. "Trapping him in a circle isn't much better than leaving him stuck inside Ezra. I don't see him agreeing to a regular contract-infernus-type deal."

"We can cross that bridge when we get to it," I replied vaguely, not wanting to delve into the specifics of my mission to open a hell portal and send Zylas home. "There may be options you haven't considered."

"Options like what?"

I shrugged. "We—"

A muffled shout interrupted me, the sound followed by a thump that came from the basement.

Peering at the floor as though she could see through it, Tori asked sharply, "Where are the guys?"

"Where's *Zylas?*" I yelped, shooting to my feet.

As another shout erupted, Tori streaked out of the dining room. I ran after her, Amalia on my heels. We sped into the compact kitchen and through a door tucked in a nook near the fridge. A straight staircase led downstairs.

Tori barreled down the steps, then pulled up short. I almost crashed into her back as I skidded to a stop.

The basement had been converted into a gym, the floor space packed with exercise equipment, weights, a punching bag, and a sparring area. My gaze whipped across it until I found my demon—along with the three mages. All four of them were standing among the weightlifting equipment.

"No way. It's impossible."

"But he just deadlifted six hundred pounds like it was nothing."

"He's shorter than you. It just isn't physically possible."

As Aaron and Kai debated, I noticed the loaded barbell sitting on the floor in front of Zylas. I wasn't sure how much weight was packed onto it, but the metal plates were huge.

"You have no idea what a demon can do," Ezra told his friends with quiet amusement.

Zylas gave the barbell a look like it had just called him a liar. With an annoyed snap of his tail, he grabbed the bar and heaved it up to chest height with about the same amount of effort I expended lifting large bags of flour at the grocery store.

My stomach dropped at the sight.

"Holy shit," Aaron muttered under his breath.

"What is the point of this?" Zylas asked grumpily, holding the barbell with no apparent strain. "Lifting heavy things?"

Ezra's mouth twitched as he suppressed a smile. "Humans do it to make themselves stronger."

"This makes *hh'ainun* stronger?"

Zylas didn't need any help becoming stronger, I thought faintly, unable to tear my eyes away from the tight, hard muscles in his arms.

"Can you lift it over your head?" Aaron asked almost warily.

Widening his stance, Zylas pushed the bar upward. As it rose over his head, slow heat flushed through my body, climbing from my toes up to my face until my cheeks were throbbing with it.

Holding the weights above his head had engaged every muscle in Zylas's body. Arms, shoulders, chest, abdominals, thighs, calves. Hard, lean, defined muscles beneath that beautiful, smooth, dusky-red skin. My mouth went dry, my head swirling, my thoughts fuzzy.

As he lowered the barbell, an elbow prodded my ribs, jarring me out of my trance. I darted a petrified glance at Tori.

"What did I tell you?" She arched an eyebrow. "Perfect abs."

Had she noticed me gawking at him? My cheeks burned. "I dare you to say that to his face now that he can talk back."

Not that she needed to repeat herself. Even whispering, she hadn't spoken quietly enough for Zylas's sensitive hearing to miss her observation.

A flicker of his irritation touched my mind, and I peeked at the demon again—just as he bared his teeth at Tori from across the room, a silent threat.

Maybe I should've warned her not to tease Zylas. Familiarity from humans he didn't trust wasn't something he wanted or tolerated. Plus, he didn't like being stared at.

"Okay."

Aaron's decisive voice snapped me back to the present.

"Let's find your limit, demon," he said, sliding another huge plate off the weight rack. Kai moved to help him, while Ezra hung back, caught halfway between amusement and exasperation.

Flicking his tail, Zylas straightened a strap on his armor that had shifted during his last lift. "Why? It is stupid."

"You can prove how much stronger you are than a human," Ezra explained helpfully.

"I already know *hh'ainun* are weak."

I wasn't sure whether to laugh or cringe at his bluntness. "We, uh, should probably get going."

Aaron flashed me a charming grin as he passed another plate to Kai. "Just one more. All males like to show off their strength. Whoever can lift the most wins."

My nose scrunched.

"*Ch*," Zylas huffed. "There is no victory in this. It is only strength. *Hh'ainun* are stupid."

I coughed back a laugh. "Brawn over brains" psychology was the last thing that would work on Zylas. He owned his reputation as a cowardly fighter, satisfied with victories gained through wit and cunning instead of brute power.

Ignoring the demon's lack of enthusiasm, Aaron and Kai stuffed as many plates onto the barbell as they could fit.

Zylas eyed the barbell as the two mages stepped back with an air of expectation. I could practically see the demon considering his options. He didn't care what the humans thought of him, but he *did* care about the *Dīnen* of Dh'irath, who was watching him from behind Ezra's pale iris.

Scowling, Zylas leaned down to grasp the bar. My heart climbed into my throat as he set his feet and lifted. This time, the weights came up slowly, the steel bar bowing from the pressure. Muscles bunched in his arms and his breath rushed through his clenched teeth. With a rough half-growl, he heaved it up to his chest.

My stomach did that dropping thing again.

The demon got one triumphant moment before a clip on the end of the bar gave way. The mages leaped forward as Zylas staggered and a plate slid off, crashing to the floor. Ezra grabbed the bar, taking a portion of the weight, while Aaron and Kai heaved up on each end of the barbell, stopping more plates from sliding off.

Together, they lowered the barbell to the floor. Zylas stepped back, puffing and rolling his shoulders as Kai began counting the weights. I bit my lip, hoping Zylas hadn't hurt himself.

"Tired?" Aaron asked the demon, amused.

Crimson eyes swung to the mage. His fingers closed around the front of the taller man's shirt and, with one arm, Zylas lifted Aaron off the floor. The mage grabbed his wrist, eyes wide with alarm.

"It would take more than that to make me tired," Zylas growled.

He opened his hand and Aaron dropped to the mats. The mage took a quick step back, putting himself out of the demon's immediate reach.

Ezra shook his head. "You just don't know when to keep quiet, do you, Aaron?"

"What?" Aaron muttered. "I was just asking."

"You're lucky he even played along with the weightlifting thing. He could've just brained you with a hundred-pound plate."

"I do not need a weapon to kill him," Zylas corrected.

Amalia snorted in amusement and I sighed. Well, it wasn't like demons were known for their friendliness or charm.

Turning to Tori, I found her worrying her lower lip, but I wasn't sure if she was watching Ezra or Zylas.

"As soon as you have a location," I told her, "we can begin."

She dragged her attention off the men and focused on me. Her hazel eyes were tight with uncertainty but her jaw was set with determination.

"Give me twenty-four hours."

8

AMALIA BLEW ON HER HANDS, her breath fogging in the chill air.
"What's taking so long?"

Huddled in the bus stop shelter, I peered down at my phone.
Ezra's message from two hours ago glowed on the screen,
instructing us to meet him at a downtown coffee shop in an
hour. That hour had come and gone, and the coffee shop had
closed for the night, leaving Amalia and me lingering on the
dark street.

I'd sent him three texts and tried calling him, but no
response.

"Should we keep waiting?" I mumbled. "Or just go home?"

Amalia shifted her weight. "What about Tori?"

I flipped to her name, bringing up our chat history. At ten
this morning, she'd sent me a message: *Got a lead on a location
for our special event! I'll let you know how it goes.*

After that, nothing. She hadn't responded to my follow-up messages.

Fidgeting with the chains around my neck, I peered up and down the street. Part of me was tempted to call Zylas out of the infernus, but a handful of pedestrians moved along the sidewalks, bundled in their jackets, and I couldn't risk anyone seeing him.

A flicker of impatience in the back of my mind—Zylas wasn't enjoying the suspenseful wait either.

"I just want to get this over with," Amalia said with a sigh. "Then we can focus on the Vh'alyir Amulet and the portal magic."

"And Xever," I added, preferring not to dwell on the task of sending Zylas home.

She tugged her knitted hat lower over her ears, the gesture almost disguising the measuring look she cast over me. "Do you want to deal with Xever before trying to open a portal to send Zylas home?"

"We don't stand a chance against Xever and Nazhivēr without Zylas."

"That's true," she allowed.

"Do you think I'm stalling on sending him home?" I asked irritably. "Maybe you don't remember, but I didn't try to stop him from using Saul's portal. I told him to go."

"I remember." She glanced at me, then stared determinedly at the intersection where a traffic light had just turned green. "I get that Zylas is important to you, but ... look, don't freak out, okay? But are you sure your attachment to him isn't coming from an unhealthy place?"

"What?" I snapped.

"Your parents died less than a year ago, and you were left basically on your own. I wasn't any help to you early on, right? What if you're … using him as an emotional surrogate to cope with your feelings of loss and loneliness?"

My gut twisted unpleasantly. "Have you been talking to a therapist about me or something?"

"No!" She stuffed her hands in her pockets. "I read some blog posts about grief and co-dependency."

"You think Zylas and I are *co-dependent?*"

"No, actually. It doesn't really fit. I was just trying to understand what's going on with you."

I glared at her.

"I'm worried!" she added defensively. "You've always had this naïve view of Zylas, like he's fascinating instead of terrifying. You were feeding him cookies and reading him books before you even had a contract."

"I didn't read him books."

"And your contract doesn't even *work!* Doesn't that bother you? Why hasn't he killed either of us?"

My fingers pressed against the front of my jacket where the infernus was hidden. "Because he promised."

"Prom—" She bit off the word. "There you go again, Robin. He's not a guardian angel who happens to have demon horns."

"I didn't say he was. If you think he's so awful, then explain why he's been honoring his promise to protect me all this time? Even when it's nearly gotten him killed?"

Her mouth bobbed open and shut.

"We came back for you, remember?" I said quietly. "He could've escaped the *īnkav* if he'd kept running, but he went back to save you."

She huffed. "Okay. Okay, you're right. It's not fair of me to keep painting him with demon stereotypes."

A painful weight in my chest lightened.

"But," she added forcefully, "that doesn't change the fact he's still a demon, and you don't want his demon dick anywhere near you."

I recoiled with a shocked squeak, my face instantly on fire.

"Trust me, Robin," she said with a sage nod. "Virgins see everything with innocent eyes, but it's not all sweetness and roses, especially when—"

"I'm not a virgin."

The words echoed through the bus shelter. Realizing what I'd just blurted, I clapped a hand to my mouth.

Amalia stared for a second, then snorted. "Please. You're the most virginy virgin I've ever seen. I always know when your books get steamy because you blush while you're *reading*."

"I'm not!" I clenched my teeth, praying that Zylas wasn't picking up on any of this. "I met a guy in my History 202 class and we dated for a semester." My cheeks burned hotter. "We slept together a few times."

"A few," she repeated dubiously. "Was it good?"

"Um … I guess so?"

"That means it wasn't good," she said dryly. "Why'd you stop seeing him?"

"Well, he was a philosophy major."

"Ah. Say no more." She squinted at my beet-red face. "Why are you so prudish, then?"

"I'm not prudish! I'm just … just shy." I folded my arms. "Anyway, I know what s-sex is, okay? You don't need to lecture me."

She snickered at my inability to say "sex" without stammering. "Did you try anything besides missionary with your boyfriend?"

"We are not having this conversation."

"Oh, come on. I'm curious. Did he go down on you?"

Losing all sense of dignity, I pressed my hands over my ears.

"Ever had an orgasm?" she asked loudly, grinning at my squirming embarrassment.

I pushed harder on my ears, attempting to block out reality. If she asked one more inappropriate question, I would—

"Am I interrupting?"

Amalia and I whirled around. Ezra stood just outside the bus shelter, a black toque hiding his curly hair. My level of mortification skyrocketed, and I almost cowered behind my taller cousin.

"Girl talk," she said offhandedly. "Where the hell have you been? We've been waiting for over … uh, are you okay?"

When her sharp impatience switched to cautious concern, I looked at Ezra properly—and realized there was no humor in his face. His jaw was set, and a frightening sort of blankness filled his eyes.

"My phone died," he said flatly. "Kai and I had to sweep the area, and it took longer than expected. Come on."

He strode away from the bus shelter, and I exchanged a quick, worried glance with Amalia before rushing out after him. I trailed behind for a few steps, then jogged to his side.

"Ezra?" I asked hesitantly. "What's wrong?"

He kept walking, staring straight ahead. "I'm not calm enough to talk about it right now."

"Oh." I paced beside him, having to stretch my legs to keep up. "Is Kai still around?"

"No, he went back."

"Back where?"

Ezra's jaw flexed. "This way."

He turned into an alley, leading us past three buildings before stopping beside a chain-link gate that protected a garage-like opening in the back of a two-story brick structure. He withdrew a key from his pocket and unlocked the padlock on the gate.

The gate rattled as he slid it open, the noise echoing in the quiet alley. Amalia and I followed him through the garage.

Inside, the air had a musty smell. I turned on my phone's flashlight, keeping it pointed at the floor. The hall was plain and beige, giving no indication of the building's use, but when I peeked through a doorway, I found a small room lined on one side with floor-to-ceiling glass displays, behind which stood mannequins dressed in dark uniforms.

"What *is* this place?" I whispered sharply.

"A police museum." Ezra opened a door marked with a staircase sign. "It's closed, so no one will show up out of the blue. And who would expect criminal activity in a police-owned building?"

No one—because breaking the law in the police's backyard was ridiculously foolhardy. Considering Ezra's mood, however, I decided not to point that out.

He led us into the basement and swiped his hand over a panel of light switches, turning them on all at once. Rows of fluorescent bulbs flickered to life, illuminating a long stretch of open concrete. Storage shelves, filled with boxes, lined the walls. No windows. No other exits. Completely private.

Pocketing my phone, I walked past him, scanning the floor as I went. The cracks and divots would need to be filled, since any imperfections could interfere with the magic, but the space was large enough for the ritual array.

"Will it work?" Ezra asked.

"Yep," Amalia answered with a mixture of surprise and satisfaction. "This is actually kind of perfect."

"Good. Kai and I picked up the supplies you talked about last time. We weren't sure exactly what you'd need, so we got everything we could remember."

I turned to find him gesturing at an oversized duffle bag beside the door. Several plastic bags from a hardware store peeked out the top, and a mop and bucket leaned against the wall.

"Concrete crack filler, diamond sanding blocks, sponges …" Ezra recited. "Alchemic paint and paint remover, a measuring tape, straight rulers, angle rulers, protractors, compasses."

I lifted a two-gallon bucket with a plastic top out of the duffle bag. Someone had written "Remover" on it in black marker. "Did you get all this from the guild?"

"No, we didn't want to draw attention to ourselves. Kai sourced it." Ezra shrugged his jacket off and pushed up his sleeves. "The crack filler needs a couple hours to dry, so we should apply it immediately. Where do you want me to start sanding?"

"We need to mark out the circle first," Amalia said. "Grab the measuring tape."

As I pulled a generic construction measuring tape from the bag, crimson flared out from my jacket's front. Zylas appeared beside me, his nose wrinkling at the musty air. His glowing stare flashed around the space as he did his usual high-speed escape-route planning—part of being "smart prey."

He pivoted to face Ezra. "One way out."

"And only one way in," he replied. "If you're concerned about being ambushed, keep watch outside."

Zylas scowled.

Ezra and I stretched the measuring tape across the floor, and Amalia marked the center point. She then used the largest compass kit to trace out a twenty-five-foot-wide circle. Zylas alternated between observing our efforts and investigating the storage shelves along the wall.

With a sanding block in hand, Ezra got to work evening out the floor. I grabbed the bucket for the mop and ventured up the stairs, searching for a bathroom where I could fill it with water.

Zylas followed me, his tail lashing. "*Hh'ainun* magic is slow."

"Yes," I agreed distractedly, pointing my phone's flashlight up and down the hall. "This will take a while."

I found a bathroom, filled the bucket with hot water, then returned to the basement. As I dunked the mop into the water, Ezra sat back on his heels and gave Zylas, who was loitering behind me and oozing impatience, a long look.

He tossed his sanding block to the demon, and Zylas caught it, glancing at the unfamiliar object in confusion.

"Make yourself useful," Ezra said, rising to his feet. "The faster we work, the sooner we can leave."

The demon mage trudged back to the bag, grabbed a second sanding block, and returned to his spot. Zylas watched him for a moment, then sank into a squat and started scraping his block over a rough spot on the concrete. He and Ezra worked steadily across the floor, and I followed with the mop, scrubbing away the dust and dirt. Armed with the crack filler, Amalia repaired every imperfection.

By the time we made it across the circle, the crack filler in the first half had dried. Ezra and Zylas went over it again with their sanding blocks, and I mopped up with clean water.

Finally, I returned the mop to its original spot, my back aching. Ezra and Zylas chucked their sanding blocks in the duffle bag, their hands coated in white concrete dust.

"One of us will meet you at the same bus stop tomorrow at nine," Ezra said. "We need to check the area each time before you go near this building."

"Check the area for what?" Amalia asked.

"Cultists." Ezra clenched and unclenched his jaw, then exhaled heavily. "A cultist attacked Tori after she stopped in here this morning. We don't think they know about this location, but we're being extra cautious."

"Is Tori okay?" I asked, fearing the answer.

"She … it looks like she'll pull through. I'm heading back to the hospital now."

The hospital? Not a good sign when most mythics got first-aid treatment from healers. "Keep us in the loop, please."

"I'll have Kai text you updates. He'll probably be the one to meet you tomorrow since Aaron is tied up with work at the guild."

Zylas returned to the infernus, and Ezra escorted me and Amalia out of the building and onto a well-lit street a block away. As he turned to leave, I caught his hand. Mismatched eyes snapped to me, cold and angry and shadowed with helplessness.

"It isn't your fault, Ezra," I said softly. "It's Xever. He's the one causing all of this."

His expression didn't change, but his jaw loosened slightly.

"Take care of yourself, okay?"

He nodded. "You too, Robin. This will all be over soon."

I watched him stride away, my lower lip caught between my teeth. Soon. A week, maybe a little less, but the cult had already nearly killed Tori—and a week more might be a dangerously long delay.

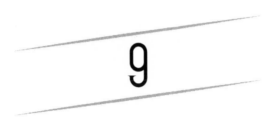

9

AFTER FOUR NIGHTS of intensive effort and seventy-two hours for the ritual array to charge, our work was done.

I stood beside Amalia, examining the results of our labor. The array, spanning half the room, comprised one large circle with two smaller ones inside it. Lines at precise angles intersected the rings, directing the magical forces. Runes—both arcane and demonic—dotted the intricate tangle.

"If this works," Amalia remarked, hands planted on her hips, "we'll make history. Not that we'll ever get credit for it."

"Are you ready to perform the ritual?" I asked.

"It's not *that* different from a regular summoning, and I've been practicing those incantations for years. I can handle it." She tapped her chin. "But there's a big downside to all this."

"What's that?"

"We won't have a demon mage helping us anymore."

"If we play our cards right, maybe we'll have Eterran's help instead, and he'll be more powerful on his own."

"Will you promise him a ticket home too?"

"Maybe. Why not, I guess."

As I spoke, I glanced around, half expecting Zylas to storm into the room complaining that I couldn't open a portal for the Dh'irath demon.

But he didn't appear. He was patrolling the building, as he'd done every night we'd been here. This time he was being extra thorough; it was our first visit to the museum without one of the mages escorting us.

Amalia let out a long breath. "I don't know about getting Eterran's help. Something tells me it won't be that simple."

"What do you mean?"

"It's just a feeling." She shrugged. "Call me a pessimist, but—"

She broke off as the sound of scuffing footsteps reached us. Someone—definitely not Zylas, who'd never make that much noise—pattered down the stairs into the basement. In a flash of wild red hair, Tori careened through the doorway.

"Whoa!" she gasped, coming up short at the sight of the massive summoning circle. "Holy shit, look at that!"

I couldn't help but grin at her amazement. A few steps behind her, Aaron breezed into the room, hands in his pockets and a smile curving his lips—a relaxed expression I hadn't seen from any of the mages all week.

Tori turned toward me, eyes bright with hopeful energy, but her optimism wasn't enough to disguise her pale complexion.

"You two did all of this?" she exclaimed. "You girls are Demonica rock stars!"

Amalia scoffed, almost managing to hide her pleasure at the compliment. "It's not that big of a deal."

"Seems like a big deal to me," Tori said brightly. "Is it charging up? How much longer?"

I brushed my hair away from my eyes. "It's ready."

"Ready?" Her gaze flicked between me and Amalia, her excitement unexpectedly fizzling out. "As in, we can start the ritual right now?"

"Uh …" I frowned, unsure why she wasn't happier that the wait was over. "Technically yes, but I don't think we should attempt the ritual in broad daylight."

"We should wait for tonight," Aaron said firmly, moving to Tori's side. "After midnight, at least. And I want Kai here too, just in case."

A smart plan. We needed to ensure there were no interruptions that could spoil the ritual. Otherwise, we'd have to let the array charge and start all over again.

The electronic blare of a ringing phone erupted, the sound bouncing off the concrete walls. Aaron whipped out his cell.

"Hello? Oh, hey Girard." A pause as he listened. "Okay, yeah, I figured ice artifacts would be difficult to find … No, the teams I sent out haven't found any vampires. All the usual nest spots are empty."

I blinked in surprise. They were searching for vampires? And cold-inducing artifacts? Had Aaron actually taken my suggestions on how to fight demons seriously?

"What about frost-bombs?" he asked, walking toward an empty corner of the basement. "Has Katherine had any luck making one?"

The warm feeling of his trust filled me as I swiveled back toward Tori. She was staring after Aaron with her hand pressed to her stomach, her face paler than before.

Concerned, I stepped closer to her. "How are you feeling?"

She started, her gaze snapping to me.

"Your injuries …" I hesitated. "Have they healed okay? Do you want Zylas to check them?"

Her mouth dropped open. "*Zylas?*"

I smiled encouragingly. "He's very good at healing. I could probably convince him to fix you up if you need it."

"Probably" being the key word there. "Possibly" or "a slight chance" would be more accurate, but I'd nag Zylas all afternoon if I had to.

"Uh." Tori blinked a few times. "That's very considerate, but I'm just tired." She shook off her bleak mood. "How are you? According to the guys, you've been out here every night."

"It's the least I could do. Even without the amulet to trade, I would've helped Ezra."

Yes, this had delayed our efforts to unravel the mysteries of the Vh'alyir Amulet, figure out portal magic, and hunt down Xever, but I still wouldn't have refused to help. Ezra might have his own motivations, but he'd helped me more than I would've ever asked for or expected.

"He saved Zylas's life," I added softly.

Tori rocked back on her heels. "He did?"

"Yes." Memories flashed through my head—Zylas caught in the *īnkav*'s jaws, his cry of agony as the beast bit down on him, his blood spreading across the cracked concrete of the helipad. "I almost lost him."

"Your demon means a lot to you, huh? What exactly is your relationship?"

My heart stopped.

"Wh-what?" I gasped with a sharp stab of panic. What expression had been on my face just now? "Our *relationship?*"

"Like … do you have a contract?" she asked, faintly puzzled. "Can you command him or what?"

Oh. *Oh.* She was referring to our unusual contract, not our … unusual closeness.

"We have a contract," I said hurriedly, battling a resurgence of the humiliation I'd felt after Amalia had caught me and Zylas together. "But I don't command him. We work together."

Her expression shifted to intrigue. "How did that come about?"

"We …" A dozen different replies spun through my head, but only one slipped past my lips. "We saved each other."

A soft wave of emotion rolled through me as I said it. We'd *saved* each other. Not just on that horrific afternoon when we'd formed our contract, but before that, when I'd given him life-sustaining food and he'd distracted me from my overwhelming grief and loneliness. And after that—every day after that, we'd been protecting each other in our own way.

Suddenly, the desire to see him was so strong I almost ran for the stairs.

Zylas, where are you?

A distracted flicker answered me. He was focused on something.

I returned my attention to Tori. "Are you concerned?"

"About what?"

"That I don't command Zylas."

"I won't pretend he doesn't frighten me," she replied with a shrug, "but Eterran frightens me too, and he's not *that* bad … for a demon."

"You sound like Amalia. That's how she describes Zylas." Needing to know what my demon was so intent on, I headed for the stairs. "Speaking of Zylas, I should find him. He wandered off again."

Tori trailed after me. "I didn't realize he was out."

Explaining that he was prowling the grounds for potential prey didn't seem like a comforting revelation, so I said, "He doesn't like spending hours and hours in the infernus."

Aaron's voice disappeared behind us as we climbed the stairs to the main level.

"What's being inside an infernus like?" Tori asked.

"I'm not sure, but the gist of it seems to be 'boring.'" Pushing open the door, I led the way into a dusty hall. "Are you ready for tonight?"

It took me a second to realize my question had stopped Tori dead in her tracks.

"I'm terrified," she admitted quietly. "I'm terrified to lose him. It feels like we're ushering him to his own execution."

"You aren't ushering him," I told her. "He decided this himself, didn't he? There's a big difference between being forced to do something and choosing your own path."

Why did you protect me all this time?

Because I promised.

I shivered at the memory of Zylas's husky answer. His promise. His choice.

"Choosing ... means something," I whispered.

Zylas had chosen to protect me. He'd chosen *me*. And I still didn't understand why.

Tori waved her hand in front of my face. "You all right there?"

I jolted. "Y-yes. Sorry. Just ... just remembered something, that's all.

"So, do you wanna call for him, or what?"

"Hm? Oh, he already knows I'm looking for him." I resumed walking. "He's got some reason for not coming to find me. Let's check the second floor."

Blips of Zylas's thoughts leaked into my head, and I knew he was somewhere above me. We returned to the stairwell, and I led the way to the upper level. The museum displays continued, the old offices converted to a new purpose. If I hadn't been intent on locating Zylas, I might've been tempted to snoop around.

When Tori and I turned into a corridor lined with windows, I knew we were in the right spot—because a flash of Zylas's annoyance hit me.

The shadow atop a tall cabinet came to life and the demon sprang off it.

I had one second to realize what he was doing, then he landed on me. His weight shoved me down, but he grabbed the back of my jacket and pulled me up just before my face hit the floor. A yelp told me Tori hadn't escaped his pounce either.

"*Zh'ūltis.*" His growl was quiet, almost a whisper. "Walking into the sight of hunters? I taught you to be smarter, *vayanin.*"

I scowled at the carpet in front of my nose. "Zylas, get off me. And what hunters?"

Crouched above me, he stretched his head up to peer over the windowsill to the street beyond. "They are watching."

"Someone is spying on us?" Tori demanded, pushing up on her elbows. "Who?"

Zylas shoved her back into the floor. "Humans. Three. They try to hide among the others, but they stay in one spot and watch, watch, watch. Hunting. Planning. They will ambush us."

Were they cultists, sent by Xever to watch us? The mages had checked every night for signs of trouble. Had they missed these men?

Moving cautiously, Tori peeked out the window. I would've looked too, but Zylas had a foot on either side of me and a solid grip on my jacket. If I tried to get up, he'd probably sit on me.

"What are we going to do?" Tori whispered, ducking back down. "Finding a new location and starting again now, when we're so close …"

Zylas, I silently warned, then scooted out from under him. He allowed it, his crimson stare flashing down to me before returning to the window.

"You haven't seen anyone watching us before this, have you?" I asked him, crouching beside Tori with my head below the sill.

"No. They came today only."

I could sense his certainty. This telepathic connection was actually kind of handy.

Straightening my glasses, I turned to Tori. "The ritual is ready. It'll all be over tonight. We should stick to the plan, and if they're here when we return at midnight—"

"—I will hunt *them*."

At Zylas's growling promise, I suppressed a shiver, hoping those men didn't return. They had no idea what waited for them if they did.

IO

THE WINTRY NIGHT AIR nipped at my cheeks as I lay on my stomach on the museum rooftop. Zylas lay beside me, unbothered by the cold even though half his skin was bared to the frigid wind. I discreetly inspected his upper arm, slightly unnerved by the smooth texture. Demons didn't get gooseflesh.

No goosebumps, no visible pores, no sweat. Amalia's reminder that his body was part magic lurked in my thoughts.

"Anything?" I whispered.

He poked his head above the concrete lip at the edge of the rooftop, eyes slitted to reduce their telltale red glimmer. He scanned the street below, then ducked down again. "I can't see anyone."

I let out a relieved sigh. "We're good to go, then."

"You will call me when Eterran is free?"

"I'll keep you updated the whole time." I smiled wanly. "Just listen for my thoughts."

"I am always listening."

My gaze darted nervously toward him, but he was peeking over the roof's edge again. *Always listening.* Did that mean he'd heard my uncomfortable conversation with Amalia—and the disquieting thoughts that had followed? He hadn't mentioned it, but that didn't mean he hadn't been mulling it over for the past week.

Busy worrying, I forgot where I was and pushed up onto my hands and knees.

With a sharp hiss, Zylas lunged for me. My back hit the concrete as he pinned me down. He shot a quick look at the street, then glared at me.

"Not seeing a hunter does not mean the hunter isn't there," he berated in a rough whisper.

My mouth opened but my voice had vanished.

He scowled at me, our faces inches apart. "You need more lessons on being smart prey."

"Sorry," I breathed. "I forgot."

Quiet stretched between us. Somewhere in the distance, police sirens wailed.

"You are blushing," he observed.

Yes. Yes, I was. Because he was lying on top of me, his weight pressing down on my body in a way that felt … good. Way too good. Even with cold concrete under me and the bulk of my jacket between us, I could feel his firm strength.

And his face—so close. And his eyes—softly glowing, the vibrant red broken by dark, dilated pupils.

"You can get off me," I said hastily. "I won't stand up this time."

His expression grew distinctly calculating.

I narrowed my eyes. "Don't make me use the infernus."

His muscles tensed, but instead of sliding off me, he leaned down—and pressed his warm face against the side of my neck.

I sucked in a sharp breath. "What are you doing?"

He nuzzled my throat and I grabbed his shoulders. For a second, just a second, I couldn't make my muscles obey—then I shoved. He moved easily, sliding off me, then rolled sideways and landed on his back.

Pushing up on one elbow, I glowered at him. "What was *that?*"

"You are not afraid of me."

My anger fizzled. "I'm not?"

"No. You are …" He searched for the right word. "You are nervous, *na?* Your heart was beating fast, but it was not fear."

I blinked again, my cheeks hot.

"You are not afraid," he concluded—and then he smiled.

The air disappeared from my lungs. My limbs weakened, and something strange happened to my heart—it was lurching, or swelling, or … heating. I didn't know. All I knew was that *Zylas was smiling.*

Not a wolfish smirk. Not a vicious grin. Not an aggressive baring of his teeth.

A smile of pleasure.

The soft expression only lasted a couple seconds, then he rolled onto his stomach and peeked toward the street again. "Tell the others to begin now, *vayanin.*"

"Right," I whispered, the sound squeaking through my tight throat.

Remembering not to stand, I scooted across the rooftop to the open access door and climbed down the ladder. Lost in a stunned haze, I passed through the halls without seeing them.

Zylas had smiled at me. A happy, pleased smile. Sweet. Soft. Things I didn't associate with him. And all because … because I wasn't afraid of him anymore?

The quiet murmur of voices roused me from my thoughts, and I blinked in the bright fluorescent lights, surprised to find myself standing at the bottom of the stairs, staring across the transformed museum basement.

Ezra stood at the edge of the circle, surrounded by Tori, Aaron, and Kai. They were all dressed in combat gear and armed with weapons—except for Ezra, who didn't have any weapons aside from the long gloves he wore, the knuckles and elbows reinforced with steel.

Amalia was crouched beside my backpack. Rolls of paper stuck out the top, and the open case of Nazhivēr's blood sat beside it. She had the cult grimoire open on her lap, her lips moving as she silently recited an incantation.

I cleared my throat. "Zylas doesn't see any signs of trouble. He says we can begin."

In almost perfect unison, Tori, Aaron, and Kai reached out, each of them touching Ezra—his hand, his shoulder, his arm. The demon mage drew in a deep breath, his shoulders pushing back.

"Let's do this," he said.

We took our positions: Ezra in the center of an inner circle; Amalia across from him, just outside the outer ring; Tori, Aaron, and Kai on the left side of the array; and me on the right, beside the case of demon blood.

Amalia balanced the grimoire on her outspread palm. "Ready?"

Ezra nodded.

"Once I begin, you can't move or speak," she warned, then added to the other three, "Same for you. I have to recite each line perfectly. Don't distract me."

Tori bobbed her head, her face white. As Amalia breathed deeply, centering herself before beginning, Tori clasped Aaron's and Kai's hands.

Raising her chin, Amalia began to chant. Her voice filled the large room, the Latin words flowing without hesitation. Admiration welled in me. I was the more obviously studious one between us, but the amount of dedication it took to reach that level of proficiency far outshone the time I put toward my fleeting passions.

She uttered incantations one after another, the ancient words calling upon and directing the deep, mysterious energies of the natural world. I tried to focus, but the memory of Zylas's smile kept pushing out other thoughts and I squinted at Amalia, trying to follow along.

Sharp alarm hit my mind like a splash of cold water.

Zylas? I gasped silently.

His ebony presence roiled inside me—*Not now—why is he here—too close—enough time?*

Zylas, I mentally shouted. *What's wrong?*

His focus shifted inward, toward me. *Do not stop the vīsh.*

My hands clenched. *Tell me what's happening!*

A fizzle of his trepidation, then his thoughts went dim and fuzzy as though he'd spun the tuning dial on a radio. He was blocking me out.

Amalia's voice rose, then cut off. She gestured at me.

Zylas had said to keep the ritual going, so that's what I'd do. Kneeling, I flipped open the case of Nazhivēr's blood and lifted out a vial. The others watched in terse silence as I walked to the edge of the array and stepped over the outer ring.

Magic vibrated into the sole of my foot. I moved to the center of the second, empty circle where a large rune waited. Tugging out the cork, I stared at the thick blood I'd stolen from my greatest enemy, which I would now use to save the life of a man he'd condemned to a horrific death.

I tipped the vial. The blood dribbled onto the rune, and as described in the grimoire, it clung to the silver lines, not a single drop touching the unmarked floor.

I glanced up at Ezra, who stared back at me—him and Eterran both—then returned to my spot outside the circle, stuck the empty vial in the case, and clasped my hands together. In the back of my head, Zylas's muffled tension crackled like static, a building electric charge.

"*Te tuo sanguine ligo, tu ut vocatus audias, Eterran of the Dh'irath House!*"

With Amalia's declaration, rippling crimson spread outward from the bloody rune, rushing across the silver array. The lines gleamed with iridescent magic as the power spread to the spot where Ezra stood.

He went rigid, his left eye glowing.

I held my breath. Had it worked? Had Nazhivēr's blood linked to Eterran's spirit?

Eyes alight with triumph, Amalia launched into the next phase of incantations, then pointed at the red-tinted line in front of her toes. "*Terra te hoc circulo semper tenebit!*"

The scarlet sheen whooshed upward, forming a brief outline of the dome barrier, over double the size of the barrier that had enclosed Zylas during his imprisonment in the library summoning circle. Ezra and Eterran were trapped now. No going back.

We were close. A few minutes more.

A sudden movement—Tori. She'd pulled out her phone. Aaron and Kai leaned toward her, and I caught a glimpse of the device's lit-up screen. Was someone calling her? Now, after midnight? Why—

Not yet, not yet!

Zylas's frustrated fury hit me. An image flashed through my head: a high view of the street in front of the museum. Zylas was on the rooftop, looking down at … people. Men in dark clothes—no, men in *combat gear*, slinking toward the building in small groups.

Tori was whispering quietly. She had her phone to her ear, horror stamped across her face. Amalia's eyes darted around but she didn't slow or falter, plowing through the next line of Latin.

Should I stop them?

Another vision hit me—Zylas was inside now. A dark hallway, so dark I shouldn't have been able to make out anything, but every cabinet and door and framed picture was sharp and clear.

Dim lights flashed at the end. Men in the museum corridor, one of them pointing sharply while the others crept past him, moving deeper into the building.

With doubled vision, I saw Amalia point at the blood-drenched rune as she called out another incantation.

Too many. Zylas's rapid assessment. *Can't stop them without vīsh.*

A dark stairwell. Silent feet rushing downward.

The scarlet glow of the array darkened to blood red. The bittersweet tang of magic coated my tongue, and I felt it in my chest, power building toward its ultimate release.

Amalia drew herself up. "*Tenebrarum auctoritatem da mihi, da super hunc imperium sine fine! Eterran of Dh'irath, bearer of the power of Ahlēa, wielder of the king's command—*"

Zylas streaked through the doorway.

"*—by your blood and your oath, I summon—*"

Springing toward Amalia's back, he clapped his hand over her mouth, interrupting the final words. The power in the array swelled, electric and intense, then faded.

Interrupted. Ruined. Extinguished.

"They are inside," he growled.

Silence pulsed through the room.

"Who's inside?" Kai demanded.

"Odin's Eye," Tori answered in a choked whisper.

My head snapped toward her. Odin's Eye? The guild? How did she know that? Even Zylas didn't know who the intruders were.

Aaron jolted like he'd been electrocuted. "We have to get out of here!"

He, Tori, and Kai pivoted toward the basement's only exit, but I didn't move. Because I already knew. I'd already seen it through Zylas's eyes. The enemy had been heading for the stairwell. They knew exactly where we were and how to trap us.

A hand closed over my arm. Zylas swung me toward Amalia, then sank into a half crouch in front of us, fingers curling and claws unsheathing. His thoughts flickered across mine.

He could hear them. Footsteps on the stairs. Rustling clothing. The heavy breaths of large men.

"Aaron Sinclair. Kai Yamada. Tori Dawson." The deep voice called through the doorway, the Odin's Eye team just out of sight. "You've been charged with harboring a demon mage, a capital offense under MPD law. Surrender now, or we will attack with lethal force."

Reaching out, I grabbed Amalia's hand, my fingers digging in. They *knew*. They knew Ezra was a demon mage. *How?*

"Ezra Rowe," the man continued in a rough half-shout. "You've been identified as a demon mage and the MPD Emergency Judiciary Council has ordered your immediate execution. If you have any integrity or humanity left, you will surrender as well."

Amalia squeezed my hand so hard it hurt.

Ezra stood as motionless as a statue. He hadn't moved from his spot in the circle, his expression terrifyingly blank and the gleam of demonic power gone from his left eye.

Tori whipped her arm out, flinging a small glass orb at the floor.

At the exact same moment, Zylas leaped toward the summoning circle. He slammed his fist into the floor, shattering the concrete—and the runes inscribed on it. Breaking the circle. Freeing Ezra.

Tori's glass ball smashed an instant later and smoke billowed out from the shards, rushing to fill the room. My vision went white.

With roaring shouts and thundering steps, the unseen mythics charged into the basement.

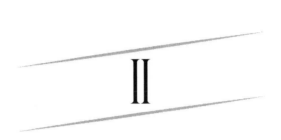

MAGIC EXPLODED EVERYWHERE, flashes and booms within the mist. A burst of orange light briefly illuminated Aaron's silhouette.

Panic screeched in my head. What should we do? Fight them? *Kill* them? But they weren't rogues or cultists—they were bounty hunters trying to bring down a lethal demon mage. There was nothing evil or immoral in that.

"Robin!" Amalia shouted in my ear, clutching the cult grimoire. "The circle!"

The circle. Drawn across the floor was twenty-five feet of evidence that we'd been engaging in illegal Demonica magic. To have any chance of getting out of this without a death sentence, we had to get rid of the circle.

I launched toward the corner where we'd left all our things. A shadow loomed across my path—a bearded man with a battle axe in hand.

Zylas shot past me. He slammed into the mythic, driving him back, and I rushed forward, Amalia right behind me. *There.* My backpack and the duffle bag. I skidded to a stop and dropped to my knees. Amalia shoved the cult grimoire into my backpack while I dug into the duffle bag.

An explosion hit us, throwing me into Amalia. We sprawled on the concrete as two mythics ran out of the fog, one with a sword and the other holding a key chain that rattled with small artifacts.

Zylas darted in behind them. Before they realized he was there, he'd swept his leg into their ankles. As they crashed down, he sprang onto their backs, grabbed their heads, and slammed their faces into the floor.

Don't kill them! I shrieked silently, praying he would listen because I didn't have time to explain why we couldn't use lethal force in this fight.

Lurching toward the duffle bag, I got my hands on a thin metal handle. I yanked and the two-gallon bucket of "remover" lifted out of the bag. I pried off the lid, threw it aside, and heaved the bucket up. The clear liquid inside sloshed wildly.

Heedless of the nearby shadows of mythics obscured by the smokescreen, I ran to the circle and flung the potion onto the floor. It splashed over the concrete, and wherever it ran, the red-tinged lines of the Arcana array vanished.

Amalia appeared beside me, holding the mop bucket, full of old water from when I'd cleaned the floor. She pitched the water into the circle. It sloshed into the remover potion, the two liquids mixing, and as it spread farther across the circle, the markings blurred and melted away, leaving indistinct smears.

Dropping the bucket, Amalia dove back toward our bags.

A gust of wind whipped across me, smoke swirling in its wake. Ezra rushed out of the haze, lunging across the wet floor at a group of Odin's Eye mythics.

"Mario!" The shout cut through the chaos. "Get your demon over here!"

A demon? There was another contractor here?

With a flash of crimson, a beastly shadow appeared, moving toward Ezra. More mythics had surrounded him. He was trapped—and in moments, he'd be overwhelmed.

Zylas!

He didn't need my prompting. His agile form shot past me, then he was smashing into the wall of mythics encircling Ezra. A man went down, knocked off his feet, while Zylas leaped for the next in line. Swinging off the heavier man's shoulders, the demon kicked a third mythic into the wall.

As the mythics reeled back from the demon, magic gleamed off something silver on the floor a few steps away from me— the case of Nazhivēr's blood, abandoned on the concrete.

"Ezra!" Aaron shouted. "Whirlwind!"

A shrieking gust erupted through the room, whipping grit into my face. Squinching my eyes, I dove for the floor and grabbed the case with both hands.

The howling whirlwind exploded into flame.

I screamed—then weight landed on my back. Zylas covered me with his body as the inferno tore through the room, carried by Ezra's tornado. As heat buffeted us, all the hair on my body stood on end.

Zylas scooped me up and leaped off the floor, wrenching me into the air—right as the fluorescent lights lining the ceiling exploded with electricity. Bolts flashed from the ceiling to the floor. Cries rang out as the crackling power found its targets.

Landing on the wet floor, Zylas slipped on the slick surface, recovered, and sprang toward the corner where Amalia cowered with her arms over her head. He swung me under one arm while I desperately clutched the case of demon blood, then grabbed Amalia. As he heaved her over his shoulder, I stretched my hand out.

My fingers snagged the strap of my backpack, the top open and a corner of the grimoire sticking out.

Wind roared, fire flashed, and electricity crackled, the entire basement consumed in a hellscape of raging elements. As I swept the backpack up and stuck my arm through the straps, Zylas whirled. He sprinted along the wall, keeping out of the worst of the elemental storm.

The doorway loomed just ahead—and fire blasted out of it.

Zylas dove. Cold swept over him as he sucked the heat in before it could burn me and Amalia. The inferno roiled over us and we slid into the small landing at the base of the stairs.

Spinning, Zylas threw me into a strong pair of arms—Aaron's. I gawked up at him, his body radiating heat.

A scream of agony pierced my shock. I twisted around—Zylas was gone. He'd vanished back into the haze of smoke to buy us time.

"Go!" Aaron yelled, pushing me ahead of him.

As I stumbled, I realized Ezra, Tori, and Kai were here too. Together, the six of us sprinted up the stairs, Tori leading the way while I raced right behind her. She flung the door at the top open.

Dark shapes—more mythics waiting for us.

Tori punched the first man in the face. Right on her heels, I grabbed her shoulder and shouted, "*Ori eruptum impello!*"

The silvery dome of my artifact spell whooshed out, blasting the mythics through the wall behind them and into another room.

"Go left!"

At Ezra's command, we ran left. Ezra sprinted past me and Tori, heading for the tall window at the end of the corridor. With a thrust of his hands, he used a blast of wind to blow out the glass, then sprang through the opening.

Without breaking stride, Tori jumped out after him.

I clutched my backpack and the case of blood. No choice. Praying for a moment of athleticism, I ran for the window and leaped. Barely clearing the sill, I plunged down, no time or breath to scream, then Ezra caught me. He shoved me toward Tori and spun to catch Amalia as she jumped out after me.

Tori caught my shoulders as I collided with her, and the case of blood slipped from my arms. It crashed to the pavement—we were in an alley, the dark asphalt lit by a dim security light.

I let the backpack fall and seized my infernus.

"You—you grabbed it—" Tori gasped, reaching for the metal case.

I scarcely heard her, my attention focused inward. Panic pounded in my head. How long had Zylas been down there, fighting all those mythics by himself?

Daimon, hesychaze!

The infernus vibrated under my hand. A second later, Zylas's power burst through the nearest wall and launched into the silver medallion. With another flare, he burst back out and reformed into solidity.

I barely had a chance to check him for injuries before he threw me over his shoulder. He grabbed Amalia, and she yelped as he clamped her against his other shoulder.

"*Run*," he snarled at Tori.

His urgency pounded through my head—then he was running at full demon speed, or as close as he could get with two passengers. He streaked straight for a chain-link fence, and I felt his muscles coil with power.

He leaped the fence. Three strides, then he bounded onto a van. Another jump, and he landed on a rooftop.

Behind us, the other four bolted down the alley, my backpack over Tori's shoulder as she fled.

Zylas sprinted across the roof. The edge loomed, and without slowing, he vaulted over it. We plummeted two stories and his feet slammed down on a sidewalk, his knees bending to take the impact. Amalia yelped, struggling to brace herself on his shoulder. Headlights flashed past us—a four-lane road dotted with traffic. A city bus lumbered to a halt at a stop across the street.

Zylas dashed across the asphalt and veered toward the bus. I choked back a shriek as he vaulted onto the roof with a clang— then leaped across the gap, aiming for a one-story building squeezed between two taller structures.

We landed on the roof. Zylas stumbled, his arm briefly crushing my ribcage, then pushed forward.

No way the Odin's Eye mythics could follow our route. No sign of them behind us. But urgency bordering on fear pulsed through Zylas, and he didn't slow. Across the roof, leaping down into an alley—

Getting closer.

—careening left, darting across another street—

Closer, closer.

—speeding into another alley, flashing past power poles and graffitied walls—

Too close!

Zylas skidded to a violent stop. Dropping me and Amalia, he whirled around, crimson power blazing over his arms. As I dropped onto my butt, the glow of his magic burned brighter—and another gleam of red magic ignited in the sky above us.

Zylas thrust his hands up, his spell forming a curved shield an instant before a blast of demon magic hit it. Concussive force threw me onto the pavement.

A dark shape plummeted out of the sky.

Zylas leaped sideways and the winged demon slammed into the ground where he'd just been. Nazhivēr straightened, huge wings sweeping out.

Phantom talons glowing over his fingers, Zylas slashed at the demon, forcing him back a step.

Get away!

His silent command cut through my panicked thoughts, and I scrambled up—but before I could retreat, another shockwave from colliding magic hurled me off my feet. Zylas crashed down on his back a few yards away.

Eyes glowing and arms veined with magic, Nazhivēr extended a hand toward the Vh'alyir demon. A jagged pentagon flared around his outstretched fingers.

Daimon hesychaze!

Zylas dissolved into crimson light—and Nazhivēr's spell struck the pavement. The asphalt shattered, water flooding out of the hole from a broken water main.

The streak of Zylas's power hit the infernus and bounced out again. He reformed in front of me, knees bent in a defensive half-crouch. Across the alley, Amalia scooted backward toward a chain-link fence topped with barbed wire.

Nazhivēr pivoted toward Zylas, his teeth bared in a grin that was part amusement, part disdain for his pathetic Twelfth House opponent.

Zylas sank lower, then sprang across the distance between him and the larger demon. Attacking instead of defending—because he didn't want Nazhivēr getting too close to me. I could sense his urgent need to keep Nazhivēr away.

The two demons slammed together, claws flashing. I retreated unsteadily, my heart pounding in my throat. Crimson blazed in Nazhivēr's palm, a sizzling orb of demonic power. He drew his arm back, aiming for Zylas, and panic jumped through me.

Daimon hes—

Faster than my human brain could comprehend, Nazhivēr flung the orb of power. But not at Zylas.

My vision filled with red light.

Robin!

It hurt. Everything hurt. My whole body. My head throbbed the worst, sharp torment implanted in the back of my skull. Darkness filled my eyes. The air hurt my bruised lungs.

"Robin! Oh my god, please wake up. *Please!*"

A hand gently patted my cheek, and pain clanged through my skull like strikes of a hammer. I groaned and squinted my eyes open. A blurry face surrounded by blond hair hovered above me.

"Robin!" Amalia's voice broke on a panicked sob. "He's going to kill Zylas!"

Adrenaline dumped into my veins and I sat up so fast the whole world spun, my vision flashing with black and red at the agony in my head.

No, not my vision. Crimson flickered and flared in the darkness.

Nazhivēr and Zylas fought in the center of the alley, darting evasions, powerful blows, slashing talons. The larger demon's wings flared with his strikes, his tail sweeping out for balance.

I didn't see what happened—what mistake Zylas made. One moment he was dancing away from Nazhivēr's talons, then he was falling. His back hit the ground—and Nazhivēr pounced. The heavier demon landed with a knee on Zylas's chest and slammed his fist into Zylas's head.

My mouth opened in a silent scream. *Daimon hesychaze!*

Nothing happened.

Zylas drove his six-inch phantom talons into Nazhivēr's side. Without flinching, Nazhivēr smashed his knuckles into Zylas's cheek again, ramming his skull into the pavement.

I grabbed at my chest, finding no chain. "My infernus!"

Nazhivēr hit Zylas again, the sound of the impact like a blow to my gut.

Zylas's crimson talons flickered out. He wasn't struggling. He wasn't moving.

Amalia disappeared from my side. I tried to push onto my feet and pitched forward, retching. Bracing myself, I looked up again.

His knee on Zylas's chest, Nazhivēr held a small metal object—a steel vial. Lifting Zylas's limp arm, he raked his claws over the demon's inner elbow. Dark blood bloomed across his skin.

"Robin!"

Amalia beside me. Amalia shoving something into my hand—a flat disc on a broken chain. The infernus.

Nazhivēr held the vial to Zylas's bleeding arm.

Daimon hesychaze!

Zylas shimmered into light, and Nazhivēr's armored knee hit the pavement with a crunch. Crimson power streaked across the alley and filled the infernus, the silver medallion buzzing as Zylas's spirit entered it.

This time, he didn't burst back out to defend me.

Nazhivēr rose to his full, terrifying height and turned toward me, that steel vial still in his hand. His dusky lips curved in a mocking smile.

Zylas!

In answer to my mental cry, the dark flare of his mind met mine. Heat flowed through his presence—and it flowed through me. Fire in my veins, scorching my innards.

Power pulsed between us, and my pain faded to the background of my awareness. I raised my arm, palm pointed toward Nazhivēr.

Crimson veins streaked over my hand and ran across my wrist.

Nazhivēr's eyes widened with shock—and in that instant when he hesitated, I imagined a five-foot-wide rune in the space between us. It appeared in glowing red.

"*Impello!*" I yelled.

The invisible blast flung Nazhivēr back. He twisted in midair, wings flaring for balance, and landed on his feet with his tail lashing. Magic blazed over his hands for a counterattack.

I created another rune, even larger, my magic faster than his. "*Impello!*"

It hurled Nazhivēr backward.

I created a third one. "*Impello!*"

He smashed into a building, the bricks cracking with the impact of his body. As he lurched off the wall, I summoned a fifteen-foot-wide rune right in front of him and screamed, "*Impello!*"

The wall exploded inward, Nazhivēr disappearing with it. Bricks tumbled from the jagged edges of the hole.

The heat of Zylas's magic burned down my arm and scorched my chest, but I ignored it as I called up one more rune—a different rune. It appeared on the side of the building, spanning the entire wall.

"*Rumpas!*" I shouted.

The wall shattered. Brick and concrete collapsed with a cacophonous roar, a cloud of dust billowing outward.

I didn't wait to see if Nazhivēr would reappear. Grabbing Amalia's hand, I bolted in the opposite direction, leaving the toppled wall and unseen demon behind.

12

EVERY STEP jarred my aching bones, but I kept walking. Amalia paced beside me with her arm around my shoulders to steady me. My infernus, tucked safely in my jacket pocket, clinked quietly against my *impello* artifact.

"Okay." Amalia blew out a long breath. "Okay … are we going home?"

I squinted blearily at her. My glasses hadn't survived Nazhivēr's attack. "Isn't that the direction we're walking in?"

"Yes, but maybe we shouldn't go back. It might not be safe."

"I don't think Nazhivēr is following us. He would've attacked already."

She shoved her tangled hair away from her face. "Not what I meant. I'm talking about Odin's Eye. They knew Ezra was a demon mage, and they saw us in that basement with him. And what if they saw the huge-ass Demonica ritual all over the floor? If our names weren't on their bounty list before, I bet they are now."

The winter night suddenly felt much colder. "But that means …"

"I don't know what MagiPol will charge us with—illegal Demonica, an illegal contract, or even harboring a demon mage—but the guilds are going to hunt us too."

"So … we're rogues now?"

"More or less, yeah." Her jaw tightened, then relaxed. "My dad drilled us on this stuff. I know what to do. To start—oh! Right. Give me your phone."

Stopping on the sidewalk, I felt around in my pockets and located my cell. The screen was cracked, but I could just make out the time: 3:32 a.m. I passed it to Amalia.

She stuck her arm over the curb and let go. My phone plunged straight through a sewer grate. A clang rang out as it hit something under the surface.

"Amalia!" I gasped.

She fished out her phone and dropped it too. It followed mine into its subterranean grave. "First rule. Phones can be tracked. We'll pick up a burner in the morning."

"But you didn't give me a chance to write down any phone numbers!"

Her look was incredulous. "You don't memorize them?"

"Uh … no?"

"I memorize every phone number. Dad taught me that when I was, like … five, I think? I know all the important numbers."

"Even Ezra and Tori and—"

"All of them."

"Oh." I peered miserably at the grate. "Should we have turned them off first?"

"They won't last long down there anyway. Let's go." She steered me back into motion. "Normally, we'd head straight for a safe house, but—"

"But we're not leaving the Athanas grimoire," I interrupted fiercely.

"Exactly. And I have to get some stuff. Also, we can't abandon Socks."

"Absolutely not," I agreed.

"Then it's decided. We go home first, get everything we need, then get to a safe house."

"Do we have a safe house?"

"The safe houses are technically Dad's, but yeah." She glanced both ways, then crossed a quiet street a block from our apartment. "There could be an ambush waiting for us at our building."

I struggled to concentrate through the pain in my head. "We used a fake address in the MPD database."

"But those two agents found us, remember? The abjuration sorceress and her snarky sidekick."

"Lienna and Kit," I mumbled. "That's true. I was so shocked when they showed up that I didn't think about *how* they showed up. Did Ezra give them our address? He'd filed a report that included our names ..." I trailed off uncomfortably.

Amalia frowned for a few steps—then jolted to a halt. "Oh *hell* no."

"What?" I gasped.

"It wasn't Ezra," she groaned, slapping a hand against her forehead. "It was *me*. My patent paperwork. I didn't put our real address on it, but I *did* put my real name. I should've realized they'd processed it too fast!"

"What are you talking about?"

She looked at me guiltily. "I think the agents followed me home after I picked up my patent approval."

My mouth dropped open. "You—you're right! They knocked on the door *minutes* after you got back."

"Ugh. I'm so sorry. Dad wasn't kidding when he said never cross paths with MagiPol."

We started walking again.

"So," I said heavily, "the question, then, is whether Lienna and Kit reported our real address. If they did, we're screwed."

"And there might be a guild parked outside our apartment," Amalia agreed. "But it's only been, what, thirty minutes since Odin's Eye crashed our ritual, if that? Their guys are probably all still chasing Ezra."

"I hope they're okay."

"Did you see what those mages did in the basement? They can handle themselves." Her gaze flicked toward the infernus in my pocket. "I'm more worried about us. How long will Zylas need to get back in fighting shape?"

"I don't know." His thoughts had gone quiet after we'd gotten away from Nazhivēr, and as much as my panicky side wanted to prod him mentally every two minutes to make sure he was okay, I resisted.

Remembering Nazhivēr pounding Zylas's head into the pavement, I shuddered, sweaty and nauseous. "Nazhivēr wasn't trying to kill Zylas. He knocked Zylas out so he could—could take Zylas's blood. Why?"

Deep creases formed around Amalia's mouth. "We were using Nazhivēr's blood to summon another Second House demon. Could Xever want Zylas's blood to …"

"To summon another Twelfth House demon?" I finished, horror choking me. "Could he use blood to get around not having the Vh'alyir name's demonic spelling?"

"Maybe. My dad should never have let that scheming bastard know *any* part of the Twelfth House name."

Our dreary apartment came into view, and we let the topic drop as nervous tension crackled between us.

We cautiously circled the building, then entered through the back entrance. All was quiet except for the tenant on the second floor who liked to sing country-music karaoke in the middle of the night. The off-key vocalist grew muffled as we crept up to the third level and cracked open the fire door. The hall was empty.

Clutching my *impello* artifact, which hadn't had time to recharge fully since our escape from the museum, I unlocked the apartment door and pushed it open as quietly as possible.

"*Meow.*"

I jumped half a foot in the air, accidentally knocking the door all the way open. Socks let out another loud meow and rubbed against my ankle as she waltzed past, sighting freedom.

Amalia scooped the kitten up before she could escape down the hall. We exchanged half-fearful, half-relieved looks, then ventured into the dark apartment. We quickly checked the bedrooms and bathroom for intruders, then returned to bolt the door.

"We're good—for now," Amalia declared. "We don't want to linger, but Zylas needs as much time as we can give him."

"I'll get him into the shower. You should start packing up."

Nodding, she disappeared into her bedroom, still carrying Socks, who was squirming impatiently.

In the bathroom, I closed the door before turning on the light, not wanting the telltale glow to leak through the apartment windows, then cranked the shower to its hottest setting. Waiting for the water to warm, I peeked at my reflection in the mirror—my face pale and splattered with red droplets. My hair was matted with blood at the back.

My stomach lurched unhappily. Nazhivēr's blast had hit me like a truck, but my impact with the pavement might've done more damage. I was lucky I hadn't split my skull open.

I held the infernus up by its broken chain. "Zylas? Time for a hot shower."

Red flared over the medallion and he took form in front of me. My innards twisted with muted horror—bloody gashes crisscrossed his limbs and his cheek was split from Nazhivēr's knuckles.

"*Vayaaanin*," he slurred, reaching for me—then he pitched forward.

I caught him under the arms, bracing against his weight. He staggered, his tail smacking the wall and the barbs gouging a chip out of the paint.

He pressed his hand to the side of my head. "You're bleeding."

"I'm okay for now," I assured him, peering anxiously into his face. His eyes were dark scarlet and his pupils were dilated—way too dilated for the bright bathroom. "Zylas, can demons get concussions?"

"I do not know that word."

I nudged him toward the tub. "Get under the hot water. You need your strength back."

He grumbled something incoherent that probably wasn't English and stepped into the tub. The water turned red with his blood, swirling down the drain in macabre patterns. He stood under the spray for a long moment, then sank down, folded his arms over his upraised knees, and rested his forehead on his arms, water drenching his hair.

I washed my hands, then got out my contacts and a bottle of solution. My head throbbed as I put in my contacts. I tucked their plastic case and the solution bottle in my toiletry bag to bring with me when we left for the safe house.

Gazing at the mirror, I pinched a lock of my blood-caked hair. I couldn't walk around the Vancouver streets like this. I considered the sink, but it was tiny. Time was of the essence, and the fastest way to clean up was in the shower.

My heart gave an extra hard thump as I shrugged my jacket off and set it on the counter. My sweater followed. I toed off my shoes, then tugged off my socks.

I stood with my fingers on the waist of my jeans for a long moment. Zylas's face was hidden, still pillowed on his arms. Gulping, I popped the button, unzipped the fly, and pushed my jeans down.

Zylas's head came up. His unfocused gaze swung to me.

My cheeks flushed as I stepped out of my jeans. "I need to wash off and we don't have time to take turns."

He blinked slowly. If he hadn't been suffering from a head injury, I suspected his reaction might have been different.

I tugged my tank top off, shivering as the steamy air met my bare skin. My sports bra and panties were staying right where they were. I'd just have to change after showering.

Dark scarlet-tinged eyes watched me approach the shower. I tested the water, hissed at the scalding temperature, and fiddled with the taps until it was bearable. Then, teeth gritted, I stepped into the tub in front of Zylas.

Water splashed down on my back and I stuck my hands in my hair, intending to scrub the blood out as quickly as possible—but the instant my hands touched my scalp, agony burst through my battered skull. I gasped, inhaling as much water as air. A violent cough racked me and I staggered, tripping on Zylas's feet.

I pitched forward, reaching out to catch myself—and came to a sudden stop that made more pain shoot through my skull.

My hands rested on Zylas's shoulders. His hands were on my hips, steadying me, his fingers pressing into the bare skin above and below the thin strip of my underwear.

I stared at his upturned face, my heart thudding, then hurriedly pushed off his shoulders, checked my balance, and kneeled on the tub floor. I gingerly slid my fingers into my hair and began rinsing the blood away.

Zylas didn't speak, his gaze roaming over me. Down my front, across my thighs. Back up. Lingering around my midsection. Up a little higher to examine my bra.

My face burned, but I couldn't get my thoughts in order enough to tell him to quit staring. I gently but hastily scrubbed my hair clean, skipping shampoo so I didn't get it in the cut, then climbed out of the tub. My head throbbed sickeningly as I grabbed a towel, wrapped it around myself, scooped my things off the counter, and slipped out of the bathroom.

Though I didn't look back, I felt Zylas watching my every movement.

I ducked into my room, shut the door, and stripped out of my soaked bra and underwear. As I peeled the fabric off my wet legs, ridiculous thoughts kept popping into my head. Like whether Zylas had ever seen that much of my skin before, or whether he found my soft, pale human body attractive compared to a *payashē*.

Banishing the topic from my mind, I dried off and opened my closet. Sturdy jeans, long-sleeved shirt, sweater with a hood, warm socks. I dressed quickly, then pulled my wheeled suitcase from the back of the closet. The sight of it sent anxiety spiraling through my chest.

I remembered packing it the night before I left my childhood home forever. I remembered living out of it while interloping in Uncle Jack's home, miserable and unwelcome. I remembered it bouncing along behind me as Amalia and I fled Tahēsh, venturing in the dark city on our own.

Grabbing my favorite books, I stacked them at the bottom, then pulled clothes off hangers and stuffed them in next. Tossed in my toiletry bag. Selected a few other small items from around my bedroom. Ducked into the main room to get Zylas's landscape book.

I slid it in with my other treasured belongings, then tugged the all-important metal case from beneath my bed, whispered the incantation, and opened the lid.

The Athanas grimoire sat in its nest of brown paper, and lying atop it was the Vh'alyir Amulet. I snapped the lid shut, then tucked the case alongside the landscape book.

As I zipped my suitcase, the sound of running water cut off with a clunk of the tap. A moment later, my bedroom door opened and Zylas came in, a purple towel hanging over his head as he rubbed the water from his hair. His steps weaved as he walked to the open spot in front of my bed, tossed the towel aside, and sat on the carpet.

Crimson power lit his hands and arms, and I backed out of the way, pulling my suitcase with me. The glowing circle of demonic healing magic appeared—but unlike the usual rock-steady lines, it wavered and blurred.

He huffed out a breath, eyes squinched as he struggled to focus with a concussion—or the demony version of one.

I held my breath while he painstakingly brought the magic into focus, then lay back. Power flashed, the glowing magic rushing over his body, and he arched up in agony as his wounds filled with crimson light, then shrank and disappeared.

He sagged onto the floor, breathing hard, and his eyes cracked open. Dim coal-red, not bright crimson. He was still running low on magic.

Sitting up, he flicked his fingers at me. "*Vayanin.*"

I walked over and sat facing him. He cupped the sides of my head. His cool magic tingled through me, and under the guiding pressure of his hands, I stretched out on my back, my eyes closed.

His magic was cool, but also warm, rushing through me in waves of differing temperatures. His touch was gentle as he used the rare skills he had learned from an unknown master to repair the damage to my fragile human body.

So breakable.

Dark thoughts, tinged with dread, swirled through my psyche.

Nazhivēr knows. He will break her.

The magic flowing over me flashed hot, and agony burned my body, concentrated in my skull where it had struck the pavement. The pain softened, then disappeared, leaving a dull ache in my head. I drew in a deep breath.

I am not strong enough.

My eyes opened, finding scarlet eyes that had darkened several more shades. Zylas was leaning over me, damp hair tangled across his forehead.

"*Vayanin*, you said … if it wasn't for me, you wouldn't need protection. No one would be trying to hurt you.'"

"Did I?" I said weakly.

"Is that still the truth?"

I opened my mouth, then closed it. Where was this coming from? Why was he asking now? Was he worried about what would happen to me when he wasn't around to heal my injuries?

Forcing a smile had never been so difficult. "Once we deal with Xever and Nazhivēr, I'll be safe. You don't need to worry about me. After you go home, I won't be an illegal contractor anymore and I can go back to living a peaceful life."

A peaceful, lonely, empty life. But I couldn't say that.

His stare searched mine, a faint frown curving his lips. Flickers of his thoughts brushed against my mind, but I didn't sense any relief from him. I wasn't sure *what* he felt.

"Zylas," I began hesitantly. "What—"

His hand clamped over my mouth, and he held perfectly still, not even breathing.

Listening. He was listening for something. I sucked in a lungful of air and held my breath too. His head turned side to side, slow and careful. My human ears couldn't detect anything but the creak of cooling water pipes.

He released my mouth, uncoiled from the carpet, and ghosted through the bedroom door. Scrambling up, I rushed after him as silently as I could. He crept to the apartment door and canted an ear toward it.

His lips peeled back, baring his teeth. "There are *hh'ainun* in the hall. Males. At least four." His gaze slashed to me, then he pointed to the balcony. "We will leave that way."

Eyes wide, I rushed into my room to grab my suitcase and jacket. When I hurried out again, Zylas was striding out of Amalia's room. She was right behind him, her face pale and a roller suitcase larger than mine gliding behind her. In her other hand, she carried a small cat carrier, Socks's eyes glaring reproachfully from inside it.

Zylas slid the balcony door open, letting in a rush of icy wind.

Dropping from balcony to balcony, he took our suitcases down first, then climbed back up the same way. Next he carried Amalia down, who had a death grip on Socks's carrier. The kitten yowled plaintively at the cold breeze, and I flinched at the sound.

They reached the bottom. As Zylas leaped up again, grabbing the second-floor balcony railing, I glanced into the apartment.

The front door swung open.

I darted away from the glass doors and pressed my back to the narrow wall at the balcony's edge. Footsteps from within the apartment. Male voices murmuring. Drawing closer. The balcony door was halfway open, beckoning them.

The voices got louder, closer. I tried to calm my panicked breathing.

Zylas appeared beside me, clinging to the railing spindles. I flung my arms around his neck, and he pulled me over the metal handrail.

As we silently dropped, the glass door slid all the way open with a thump.

Zylas swung off the bottom of our balcony and landed on the one below it. He ducked into the shadows beside the unit's dark glass door, holding me tight to his chest.

A long, breathless silence.

"Clear," a rough male voice called in an undertone. "Looks like they already booked it."

The glass door slid shut, and I sagged against Zylas, feeling as much relief as despair. We'd escaped capture—but our haven was compromised and we could never go back.

13

OF UNCLE JACK'S several safe houses, the nearest one was south of the Downtown Eastside in a very old Vancouver neighborhood. The "Lee Building" was well past its prime at over a century old, but it'd been renovated ... forty years ago. And its age showed.

Our sixth-floor unit featured a tiny kitchen that offered the only access to the bedroom, a cramped L-shaped bathroom with a stacked washer and dryer in the corner, and a decently spacious living room, furnished with a dining table, sofa, coffee table, and floor lamp. Everything was liberally coated in dust.

It could be worse. It could also be way, *way* better.

Amalia and I debated who would sleep on the sofa, until I sat on it and the whole thing sagged with the obnoxious creak of ancient springs. Deciding to share the queen bed in the bedroom instead, we left Socks in Zylas's care and passed out.

Dull morning light dragged me from a restless sleep. Lifting my head off the musty pillow, I squinted at the narrow window, the drapes too old and thin to block out the light. Amalia, curled on her side with her back to the window, snored quietly.

Careful not to jostle the creaky mattress, I climbed out of bed, dressed in last night's clothes, and tiptoed through the kitchen to the bathroom. I freshened up, put in my contacts, and dragged my hair into a ponytail, then ventured toward the living room.

Zylas sat on the dusty hardwood floor beside the large window, which offered a voyeuristic view of another apartment window ten feet away, plus a sliver of unobstructed cityscape. Socks was curled up in his lap, fast asleep.

I sat against the wall beside him; the floor was slightly more comfortable than the sofa. "I wonder where Ezra and Tori are. If guilds are hunting them, I don't know how we can set up another summoning ritual to separate Ezra and Eterran."

"We can't. Nazhivēr is hunting us. Anywhere we go, Nazhivēr will go too."

I bit my lip. "Could we defeat Nazhivēr if all of us worked together?"

"Maybe, but it is too much risk. I cannot use *vīsh* where *hh'ainun* can see. Neither can Eterran."

And with bounty hunters on Ezra's tail, we couldn't keep our battle with Nazhivēr private. "We can't help them, can we?"

"No."

I fidgeted with the hem of my sweater. "What are *we* going to do, then? Nazhivēr is hunting us, but so are guilds."

He propped his arm on the windowsill. "What do we *need* to do?"

"We need to …" I pressed my fingertips to my temples. "We need to defeat Nazhivēr and Xever before they kill us. Nazhivēr is the more urgent threat, but if we stop him and not Xever, Xever will keep coming after us, especially since he seems to want your blood for something."

"Yes. Nazhivēr is the greatest threat." His jaw flexed. "If the *hh'ainun* had come later, Eterran would be free. He and I could have killed Nazhivēr."

"Is that why you waited so long to warn us that Odin's Eye had shown up?" I pressed my lips together. "You should've said something sooner. We might've been able to escape the building without being seen."

"Nazhivēr was there. He was waiting for me."

And Zylas couldn't best Nazhivēr alone. My demon-magic-fueled cantrips had held the demon off, but I wasn't naïve enough to think *I* could defeat him. I wouldn't have the advantage of surprise again.

"Together," I said, "do you think we could defeat Nazhivēr? If we both use your magic?"

Zylas considered that. "If I am close to Nazhivēr, you cannot attack him without hitting me. But if we attack together before Nazhivēr is too close … maybe. But it would not be *dh'ērrenith*."

"Running away from Nazhivēr doesn't work, though," I pointed out bleakly. "He can fly. It'd be better if we went after him instead of always getting ambushed, but how do we *find* him?"

"Maybe with the book. But she took it."

"Who … *oh*." I squeezed my eyes shut, furious with myself. "Tori took the cult grimoire. Why didn't I grab it? That's our only clue about what Xever is trying to do!"

"He wants to open a portal. We have information about the portal—more than him. We have your grimoire and the *imailatē*."

Right, the Vh'alyir Amulet. It contained a portal-magic spell.

Pushing to my feet, I hurried back to the bedroom. Amalia lifted her head groggily as I dug into my suitcase and pulled out the Athanas grimoire's metal case.

Returning to the living room, I set the case on the coffee table. "*Egeirai, angizontos tou Athanou, lytheti.*"

A pale shimmer ran across the steel. As I opened the lid, Zylas sat beside me and deposited Socks on his lap again. She poked her head up, whiskers twitching as she sniffed toward the case.

I lifted out the amulet and set it in front of him, then withdrew the Athanas grimoire, laid it on the table, and opened it to the matching illustration.

"Okay …" My burst of determination waned. "Where do we start?"

He flipped the amulet to its back, where tiny, intricate arrays were etched. "The portal *vīsh* is connected to the demon spell."

"Is it?"

"That is my … guess." He scowled in obvious dislike for any speculation where magic was concerned. "I do not know how to make the spell awaken. The words do not work."

"You mean the '*evashvā vīsh*' incantation?"

"*Var*. It means ... *magic release*. It awakens all spells, except special ones." He prodded the amulet. "This spell is a special one."

"Do you have any idea what the incantation could be?"

"No."

"Maybe there's something similar in the grimoire." I started turning pages. "Anthea couldn't have created that demonic spell until she'd discovered the demon world, so let's jump to right after she perfected the portal spell."

I navigated back to the portal spell, then flipped ahead to Anthea's next experimental array, the precursor to the modern summoning array. Zylas shifted closer, his arm bumping mine as he leaned over the book. A tingle ran down my spine at the innocent contact, and an abrupt memory filled my mind: Zylas's dark stare roving across my near-naked body in the shower.

I frantically banished the memory and focused on the page in front of us. Faithfully copied notations filled the page, including neatly crossed-out corrections and Anthea's notes to herself.

"It's strange, isn't it?" I murmured as I turned to another page of experimentation. "Anthea managed to open a portal and ... I'd guess she at least *saw* a demon, right? She'd just discovered a new world populated by a whole race of never-before-seen magical beings ... and the very next thing she did was start working on a spell to abduct them from their home and enslave them. Why would she do that?"

"Power," Zylas rumbled. "*Hh'ainun* are weak. She wanted our power."

I'd marveled at Anthea's genius and dedication, but my admiration steadily soured the more I discovered. I flipped another page. "Slavery was common in her time. Maybe she didn't see anything wrong with it, but I still don't understand why her first—"

His hand covered mine, stopping me from turning the page. Several lines of demonic runes had been carefully drawn out, with arrows indicating where they would appear in the array.

"Is that part of the amulet magic?" I asked eagerly.

"No." An emotion I couldn't identify edged his quiet voice. "It says, '*Enpedēra dīn izh.*'"

That sounded vaguely familiar.

"It should be '*Enpedēra dīn nā.*'" He snarled, the sound rough and throaty—and furious. "'*Izh*' is him. *Enpedēra dīn izh. Kasht!*"

He shoved away from the table, dumping Socks off his lap. The kitten darted under the sofa as he stormed across the room, his tail slashing back and forth.

I scrambled to my feet, eyes wide. "Zylas, what's wrong?"

"I did not see it! *Esha hh'ainun raktis dahganul īt menirais thāanus īs!*" He pivoted on one foot, facing me with his teeth bared and eyes glowing with rage. "*Ahlēa* gives power to *Dīnen*. It is a special *vīsh*. It is … *King's Vow*. Other demons of our House swear to us—to obey the command we give them. If they disobey, we know. We feel their betrayal."

His nostrils flared as he sucked in air. "When *Dīnen* swear a King's Vow, *Ahlēa* will not let us break it. We *can't*."

"And the … the King's Vow is in the grimoire?" I asked. "In the summoning ritual?"

"The King's Vow is '*enpedēra dīn nā.*' King's Vow bind *me*. This"—he jabbed a claw at the grimoire—"says, '*enpedēra dīn izh.*' King's Vow bind *him*. *They use our own magic to enslave us!*"

He shouted the final words, his rage fueled by millennia of injustice, persecution, fear, and the slow destruction of demonic society.

"Oh my god."

The faint voice came from the hallway. Amalia, her hair messy from sleep, stood in the threshold, her hand braced against the wall as she stared at Zylas.

"That's why demons can't disobey their contracts," she whispered. "Not because of *our* magic, but because of *theirs*."

"And ..." I swallowed. "And that must be why only *Dīnen* are summoned. They're the only ones who *can* be summoned, because only *Dīnen* are bound by the King's Vow." As tears stung my eyes at the horrific unfairness of it, I hesitated. "But Zylas, didn't you say the power of *Dīnen* leaves you when you're summoned?"

His hands curled into fists. "I knew that *Ivaknen* return without power. But when Eterran and I swore the King's Vow to each other, the *vīsh* was there. We lose it when we return. *Ahlēa* must take it back then."

Jerkily, he turned to face the window, his back to us. He was so furious his tail wasn't even lashing, his entire body tense and limbs rigid. How much did he despise humankind right now?

"The Twelfth House is exempt from contracts, though," Amalia said uncertainly. "Is your *Dīnen* magic different?"

"No," Zylas growled without turning. "I do not know why I am not bound."

Amalia disappeared down the hall and returned holding a thin book with a leather cover that I recognized as her grimoire. Joining me, she opened the book to a detailed drawing of a summoning array.

"This part here," she said. "Is this line of demonic runes what invokes the King's Vow against the demon when he's summoned?"

Zylas stalked over, stopping on her other side. "Yes. And this"—he pointed to another set of runes—"is *Ahlēvīsh*."

Chewing the inside of my cheek, I considered what Zylas had revealed. "I don't think Anthea came up with all this on her own. She could've studied demon magic for decades and never come close to understanding the complexities of King's Vows and *Ahlēvīsh*, let alone figured out how to pervert them for her summoning spell."

"But clearly she *did* do that," Amalia said, gesturing at the ancient grimoire.

Sinking to the floor, I picked up the Vh'alyir Amulet, turned it over, and set it gently on the Athanas grimoire with the Twelfth House sigil facing up. "This amulet is described in the grimoire, and it contains a spell that's entirely demon magic. Anthea didn't add that herself. A demon added it."

"Willingly?" Amalia asked, kneeling beside me.

"I don't know, but the entire Vh'alyir House is exempt from contract magic. Everything else works, so it seems—doesn't it seem deliberate? Their exemption?"

A sound rasped from Zylas's throat—a furious, despairing snarl different from his usual angry growls. He swept away from us, hands clenched into fists again. Stopping at the window, he stared out at the narrow strip of cityscape and gray sky.

"Coming up with unprovable theories about the past isn't useful," Amalia said abruptly. "Let's look at the portal spell again."

"Right. Sure." I bobbed my head, eager to change the subject, and reached into the grimoire's metal case for my notebook. "We can look for …"

My hand dug through the brown paper that normally wrapped the fragile grimoire. I rose onto my knees and shuffled it more urgently, then pulled all the paper out of the case. A few sheets of scribbled translations fluttered onto the coffee table.

"Uh, Robin?" Amalia quirked an eyebrow. "Something wrong?"

I stared at the empty metal case, nausea building my stomach. So clearly, I could see it in my mind's eye: my notebook sitting on the nightstand in my bedroom. The evening of the guild meeting, I'd pulled it out to reread my translation of Myrrine's journal entries, and when Amalia had come in, I'd hastily dropped it on the nightstand instead of putting it away.

Since then, I'd been using a different notebook while working on the cult grimoire. I'd never put my most important notes back where they belonged.

And now they were in our apartment where anyone could discover them—and all my family's secrets.

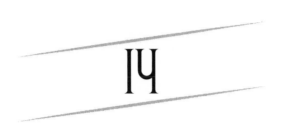

I CROUCHED BESIDE ZYLAS, shivering in the cold as we peered over the edge of the rooftop at the shorter building across a narrow alley. Our apartment.

Night had fallen, and in the darkness, bulky shadows prowled up and down the surrounding alleys.

I'd assumed the men who'd broken into our unit last night were from Odin's Eye, but I recognized those burly, leather-clad mythics with their bushy beards and arrogant swaggers.

The Grand Grimoire. Our former guildmates were hunting us.

My gaze darted to our balcony, light leaking through the glass door. That didn't mean anyone was in there; we might've left a light on during our urgent escape. It also didn't mean the place hadn't been searched top to bottom and all valuables claimed as "evidence" for whatever charges the MPD had brought against us.

Leaving my notebook exposed all day had been torture, but it'd been too risky to show up in daylight. This was our only chance to reclaim it before it fell into the wrong hands—if it hadn't already.

"Eight *hh'ainun*," Zylas said in a low voice. "They walk around and around but do not go inside. They are waiting for you to return like a human would, *na*?"

"Their demons are all clumsy brutes who can't sneak anywhere," I whispered. "Those guys probably can't imagine going across rooftops or climbing balconies the way you do."

His canines appeared in a brief, vicious smile, then he tugged my sleeve. "We will go now."

"Any sign of Nazhivēr?"

"No."

Relieved, I scooted behind him and climbed on his back, my legs clamped tight around his waist. Nazhivēr's absence was a comfort, at least. Demons were so magical that they couldn't hide their presence from other demons once they got within a certain range. Zylas could sense Nazhivēr coming—if he was paying attention.

He crouched on the rooftop's edge, hands braced on the concrete between his feet, then launched us across the gap. Landing on the building, he slunk along the ledge until he was above our unit.

Without a glance at the drop below, he hopped off.

I gasped as we plummeted, but he caught the ledge above a tall, narrow window. Hanging from one hand, a foot braced casually against the brick, he slid the window open. I peered over his shoulder into my dark bedroom.

"Is this how you come in every night?" I whispered. For some reason, I'd always assumed he climbed *up* the wall, not dropped off the roof.

He leaned across the sill, inhaling through his nose. After a cautious pause, he swung inside and landed silently on the carpet. I clutched his shoulders, scarcely breathing as I surveyed my room. Dark and empty. My closet door hung open, several of my belongings scattered across the floor, but I wasn't sure if I'd made the mess while frantically packing.

Sliding off Zylas's back, I hurried around my bed. A book sat on the nightstand: a study of Latin usage in Demonica that I'd borrowed from Amalia while we'd been working on the ritual to save Ezra.

I lifted the textbook—and there was my notebook. Exhaling in relief, I unzipped my coat and stuffed the notebook down the front of my shirt, its cover cold against my stomach. With my shirt tucked in, there was no way I could drop it while Zylas leaped across three-story-high gaps.

I zipped my coat and grinned. "We got it. Let's … Zylas?"

Eyes narrowed and nostrils flaring, he prowled to my open bedroom door and stopped, staring into the living room. I crept after him and peered over his shoulder.

The living room looked like it always did. Had the Grand Grimoire team even searched it? My focus darted from the breakfast bar to the sofa, remembering all the times Zylas and I had sat there. Sorrowful nostalgia stole over me as I realized those comfortable afternoons belonged to the past. We'd never spend time here again.

"I smell Nazhivēr," Zylas growled. "But I do not sense him."

"Smell him? You mean he was here?"

Zylas slid into the room, and I minced after him, revolted by the suggestion that our enemy had been here, looking at our home and touching our things.

Scenting the air, Zylas headed toward Amalia's bedroom. I waited where I stood, scrutinizing everything.

A glint of metal in the dark room. My brow furrowed. I took a few steps closer to the coffee table. Lying across the wood, a chain neatly coiled around it, was an infernus.

My hand jumped to my chest as, illogically, I assumed I must've forgotten mine. But of course I hadn't. Mine was hanging around my neck on the repaired chain.

The sigil etched on the infernus's face was wrong. Unfamiliar. Alien … but I'd seen it before.

"Robin!"

I reeled backward at Zylas's warning snarl—and crimson light swept across the strange infernus.

Power ballooned from the medallion and took form directly above it, stretching upward, expanding into the shape of unfurled wings. The coffee table creaked warningly as heavy weight settled atop it.

As I backed into Zylas, Nazhivēr solidified before us, the infernus between his feet. His lips curved, flashing white canines, then he scooped up the infernus and hooked it on his belt.

His glowing eyes rose to me and Zylas. "It is difficult to sense anything from inside the infernus. I was not certain you had come, Vh'alyir."

We have to attack together, I told Zylas desperately.

I felt his instant alarm—that Nazhivēr was too close, that it wouldn't work—then a surge of determination.

Get back, then attack.

Obeying his silent instruction, I retreated in a scramble, keeping my eyes on Nazhivēr while I ran through possible cantrips to use against him.

His lips curving in a venomous grin, the winged demon launched off the coffee table, the force of his leap collapsing the wooden legs.

Crimson streaked over Zylas's hands, forming his phantom talons. The two demons met—and I gasped as Zylas's talons plunged into Nazhivēr's lower gut. That easily, he'd landed his first strike.

Zylas's fear slashed across my mind—the realization that he'd made a critical mistake.

Nazhivēr's elbow smashed down between Zylas's shoulder blades, throwing him into the floor. I flung my hand up, crimson sparking over my fingertips as I called up the image of the *impello* cantrip.

I expected Nazhivēr to attack Zylas, crumpled at his feet. To stomp on the smaller demon before he could retaliate. To do *something* to his more dangerous opponent.

But in that single, miniscule instant, the Dh'irath demon turned his attention to me.

He was across the living room in a flash, and his blow struck my chest.

I flew back and crashed into the refrigerator. I was in the kitchen now? The thought flittered across my dazed, pain-racked brain—then a huge, powerful hand closed around my throat, squeezing my windpipe.

A tearing tug against my chest, a slash of pain across the back of my neck, then the world spun as I flew through the air.

Arms caught me. I thudded against Zylas, gasping and coughing. As his grip on me tightened, I lifted my tear-blurred gaze.

Nazhivēr stood in the kitchen, a chain dangling from his fist. My infernus. He'd torn it off me so I couldn't use it to call Zylas out of danger or tap into his magic.

The demon smirked mockingly as he raised his other hand and closed it around the swinging medallion. Crimson flared across his fist.

Terror washed through me in an ice-cold wave. Zylas's horror mirrored mine, a dark swirl in my mind.

No, I silently gasped.

No, he furiously snarled.

Magic blazed over Nazhivēr's hand, and his fingers clenched. Canines flashing in a sneer, he opened his fingers.

The broken shards of my infernus tumbled from his hand and pattered to the floor. I scarcely heard the faint clink of metal on tile, consumed by the sudden, deafening emptiness inside my head.

15

ZYLAS? Zylas? Zylas?

No matter how forcefully I thought his name, I got no reply. I couldn't hear him. I couldn't sense him. His arms were still around me, but he was gone from my mind—and his power was gone from my body.

Nazhivēr dropped the infernus chain atop the rubble of the medallion. Wings flaring, he charged us.

Zylas threw me out of harm's way. I landed on my hands and knees, then scrambled across the carpet as the demons collided. Panting with desperation, I crawled into the kitchen and grabbed the largest piece of the infernus—a shard the size of my thumb, the edge of the Vh'alyir sigil etched on it.

Daimon hesychaze! I mentally shouted, clutching the bit of metal.

Zylas dodged Nazhivēr's slashing talons and landed on the sofa. He grabbed the floor lamp and swung it at the larger demon. The shade flew off as it grazed Nazhivēr's horns, and Zylas jabbed with it like a spear.

Nazhivēr ripped it out of his hand, and Zylas seized a throw pillow. He chucked it at Nazhivēr's face, then dove for his enemy's leg. He raked his claws across Nazhivēr's ankle as he slid past.

Zylas rolled back onto his feet. Nazhivēr spun around—and with a crash, the floor lamp tumbled after him. Somehow, Zylas had looped the cord around Nazhivēr's leg.

Ignoring the lamp, Nazhivēr called on his magic. Crimson power blazed as he surged toward Zylas.

A crackling orb flew past my head and smashed into the fridge door. I plastered myself to the carpet as the demons broke apart, holding handfuls of sizzling magic that they had no time to form into spells. They hurled their magic and the glass patio door shattered. Another spinning orb flew past me and hit the electric range, exploding against the stovetop.

I scrabbled across the floor, infernus shards jabbing my hands. As I snatched up my *impello* artifact, caught on the broken chain, I smelled it—smoke.

A roll of paper towel had toppled on the mangled stovetop where the element coil had torn halfway from its socket. Sparks jumped at the connection point, and flames licked at the top of the paper towel roll.

I shot a panicked glance over my shoulder at the battling demons, then flung open a kitchen cabinet and seized a bottle of olive oil. Leaping up, I threw it as hard as I could into the stovetop. It shattered, oil splashing across the burning paper towel. Flames whooshed up—but didn't roar across the oil like I'd expected.

Cursing, I grabbed the bottom of the oil-soaked paper towel roll, spun around, and flung it. The fiery projectile arched over the breakfast bar and landed in the middle of the sofa. The smoke alarm went off with a high-pitched keening and both demons flinched.

As flames caught on the edge of the cotton blanket I'd left across the back of the sofa, I opened another cupboard and heaved out a half-full bag of flour. Ripping the top open, I flung the flour at the sofa in a wide arc. White powder poofed through the air, drifting down toward the open flame.

It exploded into a fireball.

I was already ducking behind the breakfast bar as the roaring flames rushed through the cloud of flour. Heat blasted my arms as I shielded my head, but the fire was short-lived.

I shot up again, a hand pressed to my stomach to ensure my notebook was still safely tucked in my shirt. Zylas and Nazhivēr had separated, diving to opposite ends of the room to avoid the explosion I'd unleashed. The sofa was engulfed in flames, black smoke roiling across the ceiling and hazing the air.

Bang.

The apartment door, three feet away from me, flew open.

I glimpsed an unfamiliar demon barging through and screamed, "*Ori eruptum impello!*"

A silvery dome burst off my artifact and hurled the demon back out into the hallway—and into the contractor behind him.

I rushed away from the door, panting—coughing. Shimmering fire crawled across the walls, spreading fast, the heat beating against me. The room was growing darker by the second.

Eyes and throat burning, I dropped to my hands and knees. *Zylas!*

But he couldn't hear me that way.

"*Zylas!*" I screamed hoarsely.

A shadow in the smoke. Zylas skidded out of the haze and scooped me up with one arm, crimson magic blazing up his other arm. A five-foot-wide spell circle flared off his wrist, pulsing with power.

Across the apartment, Nazhivēr stood in front of the shattered patio door, smoke billowing around him as it rushed out the opening.

Zylas's spell erupted—a howling beam that tore across the room. A booming crash pierced my ears and a rush of cold swept in through the obliterated wall.

The hungry flames devouring the sofa surged across the ceiling. Everything was fire and smoke, and I couldn't breathe to tell Zylas my plan. I pointed at my bedroom.

Obediently, he shot into the room. He must've figured out my intent, because without direction, he ducked into my open closet, shoved a bundle of fabric into my arms, then rushed to the open window. His arm squeezed my middle as I clutched the clothing, my notebook pressing into my stomach beneath my jacket.

Blessedly cold air hit me as Zylas swung out the window and dropped. He caught the sill below to halt our fall, then let go. Dropped to the next window. Then dropped to the ground.

In the dark, narrow gap between buildings, he pressed me into the wall.

"Robin," he whispered urgently.

I gasped over and over, fighting the need to cough so my lungs could absorb some oxygen. His hands slid into my hair and his magic flowed through me.

"You are not injured badly."

Nodding, I sucked in more air. "Nazhivēr?"

"Nearby."

I lifted my chin, listening for the sound I was desperate to hear—the reason I'd spread an inferno through my apartment.

The wail of sirens pierced the quiet night, growing louder, and I let out a relieved breath. Hands trembling from post-adrenaline weakness, I held out the bundle of fabric to him.

He lifted a pair of baggy sweatpants and stepped into them, tugging them up his metal greaves and dark shorts. Pulling the black sweater on, he drew the hood over his horns, then looped his tail around his waist, hiding it beneath the sweater's hem.

I checked one more time that I still had my notebook, then grasped his hand and dragged him out of the shadows. Tenants streamed out of the apartment building, some in pajamas and housecoats, and we joined them as a line of firetrucks rolled down the street, lights flashing and horns blaring to clear the traffic.

Zylas walked beside me, eyes downcast to hide their telltale demonic glow. No one gave him a second glance as we followed the other tenants into the street. He wasn't the only barefoot refugee of the fire.

The blare of firetrucks and alarms battered my ears. Flames boiled from the gaping hole in the building's wall that marked our unit, smoke billowing toward the dark sky.

As firefighters poured out of the trucks, a few of them shouting at everyone to get back, I spotted a small group that stood out in all the wrong ways: four burly men in leather, two with round pendants glinting on their chests. They lurked near the alley, scanning the stragglers fleeing the apartment's main entrance.

Tightening my grip on Zylas's hand, I pulled him deeper into the growing crowd. Some people had their phones out, cameras pointed at the spreading fire. We squeezed into the mix of displaced tenants and spectators, and I rose onto my tiptoes to look for the Grand Grimoire bounty hunters again.

Zylas pulled me against his chest.

I gasped as he wound his arms around me. His glowing eyes met mine, then flicked to our left. A young couple stood nearby, the man holding his girlfriend close while she sniffled quietly.

Ah. He was mimicking them to help us blend in. Smart.

As I leaned into him, the chaos swelling and nameless people jostling us, I slid my hand into my pocket where I'd stuffed my *impello* artifact. My fingertips brushed against the infernus shard, and a tremor ran through me.

I buried my face in his chest, telling myself it was just an act—but it was harder to convince myself that the tears on my cheeks were for the benefit of the crowd around us.

ZYLAS AND I STOOD at a bus stop.

An hour ago, taking public transit from our safe house to the apartment had been easy. Thoughtless. The natural decision.

Now, I had to concentrate on breathing so I didn't hyperventilate and faint. The middle-aged man standing a few paces away, also waiting for a bus, kept glancing at Zylas's half-bare feet. Had he noticed the unusual tone of the demon's skin? Was he suspicious? Would he say something?

I'd jokingly promised to take Zylas for a bus ride once, hadn't I? What a ridiculous, risky idea.

I stared down the dark, quiet street as though concentrating hard enough would make a bus appear. We were three blocks from the burning apartment building. No bounty hunters were likely to wander this far afield, and even if they did, why would they glance twice at a couple with their hoods drawn up against the cold?

My hand was wrapped around Zylas's warm fingers. I wasn't sure why. So we'd look more natural and couple-like? So I could squeeze his hand in warning if he did something too demony? So I could feel like we were connected in some small way?

The distinct wheeze of a bus engine reached my ears, and the large vehicle turned the corner. I gulped as it rolled to a stop and the doors slid open.

Clutching Zylas's hand, I stepped inside the bus and stuffed two tickets into the receptacle. The middle-aged man didn't follow us onboard, and the doors slid closed. A group of teenagers sat near the front, chatting loudly. They didn't spare us any attention as I nudged Zylas ahead of me, pushing him toward the rear doors.

The bus accelerated away from the curb. At the sudden movement, Zylas wobbled—and his tail appeared as he instinctively swung it out for balance.

He snapped it up around his waist again almost as fast, and I glanced over my shoulder in a panic. The teens' chatter went on. They hadn't noticed.

We moved into the gap beside the rear doors, Zylas's back to the driver and group of teens. When I wrapped my hand around the center pole, he copied me, the bus's dim overhead light washing the red undertones from his skin. He raised his eyes, two crimson spots reflecting on the window as dark storefronts slid past outside it. The bus trundled to a stop at a traffic light.

"You are not there."

My gaze flicked from the window to his face.

"Since I left the circle …" The engine's low roar almost drowned out his husky voice. "… you have been in my mind. Always. Sometimes quiet, but always there."

We swayed in unison as the bus slowly took a corner.

"I'd only just gotten used to hearing you in my head," I mumbled. "Now you're gone. Our connection is gone."

He slid his hand down the pole until it touched mine.

I let out a shaky breath. "I can't share your magic anymore. We can't communicate mind to mind. You can't hide in the infernus."

In other words, all our special advantages were gone. We were just a demon and a human, separate and independent of each other. Our special link, our intimate bond, had been erased.

Why did losing the infernus feel like a piece of my soul had been severed?

"We have to replace it," I whispered, my panic spiking. "As soon as possible."

He gazed at me, then tugged on my jacket, pulling me closer. As I tipped into him, my eyes widening, he leaned down. His nose touched my cheek, his breath warm on my skin.

"You are afraid."

I said nothing. Didn't know what to say. I'd never been more helpless to read his meaning or his mood.

Somehow, standing on a bus dressed in human clothes, he seemed as mysterious and incomprehensible as he had the first time I'd seen him in the summoning circle in Uncle Jack's basement.

16

THE SAFE HOUSE DOOR banged shut. I leaped off the sagging sofa and hurried toward the hall.

Amalia strode to meet me, her jacket zipped up to her throat and a plastic bag hanging off her arm. She waved me back into the living room and dropped her purse on the floor.

Zylas looked over. He sat in his new favorite spot by the window, still wearing his black hoodie. Not the sweatpants though. He'd forgotten about his greaves and the metal armor had torn the knees out of the cotton pants when he'd sat down.

"Got one," she announced, pulling a cheap cellphone out of her bag. "Thank god for twenty-four-hour stores."

I bounced nervously on the balls of my feet as she pried the packaging open, inserted a new SIM card into the phone, and turned it on. The few minutes it took for the phone to boot up and connect to the network made my skin itch.

"Calm *down*, Robin," she muttered. "You're making me jumpy."

"Sorry."

She finally dialed, and the phone rang on speaker. Six rings, and it went to voicemail. She redialed. It started ringing again—and the line clicked.

"Who is this?" a gruff male voice demanded.

"Your daughter," Amalia said, rolling her eyes. "My first burner phone. You should be proud, Dad."

"Where are you?"

"The Lee Building apartment."

"Is Robin there? Are you two okay?"

"I'm here," I said quickly, a warm feeling pushing through my anxiety. Uncle Jack actually sounded worried about us. "We're fine."

"And is … uh … Zeelas there?"

"*Zuh-yee-las*," Amalia corrected. "Get his name right, jeez. And yes, he's here."

Uncle Jack puffed out a breath, and a rustling noise suggested he was repositioning. Considering it was after midnight, he was probably in bed. "So, what happened?"

"We were helping some guildmates with illegal Demonica shit and got busted by Odin's Eye," Amalia summed up with admirable succinctness.

"Illegal shit like a *demon mage*? What were you thinking, Amalia?"

"How do you know about that?"

"MagiPol pushed the bounty alert to every mythic in the city. You've been charged with harboring a demon mage and performing prohibited Demonica magic. There's a sizable bounty on you both."

Amalia swore.

With my gut sinking at the confirmation of my fears, I asked, "Do you know if Ezra's been captured?"

"Not yet, but the combat guilds are searching for him and his buddies—and once they're dealt with, the guilds will be coming after you two." He cursed under his breath. "I taught you better than to get involved in this kind of thing, Amalia! Didn't I tell you—"

"Yeah, yeah," she interrupted. "Let's come back to that. First, I need to know if an infernus can be replaced."

"Replaced? You mean, if an infernus is damaged?"

"Yeah."

"Typically not, no."

"Why not?" I demanded.

"Legal contracts, and most illegal ones, don't allow the demon to regain its autonomy under any circumstances. If the infernus magic ceases to function, the demon can't act on its own and basically freezes up."

"Ah, shit," Amalia muttered. "You can't set up a new infernus without the demon accepting it, and if the demon is frozen, it can't do that."

I looked from the phone to Amalia and back. "Frozen? You mean, the demon just … turns into a statue? And it'll just stand there forever?"

"No contractor would just *leave* it there," Uncle Jack corrected. "But yes. There's nothing to do but put the demon down."

Bile rose in my throat and I swallowed hard. "That's barbaric. It isn't the demon's fault if an infernus breaks."

"It's necessary." Impatience sharpened Uncle Jack's voice. "Otherwise, the demon would be free to kill its contractor—or anyone else nearby."

I pinched the bridge of my nose. "What about a demon that hasn't frozen up?"

"Then you could theoretically repeat the infernus ritual, assuming you can make the demon agree to—wait, are we talking about *your* infernus? With Zeelas?"

"*Zuh-yee-las*," Amalia repeated in exasperation. "And yeah. Claude's demon smashed it."

I glanced toward Zylas, who still sat by the window, watching us. He hadn't said a word since the phone call had begun, his expression oddly closed off.

A sudden thought hit me: *Would* he agree to be bound to a new infernus?

He hated being stuck inside it all the time, and he *really* hated it when I forced him to return with the command phrase. Since escaping Nazhivēr, he hadn't actually *said* we should get a new infernus, or implied he agreed with my urgent plan to acquire a replacement.

"So we just need a new infernus, then?" Amalia asked, missing my alarm.

"Yes," Uncle Jack replied brusquely. "And I'd recommend redoing the entire contract ritual to ensure there are no blips. Do you have a blank infernus?"

"Nope. Lost 'em when our house burned down. Where can I get one?"

"Depends on whether you want a prepared one."

"That'd be preferable since I don't have two weeks to waste drawing an array and charging it."

Uncle Jack chuffed a brief laugh. "I'll ask around. Not letting you anywhere near my associates while you have bounties on your heads. You'll get them arrested."

"Gee, thanks, Dad," Amalia retorted dryly. "Learned anything about Claude lately? 'Cause *we* found out he's actually the secret leader of a demon-worshipping cult."

"He's a *what?*"

While she updated her father on Claude's true identity, I sank down on the sofa and dropped my face into my hands. A new infernus. Uncle Jack would find one for me.

Then I just had to convince Zylas how vitally imperative it was that he agree to bind himself to it.

I peeked at the demon through my fingers. He was staring out the window again, looking unusually bulky with the loose sweater draped over him. It was disconcerting when I was so used to seeing him half nude.

"Okay."

I lifted my head, realizing Amalia had ended the call with her father.

She bounced the phone on her palm. "While we wait for Dad to find a replacement infernus, we need to plan our next move."

"What move? We're staying right here until we have an infernus."

Her eyebrows drew down. "That could be days, even weeks. We can't just wait around while Nazhivēr hunts us."

"I don't have an infernus." I emphasized each word since she didn't seem to get it. "Zylas can't move around in daylight, and at night, it's still a huge risk. Like your dad said, no infernus means no contract for a legal contractor."

"Well, yeah, there are additional challenges." She pushed her hair off her shoulders. "Xever is moving on his plans to open a portal, and Nazhivēr is after Zylas's blood for whatever reason. Zylas can't hide in the infernus, and since demons can sense each other, that means Nazhivēr is gonna find him eventually."

I bit my lower lip. "But … but what can we do while there's a bounty on our heads?"

"Zora said she was tracking suspected cultists and trying to get a lead on Xever." Amalia started punching a number into the phone. "Let's see what she knows."

"Wait, no, you can't contact her while we're—"

The phone was already ringing on speaker, and Amalia slapped it into my palm.

A click, a clatter, then a sleepy, "Hello?"

It was the middle of the night. Why was Amalia calling people *in the middle of the night?*

"Uh …" I gulped. "Zora?"

"*Ro*—" She cut herself off. "One sec—no, Felix, go back to sleep." A rustle, then the sound of a door. Footsteps, then another door clacked. "Okay, I locked myself in the Arcana Atrium. Robin, are you okay?"

"More or less," I answered, rubbing my aching throat. "Are you at the guild?"

"*Everyone* is at the guild, and it's damn crowded. Is Amalia with you? What about Tori and the guys?"

"Amalia, yes. The others, no."

Zora cursed under her breath. "Are you safe? You need to find somewhere to hide. Bounty hunters are everywhere, and it's looking ugly. The cult is playing us."

"The cult? What do you mean?"

"They doctored some video footage to frame Ezra as a demon mage. He's got a death sentence on his head, and the MPD put bounties on everyone connected to him—which is basically our entire guild. We're in lockdown so the other guilds can't pick us off."

Amalia and I simultaneously winced at her comment about Ezra being "framed," and I squashed my guilt for saying nothing. It wasn't my secret to blow.

"What does that have to do with the cult, though?" I asked.

"The Keys of Solomon guild reported Ezra, but Darius says the cult is behind the bogus video. They're pulling strings to take the heat off them and put it on us instead." She paused as though gathering her thoughts. "The bounty on you and Amalia doesn't say anything about an illegal contract. As long as you and Zylas keep up your act, you'll be fine once we prove Ezra's been set up."

Clearing Ezra's name wasn't happening unless Tori somehow prepared and completed the summoning ritual without me and Amalia. And faking my contract with Zylas was all but impossible now too, at least until we replaced the infernus.

"What about Xever?" Amalia jumped in. "Do you have a lead on him yet?"

"Not Xever specifically, but before the whole guild went into lockdown last night, we were tailing several cultists to find out how they're communicating with the cult leaders. We'd just identified someone we think is a cult lieutenant when shit hit the fan."

"Who?" I asked. "And where?"

"Nuh-uh. I'm not giving you that information so you can barge in on this guy alone."

"Zora …" My hand clenched around the phone. "I don't know what the cult's goal is, but I'm pretty sure Xever intends to open a portal to the demon world. We need to know everything you can tell us."

"I'm sorry, did you say open a *portal* to the *demon world*?"

I wished I could laugh. "Yes."

Zora muttered a string of profanity that made Amalia's eyebrows shoot up in an impressed way. "All right. I'll talk to Darius."

"Talk to Darius about what?"

"About sneaking me and my team out of the guild." Her voice hardened. "Nothing will change if we keep hiding. We need to find the cult, and that means making a move on the cultists we've been tracking."

"But if there are bounties on you ..."

"We know how to move around undetected. Can I reach you at this number?"

"Yes."

"All right. I'll call or text as soon as I have an update. You and Amalia be careful, okay?"

"We will."

With a quick farewell, Zora disconnected. I lowered the phone.

"Well ..." Amalia puffed. "I guess all we can do is wait, then."

I stared at the phone. Waiting. Letting others do the work. That was all we were good at. We hadn't separated Ezra and Eterran like we'd promised. We couldn't defeat Nazhivēr. We couldn't get a new infernus on our own. And now Zora was putting herself at risk to find a lead on Xever for us.

But then, was I really surprised? I was a twenty-year-old college dropout who'd spent most of her life running from anything resembling magic, whose only accomplishment was an accidental contract with a Twelfth House demon.

And without the infernus, I didn't even have that.

"**NOT AGAIN!**" Amalia's furious shout reverberated through the wall. "How is it jammed *again*?"

"You are too loud." Zylas's low, complaining tone was almost indiscernible.

"Shut up."

I blinked slowly at the bedroom wall, then refocused on the ancient grimoire sitting on my lap. My notebook was open beside it, but I could hardly look at its lined pages. Saving it had cost me far more than I ever could have guessed.

The whir of Amalia's new sewing machine resumed. She'd bought it from a department store this morning to finish the hex-gear outfit she'd started for Zylas several weeks ago, salvaged from her room before we'd fled the apartment.

Latin handwriting swam in my vision as I scanned the text. I was supposed to be looking for information about the Vh'alyir Amulet and portal magic, but instead, I was aimlessly turning pages, my thoughts in a disorganized haze.

Xever and Nazhivēr. The portal they needed for unknown reasons. Their new desire for Zylas's blood. What did they want? What were they trying to accomplish?

And did we have any chance of stopping them?

No word from Zora yet. Was she out on the streets already, searching for the trail of those cultists?

A mechanical popping noise interrupted the whir of the sewing machine.

"*Ugh!* I hate this thing!"

I sighed and flipped another worn page.

The bedroom door swung open. Zylas walked in, grumpiness all over his face and Socks hanging off his shoulder.

"She is noisy," he grumped. "More noisy than the *sewing machine.*"

"Hmm," I murmured vaguely, returning my attention to the grimoire. He'd removed his hoodie—probably so Amalia could measure him some more—and the Vh'alyir sigil on his breastplate glinted.

He scooped Socks off his shoulder and dropped her on the foot of the bed, then climbed onto the mattress. Stretching out on his stomach beside me, he pillowed his cheek on his folded arms, eyes skimming lazily over me.

"What are you thinking?" he asked.

"Nothing."

"You are always thinking." The end of his tail flicked side to side. "I could not always hear your thoughts, but I could *feel* you think, think, think."

I scowled. So maybe I was prone to anxiety-fueled overanalysis. Lots of people—human people, at least—spent a lot of time thinking.

"Are you happy to be rid of my thoughts in your head?" I asked, trying to sound playful. It came out defensive instead.

"No."

I squinted sideways at him. "No?"

"I like knowing what you think. You let me hear more since you gave me your strawberry to eat."

A slow flush rose up my cheeks. How could he mention that so casually?

Another flick of his tail. "Did you like hearing my thoughts?"

"Yes," I admitted. "I wish I could've heard more. It was hard to get any detail. You think really fast."

His wolfish grin flashed. "*Hh'ainun* are slow in all ways."

I wrinkled my nose. "Demons are rude in all ways."

"Rude?" He considered that. "That is the opposite of *nice*?"

"Yes."

"We are rude," he agreed shamelessly.

Snorting, I turned another grimoire page. It was the notation with demonic runes that had upset Zylas yesterday— the invocation of the King's Vow that twisted their magic against them.

I'd learned early on that demons didn't lie, but I'd given little thought to how their society viewed honesty. Zylas valued his word enough to risk his life to keep the promise he'd made me, and demon leaders were held to an even stricter level of integrity than the average demon. There was so much violence in their society, but it was defined by a brutal frankness.

"What will you do when you're home again?" I asked softly, flipping past the damning page. "Will you … raise children like other *Ivaknen*?"

Why had I asked *that*? The question had just popped out.

He rolled his shoulders, working out stiffness. "No."

"Why not?" I lightened my tone. "Because you're scared of female demons?"

He chuffed dismissively. "All males fear *payashē*. I will not have young until I am strong enough."

"Strong enough for what?"

"To be a good sire." He closed his eyes. "If I am not strong, I might die before I can teach my sons to be smart warriors who will survive."

My teasing smile melted away. His father had died when he was young, leaving him alone in a mercilessly deadly world. I still didn't know how he'd made it to adulthood.

Turning around, I set the grimoire on my pillow and stretched out on my stomach beside him, cheek resting on my arms to mirror his pose. As he cracked his eyes open to watch me, I searched his face, questions piling up in my head.

"Will you have any young?"

All my queries vanished like popped bubbles. *He* was asking *me?*

"I always assumed I would, someday, so I could pass the grimoire down to my daughter ... like my mom did for me." Resting my chin on my folded hands, I scrutinized the ancient book. "But now I don't know. Anthea accomplished incredible magic, but her legacy is tainted by what she did with it. Part of me wonders if ... if the grimoire should be destroyed."

Even as I said it, I shook my head slightly, unable to imagine destroying such a momentous piece of mythic history.

"Destroying it would not erase summoning," Zylas pointed out quietly.

"No ... but I'd erase summoning if I could." Puffing out a breath, I dropped my cheek back onto my arms. "As for having kids, I don't know. I haven't thought about it much."

"*Hnn.*" He tilted his head slightly. "There are many things to do and see and learn in this world. Will you do those things instead of raising young?"

I'd always imagined my life as a carbon copy of my mother's—a quiet, domestic life with my small family and a quiet, simple job that I enjoyed. Preferably one involving books.

But picturing that now, it felt so ... flat and empty.

"Maybe," I answered softly. "I think there are things I'd like to see and learn. Apprenticing with a sorcerer and learning Arcana properly. Visiting ancient, famous libraries. Seeing history for myself. Maybe ... writing a book about it all."

Creating my own compilation of words and thoughts to add to humanity's accumulation of knowledge—before all this began, I'd never have considered it. After all, what new knowledge and experiences could I have offered? But now ...

I smiled hesitantly. "There's also your book of landscapes. I'd like to see some of those places."

A shadow moved through his crimson eyes.

"Maybe we could see one or two?" I suggested, insecurity leaking into my tone. "Before you go home? Once we have an infernus again, we could ... figure it out."

He was silent for a long moment.

"Infernus," he repeated. "Do we need the infernus?"

"Of course we do."

"I can pretend to be human. They do not look at me."

"Last night it was dark and late, and we got lucky. Mythics aren't as easy to fool as regular humans. All it would take is one of them to realize you're a demon. We *need* an infernus so we can pretend you're contracted. Not only that, but we need it for the mind-reading and the shared magic and—"

"And the command. To make me return to the infernus."

I forced my jaw to unclench. "That too. It's useful in a fight."

He studied me, then pushed up on his hands and knees. As the mattress bounced, I expected him to climb off the bed and stalk away.

His hand flashed out. He grabbed my shoulder and rolled me over—rolled me *under him*.

I gasped as I landed on my back, his fists braced near my head, his knees on either side of my hips. My heart crashed into my ribs.

His glowing eyes flicked over me, then he dropped onto his elbows and pressed his face against my neck.

"Zylas!" I pushed on his shoulders. "Get off me!"

He didn't move, his breath hot against my skin. I shoved harder on his shoulders, my lungs heaving as I felt his inconceivable strength. I couldn't shift him. Couldn't move him. Couldn't do a damn thing to stop him.

Panic burst through my head, obliterating any remnant of logic. I didn't have the infernus command. My only slight, temporary power over him was gone, and I was helpless. Trapped. *Trapped by a demon.*

I hammered my fist into the top of his shoulder. "*Zylas!*"

He lifted his head—and then he was off me. Off the bed. Standing beside the mattress, towering over me, his expression unreadable. I panted for air, my hands trembling.

"Fear," he said.

He stretched his hand out. I flinched, but he wasn't reaching for me. He scooped Socks off the foot of the bed. The small kitten purred happily as he carried her out of the room.

I stared at the empty threshold, his stony expression burned into my mind. Fear, he'd said.

And I remembered his soft, pleased smile from two nights ago. *You are not afraid.*

I bit hard on the inside of my cheek, tears stinging my eyes and regret heavy in my chest.

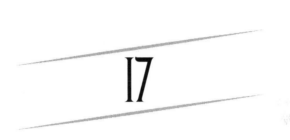

17

I BOUNCED ANXIOUSLY from foot to foot. "Amalia, we need to *go*."

"I know, I know! It's just—not—sitting right! Why are you so flexible?"

She shot the accusatory question at Zylas, whom she'd ordered to bend over. He had his hands pressed flat to the floor, and the hem of his jacket had lifted too high, revealing his tail looped around his waist.

The new outfit was an improvement over the baggy sweats and hoodie he'd been wearing before. The loose-fitting pants were stretchy without *looking* stretchy. His greaves hid beneath them, with one alteration: Zylas had reluctantly sheared the pointed tops off the shin guards so they wouldn't tear his outer layer. Amalia had even added a loop on the waistband for him to hook the barbs on his tail through.

She tugged fruitlessly at the top's hem, then allowed him to straighten. The black jacket featured a deep hood and patches of durable leather mixed with angular panels of elastic fabric that wouldn't hinder his agility.

I pointed at the floor. "You have to put the shoes on."

He scowled at the pair of brand-new slip-on runners. "They are *zh'últis*."

"You can kick them off if there's a fight," I said impatiently. "We're already late, so just do it."

Scowl deepening, he dropped to sit on the floor and picked up a shoe like it was decomposing garbage I'd fished out of a dumpster for him to wear.

Amalia fussily adjusted his hood, then wrung her hands together. "You have the phone?"

I tugged it from my pocket and held it up. My outfit was simpler than Zylas's—sturdy jeans, sneakers, and my leather jacket over a tank top and sweater. Someday, I would get a full combat outfit.

"I should've bought two phones," Amalia fretted. "How will I know what's going on? I just have to sit here and hope you two don't die."

"We'll be fine," I assured her, pretending I wasn't worried. "We'll be with Zora."

Zylas stood up. Amalia fished a pair of reflective sunglasses out of the shopping bags scattered across the sofa and passed them to him. He slid them on his face, hiding his eyes, then tucked his hands in his pockets and relaxed his shoulders.

"Do I look human?" he asked.

I stared at him, my mouth dry. The fitted garments looked surprisingly good, and the reflective sunglasses and hood lent him a vaguely dangerous air. But most shockingly, he really *did* look human. Against the dark clothing, the reddish tone of his skin had almost disappeared, leaving it a warm russet brown instead.

"The clothes aren't actually black," Amalia said, watching my reaction. "The fabrics are a very dark scarlet. Since the color is more saturated than his skin, it tricks the eye into seeing black and brown."

"Oh," I stammered. "Wow."

"Yeah, worked pretty well. Now get going before Zora busts the cult without you."

I gulped at the reminder of our mission.

Instead of risking a crowded bus, Zylas and I took a cab downtown. Darkness had fallen, but traffic zoomed along the streets. Zylas watched out the window, stiff in his seat. He didn't seem to like the lurch and heave of the moving vehicle.

As towering skyscrapers surrounded us, I peeked at the text Zora had sent early this evening.

```
Meet in alley behind Lennox Pub @10pm.
Dress to blend in but be prepared for
combat.
```

Amalia and I had begun immediate preparations—mainly, preparing Zylas for exposure to humans. It'd been so much easier when I could carry him around in the infernus.

My gaze flicked to his profile, his eyes hidden behind those reflective sunglasses. Now that he was free of the infernus, he didn't want me to have power over him again, even such a small power as the recall command.

Fear.

I squashed the memory of his flat voice. This wasn't the time to worry about the gaping chasm that was yawning wider between us with every passing hour.

The cab dropped us off in front of the Lennox Pub, a narrow restaurant tucked into a building otherwise dominated by a two-story shoe store. For once, we weren't traipsing through a disreputable neighborhood—and there were pedestrians everywhere, mostly young twenty-somethings celebrating the end of the workweek.

Zylas's sunglasses got a few strange looks as we followed the sidewalk alongside the pub. The alley was just ahead, and I sped up, drawing in front of Zylas as I mentally prepared an explanation for Zora about why my demon was out of his infernus and dressed like a human. Luckily, she already knew his contract was nonstandard.

I swung around the corner. In the alley, a group of people stood beneath the security light above the pub's rear door, and I peered past them, expecting Zora to have found a more private spot to wait for me.

Or that's what I thought until she stepped out of the group, her short blond hair pinned off her face and a long black case slung over her shoulder.

At the sight of her, the other four people belatedly registered as familiar.

My brain tripped over itself and landed in a useless sprawl. Zora *knew* my demon was in an illegal contract and couldn't use magic if there were witnesses! Why hadn't she come alone?

"Robin!" Grinning in relief, she rushed over and grabbed me in a brief hug. "I'm so glad you're safe. Any trouble getting here?"

"No," I whispered faintly.

"Good." Her attention shifted over my shoulder. "Who …"

She trailed off, her eyes going wider and wider as she stared at the demon. Zylas's build and non-nighttime-appropriate eyewear must've tipped her off.

"My infernus is broken," I hissed under my breath. "I thought you'd be alone!"

"We're investigating a *cult*," she hissed back. "That isn't a job for one or two people! I told you I had a team, remember?"

No, I didn't remember that ... but I'd been under a lot of stress lately and my memory wasn't at its best.

She flicked a glance over her shoulder at her teammates. "We'll just have to wing it."

"But—"

"Play along," she said, directing the command more at Zylas than me, then waved her team over. "Okay, we're all here. Robin brought some help, too."

The Crow and Hammer mythics approached, some offering smiles I was too nervous to return.

Zora held up her hand toward Zylas as though presenting a prize in a game show. "This is Zee. He's, ah, shall we say *private*, so no questions, okay? He'll be useful, I promise."

A few eyebrows rose.

"Zee, I'll run through the team for you. This is Andrew, one of our best sorcerers. Excellent on defense and offense."

Andrew, a lean man in his fifties who radiated dependability, smiled welcomingly at Zylas.

"This is Gwen. Defensive sorcery. *Aggressive* defensive sorcery," Zora added with a chuckle.

Gwen grunted in response, which was actually a relief. The tall, beautiful blond sorceress looked like a posh CEO but had such a filthy mouth she could make *Amalia* blush. I usually avoided her.

"Drew is a telekinetic," Zora continued, waving at the stocky, well-muscled psychic on her left who'd gone into the storm drains with us back in December. "We work together often. And this is Venus, a combat alchemist."

I hadn't known our guild included a combat alchemist. Venus was of average height, with long black hair in a braid and a complexion that looked very similar to Zylas's in the dim light.

Zylas nodded in response to each introduction, saying nothing. Zora paused, a faint sheen of perspiration on her forehead despite the chill February air, then cleared her throat.

"The last member of the team is Taye, our telethesian. He's already in place since he's been under deep cover for over a week now." Her voice gained confidence. "You all know the plan. Our guild is counting on us. Let's make this happen!"

The others nodded, then swept past us. At the mouth of the alley, they parted, Andrew and Gwen going one way, Venus and Drew going the other way.

"Where—" I began.

She pulled out a small black device with an earpiece hanging from a curly cord. "Put this on. I only brought one extra, sorry."

I took the radio.

"We've got a location," she said as I fumblingly inserted the earpiece. "Or, at least, we're pretty sure we do. Taye tracked the lieutenant cultist to the One Wall Center, which is a few blocks away. But we don't know where to go from there."

She flipped a couple buttons on the device, and sudden noise filled my ear.

"*I'm at the back door, Taye.*"

I recognized Drew's voice.

"We're muted," Zora added, seeing my surprise. "The lieutenant from One Wall is at a nearby nightclub where he regularly meets other cultists—passing on instructions, we suspect. Come on."

She swept out of the alley and onto the sidewalk. I hurried on her heels, Zylas gliding after me.

"*I'm inside,*" Drew murmured, his voice crackling through the tiny speaker in my ear. "*I can see the target.*"

Zora pressed a button on the cord of her earpiece. "Is everyone in position?"

"*Gwen and I are out front,*" Andrew replied.

"*I've got eyes on the back door,*" a female voice—Venus, I assumed—said. "*I set off a little something to keep loiterers away.*"

"*Is it that god-awful stench bomb you used back when we—*"

"No chatter," Zora said, interrupting Gwen's question. "Drew, Taye, keep us updated."

I walked beside Zora, wanting to ask a hundred questions about what we were doing, what was happening with the guild, and if she knew anything about Ezra's or Tori's whereabouts, but I wasn't sure if that counted as "chatter." Other pedestrians passed us, and I was surprised that Zora's black leather didn't stand out—though her sword case was still conspicuous.

"*Target is at a table with eight others.*" Taye's South African accent was easy to identify. "*Drew is positioned nearby.*"

"What's the plan?" I whispered to Zora as the low thump of bass music reached my ears. Zylas trailed behind me, a shadow in my peripheral vision.

"Information is our top priority, but also—"

"*Another man just joined the table,*" Taye said, his mic picking up the same thudding music. "*The others all sat up like the Pope just walked in.*"

"*Looks like he might be a big fish,*" Drew added.

"Description?" Zora murmured, quickening her pace. The club was just down the street, identifiable by the clubgoers lined up in front of it.

"*Over six feet tall,*" Taye reported. "*Dark brown hair, fair skin, looks like a—I think a scar on his chin?*"

I gasped. Zora looked at me sharply.

"Xever," I whispered to her. "That's Xever."

Her eyes popped wide. "Heads up, team. The scarred man may be Xever, the leader of the cult. Drew, Taye, can you get a better look to confirm?"

"*I'll do a walk by*," Drew said. Muffled music thumped through his mic. "*I think it's him. He matches the description Darius gave everyone.*"

"Stand by." Zora flipped the switch on her earpiece, muting herself, then scooted into the doorway of a closed Vietnamese restaurant. "We aren't prepared to take on Xever. This is the wrong team for combat against dangerous mythics."

"I do not sense Nazhivēr," Zylas said, moving to my side. "But he could be with Xever in his infernus."

She blew out a breath. "Maybe we should withdraw."

My gut clenched but I didn't disagree. For the first time, we'd found Xever instead of him and Nazhivēr ambushing us, but surrounded by cultists in a public venue, we couldn't take advantage of catching him unaware—nor were Zylas and I in any shape to take him and Nazhivēr on.

"This is not *dh'ērrenith*," Zylas said, echoing my thoughts. "Better to keep away and plan our attack."

Zora nodded and reached for her mic to unmute it.

"*Our target just left the table,*" Taye said sharply. "*I think he's getting a drink. Drew, are you ready?*"

"*Ready.*"

"Wait—" Zora cursed and jimmied her mic. "Hold on, you two!"

"*Taye is approaching*," Drew reported in a whisper. "*What's wrong, Zora?*"

She let out a hissing breath. "Be careful."

"*Taye is down the bar from him. The target is ordering.*"

Zylas tilted his head toward me, listening in.

"*He's reached into his pocket … pulled out cash from his wallet … got it!*"

"Got what?" I asked, startled.

"*Target is looking for his wallet. He thinks it fell under the bar. And … bingo! Taye has it now.*"

I clued in to what was going on: as soon as the target cultist had withdrawn his wallet, Drew had used his telekinesis to knock it from the cultist's hand and move it into Taye's reach.

"*Done*," Taye said. "*Got it again, Drew?*"

"*Yep.*" A short pause. "*Moved it under a stool. Give him another few seconds … target found it. Put it back in his pocket, not even suspicious. Perfect!*"

"*Meet me near the door, Drew*," Taye said.

I gave Zora an astonished stare, and she smiled ruefully. A minute passed, then the speaker in my ear crackled again.

"*I'm out*," Drew declared, "*and I've got the target's key fob. Let's do this!*"

Zora zoomed out of our shadowed nook. "Taye, keep your distance and watch them. I want to know if they move. Everyone else, head toward One Wall."

She strode down the sidewalk at a speed that should've been impossible for her short legs. I had to jog a couple steps to catch up, then puffed after her. Zylas followed in my wake like a shadow.

We reached an intersection and Zora blazed right into the road, earning a furious honk from an oncoming car. We continued onto the opposite sidewalk, heading northwest. The street, lined by large trees, widened as the short, dense commercial buildings gave way to a sprawling business district with modern structures broken up by courtyards and open plazas.

Reaching another intersection—a much busier one—Zora drew to a halt. A moment later, a woman drifted over to join us: Venus. Andrew and Gwen stopped on our other side, and scuffing footsteps announced Drew's approach.

"There it is," Zora murmured. "One Wall Center."

She could only mean the building directly ahead of us on the opposite street corner, and my lips parted with disbelief as I tipped my head back, looking up—and up, and up.

A skyscraper, majestic and solitary, rose far above the surrounding structures. Its sides gently curved, forming a sharp point aimed at the intersection, and its entire exterior was covered in dark, reflective glass.

A tower crane anchored to the side of the building dampened the sleek look. Fifty stories up, the crane's steel jib floated over the rooftop, where some sort of construction was underway.

"You *stink*."

My gut plunged with alarm before my brain caught up to the fact that *Zylas* was speaking. I jerked toward him.

He had a hand over his nose, his dark sunglasses turned toward Venus.

She arched her eyebrows at him, then sniffed at her shoulder. "Do I?"

"Did you get that stink bomb on yourself?" Andrew asked in amusement.

Drew stepped closer to her and inhaled loudly through his nose. "I don't smell anything."

Zora cleared her throat. "Focus, guys. Let's go."

The crosswalk light had changed, and as the others followed her, I fell into step beside Zylas at the back of the group.

"She smells like *thāitav kranis*," he growled under his breath. "*Gh'akis*."

"I'm sure it's awful," I muttered, "but don't complain. No one else can smell it."

One Wall's lobby was huge, the surfaces pale and shining, the ceiling two stories high. A pair of escalators led up to the second floor, where the open front of a restaurant emitted delicious aromas, and a hotel-like sitting area with slim, angular sofas was arranged near a long concierge desk.

Zora scanned the spacious lobby, then unmuted her mic. "Taye, report."

"They're at their table, deep in discussion. I'm keeping well away."

"Good. We're in One Wall now. Keep us posted." She muted her mic again. "Venus, take care of the concierges."

Venus strode to the front desk, where two men in suits were peering suspiciously in our direction. I couldn't blame them. Our group was wearing a lot more leather than was typical, and we were just standing around.

She slid a hand into her pocket, then set her fist on the counter and opened her fingers. A white puff of what looked like steam ballooned outward, and the two men recoiled.

Venus murmured something, and the concierges nodded, relaxing. She spoke again, one of them replied, and they both smiled as she turned away.

"Done," she said as she rejoined us. "They said the elevators are all keycard activated. The first two are for the hotel, the second two are for the condos, and the VIP elevator accesses the top six floors only."

"What did you do to them?" I asked uneasily.

"Extra strong, aerosolized soothing potion. I took the antidote before setting it off so it wouldn't affect me."

"A *soothing* potion?"

"Soothing potions are completely legal." She smiled in a slightly unnerving way. "But my dosage is … intense. They're so relaxed that nothing will bother them for another hour or so."

"But we still can't waste time," Zora said. She gestured toward Drew. "The key fob?"

He pulled a small plastic fob from his pocket and strode to the nearest elevator—a lone stainless steel door surrounded by black marble—and tapped it against the panel. A green light flashed. He pressed the call button. It lit up and a distant hum echoed through the shaft as the elevator began its descent.

We waited in silence—Zylas with his hand over his nose again—then the elevator chimed and the door slid smoothly open, revealing an interior covered in the same black marble. We piled in and the door slid shut.

Zora peered at the six button options—floors forty-two through forty-seven. "Let's see where we end up."

Drew tapped the key fob to the panel inside the elevator, then Zora pushed the button for floor forty-two. Nothing happened; the key fob didn't have clearance for that level. She pressed the button for forty-three. Nothing again.

She kept pressing the buttons, and I held my breath, somehow certain which one it was.

The light for floor forty-seven, the penthouse level, glowed beneath her thumb. The elevator launched upward, shooting for the top of the building. Zylas stiffened at the sudden movement.

Jitters ran through me, my brain throwing random facts through my head. Almost fifty stories meant this building was around five hundred feet tall. How long did it take to fall five hundred feet? Terminal velocity for a human was achieved in twelve seconds, so maybe … half that? What was the terminal velocity of an elevator?

Why was I even thinking about this?

The elevator slowed to a speed that didn't compress my brain inside my skull, then floated upward until the digital number above the door read forty-seven. Another chime, and the door slid open to reveal a small lobby with straight halls leading off each side.

Directly ahead was a pair of sleek double doors.

We crept out of the elevator. Tension vibrated my limbs as I stared at those doors. The penthouse condo. I'd bet my entire savings account that this wasn't a mere cultist hideout.

It was *Xever's* penthouse.

18

THE LAIR OF MY ENEMY. Not a humble townhouse or a modest apartment, but a one-of-a-kind abode with luxury, sophistication, and a price tag that put Uncle Jack's gaudy mansion to shame.

I looked at Zora, her lips pressed thin as she stared at those doors. She, too, had realized we were about to set foot in an enemy stronghold.

"This place may not be unguarded," she warned in a whisper. "We need to be quick and careful. Andrew, Venus?"

Andrew slid a black case from his pocket, revealing a set of lockpicks. As he knelt in front of the bolt, Venus pulled out what looked like a bottle of clear nail polish. She gave it a quick shake, then used the little brush to swipe the liquid across the top edge of the door.

I leaned toward Zora. "What's Venus doing?"

"A magnetic solution," she whispered. "If there's a security system, it'll prevent the alarm from tripping when the door opens."

The bolt clicked. Andrew nudged the door open by a fraction, and loading her small brush again, Venus slathered more liquid across the inner frame. As she capped her bottle, he swung the door farther open.

Slipping inside, we were met by a two-story foyer with a grand, curved staircase and towering windows that offered a stunning view of the distant mountains, scarcely visible against the dark sky. To our left was a large dining room with a black table and ten chairs, partially open to the foyer. To our right, a short hall with a corner of a kitchen counter visible.

The silence was broken only by our quiet breathing. The place seemed abandoned.

"Taye," Zora whispered, unmuting her mic. "Any change?"

"*Nothing.*"

"Mics open, everyone," she instructed, then pointed at Andrew and Gwen and gestured to the left. She directed Drew and Venus up the stairs, then waved at me and Zylas to follow her to the right. We entered the glossy white kitchen with a long island in the middle.

A sudden noise behind me made me leap half a foot in the air.

Zylas pressed a hand to his nose, having just muffled a sneeze. "I can't smell anything but that *hh'ainun*'s stink," he complained. "But I do not hear anyone."

"Keep moving," Zora ordered, several steps ahead of us.

Heart pounding, I followed after her. The floorplan curved with the outer wall of windows, and we proceeded into a spacious family room with a fireplace. Though poshly decorated, the room was impersonal. Nothing cultish in sight.

Doubts flitted through me. Was this not a cult base? Why wasn't it guarded?

A wide hall led us past the open doorway of a spare bedroom and into a large room—an office that filled one end of the penthouse. A custom-made desk was fitted into the far corner and a long table was pushed up against the floor-to-ceiling windows that formed the entire outer wall.

Papers, folders, maps, and documents covered the table.

"*There's nothing at this end,*" Andrew reported. "*We're heading your way.*"

"*Just checking the master bedroom,*" Venus said. "*Doesn't look like there's anything up here either.*"

"The jackpot is in the office." Zora glanced warningly at me. "Don't touch anything."

Zylas stayed near the hallway, keeping watch while Zora and I approached the table. The quiet in the penthouse pressed in on me, my pulse beating in my ears like a clock ticking down. I reminded myself that Xever was at the club, and Taye would warn us if he left. We'd have time to get out.

I halted in front of a large map of Vancouver and the surrounding area, with markings in different colors all over it. A slow prickle ran through me.

Leaning over the table beside me, Zora pointed at an orange circle. "That's the building where we found the vampire nest."

The building where Zylas and I had first encountered Vasilii—and nearly died.

"And here ... that's the nest you uncovered after getting washed down the storm drain."

Another location where I'd almost perished.

She scanned the map. "And these three here ... locations where we've found vampires in the past."

My gaze slid up past North Vancouver. On the west side of Mount Seymour was a wide circle around Uncle Jack's hideout, where we'd fought and killed Vasilii—and where Nazhivēr had stolen the grimoire pages.

My attention shot back down and stuttered on a purple ring on the northern coast. I pointed. "Is that—"

"The stevedoring facility where we fought Varvara Nikolaev's rogues," Zora said in a low growl.

And where Nazhivēr had almost killed her.

I skimmed across the map, picking out different spots. Uncle Jack's mansion. Xever's townhouse. His apartment. *My* apartment. All of them were circled and marked with a red X— meaning compromised or destroyed, I was guessing. The locations where we'd encountered Vasilii, where we'd fought Nazhivēr, and where we'd found Saul and his sons had all been crossed out.

The Grand Grimoire. The Crow and Hammer. Odin's Eye, the Pandora Knights, the SeaDevils. Only the latter was crossed out—because their headquarters and the helipad had both been destroyed.

But there were more circles, many more, some with X's and some without.

I scanned again. There, south of the Eastside—Aaron's house. A few more blocks south, another address was circled, but I didn't know why. I swallowed the bile in my throat, fighting back a wave of dread.

"What's the color code?" Zora muttered in terse frustration. "What does red mean?"

I looked back toward downtown. She was staring at the Crow and Hammer, circled in bright red. More circles in orange, purple, and blue had been drawn nearby.

"Whoa."

The voice came from nearby at the same time I heard it through the speaker in my ear. Andrew, Gwen, Venus, and Drew walked in, eyes wide.

"Start taking photos," Zora said, "and don't touch anything."

As the others spread out through the room and Zora aimed her cellphone camera at the map, I moved down the table, passing Arcana notations, and stopped on a lunar chart for February. The full moon had been circled, and the next seven nights had been counted. The eighth was circled again, and beneath it was a time: 6:57.

A strip of another map peeked out from behind the lunar chart. With a quick glance at Zora, who was rapidly snapping photos, I slid the lunar chart aside.

A topographic map. It showed a mass of land bordered on two sides by water. At the peak of a broad hill, a meticulous circle had been drawn, intersected by straight and curved lines that streaked across the map at various angles.

Those were anchor lines for planning an Arcana array that needed to be precisely oriented in relation to polar north or an astral alignment—an array like Anthea's portal spell. And positioned on a hilltop—perfect for ensuring the spell would be exposed to unobstructed moonlight.

My gaze darted to the lunar chart, then back to the map. This had to be the location Xever had chosen for his second portal attempt. But where—

"What the hell is this?"

I jolted at Drew's sudden half-whisper. He and Venus stood in front of a metal case at the far end of the table, the lid open.

"I told you not to touch anything!" Zora barked.

Inside the case, a foam insert held a collection of vials just like the case of Nazhivēr's blood I'd stolen from Xever—but this one held many more vials.

"Is that blood?" Venus asked, squinting. "It looks too dark."

My pulse pounded in my ears. "How many vials?"

"Uh." Drew counted. "Eleven. The twelfth one is empty."

I sucked in air as my head spun. My eyes darted to Zylas. He waited by the hall, his face turned toward me. Spinning back toward the map of the portal location, I shifted papers and folders out of the way.

"I said not to touch anything!" Zora said angrily. "Taye, give me an update on Xever and the cultists."

Ignoring her order, I lifted a heavy Latin text and set it aside. I needed to know where they were building the portal.

"Robin, stop that!" Zora hissed. "Taye, update!"

My hands paused as the silence in my earpiece stretched out.

"Taye? Do you copy?"

We all stood perfectly still, waiting.

"Taye? Taye, do you copy?"

When she received no answer, Zora pivoted to face the rest of us. "We're leaving. Out. Now!"

The others rushed into the hallway. I cast a wild look at Zylas, then whipped back to the map and grabbed the bottom edge. I pulled, but part of it was still buried under heavy texts. Instead of sliding across the desk, the map tore.

I stared in horror at the long rip—then yanked the corner of the map free and ran after the others. Zylas joined me and we raced down the hall for the penthouse doors.

"Stop!" he barked.

Halfway across the sitting room, Zora and her team slid to a halt—and in the quiet, the rumble of a male voice echoed through the unseen foyer. A door clacked.

Someone was inside.

Zora gestured silently, ordering us back. As we retreated into the hall, I stuffed the torn corner of the map in my pocket.

The murmuring voices grew louder, coming this way.

Zylas grabbed my arm and pulled me through the open door of the bedroom. A large bed filled half the space, and like most of the penthouse, the outer wall was made entirely of windows, the view ruined by the dark steel beams of the tower crane running up the side of the building.

The others followed us, and we crowded into the corner alongside the door, where we could only be seen if someone entered the bedroom.

The muffled voices gained volume.

"… attention is on Enéas, as we expected."

That rough male voice sent a violent shiver rippling through me.

"But," the man went on, "if he's captured alive and confesses—"

"He'll fight to the death."

The two speakers passed the bedroom door, and the dark windows reflected their silhouettes—Xever's tall form accompanied by a man with pale skin and white hair.

At the sight of the second man, a wave of vivid memories assaulted me. Saul on the helipad, standing over the portal array and chanting in a harsh, powerful drone. Amalia looping her hex-scarf over his head and the fabric bursting into flame. My demonic-sized *impello* cantrip blasting the screaming man off the helipad and into the dark ocean water.

Saul was alive.

"Are you sure Enéas will go that far?" he asked as the two men continued past the bedroom and into the office.

"He's always been staunchly unswerving once he commits himself," Xever replied. "It made him a perfect demon mage."

"Get ready to move." Zora's whisper was almost soundless. "We'll make a run for the exit as soon as—"

"Xever."

Saul's sharp exclamation silenced Zora.

"Look at this," he said.

A moment of quiet. Tension gripped our small, hidden group, and the torn corner of the map in my pocket seemed to weigh a hundred pounds.

"Hmm," Xever mused. "Someone unexpected has been here."

"We were gone for less than an hour."

"Yes," Xever agreed thoughtfully. "I wonder … if they might still be nearby?"

Fresh panic gripped my chest at the cold amusement leaking into his tone.

"*Daimon hesychaze.*"

The Ancient Greek hissed off Xever's tongue—and crimson light blazed through the bedroom where we hid. Illogical terror hit me and I lunged for Zylas, but he was already dissolving. Red power streaked through the bedroom wall.

My hands clutched his empty jacket, still warm from his body heat.

19

DROPPING ZYLAS'S JACKET, I sprinted for the bedroom door.

"Robin!"

I scarcely heard Zora's low warning call as I careened through the doorway and shot down the short hall.

"*Ori novem!*"

Saul's incantation rang out as I burst into the office. Crimson blazed across the windows—Zylas was taking form in front of Xever.

Purple magic flared and Saul's semi-transparent harpoon struck the demon's chest the instant he solidified. Saul rammed it into Zylas, driving him down onto the table behind him. He hit it on his back, the violet shaft sticking out of his sternum. His limbs spasmed, claws ripping across the large city map.

As I slid to a horrified stop, Xever turned to me. The scar that ran up his chin and into his lower lip twisted as he smiled.

Running footsteps—then Zora appeared beside me, her sword out of its case and the long length of steel shining. Drew halted on my other side, a steel ball the size of a grapefruit resting on his upturned palm, and more footsteps told me the others had come too.

I was simultaneously furious that Zora hadn't led the others to safety and grateful I didn't have to confront Xever and Saul alone. Together, we faced the two men, our standoff reflected in the glass walls of the office, the city lights twinkling far below.

Crimson flashed over Xever's chest. Power leaped to the floor, then flowed upward and solidified. Nazhivēr stretched his wings out, filling half the room, before furling them against his back, his glowing stare moving from Zylas to me and my group of mythics.

Zylas dragged his arms up and grabbed the harpoon shaft, trying to dislodge it from his chest, his breath rushing loudly through his clenched teeth.

"Welcome, Robin," Xever murmured, safely behind Nazhivēr. "Thank you for returning my demon."

My fingernails cut into my palms. "He's *mine*."

"Is he? Then why not call him into your infernus?"

He knew. That bastard knew Nazhivēr had destroyed my infernus.

"Zylas is my demon now—as disobedient as he is." Turning, Xever walked casually over to his desk. He lifted a vial from the case of demon blood. "I'm curious as to why my contract with him failed."

"If only you had an ancient grimoire with thousands of years of Demonica history to provide answers," I spat.

Xever opened a desk drawer and withdrew a short combat knife. My gut dropped as he joined Saul at the table where the glowing harpoon pinned Zylas.

Panting, Zylas pulled desperately at the abjuration spell.

"All twelve Houses," Xever murmured, raising the knife. "I've waited a long time."

He slashed the knife down—Zora grabbed my elbow as I lunged forward even though there was nothing I could do. Nazhivēr's wings twitched at my movement, the demon ready to intervene.

Dark blood welled in the slice Xever had cut across Zylas's thigh. The summoner held the empty vial to the wound and blood trickled into it. When it was full, he capped the vial.

"You have what you need, Xever."

Saul's voice came out in a harsh rasp, and my attention darted to him. His venomous stare was fixed on me, his teeth bared and chest heaving. Faint white scars webbed his pale skin, covering every inch of his face and over his short hair, where patches were missing entirely.

"Now let me kill her. I'll peel her skin from her flesh for what she did to my sons."

"No, Saul." Xever tucked the vial of Zylas's blood in his pocket. "Not until I've confirmed whether she and the demon have a banishment clause."

My jaw clenched. Xever had threatened to kill me before, but that must've been a bluff—one I hadn't doubted at the time.

Twirling the blood-smeared knife, Xever assessed the five mythics flanking me. "But we do need to deal with these interlopers. Saul, keep Zylas under control. Nazhivēr will handle the rest."

Beside me, Zora hissed an incantation under her breath, her knuckles white around the hilt of her sword.

"Kill everyone but Ro—"

Before Xever could complete the order, something the size of a marble flew over my head, arcing toward Nazhivēr's face. Sneering, the demon swatted it away.

The instant his hand touched it, it exploded.

As the blast knocked the demon back, Drew's steel sphere rose off his palm, then shot at Nazhivēr as though fired out of an invisible cannon. It hit the demon in the chest with a dull thud, knocking the demon back another step.

Nazhivēr's lips curled, then he launched toward us.

The Crow and Hammer mythics scattered, Zora yanking me with her. I fell onto my knees as she pivoted, sword swinging. Venus lobbed another potion at Nazhivēr. As he ducked it, Drew gestured. The potion shot straight down and exploded between the demon's shoulder blades, knocking him onto one knee as his blood splattered the floor.

Scrambling up, I ran toward Zylas as the demon wrenched the spell out of his chest.

"*Ori novem,*" Saul said. Another violet harpoon shimmered into his hand.

"*Ori eruptum impello!*" I gasped.

As the sorcerer swung the harpoon down toward Zylas, my spell flashed out. Papers flew into the air, blown off the desk, and Saul hurtled backward. The silver dome expanded into the window behind the desk, and cracks burst across the floor-to-ceiling glass.

Zylas rolled off the desk, landed on the floor, and launched into an attack—away from Saul and toward Nazhivēr. The winged demon was choking Andrew with one hand and had just lifted Venus off the floor by her arm with his other hand. Her scream rang out as his powerful grip snapped her wrist.

Crimson talons forming on his fingers, Zylas sprang at Nazhivēr's back and rammed his talons down into Nazhivēr's shoulder.

Snarling in pain, the winged demon dropped his human victims and reached back for Zylas. As Andrew fell to the floor, Drew darted in with a thrust of his hand. His steel sphere flew out of nowhere and slammed into the pit of Nazhivēr's stomach. Clinging to his back, Zylas sunk his other talons into Nazhivēr's opposite shoulder, and Zora swung her sword, slicing the membrane of Nazhivēr's wing.

Silver runes from her blade flashed up the demon's wing. The appendage sagged as though it had gone numb.

A hand grabbed my hair.

Saul threw me down on the table and closed both hands around my throat, cutting off my air. I grabbed his wrists, my fingers slipping on the silver rings that ran up his arms.

"Pathetic, mewling *bitch*," he hissed. "I don't care what Xever wants. I'll kill you for what you did to my boys."

My lungs screamed, limbs spasming. Teeth bared, Saul glowered hatefully into my eyes—then lurched back as a long blade swept through the spot where his head had just been.

Zora spun into a roundhouse kick, her foot slamming into Saul's chest. The sorcerer staggered back, and she slashed with her blade again, forcing him to dive away. He slipped on scattered papers and fell.

In the far corner of the office, Xever tugged on a handful of chains around his neck—and no less than five pendants appeared from beneath the collar of his shirt. He selected an infernus from the collection.

Red light blazed, and a new demon took form—seven feet tall, lean and powerful, with a hairless skull adorned with bony ridges. His long tail lashed as he fixed his glowing eyes on Nazhivēr and his attackers.

Panting and coughing, I sat up on the table and grabbed Zora's arm. "Get the others out of here!"

She shot a fearful look at Xever's second demon, then rushed toward her comrades.

As the new demon advanced on the battle, crimson force exploded off Nazhivēr, ripping through the office. Gwen shouted an incantation and a crackling barrier of light arched over Venus and Andrew—but Zylas and Drew were hurled in different directions.

Zylas twisted in midair and landed in a crouch on the table beside me, skidding on the scattered papers. Red power flashed up his hand, and he swung his arm to point at Xever. A spell circle flashed around his wrist, power pulsing—

"*Ori quinque!*" Saul spat.

Zylas's spell erupted, blasting toward Xever, and at the same moment, Saul's silvery force hit Zylas, flinging him back. His arm caught me in the chest and I pitched backward with him.

He hit the window behind us, the sound of the impact so horrifying it consumed every ounce of my attention: shattering glass.

Sparkling shards danced all around me.

Zylas yanked me into his chest as we plunged through the broken window. A gale of icy wind hit us, propelling us like weightless leaves. We were spinning, falling, plummeting. A dark, reflective wall flashed past, the city lights whirling, Zylas's arms the only thing that felt real.

Howling wind—a dark shape—then we slammed to a halt.

The force wrenched me from Zylas's hold. I plunged down, then agony jarred through my arm as he grabbed my wrist. I jerked to a stop for a second time in as many seconds, hanging from one arm.

The sudden jolt caused Zora's little black radio to fall from my pocket. The tiny earpiece yanked from my ear as the device plummeted.

Zylas clung to the side of the tower crane, one hand gripping a steel support and the other clutching my wrist. The roaring wind buffeted me, blowing me away from the structure, trying to tear me from his grasp. My feet swung through empty air, five hundred feet above the miniscule cars creeping along the roads below.

Five hundred feet. Six seconds. If Zylas's hold slipped, I'd be a splatter on the pavement in six seconds.

Baring his teeth, he pulled me up. I stretched my hand out and grabbed his belt, then clambered onto his back and wrapped my legs around his waist, clinging to him so hard my limbs ached. I panted, my senses overwhelmed by the howling gale that beat at us. Inside the building, it'd been so quiet, so peaceful, while this windstorm raged on the other side of the glass.

Zylas craned his head back, peering up. Terrified to look down again, I looked up too.

Two stories above, the shattered window was a dark hole in the reflective glass that covered the skyscraper. And in that opening, Nazhivēr stood, leaning out, watching us with glowing eyes.

Zylas began to climb the outside of the steel structure. The icy drafts rammed us, trying to hurl us off our desperate perch. I clamped my arms even more tightly around his shoulders.

Painstakingly, he carried us up to the penthouse level. There he paused, staring along the curving glass wall to the shattered panel. Nazhivēr stood in the opening, still watching, but he didn't fly at us. His left wing drooped—still numb from Zora's spell.

The room beyond Nazhivēr seemed quiet. Had Zora and the others fled like I'd told them?

Movement behind the glass. Xever appeared beside Nazhivēr, watching us with his scarred lips twisted.

Zylas's muscles tensed and I clutched him, waiting for whatever would happen. If Xever called Zylas back into his infernus, I would fall to my death. Would Xever gamble on the possibility that Zylas and I had a banishment clause?

Several long seconds passed, then Zylas reached up for the next steel bar. He resumed his climb, leaving Xever and Nazhivēr watching from the broken window.

Zylas kept going. Heading for the roof. There would be access into the building somewhere at the top. There had to be. Our enemies would be waiting for us inside, but anything was better than this.

The upper ledge of the building loomed ahead. He heaved us up another half dozen crisscrossing bars that supported the outer frame of the crane tower. We drew level with the edge.

My hammering heart lurched with denial.

The edge wasn't a rooftop. The peak of the skyscraper curved inward, narrowing to a roof half the circumference of the main walls. The sides were steep and slick, impossible to traverse.

Zylas paused, clutching the crane tower, then continued upward, seeking the top of the crane where the long jib hovered above the flat section of the roof like a reaching arm.

We could cross that perilous bridge and jump down onto the rooftop.

I'd never seen anything that looked more dangerous in my life.

Up another story, then another. The operator cabin loomed overhead. Zylas climbed past it and clambered onto the jib. The crane's apex rose above us, suspension cables running from its top to the end of the long jib ahead of us and to the shorter counter jib behind us.

I gingerly uncoiled my legs and stretched them down until my feet pressed against the steel beneath us. The whole crane swayed in the endless wind. Holding me tight to him with one arm, he gripped the apex with his other hand, maybe calculating the safest way to venture onto the long jib. The footing would be treacherous at best. We might need to crawl across it.

Pulling me up his body so my feet lifted off the steel again, Zylas swung around the apex toward the long jib—then lurched back. The wind flung us sideways and he half leaped backward, one arm stretched out for balance.

With a flare of his wings, Nazhivēr sprang up from behind the operator cabin. He landed on its roof, gripping the steel apex with one hand. Grinning viciously, the demon hopped onto the counter jib.

Zylas scrambled backward, stepping rapidly across the steel braces as the gale tore at us. Tucking his wings against his back, Nazhivēr advanced, eyes glowing and tail snapping side to side.

"Pathetic, Vh'alyir," the demon roared over the wind. "You are a cowardly child like the rest of your House."

Zylas retreated down the jib, carrying me with him, and all I could do was clutch him as he backed out over open space, that five-hundred-foot drop yawning below our feet.

"Have you ever finished a fight?" Nazhivēr taunted. "Or do you only know fearful escapes?"

Zylas halted. I darted a glance backward—and saw why. We were at the end of the counter jib. A foot behind us was *nothing*.

Coldness overtook Nazhivēr's sharp features. "I thought you would be there. When Xever claims *his* victory. But you are too weak and too rash."

Zylas's arm tightened, crushing me to his side. We were helpless. One misstep and we would fall to our deaths. We had no choice but to surrender—or die.

Five paces away, Nazhivēr spread his arms, the wind whipping his ponytail out behind him. "How will you escape me this time, Vh'alyir?"

"*Vh'renith vē thāit.*"

Nazhivēr barked a laugh. "Death is for fools."

The wind shrieked over us, enraged by our resistance to its buffeting force. Zylas lifted his hand, fingers outstretched and palm aimed at Nazhivēr.

"I will die," he snarled, "before I surrender like you did."

Crimson blazed over his hand and raced along his arm in twisting veins. It snaked over his shoulder, up his neck, and across his face. The glow in his eyes brightened, power bleeding out, shining through his skin.

A spell circle bloomed in front of his palm, eight feet across and filled with runes. Nazhivēr's eyes widened. He stepped backward as Zylas's spell flashed brighter.

The spell exploded from the incandescent circles. Three beams of crimson power twisted together as they screamed toward Nazhivēr.

The demon flung his wings open.

The wind and the spell caught him at the same time. He whipped backward, flung away by the raging gusts—and Zylas's spell hit the apex where the crane's jibs met its central tower. Metal shrieked and tore, the counter jib beneath us lurching violently.

And the wind, finally, won its battle against us.

Zylas and I pitched sideways—then we were falling. This time there was no skyscraper beside us. No tower crane within reach. Nothing but open space.

Six seconds.

We plunged through nothingness, spinning in the violent wind. A gale wrenched at me and I flew away from Zylas. He grabbed my forearm, claws piercing my jacket sleeve and biting into my skin.

Five.

Crimson burned in my vision. Veins of power snaked over Zylas's arms, magic flowing to his shoulders, building, pulsing. His eyes were twin pools of demonic essence, wide and unblinking, pupils indiscernible.

Four.

His mouth was moving. Words that the wind whipped away, but the shapes his lips formed weren't English. The dark side of the skyscraper rushed past.

Three.

Red light burst out of him, blinding me. A wrench on my arm. A surge of air, my stomach lurching, sweeping, rising—*rising.*

The skyscraper whipped past, then it was gone. Lights. City lights flashing past us. We weren't falling. We were—we were—

Zylas clutched my arm, pulling me with him as we soared ... soared on the ruby wings arching from his back. Semi-transparent like his phantom claws. Veined with power, streaks of magic pulsing through them as they stretched wide, as large as Nazhivēr's and infinitely more beautiful.

The downtown streets streaked by, two hundred feet below us. As we glided, we lost speed and altitude. He canted his ghostly red wings and we swept between two high-rise apartments. A wide strip of darkness stretched out ahead of us— False Creek, the inlet that cut into downtown Vancouver.

We were dropping faster as our forward momentum dwindled. Zylas didn't beat his wings, but angled their rippling tips. We curved right. The ground rushed up, and he swept his wings forward.

We came to a halt in midair and dropped the last few yards. My feet hit soft ground and I slammed down on my butt, my hands sinking into cold sand.

Zylas thumped down beside me—and pitched forward onto his hands and knees. The glowing wings arched off his back as he gasped for air, his whole body shaking. The pulsing veins of magic burned brighter, and the wings lost their solidity.

With a soft hiss of magic, they dissolved into shimmering streaks that drifted away from his back. The power crawling over him faded, then disappeared. Darkness swept in, the glow of the high-rise apartments barely enough to make out his silhouette.

He collapsed into the sand.

"Zylas!"

I lunged to his side, grabbed his arm, and pulled him onto his back. His chest rose and fell with heavy breaths, his limbs quivering.

"Zylas, what's wrong?" I fumbled through my pockets, found my phone, and activated its flashlight. The bright glare hit his face and he squinted, turning his head away—but not before I saw his pitch-black eyes.

Of course they were dark. Otherwise, I'd have been able to see their glow.

I shone the light down his body, searching for injuries but finding only the slash in his thigh, then returned the light to his face. "Zylas, please! Tell me what's wrong."

He grunted between pants. After a moment more, he rasped, "*Vīsh.*"

"Huh?"

"The *vīsh* ... to fly." He grimaced. "Burns everywhere."

"Is there anything I can do?"

"Heat."

I looked around wildly, shining the light across a long stretch of sand. Water sloshed against the beach on one side, and on the other were trees, grass, and a walking path lined with benches. By my best guess, we'd landed on Sunset Beach, six blocks from the penthouse.

There was nothing here to warm him up with.

Sticking my phone in the sand so it'd stand upright with the light shining on us, I lay beside him, pressing against him and throwing an arm across his chest. I couldn't do much, but I could at least block the worst of the cold sea breeze blowing off the water.

I tucked my face against the cool side of his neck, counting the timing of his breaths. Relief stole through me as his harsh, rapid huffs gentled.

"I can't believe we survived that," I mumbled.

He grunted. "I did not know if we would."

"That magic you used ... to make wings. I didn't know demons could do that."

"They can't."

I blinked, wishing I could see his face. Silence stretched between us and he breathed in and out, lungs moving easily now.

Finally, he spoke, so quiet I wouldn't have heard him if our faces hadn't been so close.

"It is not normal *vīsh*. It is special, secret *vīsh* that no other *Dīnen* know."

His chest rose with a slow inhalation.

"It is the magic of *payashē*."

I LEANED AGAINST THE HEADBOARD, my legs stretched out. Beside me, Zylas lay on his stomach, head resting on his folded arms, naked except for his dark shorts.

He'd just returned from a thirty-minute shower to recover some magic. He usually spent longer in the shower, but the hot water here wasn't endless. The shabby furniture and weird layout weren't the only downsides to this old building.

Sprawled facedown, he was too exhausted to even twitch his tail. Socks, her green eyes blinking lazily, lay in the middle of his back, a tiny heater adding her warmth.

Our respite on the beach had lasted less than ten minutes before we'd headed back into downtown. Choosing an apartment building at random, Zylas had broken into an unfortunate person's ground-floor unit and stolen human clothing, then we'd taken a cab to the safe house.

We'd made it back. Somehow, we had survived.

My gaze flicked across his shoulders, where the phantom wings had risen, then turned to the phone in my hand. A string of text messages glowed on the screen, all from Zora.

```
I saw you and Z fall please tell me you're
alive

We made it out ok

Do you need help? We circled the building,
we can't find any sign of you

Your phone is ringing. Did you actually
fall?

Please answer
```

Guilt squirmed in my gut. At least they were safe—though she hadn't mentioned Taye. What had happened to him? Why had he stopped answering?

My thumb reached for the reply box, then I quickly turned the screen off.

Zora, Drew, Venus, Gwen, and Andrew had been in the midst of fleeing the office when Zylas and I had fallen out the window. Even if our bodies were never found, that was five witnesses who could truthfully claim they'd seen us die. As much as I wanted to reassure Zora, was it better this way?

It would be much easier to begin my new life as a rogue if the old me was dead.

The squirming guilt morphed into churning dread. Zora might be willing to overlook my illegal contract with Zylas, but the others? No way. They'd seen Zylas walking and talking like a human—then watched him turn to crimson light as he was called into an infernus. I was already being hunted for illegal Demonica activity, and now my own guildmates had witnessed my illegal contract. It was better if they all thought I was dead.

Through the bedroom wall, I heard the rattling dryer shut off. The metal door banged, and a moment later, the washing machine started up—probably to clean the clothes I'd changed out of when I got home.

Amalia pushed the bedroom door open with her shoulder, her arms full of blankets. She dumped them on the foot of the bed, then circled to Zylas's side, picked up the first blanket, and flipped it over him. As it fluttered down, he glanced toward her, then closed his eyes again.

I lifted one edge, the fabric hot from the dryer, and the Socks-sized lump under the blanket wiggled toward the opening. The kitten's head popped out, ears bent sideways in displeasure.

Amalia laid two more heated blankets over Zylas, then circled back around and sat on the mattress by my feet. "How're you feeling?"

"Exhausted." I lifted the phone a few inches, my whole hand trembling faintly. "And still shaky."

"Well, you did fall off a skyscraper." She squinted at Zylas as though imagining the wings I'd described while he was showering, then pointed toward the bedside table. "Let's take a better look at that."

I set the phone down and picked up the piece of Xever's map I'd torn off. Setting the paper scrap on the blanket between us, I spread out the crinkles. It was a six-by-eight-inch corner showing both land and water, with several lines in red pen crossing it.

"These are anchor lines," I said. "Xever had a spot marked out on a hilltop, but I couldn't tell what landmass the map showed."

"So wherever these lines intersect," Amalia said, tracing one with her fingertip, "that's where the spell is."

"Finding the spot will be difficult. The coast is dotted with islands and inlets."

"Xever probably wants another 'pure' location, meaning it could be in the middle of nowhere." She shook her head. "And he's got our favorite murdering abjuration sorcerer helping him. I can't believe Saul is alive."

His survival had caught everyone off guard. Zora hadn't realized who her team was tracking, probably because Saul's albinism wasn't as obvious as his sons'; older men often had white hair. And Zylas hadn't noticed the sorcerer's scent in the penthouse because Venus's alchemic reek had deadened his sense of smell.

"Did you learn anything else?" Amalia asked.

"There was a lunar chart with this past full moon circled, and they'd counted out seven nights. There was a number written underneath the eighth night—6:57."

"Sunrise, I'm betting." She nodded to herself. "Astral arrays that require moonlight take longer to charge when there's little to no moonlight. They started on the full moon to give it a boost, and it'll be ready at dawn."

"So they'll be able to open the portal at dawn on the twenty-eighth."

"Meaning we have five days to prevent them from opening a portal? Great." She rubbed her forehead. "What else?"

"Xever had a map of the city with a bunch of locations marked out. Places where we've fought Nazhivēr, the vampires, the golems and stuff from last month … plus a bunch of guilds, including the Crow and Hammer."

My gut prickled nervously as I remembered that red circle around our guild.

"And," I added, my sense of foreboding deepening, "there was that case of blood."

Zylas cracked his eyelids open to reveal dark scarlet eyes.

"Xever had eleven vials of blood, and he filled the twelfth one with Zylas's blood. I think we can go ahead and assume he has blood from all twelve Houses in his collection."

"But why?" Amalia combed her hair back from her face. "Our theory that he wanted Zylas's blood to cheat-summon a Vh'alyir isn't likely anymore. He wouldn't need blood to summon any of the other Houses."

"Then what?"

"Does he want to know which blood is most potent for his experiments?"

"He'd need way more blood for that." I chewed on a tattered fingernail. "It must have something to do with the portal. That's what he's focused on right now."

"Demon blood from all the Houses and a portal ... what does he get him?"

Maybe the question wasn't what he could get but what he most wanted. His ultimate goal.

"The Red Queen," I whispered. I twisted around, my eyes meeting Zylas's. "What House do *payashē* belong to?"

"They have no House."

"But when they have male children, their sons join their father's House, right?"

"*Var.*"

Which meant *payashē* had no House while still being connected to every House. "What if Xever needs blood from every House to summon a female demon?"

"He can't," Zylas replied instantly. "The summoning *vīsh* uses the King's Vow. *Payashē* do not have *dīn* magic."

"Or maybe the blood is for binding the female demon into a contract somehow." Amalia's face had paled. "The portal could be for getting at a female demon and the blood could be used to force a contract on her. He wants to make the cult's Red Queen goddess a reality."

"Then he is a fool," Zylas snapped. "A *payashē* will bring death to his *cult*."

I studied him. "You know more about *payashē* than you've let on. What did you mean when you said those wings were *payashē* magic?"

His eyes narrowed, then he turned his head away and settled into the mattress—a clear signal that he had no intention of sharing anything else. At least, not with me *and* Amalia.

Grimacing, I gave her a pleading look.

She rolled her eyes. "Okay, fine. There's a restaurant next door that's open late. Indian cuisine, decent reviews. I'll go get some dinner."

"Thanks."

She shot me a "get answers out of him" look in reply, then headed for the door. The rattling, clanking washing machine drowned out the sounds of her preparing to leave, and a moment later, the apartment door banged shut.

"Zylas?" I asked softly, watching the back of his head.

He let out a long sigh. Pushing up, he tossed the blankets off the bed and settled down on his back, half propped against the headboard beside me.

"*Payashē* are masters of *vīsh*." His expression was unreadable. "They know spells male demons don't. They teach their daughters but never sons. They always send their sons away to their sires when their magic awakens."

"But your father died."

"He died," Zylas agreed. "And I was alone in a place I had never been. A dangerous place. I knew I would die soon. Another male would kill me, or I would starve."

"Starve?" I interrupted. "But you don't need food."

"Demon young need food. We need less as our magic gets stronger, but we do not stop eating until we are almost full grown." He gazed at the ceiling, seeing another world. "After my sire died, I wandered and wandered, and then I found it."

"Found what?"

"A secret place where *payashē* live. I found it because I was small and looking for places to hide."

"What did you do?"

"I waited until morning, when the *payashē* were awake. Then I walked into their hidden *pashir*." He stared unblinkingly upward. "I walked to the middle, where the largest … largest *house* was, and I waited."

Fear zinged through me—fear for him, for his child self.

"The *payashē* gathered. Watched me. Laughed because I was small and weak and young. Twelfth House. I was not dangerous to them, and there were no young for them to protect at that time.

"Then she came out … the *payapis*."

The matriarch.

"She asked why I had come." He clenched and unclenched his jaw, the rest of his body eerily still. "I begged her to protect me."

My breath caught.

"She laughed. I told her I would do anything. I begged. They all laughed." He closed his eyes. "*Payashē* do not protect *kanyin*—young males. They will banish their own sons to die if a sire does not come."

"Then ... why did you go to them?"

He slitted his eyes open. "The *payapis* said yes."

Incredulous disbelief rolled through me.

"She would have no more young. She was bored, maybe. She said to me, 'I will protect you and you will obey every word I say. I will raise you to be strong, and when you become *Dīnen*, you will use what I taught you and change *Ahlēavah*.'"

His gaze slid to me. "I obeyed her. She taught me magic. She taught me how to fight. She taught me that it did not matter how I found victory—to find it always in any way."

He went silent, and I struggled to gather my thoughts.

"So," I began tentatively, "instead of learning from your father, you learned everything from a female demon? But you're petrified of female demons."

He scoffed in annoyance. "They are strong. Not their bodies. They are small like you, and I could push them down and hold them. You are much weaker, though," he added.

I huffed.

"But their magic, *vayanin*. Many of their spells I could not learn, even though the *payapis* tried to teach me. The wings ... that was as long as I can hold them. When *payashē* want to fly, they make wings and fly away. They do not fall to the ground in a short time like me."

I tangled my fingers in the hem of my sweater. "What was it like growing up with a *payapis* teacher, surrounded by *payashē*?"

"The *payashē* did not want me there. They thought the *payapis* was foolish to let a *kanyin* in their *pashir*."

I did a few mental gymnastics to keep up with the demonic words he was throwing around.

"They would hit me at first. Then I grew taller than them, and they stopped. They did not hate me anymore, because I was useful in small ways."

"You were? How?"

"I would collect food or watch their young. They are lazy. They made me do work for them." He exhaled slowly. "Any day, any time, they could kill me if I was trouble. I was always prey, but I was safer with them than alone, so I did what they wanted."

How nerve-racking would it have been to grow up in a community where anyone could slaughter you at any moment?

"When I was older and stronger, I would go out at night and protect the *pashir*. I liked that better because I was away from the *payashē* more. I killed many males who came too close. I was the best at ambush. They never saw me until I struck."

"I was out at night, hunting, when I felt the *Dīnen* power fill me." His hands curled into fists. "I ran."

I frowned. "What do you mean?"

"I ran far from the *pashir*. I never went back. *Dīnen* are more dangerous, and I did not know if the *payashē* would kill me if I returned."

So quickly, in a single night, his life as he'd known it had completely changed for a second time. "What did you do then?"

He pondered the question. "I tried to keep my promise to the *payapis*. I tried to change something."

"You changed things for your House," I realized. "You taught the other Houses to fear Vh'alyir demons."

"*Hnn*. She would not think that was enough." He let his head fall back against the headboard, eyes half lidded. "I tried, but it was *imadnul*. I made the others fear us, but they still kill. Vh'alyir are weak and too young. They kill us. I kill them. They kill us more. Nothing changes."

"You tried, though. And—and when you go home, maybe you can do more as *Ivaknen* than as *Dīnen*." I offered an uncertain smile. "There's no other demon like you, is there? You're the only male to have been trained by a female."

"I have never told anyone that I lived with *payashē*." He grimaced. "Other males … they would not like it."

"Why not?"

"All the reasons." He pushed his heels into the mattress, sitting up a bit more. "Do you think differently of me now?"

"Differently?" I blinked at him. "I … I'm just impressed. That you did all that. It sounds terrifying."

"*Hnn*. Lots of times, yes."

"And living with females. Not what I expected when you talk about them like they're your worst fear."

"I know better than most males how strong they are."

"Powerful," I corrected. "Not strong, since you said you could hold them d—" Breaking off, I stared at him. "Wait. Did you mean that literally? You've actually held a *payashē* down before?"

He shrugged.

"Why would you do that?" I gasped. "Did you attack one?"

He recoiled slightly. "Attack? No!"

"Then *what*?"

"She asked."

My mouth fell open.

He squinched his eyes at me. "Sometimes *payashē* want to mate when they do not want young. When I was old enough, some *payashē* of the *pashir* told me I should give them food."

Somehow, my jaw dropped even more.

"I knew they would not want young with me, because I am Vh'alyir, but ..." He shrugged again.

"But?" My voice came out in a squeak. "But *what?*"

"You are blushing."

"Well, yeah!" I blurted. "You just admitted to sleeping your way through an entire commune of females!"

"Sleeping? I do not underst—"

"Mating," I corrected loudly. "You *mated* with a bunch of females! I thought you didn't want children yet!"

"We did not make young."

"How do you know? Do demons have contraceptives? Any of them could've gotten pregnant by accident, and you never went back so—"

"Accident?" He shot me a wide-eyed stare. "Can *hh'ainun* have young *by accident?*"

Derailed, I leaned back slightly. "Yes. Are *payashē* different?"

"We choose when to have young. Many times *payashē* accept a male to enjoy mating but do not want him to be a sire. Males do not know when a *payashē* chooses young or no young."

"So some females chose you to *enjoy mating* with?"

He sat forward, hands pressed to the mattress between his knees. "Why are you angry?"

Angry? I wasn't angry. Not at all. I was ... not calm. That's all I could really tell. I was not calm, and also my heart was twisting behind my ribs like an invisible noose had tightened around it.

"When I invited you …" I began haltingly. "With the strawberry … did you accept so we could … enjoy mating?"

When he said nothing, I peeked at him. He looked more confused than ever.

The last of my anger fizzled into pain. Ah. There it was. The truth.

He'd accepted casual invitations in the past—which meant, in his eyes, my invitation had been equally casual. Which would be fine … except it hadn't been casual to *me*. When I'd held that strawberry out to him, I'd been baring my heart and soul.

And I was only now realizing how much I'd wanted his acceptance to mean something special too.

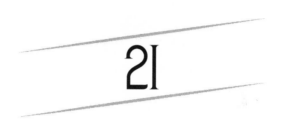

21

I PUSHED OFF THE BED. "I'll leave you to get some rest."

"*Vayanin?*"

I hurried for the door, determined to escape the room so I could nurse my bruised heart in private—and also figure out why I was hurting so badly, because my feelings weren't making a whole lot of sense.

The mattress creaked as he rolled off it, then his hand caught my arm. He spun me around to face him. The washing machine on the other side of the wall clanked and clattered as his eyes darted across my face.

"What is wrong?"

"I'm fine."

"You're lying," he growled, instantly annoyed.

I jerked away from him. "I'm leaving the room now."

He snatched the sleeve of my sweater, pulling me toward him. "Tell me what is wrong."

"I don't want to talk about it."

"I just talked to you about things I have never told anyone."

"That—that doesn't mean I have to tell you everything now."

He bared his teeth angrily. I recoiled, my sweater sleeve pulling taut between us. He yanked me back. I wrenched away, and the sound of a seam tearing shocked me.

Panic fired through my veins. "Let me go!"

He released my sleeve so suddenly I staggered. His dark eyes burned like ice as he inhaled through his nose.

"Fear," he snapped. "Fear, again. Why are you afraid?"

I stumbled back another step.

"I have not hurt you. I have *never* hurt you." His tail lashed, the barbs catching the box spring and ripping through the fabric. "How do I make you not fear me? What am I doing wrong?"

I jolted, my breath catching. My back hit the wall.

"*I* am the one with fear!" Snarling frustration roughened his words. "You break so easily. I am always afraid you will be hurt. I watch you and protect you and you still get hurt and I try and it isn't enough! Why am I this afraid for a *payilas* who thinks I will hurt her?"

With my back pressed to the wall, I stared at him with my lungs locked. Emotions boiled through me, a tangled mess I couldn't begin to sort through. All I knew was that my heart was hammering and my head was spinning and he was telling me how afraid he was that I would get hurt.

He paced away from me then swept back to the middle of the room, teeth bared. "You were not afraid when you had the infernus. I was your tool. Now I am not, and I am dangerous."

I shoved off the wall. "No! That's not it!"

His eyes narrowed.

"I'm afraid now because … because … because you're so strong, and you could hold me down and I couldn't blast you with magic like a *payashē*."

"I would not hurt you. Why don't you know that?"

I sucked in air. "When you … when you mated with a *payashē*, were you afraid of her?"

His jaw flexed. "Yes."

"You are like that to me, Zylas," I whispered. "I can't not be a little afraid."

"But those *payashē* did not want to protect me. They did not care."

I went completely still. Even my heart ceased to beat. "Do you care … about me?"

"I will protect you, not hurt you." He blinked rapidly, as though struggling for the right words in this foreign language he'd been forced to learn so quickly. "I want you to always be safe."

It took a moment, just a moment, for his soft declaration to settle in my ears—then my body was moving.

I didn't worry or wonder or doubt or *think, think, think,* as Zylas had described it. I crossed the distance between us with rushing steps, my hands reaching up. My palms found his face, fingers hooking over the back of his neck. I stretched up onto my toes.

And pressed my mouth against his.

He went rigid.

I dropped back onto my heels, breath rushing in my throat and a blush roasting my cheeks. But I kept my hands and my eyes on him.

"That's how one human tells another human that they care. And that they ... might like to ... mate," I finished weakly.

He stared at me, and my pulse jumped at the way his eyes focused on me anew, intense and almost challenging. His hands curled around the sides of my neck, palms warm and thumbs against my cheeks. Leaning down, he brought his face close to mine. The tips of our noses touched.

He pressed his mouth against mine.

My stomach dropped out of me. He waited a moment, seeing if I would panic, if I would push him away. Instead, I closed my fingers around his wrists and rose onto my tiptoes, kissing him harder—and he responded in kind.

At the firm press of his mouth, I parted my lips. He caught my lower lip in his teeth, a gentle bite—then fit his mouth to mine.

The hot slide of his tongue weakened my knees. Kissing. Tasting. My pulse raced, molten heat expanding through my core. I didn't realize he was pushing me backward until I met the wall. I gasped—and he drew away, my lips suddenly cold as his disappeared.

My hands shot up. I grabbed his head and yanked his mouth back down onto mine.

His breath rushed from his nose in surprise—then he crushed me into the wall. His hands were in my hair, holding my head. Lips and tongue and brief touches of his canines overwhelmed my senses.

Last time we'd kissed, he'd been gentle, careful, exploratory.

This time, he was intense, hungry, demanding.

This time, his mouth moved over mine, taking what he wanted, and every part of me was ready to surrender to his hands and his mouth and the fire he'd ignited inside me. He pinned me to the wall, allowing no retreat. A rough sound rumbled in his chest as I tipped my head farther back, his mouth locked over mine.

"*Holy fuck!*"

As the shrieked profanity rang out, Zylas jerked back from me. With his hands still in my hair, he looked at the bedroom door.

Amalia stood in the threshold, wearing her jacket, her face stark white. Clanks and rattles of the washer filled the silence—the noise that had concealed her return to the apartment from Zylas's sensitive hearing.

"Zylas." Amalia's hands were balled into fists, visibly trembling. "Get away from her."

He leaned back slightly, his tail lashing.

"*Get away from her!*" she shouted, fear making her voice go high and thin. "You can't do that to her! You swore to protect her! You can't—"

"Amalia—" I gasped faintly.

"—hurt her like that! You're breaking your promise! You—"

"Amalia!" I half yelled. "I kissed him!"

She broke off, her bulging eyes swinging to me. I pushed on Zylas and he stepped back, hands sliding from my hair.

"I kissed him," I repeated, my face flaming as I fought the gut-deep embarrassment. "He didn't do anything wrong."

She stared at me, shaking from head to toe. The fear in her voice—had she been prepared to challenge Zylas to protect me, knowing she couldn't defend herself if he got violent?

"Wrong," she repeated. "Nothing wrong?"

I nodded quickly. "It was me. I—"

"*You* kissed him. After what we talked about. That it was too dangerous. That it was *wrong*."

"It's not—"

"He's a demon!" she shouted.

"He's a person!" I shouted back, stepping forward, Zylas behind me. "A *person!* With thoughts and emotions and intelligence."

"A *demon* with thoughts and emotions and intelligence!"

"What's the difference?" I demanded. "If he didn't have a tail, would it be fine? If he had no magic, would he qualify as a person? Where's your line?"

"He's a different *species*."

"Based on what? The tail and the magic?"

"Don't bullshit me! We could start the list with how he can turn into a blob of energy and spend the next hour listing all the ways he's a preternatural creature from another dimension!"

My hands clenched. "Why does any of that matter?"

"Do you hear yourself? Of course it matters!"

"Why?"

"Different. *Species*," she ground out. "What *the hell* is wrong with you, Robin? You think screwing a demon will be all fun and games, a little bedroom experiment?"

"This isn't about experimenting," I snapped.

"Then what?" She stiffened her spine, glowering furiously. "Explain it, Robin. Tell me why you've lost your goddamn mind, because I sure as shit don't get it!"

I opened my mouth—but I didn't know what to say. The seconds stretched out.

"Fine." Amalia hitched her purse up her shoulder. "You know what? *Fine*. Do what you want—but I won't sit by and watch."

Spinning on her heel, she stormed away.

For a second, I was too surprised to move, then I rushed after her, passing a bag of takeout on the kitchen counter. She swept into the living room and grabbed her suitcase—already packed, because we'd decided we should be ready to abandon this location at a moment's notice.

"Amalia," I began sharply.

"Forget it, Robin! I'm done!" She pulled a heap of fabric off the dining table and shoved it into her suitcase's open top. "You nearly died tonight. Xever is days away from opening a portal and possibly contracting a female demon, and you think this is a great time to mess around with Zylas? Then go ahead. Let him rough you up."

"He isn't going to—"

She whirled on me. "You don't know that! *Fuck!* Did anything I say even register?" Jerkily turning back to her suitcase, she zipped her bag shut. "I stuck with you, Robin. For *months*. I've dealt with so much shit, so much fear, not sleeping, nightmares all the time because I've been living with *an unbound demon*, because I thought I was helping you. We were in this together."

"You—"

She yanked her suitcase upright and extended the handle. "And for what? Why should I put up with all this when you're *deliberately* putting yourself in danger?"

Tears stung my eyes. "Amalia—"

"No. I'm *done*." She turned her back to me. "Have fun with Zylas. I hope he doesn't kill you."

She strode down the hall, her suitcase rolling nosily across the floor.

"Amalia!" I burst out, speeding after her. "Would you just stop for a minute so we can talk about this?"

"We did talk about it." Not pausing, she flung the apartment door open. "I'm not risking my life for someone who doesn't care about her own safety."

Cold fear flooded me as she crossed the threshold.

"Please don't go!" I grabbed her arm. "Please, Amalia!"

She wrenched her arm away, half turning toward me. Her face was twisted, eyes filled with tears.

"I can't do this anymore, Robin. I just can't."

Turning, she sped away. I hung in the doorway, watching her go with my heart in my throat. She disappeared around the corner.

I waited, but she didn't come back.

22

I SLOWLY CLOSED the apartment door and locked the bolt. Just as slowly, I turned around.

Tears pooling in my eyes, I walked woodenly into the kitchen. The takeout bag sat on the counter, the aroma of spicy curry drifting from the containers. I automatically picked it up, but then I just stood there, holding it.

"*Vayanin?*"

Zylas appeared beside me. I stared at the take-out containers.

"Robin?"

I drew in a shuddering breath. "She can't see who you really are. When she looks at you, she sees a demon first."

Even though she'd come to like and respect Zylas, she couldn't accept that he was a being as equally capable of care and concern as a human. I remembered, less than two weeks ago, when Tori had suggested that Amalia wasn't afraid of Zylas killing her. *I worry about it every day*, Amalia had replied.

And I'd mentally shrugged over her never being comfortable with Zylas and gone right on pretending it didn't matter.

Gulping back a sob, I dropped the container on the counter and sped into the bedroom. Tears spilled down my cheeks as I crawled onto the bed and buried my face in the pillow. She was gone. The last member of my family who cared about me had left.

Would everyone leave me?

The mattress dipped. On his hands and knees beside me, Zylas leaned down to bring his face close to mine.

"Robin? Do you want me to bring her back?"

"*No!*" I accidentally shouted. "No. That won't help."

He studied me, his forehead crinkled, then shifted toward the bed's edge. Retreating.

"Wait!" I grabbed his wrist. "Don't go. I don't want you to leave."

He hesitated. "I will not leave."

Pain rent my heart. Of course he would leave. Leaving was his top priority. He wanted to return to *Ahlēavah* and resume his interrupted life as best he could. Protect his House and mate with more *payashē* and raise sons and change the demon world.

My fingers tightened around his wrist, my body trembling. "Yes, you will."

A quiet rustle—then warm solidity beside me. I blinked my vision clear.

Zylas stretched out on his back beside me. His head settled on the pillow next to mine, our arms touching.

His eyes glowed softly. "I will not leave."

I rolled toward him, tucking my body against his side, and pressed my face into his shoulder. The tears came, and I wept, shaking.

I wept with guilt and remorse—and I wept for the terrible loneliness that awaited me once Zylas left me too and I was truly, unequivocally alone.

BRIGHT SUNLIGHT dragged me from a deep sleep. A sweet, smoky scent filled my nose, and my front was warm while my back was very cold.

Only half awake, I cracked my eyes open.

I'd fallen asleep curled against Zylas's side, and we'd scarcely moved. He lay on his back, head on the pillow beside mine, eyes closed and breathing slow. Had he stayed with me all night?

My usual reaction—leaping up and running away with my face flaming—ran through my head, but I was too exhausted. Judging by the quality of light leaking through the window, it was just past sunrise, and I'd only been asleep for five or six hours.

Instead, I studied his face. The way that dull morning lit his cheekbones. The straight line of his nose and curve of his lips. He was all I had left, and soon he would be gone too.

His eyes slid open. Dark pupils contracted in the light, then he turned his head toward me, our faces a breath apart on the pillow. My forehead touched his.

Staring into his eyes, I longed for the connection we'd had, for that precious insight into his incomprehensible thoughts.

I didn't decide to reach for his face. My hand moved on its own, fingers brushing across his cheek. Eyes half closed, drowsy but strangely electrified, I traced his ear to its point, then slid my fingertips along his jaw. Down his neck. Into the hollow of his throat.

His collarbones fascinated me. Hard bone just beneath the skin. Taut tendons above. Firm muscle below.

My hand drifted along his impossibly smooth skin. I pressed my palm against his sculpted pectoral, surprised by its hardness. Its resistance to my push. I splayed my fingers, eyes closing.

His heart thumped under my palm. Solid and steady. After a moment, I slid my fingers farther down.

There were far more muscles to discover across his abdomen. Those perfect abs. He lay still, breathing slowly, as I moved my hand across his stomach, exploring every dip and curve. My hand continued its unhurried journey until it discovered the thrilling line where his lower abdominals and hipbone met to form that sexy V.

My fingers touched fabric and my heart gave a sudden, hard throb. He wasn't wearing his belt. Just sturdy fabric. I knew, from past occasions spent studying his clothing, that his shorts laced at each hip. I'd never seen him take them off.

My hand hovered at his waistline … then I slid my palm back up, away from that forbidden fabric. Back to his abs, exploring them all over again.

I was still tracing his warm skin, my forehead resting against his, when a furry weight with razor-sharp claws pounced on my hand.

My yelp rang out as Socks clamped onto my wrist and tried to disembowel my palm with her back legs.

Zylas pried her off and she switched to murdering his hand, letting out ferocious kitten growls as she gnawed on his thumb. Wincing, I sat up to examine my hand, relieved to find only a few red scratches. We should pick up some clippers and trim her claws. I'd ask Amalia to—

My brain stuttered on the thought and tears stung my sore eyes. I blinked them away, my contacts sticking unpleasantly. I probably shouldn't have slept in them.

"I think we forgot to feed Socks last night," I said, swinging my legs off the bed. "I'll get her some food."

As I walked into the kitchen, my gaze fell on the bag of takeout on the counter. Throat closing, I dropped it into the garbage. My heart seemed to fall into the bin with the spoiled food.

I curled my hands into fists. That was more than enough of this pity party. If I was on my own, then I'd just have to handle everything myself.

Five days. That's how long I had to figure out how to stop Xever from opening a proper portal to hell and summoning or contracting a *payashē*—or whatever his true plan was.

Half an hour later, after feeding Socks, showering, dressing in a light sweater and stretchy jeans, and scarfing down a granola bar for breakfast, I found Zylas in the living room, sitting by the window like usual. He hadn't redressed since his shower last night, wearing only his shorts, and my cheeks flushed as I recalled the feel of his skin.

He watched as I set up the grimoire, Vh'alyir Amulet, reference texts, torn corner of the map I'd stolen from Xever's office, and my laptop on the coffee table. Spreading a thick blanket on the floor to use as a cushion, I picked up my pencil, set my notebook in my lap … and stared at the assorted materials with my brain buzzing blankly.

The faintest scuff of a footstep. Zylas sank down to sit cross-legged beside me.

"I'm not sure where to start," I admitted.

"Know where your enemy will be. Then you can choose to be there or not."

"Right. The map first."

I fired up my laptop. While I scrolled around on Google maps, searching for a landmass that matched the map corner, Zylas picked up the amulet and resumed his examination of the spells on the back.

We worked in silence for over an hour before I heaved a frustrated sigh. "There are islands and inlets everywhere along the coast, and I don't know what the scale of this map is. It could be anywhere."

Pushing my laptop and the torn map aside, I slid the grimoire closer. Maybe I could figure out something useful from the portal array that would narrow down the possible locations. I opened the grimoire to the bookmarked page and sighed again, already overwhelmed. Anthea, for all her questionable morals, had been a genius. The intricacy of the spell was well beyond me, a challenge compounded by the fact that all the notations and instructions were written in Ancient Greek.

I opened my notebook, and the ache in my chest flared at the sight of Amalia's handwriting.

Scouring the portal array, I made some quick notes, but my attention kept returning to the missing sections—the portions Anthea had left out, erasing them from her family's history so the spell could never be replicated.

I glanced at the amulet in Zylas's hands. "Do you think the missing parts of the portal spell are in there?"

"Maybe," he murmured distractedly.

The secrets of the hell portal … concealed in an amulet likely created by a Vh'alyir demon. I flipped a few pages backward, hoping Anthea might have left a clue about the missing sections of the portal spell.

Athanas and Vh'alyir. The creator of Demonica and the reviled Twelfth House. A mysterious connection lost to time and violence.

"What is that?"

I snapped out of my reverie to find Zylas frowning at the grimoire. I'd been mindlessly turning pages and had flipped to a completely different section. His attention was on a random string of demonic runes surrounded by Ancient Greek text.

"This is …" I peeked at the preceding page. "This is where Anthea developed the infernus spell, I think."

Zylas sat forward. "*Hnn.*"

"What do the runes mean?"

"Those are not runes. It is a message."

My breath caught. "A message?"

"It says, 'The place where demon *lēvh* and human *lēvh* meet.'"

"*Lēvh?* What does that mean?"

"I think … spirit? Soul?" He canted his head. "When I go into the infernus, it is called *kish lēvh.*"

My gaze darted across the demonic words surrounded by human text. "Where demon spirit and human spirit met." If Zylas's spirit entered the infernus, did that mean …

"My soul," I whispered. "Was the infernus connected to my soul too? Is that why … why we could hear each other's thoughts? And why we could share your magic? Because the infernus connected our souls?"

"The magic tasted like your mind."

A soul bond. That had to be what an infernus was. That was how it connected contractor and demon. For a fully contracted demon, the connection created a telepathic link through which the contractor could control the demon—and created the soul link that facilitated the banishment clause.

For Zylas and I, the connection had been more than that. The closer we'd become, the stronger the bond between our souls had grown—until we could not only communicate but share each other's magic.

Tears filmed my eyes.

"*Vayanin?*"

Ducking my head, I quickly rubbed the moisture away. "Sorry."

"What is wrong?"

"Nothing." Except that was a lie and he knew it. "I was just thinking … our souls were connected through the infernus, and that's … I wish we hadn't lost that."

He propped an elbow on the coffee table, watching me. "You liked the infernus because we were … connected?"

I sniffled. "Yes."

"I liked to know what you were thinking." His nose scrunched. "You are bad at telling me your thoughts. I ask and you say, 'Nothing,' but it is never nothing."

An embarrassed flush heated my cheeks. I knew I should be more honest with him, but it was so difficult when I never knew how he might react.

"I miss that part," he added, rather grudgingly.

"But not anything else related to the infernus," I said with a quiet laugh. A yawn cracked my jaw, and I debated whether I wanted to go back to bed for a few hours.

He rested his chin on his hand, gazing down at the line of demonic. "Maybe we need the infernus."

I hesitated, trying not to hope. "Would you agree to be bound to one again?"

His tail flicked up, then thumped against the floor. "It is a good place to hide. It is easier. You need it to pretend to be a contractor."

"But I'll be able to use the commands on you."

"I don't like the command." His glowing eyes slid across my face. "Because you think you need it."

I bit my lower lip. Despite the logical and emotional parts of my brain knowing I could trust him, the subconscious part that had evolved for survival and survival alone didn't care about trust. It saw a predator.

Amalia's angry voice echoed in the back of my head, her claim that Zylas would end up hurting me one way or another.

"Maybe …" I muttered. "Maybe I was wrong."

"Wrong?"

Losing the infernus had left me feeling vulnerable because I'd relied on the feeling of control it gave me. Without it, I couldn't feel completely safe—or so I'd thought.

"Maybe I was wrong that you'll always scare me." Determination ignited in me and I scooted back from the coffee table. "Zylas … hold me down."

He blinked. "*Ih?*"

"I want to see if it scares me."

"I do not want to scare you."

"I know, but I want to see." I pressed my palms to the blanket I'd spread across the hard floor. "If I get scared, you can stop."

He squinted at me. "I do not know what you are thinking."

"Just try it."

Huffing, he rose on his knees, his lashing tail betraying his uncertainty, and reached out. A nervous prickle ran down my spine as he put his hand against my shoulder, and doubts whirled in my head.

But if I got scared, he would stop. I knew he would. It'd been so long since he'd deliberately frightened me that I scarcely recognized my memories of the two of us. His aggression and my timidity ... had we really been like that?

Well, to be fair, I hadn't fully overcome my skittish tendencies.

He pushed on my shoulder and I tipped over backward. As my back thumped gently into the blanket, his hands landed on either side of me—then he was straddling me, knees pressing against my hips. His hands closed around my wrists, and he pinned my arms to the floor above my head.

I stared up at him, eyes wide.

He assessed me, nostrils flaring as he checked my scent for that telltale tinge of fear. A rumble started deep in his chest, rasping across his throat.

My heart beat a little faster. I couldn't look away from his eyes, his hunter's stare.

He lowered his body, covering mine, pressing me into the floor. Hard, unyielding muscle. He caught both my wrists in one hand, and with the other, he pulled my hair, forcing my head back to expose my neck.

His warm breath washed over my throat.

My heart hammered, my fingers and toes tingling with adrenaline. My body was definitely reacting, but it wasn't the panic I was used to when he restrained me.

"Zylas," I whispered. "Do I smell like fear?"

He pressed his nose against my throat and inhaled. "No."

I shivered at the way he growled the word. "I think I'm a little afraid … maybe?"

He inhaled again. "No fear. That is not what I smell."

"Are you su—"

His mouth closed over the pulse in my throat.

I gasped, my body electrified with sudden tension. He slicked his tongue across my racing pulse, hot and wet—then his canines grazed the spot.

A shudder ran over me from head to toe, a tiny sound escaping my parted lips.

He raised his head. The predatory hunger in his stare stole my breath. His weight pressed me down. My arms pinned. His fist in my hair.

He dropped his head and captured my mouth with his. No gentle, tentative test. He kissed me hard, and then his tongue was past my lips, and a breathless moan escaped me.

Pinning me to the floor, he devoured my mouth, ravenous, demanding. I couldn't even squirm, completely at his mercy— and even the thought of stopping him seemed preposterous.

He pulled my head back again, his mouth finding my throat. Grazing teeth. Flicks of his tongue. He moved downward, his lips brushing my collarbones.

Releasing my wrists and hair, he braced his elbows on the floor and slid lower. His nose ran across the soft fabric of my sweater, then he nuzzled his face into my breasts. I forgot to breathe.

He moved farther down, hands dragging at my sides, until his upper body was pinning my legs and his chin was at the waist of my jeans. There he stopped, eyes meeting mine.

He placed his hand on my lower belly, fingers closing around the bottom of my sweater. He waited.

Pulse thudding in my ears, I put my hand on top of his, hesitating … then guided his hand upward. My sweater slid with the movement, baring my midriff.

His mouth was on my stomach in an instant, lips sliding over my skin, his tongue tasting me. He moved sideways and found my hipbone peeking above the waist of my jeans.

He fixated there, canines grazing the curve of bone, nose nuzzling the soft hollow. I quivered, lower lip caught in my teeth.

He shifted to my other hip, ravishing it with the same attention, then slid his nose up my waist. I pulled my sweater higher, the fabric bunching under my breasts, and he moved across my ribs, his hands joining his exploration. Hot palms running up my sides. Fingers caressing my skin.

As his nose met my sweater again, my fingers tightened around the fabric. I pulled it up to my chin.

Another rumble vibrated in his chest. His hands and mouth found my breasts, his lips gliding across the exposed skin above my sports bra. He nosed the stretchy black material—then his teeth dragged over the fabric, seeking my most sensitive skin through the barrier.

Air rushed through my lungs, and I arched up into his mouth. He hooked his fingers through the strap above my other breast, growling deep in his throat.

"Zylas," I gasped.

He raised his head. His eyes glowed faintly, his pupils fully dilated.

"Zylas, if …" My voice came out in a breathless whisper. "If I were a *payashē* who'd invited you to her bed … what would you do?"

His stare burned into me. The muscles in his arm bunched, pulling on my bra strap, and I heard a seam tear.

"You are not a *payashē*."

"What if I was?"

"I would take you now."

My chest rose and fell with deep, fast breaths as I gazed up at him arched over me—crimson eyes, tangled hair, hard muscles beneath smooth toffee-red skin, his long tail sweeping across the floor.

A demon. And I wanted him.

"Then take me like a *payashē*," I whispered. "Now."

He hesitated, nostrils flaring to check my scent one more time—then he lunged forward, the blanket beneath me sliding across the hardwood floor with the violent movement.

His mouth covered mine. A hard pull on my torso, the sound of tearing fabric. Cool air hit my chest. His hand ran up my side, then he shoved my sweater over my head, forcing my arms up with it.

Leaving the fabric tangled around my arms, he slid down and closed his mouth over my bare breast. I arched up again, my arms twisting as I tried to free them from my sweater. He licked and nuzzled, and I squirmed beneath him, gasping and whimpering. His hands roved over my skin, then down to my waist.

He pulled my hips up into his, and I felt the hard press of his arousal between my thighs. My heart lurched into my throat, pounding faster, liquid heat building in my core.

Backing up, he dragged my pants down, my underwear sliding off with them. As he yanked them off my feet, I wrenched my arms free from my sweater and bra. I lifted my arms—

He grabbed my wrists, and in an instant, my arms were pinned above my head again. My eyes popped wide, mouth opening in a gasp—and then he was kissing me. He trapped my wrists with one hand.

And his other hand slid between my legs.

I gasped again as his fingers moved over me, stroking and exploring—then his hand disappeared as he reached between our bodies, pulling at his shorts.

On his knees between my thighs, he scooped his arm under my hips, lifted them off the floor, and pulled me into him. My thighs clamped to his sides—and his hardness pressed against my core, hot and ready.

I stared up at him, my chest heaving. With one hand pinning my wrists above my head and his other arm holding my waist off the floor, he had me utterly helpless.

His eyes glowed, pupils dilated. His arm tightened around my waist.

He pulled me up into him. His hard length slid inside me, filling me, stretching me. He growled roughly—then thrust deeper.

I gasped, head spinning, eyes rolling back. Held in place, I could do nothing but clench my legs around his waist as he drove into me, deep and hard, my shoulders sliding against the floor with each thrust. Sensation rippled out from my center, scorching hotter and hotter.

Controlling my hips with one arm, he plunged into me in a measured, powerful rhythm. Pleasure rolled through me in waves, each swell more intense than the last until I was crying out, until my entire body arched.

As pleasure swept through me, he pulled my hips up, burying himself in me as deep as he could. A low sound rasped from his throat as he rocked his hips without withdrawing, milking my every panting gasp and convulsing moan.

Nerves tingling, I sagged weakly, and he sank down with me, breathing hard. Finally releasing my wrists, he slid out of me. With my legs loosely wrapped around his waist, I lay where I was, totally spent and quivering with soft ripples of pleasure.

"*Vayanin?*"

I opened my eyes, unsure when I'd closed them, and found Zylas leaning over me.

"Hm?"

My vague mumble seemed to be all he'd wanted from me, because he sat back, then gently captured my hands. Drawing them up, he nuzzled my wrists, and I was surprised to find they ached from how forcefully he'd pushed them into the floor. Other parts of me ached too as the pleasure dissipated, but I didn't mind in the slightest.

"Was that ..." The words came out fluttery and weak. I cleared my throat. "Was that how you ... mate with *payashē?*"

"*Hnn.*" He tilted his head. "You liked it, *na?*"

My cheeks heated and I was abruptly aware of how naked I was. "Y-yes."

"Do you want more?"

I glanced down. My thighs rested across his, and I could see that he was clearly ready to go again—if he'd ever been not ready.

Warmth flushed through my center and part of me almost said yes, but that ache between my legs had intensified enough to cool the fire.

"Later?" I asked, dropping my gaze, suddenly shy.

A rumble in his throat. His warm hands wrapped around my knees, then slid up my thighs to my hips. "Whenever you want me, *amavrah*."

My belly flipped as I stared up at him. "*Amavrah*? What does that mean?"

He smiled mysteriously, and with his hands on me and my body flushed with shivery warmth, I couldn't even feel annoyed.

23

AROUND THE TIME I started washing my hair in the shower, the reality of what I'd done—what *we'd* done—sank in.

I stood frozen with my hands in my lathered hair, a dozen emotions hitting me at once. Shock, embarrassment, anxiety, but also amazement, excitement, and a fresh pang of hot yearning. I lowered my arms and peered at my wrists. They were tender but my pale skin was unblemished. No sign of bruising.

He hadn't hurt me—and even while completely helpless, I'd never felt fear.

A confusing cocktail of feelings swirled through me as I hurriedly finished my shower, dried off, and hastened into the bedroom to dress in soft yoga pants and a hoodie. Thank goodness I'd packed two bras, because Zylas had ruined my other one.

Another hot pang fluttered through me at the thought.

I rubbed the towel over my hair, then tossed it in the bathroom and returned to the living room, mentally bolstering myself. The blanket was back in front of the coffee table, and Zylas sat on it, the Vh'alyir Amulet in his hands. He glanced up as I appeared, and I instantly lost my nerve.

I minced over to the table but couldn't sit beside him. Half of me wanted to run from the room, and the other half wanted to climb into his lap.

Twisting my fingers together, I coughed awkwardly. "Um … Zylas?"

He gazed up at me, waiting.

"When you said … that demons can choose when they want to have young … does that mean *you* can choose?"

"*Var.* I do not want young yet."

Relief flooded me. In the heat of the moment, I hadn't considered that particular risk. I couldn't begin to guess if it was even possible, but at least I didn't have to worry about it.

Exhaling in a rush, I picked up the shard of our broken infernus from the end table and stared pointlessly at it, my anxiety and embarrassment levels creeping up again. Why was it so hard to look Zylas in the eye now?

A hard tug on the back of my pants. I fell, landing in Zylas's lap. Tossing the Vh'alyir Amulet onto the coffee table, he wrapped his arms around me.

"You are being *zh'ūltis, amavrah.*"

"Don't call me stupid. And what does—"

"You are blushing. You have *embarrassing* thoughts now, *na*? You do not want to tell me what you are thinking."

I gritted my teeth, my hand clenching around the shard of infernus. Right on cue, my face heated again. Was he ridiculously perceptive or was I painfully obvious?

"I can't hear your thoughts anymore," he prompted.

"Good," I mumbled.

"Why don't you want to tell me?"

Because it was embarrassing—a word that was even more difficult for him to grasp than "empathy." I tried to push off his lap but he tightened his hold, pulling me back against his chest.

"I will let you go after you tell me."

"You can't do that!"

"I am stronger than you."

My jaw clenched all over again, and I squirmed helplessly. "Zylas!"

"Are you afraid?"

"No," I growled. "I'm mad."

His husky laugh made me shiver. "You like it when I hold you, *na?*"

My blush deepened. "Fine! I just wanted to know if … if you always pin *payashē* down like you did with me."

"It is safer. Sometimes a *payashē* gets scared being under a male." As though demonstrating, he squeezed me just hard enough to compress the air from my lungs. "Or she decides she does not want to mate in the middle of mating. Holding her hands makes it harder for her to attack with *vīsh*."

I blinked. "*Payashē* get scared?"

"Not from me, because I am not big like other males. But I still hold their arms to be safe."

"I couldn't blast you with magic, though."

He pushed his face into the side of my neck and his teeth grazed my skin. "No, but you wanted me to hold you down."

I flushed, my skin tingling and pulse quickening. The infernus shard slipped from my suddenly limp hands, bounced off my leg, and landed on the blanket with an almost inaudible thud.

Zylas lifted his head, peering at the broken relic. His breath caught—then he lunged forward, almost dumping me off his lap, and snatched up the shard.

"*Lēvh! Kir tūiredh'nā nul id?*"

Before I could ask what was wrong, he'd twisted the other way and grabbed the Vh'alyir Amulet off the coffee table. He held the two items side by side in front of us, and I blinked down at them, trapped in the circle of his arms.

"The marking for spirit." His words came fast, his accent thick. "It is on both. They are both places where demon spirit and human spirit meet."

Dropping the infernus shard, he caught my wrist and pressed the Vh'alyir Amulet against my palm. His hand pressed against the medallion's other side, fingers curling over mine, locking our hands together.

"Do you remember the words, *amavrah?*"

My heart drummed in a completely different way than a minute ago. I could never forget those alien words. They had saved my life. *Changed* my life. Once I'd spoken those words, I'd never been the same.

At my nod, his fingers tightened—then we spoke together, the phrase whispering across our lips in perfect unison, words last shared on that terrible, transformative day when we had bound our souls and our fates to each other.

"*Enpedēra vīsh nā.*"

The amulet burned hot beneath my palm, and the world turned to bright, bloody crimson.

A SHEEN OF RED LIGHT covered everything.

An endless, cloudless sky shone with a pale pink glow. Scarlet sand stretched away in every direction, rolling in gentle, windswept dunes. Huge clusters of tetragonal crystals jutted from the sand like gargantuan spears attempting to pierce the unreachable sky. In the bizarre red haze, they were a shade of soft rose.

It took me a long moment to realize I was still on Zylas's lap, the blanket under us and our hands entwined around the amulet. I could feel them, feel *him*, but I couldn't see them.

"*Ahlēvīsh*," Zylas whispered, his voice soft and close in my ear as he named the crystal formations. "I know this place. I have been here."

Hand trembling, I reached for the nearest crystal, a narrow spike seven feet tall. My fingers passed through it. An illusion.

The vision shimmered, the sand and sky rippling. It solidified again—and I gasped.

A demon was crouched beside us.

He stared into the distance, seemingly unaware of us. He could've been Zylas's older brother—his face leaner and harder, his muscles tough and sinewy. Instead of armor, he wore a simple wrap around his hips, tied with braided rope, and more fabric was bound around his lower legs.

His dark hair was sheared unevenly, short and pragmatic, but I scarcely noticed, too focused on the eight-inch horns, dark and ridged, curving elegantly from his tangled hair.

The demon gazed straight ahead, eyes glowing brightly, then crept forward. He kept low to the ground like a prowling tiger, hands lightly touching the sand, bare feet moving with slow, smooth grace. As he drew ahead of us, his tail hovered behind him, ending in two sharp barbs that curved back toward his body.

His prowl stilled.

Movement among the *Ahlēvīsh*. A woman walked from between two towering crystals, one hand trailing across the glossy surface. Her eyes were wide, her human face slack with awe.

Her tiered skirt fell to her ankles, each layer of fabric vivid and patterned, though the red haze of the vision erased their colors. A wide fabric belt circled her waist, and her top featured short, fitted sleeves and a V-neck that dropped all the way to her navel, exposing a bare triangle of her skin. Elaborate necklaces covered her upper chest, the dangling ends hanging between her half-covered breasts. Long, dark hair fell down her back, twisted with fabric ties.

I couldn't guess her skin tone in the red tint—she could've been olive-skinned, bronze-skinned, or deeply tanned—but for anyone who'd studied Ancient Greece, that outfit was unmistakable.

It was Minoan—a Bronze Age civilization from the island of Crete, and Europe's first truly advanced culture.

As the woman moved through the towering crystals, the demon slunk forward another step, his movements so slow that grace should've been impossible, yet he flowed across the sand.

But as stealthily as he moved, he didn't escape the woman's notice.

She whirled to face him, her hand jumping to her wide fabric belt. Gone was the soft wonder in her face, replaced with fearless steel as she whipped out a sturdy string from which hung wooden charms, each carved with a spell. Artifacts.

Demon and human stared each other down, thirty feet between them.

The Vh'alyir's tail twitched. "*Kar eshathē?*"

His mouth moved, but the sound of his words didn't come from him. They filled my ears, surrounding me like the crimson illusion.

Zylas's arm tightened around my middle. "He asked, 'What are you?'"

Holding the demon's gaze, the woman spoke—a language I'd never heard before. A language that had been lost to history over three thousand years ago when the Mycenean Greeks had overtaken Crete and absorbed the crumbling remnants of Minoan society.

Though I couldn't understand a word she spoke, the thought that she was asking if this strange place was the Underworld popped into my head.

The Vh'alyir demon, who couldn't understand her, hesitated for a long moment, then rose slowly from his crouch. The woman tensed, her hand clenched around her collection of artifacts. Did she have any idea how unprepared she was to battle a demon?

Cautiously raising his arm, the Vh'alyir pointed at her. "*Payashē?*"

She frowned, then pressed a hand to her chest. "Anthea."

Her voice, too, came from everywhere and nowhere, hollow in my ears in the same way this vision was washed of all color but red.

Eyes narrowing, the demon repeated, "Anthea."

She tapped her chest again. "Anthea."

"Anthea," he echoed flawlessly.

She pointed at him and waited.

He patted his bare chest. "Zh'rēil."

"Zh … reel," she repeated with difficulty.

"Zh'rēil," he corrected.

"Zh–ree–il."

He considered her, then warily drew closer.

Zh'rēil stopped ten paces away from Anthea, scrutinized her from her hairband down to her sandaled feet, then moved again—circling her. She turned with him, her grip tight on her artifacts.

He returned to his starting point, then stepped closer.

She called out a word, and her sharp, defiant rebuff sent him skittering sideways in a defensive retreat.

Sinking into a crouch, he slunk forward again, maybe thinking he would seem less intimidating at half her height. Anthea's eyes were wide, but she held her ground.

Zh'rēil crept close enough to stretch out a hand and touch the edge of her linen skirt. He rubbed the fabric between his finger and thumb, his tail flicking side to side. His head tilted back, eyes moving across her face as his nostrils flared.

His tail went still.

He sprang with lightning speed, knocking the rope of artifacts from her hand as he bowled her over. She slammed down on the sand and he flipped her onto her stomach and pinned her down.

I gasped at the sudden violence, clutching Zylas's wrist.

Anthea made no sound as she squirmed violently under Zh'rēil's hands and knees. Maybe she feared drawing in more enemies if she made too much noise.

He pushed on the back of her neck to hold her still, then leaned down and smelled her hair. Pulling and patting at her clothes, he seemed to be trying to get a sense of what this strange female was. Still on top of her, he flipped her onto her back and pinned her upper arms with his knees. She stretched her hand out, reaching for her artifacts in the sand, just out of reach.

Zh'rēil put his hands on her face, and she went rigid. He stroked her cheeks, touched her hair, pulled on her upper lip to see her teeth. Leaning close, he peered into her eyes, puzzling over their unusual appearance.

His weight on her arms shifted—and she snagged her string of artifacts. She whipped them toward him, shouting an incantation.

A flash of silvery scarlet threw Zh'rēil backward. Anthea rolled over, leaped to her feet, and sprinted away. The demon lunged up, unharmed, and sped after her in a slinking prowl.

The vision of *Ahlēvīsh* and sand blurred, then reformed. Same area, different spot—and this time, a new feature dominated the landscape.

A perfect circle sat upon a base of crystal. Shards of shattered quartz peppered the sand around the circle like shrapnel, as though the formation of the portal had obliterated the massive *Ahlēvīsh*.

Anthea knelt on one side of the circle. Zh'rēil knelt on the other.

Time must have passed, because Anthea's outfit and hair were different. And an even clearer indicator that this was a different day: she appeared unafraid as she watched Zh'rēil.

The demon leaned over the smooth surface of the portal, head canted and tail snapping as he peered into a pale rose sky that probably would've been blue if not for the red cast of the vision. She extended her arm into the portal as though reaching into a pool of water.

Zh'rēil peered at her unscathed arm, then back at the circle. He stretched a hand out, hesitated, then dropped his fingers in and snatched them back out.

Laughing, Anthea leaned forward and stuck her entire head and shoulders into the portal. Zh'rēil observed for a moment, then inserted his arm. Clinging to the crystal base with his other hand, he stuck his head in too.

Had his head and shoulders appeared on the other side of the portal? Was he looking into the human world, the first demon to ever glimpse Earth?

The vision rippled, reforming once more. Same spot, still the portal, but Anthea's clothing had changed again. Another day. She and Zh'rēil sat in the sand, five cautious feet between them, as she pantomimed different actions. With each gesture, Zh'rēil recited a Minoan word.

Another shimmer, a new scene. The *Ahlēvīsh* were gone, replaced by rough stone boulders protruding from the dunes. Zh'rēil walked across the shifting sand, Anthea following him.

The Vh'alyir Amulet had grown uncomfortably hot against my palm.

Dark shapes in the sand. Zh'rēil stopped, and Anthea joined him. They gazed across the barren expanse.

Dozens of bodies. Demons, their flesh rotting and bodies torn. Strange reptilian creatures darted among the corpses, scavenging for edible parts. Horns of varying lengths marked the skulls of the dead, their small stature revealing them to be Vh'alyir demons.

Zh'rēil spoke, rapid words of demonic rolling off his tongue, his voice low and growling.

Zylas's mouth brushed my ear. "He is telling her ... third rank Houses are hunting his House. Vh'alyir are killed for the fun of stronger demons … but when he told the *Naventis*, the other *Dīnen* did not care."

The *Naventis*, where the most powerful demons gathered once a year, was supposed to address issues like the slaughter of one of the twelve Houses, wasn't it?

Anthea listened to Zh'rēil's snarling frustration, then murmured something in return. The demon grimaced, then began again in halting Minoan.

The vision blurred and reformed.

Gone was the desert. Anthea and Zh'rēil stood on a rocky bluff that was far more familiar than the visions of towering crystals and portals—but in the cove below was … destruction. What must've once been a thriving port town had crumbled, the stone buildings beaten into rubble. Where land met water, the shattered keels of wooden ships draped the wreckage like huge skeletons.

Anthea was speaking, gesturing, her motions full of anger. Odd notions flitted through my head—that she was talking about huge waves striking the shore over and over, destroying everything. Then, while her people were crippled by disaster, the invaders came—and kept coming.

Ripples of crimson as the vision changed again.

Abruptly, we were inside a room. It was dark, a crude oil lamp glowing on a table. Anthea and Zh'rēil stood across from each other, the table between them layered with sheets of thick papyrus paper.

Holding the demon's stare, she spoke quietly, slowly, with emphasis. This time, the strange feeling of understanding within me was undeniable—something about the way she spoke, the intensity of each word, felt like she was whispering directly into my mind.

"*Then our pact shall be thus: we will combine our skill and magic to bind the Kings of Demons. The elder demons who have allowed the slaughter of your House will become slaves in my world, stripped of their will. I and my people will use their power to defend our island.*"

Zh'rēil's eyes glowed in the dim room.

"*We will bind our descendants as well as ourselves, for this pact will span one hundred years from this day—time for your House to recover its strength and time for my people to enforce peace.*"

Zh'rēil murmured his agreement.

The scene dissolved. The heat of the Vh'alyir Amulet scorched my palm, pain tugging at my awareness.

A new vision formed.

Anthea and Zh'rēil stood side by side at the edge of a portal, surrounded by sand and towering *Ahlēvīsh*. Anthea wore a similar outfit, but creases and wrinkles had aged her face. White streaked her hair, and she didn't stand as tall. A crude but familiar shape hung from a cord around her neck: an infernus.

I couldn't tell if Zh'rēil had visibly aged, evening shadows clinging to his darker skin. He held a rope cord, the Vh'alyir Amulet swinging from it.

"*It begins,*" he said.

"*Yes. And when the debts of our enemies are paid, my descendant will summon you to bring this to an end.*" She touched the pendant. "*Is the key ready?*"

He grasped it. "*Dūkāra Vh'alyir et Dīnen evashvā vīshissā.*"

Crimson flared out from the crystal, complex spell circles spinning around him before fading.

She gazed up at him. "*Then farewell, Zh'rēil.*"

"*Farewell, Anthea.*"

Sinking into a crouch, she put her head and shoulders through the dark portal, then climbed awkwardly through. Her sandaled feet disappeared.

Zh'rēil stood at the portal's edge, unmoving, holding the amulet in a tight fist. Minutes slipped past, then the circle began to shrink. It grew smaller and smaller until it disappeared entirely. All that remained was the flat top of the shattered *Ahlēvīsh* where the portal had taken form.

Opening his hand, Zh'rēil lifted the amulet to gaze into its etched face. "*Dakevh'il Ahlēa nā?*"

He dropped the cord around his neck, and as the amulet settled against his chest, the vista of red sand and rose crystal blurred. The crimson glare faded, and the mundane living room reappeared.

24

WITH A PAINED GASP, I tore my palm away from the scorching hot amulet. It dropped from our hands and landed on the floor with a thud.

My palm throbbed as I panted, though less from pain and more from the disorienting switch from a magical vision of the past back to the present. The drab living room seemed dull and lifeless after the scarlet-imbued illusion.

"They were right."

Zylas whispered the words, and I looked up at him, cradling my sore hand.

He stared down at the amulet. "Vh'alyir are *karkis*. We are traitors. We caused summoning."

My throat tightened with sympathy—and guilt of my own. "What one Vh'alyir demon did thousands of years ago ... it's not your fault."

I slid off his lap and sat beside him as the burning ache in my palm diminished. Cautiously, I touched the amulet. The metal was cool, and I picked it up.

"Anthea and Zh'rēil created summoning to help each other—to punish the other Houses and save Minoan civilization. But Minoan civilization fell." I pressed my fingers to my forehead, dredging up my studies of Greek history. "Around 1600 BC—that's thirty-six hundred years ago—a volcano erupted in the Sea of Crete, causing tsunamis that destroyed Crete's entire coastline. Based on that town Anthea showed Zh'rēil, I think that had already happened by Anthea's time."

The Minoans had been a mercantile people, reliant on their ships for both trade and defense. Historians theorized that tsunamis had obliterated the Minoans' port cities and fleets, crashing their economy and leaving them destitute—and vulnerable.

"Invaders from the mainland," I murmured. "The Mycenean Greeks. Anthea wanted to protect Crete from the Myceneans, but her island was overrun less than two centuries after the volcanic eruption. Enslaving demons to help fight off the invaders didn't work."

"It did not help Vh'alyir either." Bitterness infused Zylas's husky voice. "We are hunted without mercy. We are almost all gone."

I ran my thumb across the Vh'alyir symbol on the amulet. "Zh'rēil wanted to punish the other Houses for hunting his House."

"He wanted to remove the powerful *Dīnen*." Zylas twisted his mouth. "He could not kill them. He wanted them to disappear so different *Dīnen* would become powerful—*Dīnen* who would decide differently about killing Vh'alyir for fun."

Instead, Zh'rēil's attempt to save his House had doomed it. The First and Second Houses had figured out enough to blame Vh'alyir for the strange new curse upon demonkind.

"They made their pact to last one hundred years," I murmured, my gaze turning toward the grimoire. "After one hundred years, they planned to ... to *end it*."

My pulse drummed in my ears as I said the words.

"Anthea never intended for summoning to be permanent." I pressed my hand to my forehead. "It was never supposed to spread to hundreds or thousands of sorcerers, or cause hundreds of *Dīnen* to be summoned every year, destabilizing demon society."

"But they did not end it."

"Why not? Anthea couldn't have done it herself. She wouldn't have lived that long. She must have entrusted the job to her offspring ... to her daughter or her granddaughter."

"Maybe Zh'rēil died. And the First House stole the amulet."

"Maybe ..." I continued to stare at the grimoire, cold suspicion blooming through me. "But I don't think it was his fault."

I reached for my notebook of translations, pulled it onto my lap, and flipped to Myrrine Athanas's very first journal entry.

"'Why would Anthea forbid summoning of the Twelfth House?'" I read aloud. "'Why warn us of the retribution of their descendants, but fear not the vengeance of any other House? Why is the Twelfth House different? And thus I wonder: Could it be a false warning with a deceitful purpose?'"

I looked up at Zylas. "A false warning. Anthea didn't forbid summoning of the Twelfth House. She *intended* the Twelfth House to be summoned after one hundred years so her descendant and his successor could perform whatever magic was necessary to end summoning."

Zylas's eyes narrowed. "Not his *successor*. Zh'rēil could survive that long."

My mouth hung open. "He … how old do you think he was?"

"I do not know. I have never seen a Vh'alyir that old." He waved the topic away as unimportant. "Zh'rēil waited to be summoned so he and a *hh'ainun* could end the *vīsh*."

"But no one summoned him." I flipped pages to my translation of Melitta's only entry in the grimoire. "Here Myrrine's younger sister said, 'Without the lost amulet, without the secrets or the truth Anthea deemed too dangerous for the written word, we will never know why she cursed us so.'"

I tapped the page. "What if Anthea didn't purposely leave information out of the grimoire? What if, when the one hundred years was up, her daughter or granddaughter decided to wait longer to end summoning? Minoan civilization was even worse off by that time, and the Myceneans continued to invade."

"They wanted to keep the power."

I nodded. "And they waited too long. Maybe by the time they tried to summon him, Zh'rēil had died. They ended up summoning a new Vh'alyir *Dīnen* who had no clue about the origins of summoning magic—or if he did, he couldn't perform the magic to end it because he didn't have the amulet."

"He could not be bound to a contract," Zylas murmured.

"If they let him out of the summoning circle … it probably didn't go well. And whatever happened caused one of my ancestors to add that warning to never summon the Twelfth House."

I touched the edge of the grimoire. I would never know why so much was missing from it—whether pages had been lost, damaged, or deliberately altered. The Minoans had possessed their own language and alphabet, meaning one of Anthea's descendants had translated it into Ancient Greek after leaving Crete. No translation was perfect. Every time the book was copied, a little more was lost.

But there were clues still. Melitta had written, *But I ask you this, daughter of my daughter, honorable scribe, survivor, sorceress: When will it end?* Had she suspected summoning was supposed to end? Had she and Myrrine found clues hidden in the text—bits of experimentation, little messages in demonic like the one about souls in the infernus?

But those clues hadn't been enough. Something, somewhere, had gone terribly wrong with Anthea and Zh'rēil's plan, and then it'd been too late to fix.

I imagined Zh'rēil, still carrying the amulet, waiting as endless years passed. Watching more and more *Dīnen* be summoned away and chaos engulf demon society. Watching the other Houses turn on his when it became clear Vh'alyir were exempt from this new, terrible magic no demon could fight.

How long had he waited for Anthea's descendants to summon him?

"What did he say?" I asked abruptly. "At the end of the vision?"

"'*Dakevh'il Ahlēa nā?*'" Zylas's lips pressed into a thin line. "'Will *Ahlēa* punish me?'"

Punish him? Zh'rēil must have known the summoning magic was dangerous … that it was wrong. And his worst fears had come true. A pact intended to last one hundred years had become a slow genocide spanning three and a half millennia.

"Zylas." I held the amulet toward him. "Try it. See what happens."

He reached out, his fingers hovering inches from the swinging medallion. Then he closed his hand around it and rose to his feet. I scrambled to join him as he faced the open side of the living room, the coffee table behind us.

"*Dūkāra Vh'alyir et Dīnen evashvā vīshissā.*"

Crimson lit the metal amulet and flared out. I gasped as a huge spell circle expanded outward, nearly touching the walls. Runes and markings swirled across it, then faded. Another circle appeared, then faded. Yet another appeared, then faded.

The amulet went dark.

I squinted at the floor as though that would make the magic reappear. "What … happened? Was that a spell?"

"No. It was instructions."

"Instructions?"

"It is the *vīsh* to end summoning." His eyes burned as he faced me. "We can do it. We can end it. Forever."

We could? Zylas and me? Millennia of violence, of cruel magic and brutal suppression, of death and the destruction that had begun with two genius minds blinded by a desperate need to protect their people—and we could stop it forever?

But I ask you this, daughter of my daughter, honorable scribe, survivor, sorceress: When will it end?

Three millennia after Melitta had asked, I had the answer.

It would end with me.

TWENTY-FOUR HOURS later, my head throbbed from a tension headache, and my eyes didn't want to focus on anything farther than two feet away. I'd been squinting at tiny runes for too long, my contact lenses not helping with the eye strain.

Walking along the sidewalk, I breathed deeply, letting the chill February breeze clear my head, then peeked at Zylas.

He walked beside me. Amalia had grabbed her in-progress sewing when she'd taken off, but she'd left her last prototype, similar to the one he'd worn on our doomed mission with Zora and her team. The dark garments fit him exceptionally well, and he'd left his metal greaves off this time, so the pants moved more naturally with his graceful steps.

I glanced at his feet, relieved I'd bought three pairs of the same shoes, knowing they wouldn't last under demonic levels of wear and tear.

Dark sunglasses reflected the street as he scanned everything. The midmorning foot traffic flowed around us, and with each person to breeze right past him, an odd feeling tightened my chest more.

No one looked at him. No one cared. The reddish undertone of his skin wasn't eye-catching when only his face and hands were exposed. His eyes and tail were concealed. Even his retractable claws could pass as an unusual goth aesthetic—unless he slashed someone.

Rubbing my forehead, I glanced nervously skyward, but the chances of Nazhivēr suddenly appearing to ambush us yet again were slim. Not only was he unlikely to attack us on a busy street, but he and Xever had what they needed: they'd gotten Zylas's blood.

With four nights until Xever's portal opened, he was probably focused on his own plans and not on whatever Zylas and I were up to.

Unfortunately, he was right not to worry about us. I still hadn't figured out where the portal was, let alone figured out how to stop him from opening it on Thursday at dawn.

We reached our destination: a sandwich shop. Zylas didn't need to eat, but I did, and he wasn't keen on me wandering around the city without him.

I peered through the window at the lineup inside, then murmured to Zylas, "It's crowded. Do you want to wait out here?"

He nodded.

I left him outside the door. The scent of fresh-baked bread engulfed me as I entered the building and got in line. My gaze drifted back to the window where Zylas leaned, hands in his pockets, imitating a casually waiting human.

The prickly tight feeling in my chest intensified. In his lightweight armor with tail lashing and eyes glowing, Zylas's demonic-ness was unmistakable. But until recently, I hadn't considered how easily he could blend in—or how little people cared about his oddities.

I imagined bringing him in here with me. Would anyone comment? What about the grocery store? A movie theatre? A theme park?

As long as he could wear a hat and sunglasses, he could go anywhere I could go. As long as we didn't have any close encounters with other mythics who might recognize a demon, was it actually that risky?

If we *did* run into other mythics … Zora's team hadn't realized the man in black accompanying me wasn't human, and they knew my status as a contractor and had even seen my demon before.

The unexpected bubble of excitement expanding in me fizzled at the thought of Zora. I'd never replied to her texts, letting her think I was dead to protect her and her team from the consequences of associating with a rogue contractor. Why was I thinking about how easily Zylas could pass as human?

Why was the idea of him doing human things with me so enticing?

"Hey."

I started. Two guys around my age stood in line in front of me. They were both smiling at me in a friendly way. I blinked at them.

"Do you eat here often?" the blond one asked. "Got any recommendations?"

"Uh … no, it's my first time here."

"I've been twice before, and the sandwiches were great. I've never tried the soup, though."

"Oh."

His smile faded slightly and he hitched it back. "On your lunch break?"

"Yes," I lied, since it seemed easier.

"The line is pretty slow. Want to go ahead of us?"

"No thanks. I'm fine."

The guy drooped slightly. "I don't mind, but … okay."

Seeming strangely disappointed that I didn't want to take his spot in line, he turned back to his friend and they started discussing the merits of chili versus sandwiches.

I stared at their backs, puzzling over the odd interaction as the line shuffled forward. After the two guys had ordered, I requested two turkey sandwiches—one for later—and a large chocolate brownie to share with Zylas.

The cashier handed me my paper bag of food, and as I hastened toward the door, I noticed the two guys lingering by the exit. The blond one held the door open for me.

"Hey," he said again. "Uh … I don't want to bother you, but …"

I stepped out onto the sidewalk and paused, eyebrows scrunched.

"I was just wondering if I could … take you out for coffee sometime? If you're interested?"

My mouth fell open. He shuffled his feet, a pink tinge rising in his cheeks. His friend cringed, noticed me noticing his cringe, then plastered on an encouraging smile.

"Um," I began. "I …"

The blond guy's gaze flicked to something behind me—and his blush vanished as his face went white. "Never mind. I didn't realize—sorry!"

He whirled around, his buddy right with him, and they power-walked away, shooting glances over their shoulders as though expecting to get attacked from behind.

Warm breath stirred my hair.

I turned around and found myself face to chest with Zylas. He was practically standing on my heels, menace rolling off him.

"Did you scare those guys?"

He growled wordlessly.

"They didn't mean any harm," I protested.

"They were watching you. The whole time." He shot me a glower. "You did not notice."

I wilted, embarrassed by my obliviousness, then hurried down the sidewalk, heading back toward the apartment building. Zylas walked beside me, grumbling under his breath, but I was distracted by the realization that a reasonably good-looking guy had asked me out. That had never happened before. My one boyfriend had evolved from a group project at college. No one had ever flirted with me out of the blue.

I touched my nose. Was it the lack of glasses? I looked down at myself. Or the leather jacket? In what way had I become more appealing to the opposite sex?

The question occupied me the whole way back. We entered the old marble lobby of the Lee Building and headed for the stairs—Zylas had decided he disliked elevators. As we neared the sixth floor, a tug on my jacket stopped me.

I turned around. Zylas stood on the step below me, putting us almost at eye level.

"Why did you blush?" he asked.

"I ... what?"

"When the *hh'ainun* male talked to you."

I blinked. "I was embarrassed."

"Why?"

"I ... I'm not used to getting attention from guys, I guess."

He was silent. I hesitated, then pushed his sunglasses up on top of his head, revealing his glowing eyes.

"You're hiding *your* thoughts now, Zylas," I said. "What are you really thinking?"

His jaw flexed, then he puffed out a breath. "Do you like *hh'ainun* males more?"

"More? You mean more than you?" My breath caught as I clued in. "No."

"No?"

"I ..." My brain jammed, a fresh blush warming my cheeks. "I think ... you're ..." My voice shrank to a whisper. "You're more attractive than any human man I've ever met."

He didn't have any trouble hearing my mortified admission, and he smiled in a pleased way, his shoulders relaxing. I abruptly recalled that he wasn't considered desirable by demon standards. Female demons turned their noses up at the weak Vh'alyir House.

My blush intensified as we returned to the unit, but it faded quickly as I unbolted the door, unable to block out memories of arriving with Amalia. Socks's plaintive meows as Zylas and I came in without the missing member of our little family didn't help. I'd been thinking about her almost constantly since unlocking the Vh'alyir Amulet's spells, wishing I could share our new discoveries with her.

I had no way to contact her. Unless she called the burner phone she'd left with me, I would never talk to her again.

Our morning's work was spread across the coffee table and half the floor. Sheets of large drafting paper were taped together, and I'd spent hours carefully drawing out the three different spells the amulet had shown us—a feat that'd only been possible because Zylas had recreated them in glowing crimson so I could trace them directly onto the paper.

The first one was, as far as I could tell, the portal array with no missing pieces. Since step one of ending summoning forever appeared to require a portal, that explained why Anthea and Zh'rēil had included it in both the grimoire and the amulet.

Though we had the complete spell, actually opening a portal might be the most difficult part of the process.

Zylas and I had stopped for lunch just after finishing our drawing of the second and third arrays. We hadn't parsed out the details yet, but we knew the portal array needed to be activated first. The other two spells were performed on the open portal and would consume its magic in some way.

I scarfed down my sandwich, feeding a few bits of turkey to Socks, then joined Zylas at our drawing of the second array.

It was the simplest of the three and mainly Arcana, which surprised me.

As I knelt beside him, I was strangely aware that he hadn't changed out of his human clothes. The jacket's hood lay over his shoulders, his hair extra mussed from the fabric.

Watching him pore over the drawing, I bit my lip. We could *end* summoning. We could stop the enslavement of demons and destruction of their society.

Zylas kept saying he had to go home. Was that only because of his promise to the *payapis* to change *Ahlēavah*? Or was there some other reason? If he changed the demon world by ending summoning forever, would that be enough? Would he still want to return home?

Or would he consider staying?

The forbidden question rushed through my mind, and I tried to stamp it down, but now that it was loose, it refused to die. I'd been fighting that question since the day Zylas had pointed at his book of landscape photography and asked if we could see all those places.

I'd thought it was such a ridiculous question—but maybe it wasn't. Because asking him to stay didn't mean he could never return home.

We could spend months traveling North America.

We could spend years traveling the planet.

We could spend my entire lifetime exploring the world, and at the end, Zylas could return to *Ahlēavah*, become an *Ivaknen*, witness the slow recovery of the demon society for himself, and raise strong sons to help revive his House. There was no denying that his lifespan was longer than mine. He didn't have to sacrifice a future in his own world to spend more time in mine—to spend more time with me.

But did he *want* to?

I twisted the hem of my sweater as he leaned over the drawing, bringing his nose close to the paper. His tail flicked back and forth, a frown pulling at his lips.

Did he want to stay with me a little while longer? Would he even consider it?

I breathed deep, steeling my courage. "Z—"

"What is this?"

He pointed to a spot on the array. Gulping back my question, I shifted closer to look at the Arcana rune paired with the only demonic rune in the set.

"That's the rune for earth," I answered.

He turned to the third array, and I followed his gaze to a similar pattern of lines where two runes sat together, both demonic.

His breath rushed out and he sat back on his heels. Something about the blankness of his expression sent a chill rippling down my limbs.

I shuffled on my knees to face him. "Zylas?"

His gaze flicked to me, then he pointed at the array with the earth rune. "This one is earth *lēvh*." He pointed at the other array. "This one is *Ahlēavah lēvh*."

"So … earth spirit and the demon-world spirit? I don't understand."

"I think it means …" He trailed off, looking between the two arrays as though hoping for an alternate answer. "It means one *vīsh* is for the earth side. The other *vīsh* is for the *Ahlēavah* side. One spell is for you, here. One spell is for me, there. Together, they end summoning."

"For you … *there*?"

He didn't reply, staring at the arrays.

"You mean," I said, my voice strangely loud in my ears, "that to end summoning, you have to cast this spell from the other side of the portal? From within *Ahlēavah*?"

Again he said nothing.

I pointed at the arrays. "But these spells will use up the portal's power. You'd be ..."

Trapped. Cut off. Gone. He'd be out of my reach forever.

He looked up at me, his face unreadable and his crimson eyes dimmed by shadows. "It does not matter."

Doesn't matter. Doesn't matter.

Of course it didn't matter. Because I was the foolish one daydreaming about him staying. He wanted to go home. He'd wanted to go home all along.

The spell changed nothing—it merely destroyed the slight, farfetched slice of a chance that he might've stayed with me for a little longer.

25

I STOOD IN THE SHOWER, hot water pouring on my head with half-hearted pressure. I didn't need another shower, but it was the only place where I could cry without Zylas hearing me.

Soon, the hot water would run out and I'd have to get control of myself. Why couldn't the water last longer? I hated this apartment. I hated this building.

I hated my life.

My parents had been murdered for an ancient grimoire full of desperate, despicable magic that had exacted a terrible price. I'd lost my soul-deep connection to Zylas. I'd lost the special magic I'd gained with the infernus. I'd lost Amalia, the only family I had left. I'd lost the safety of my guild and all vestiges of a normal life.

And soon I would lose Zylas too.

I tried to bolster my mood with the reminder that Zylas and I had the chance to end summoning forever. If we could pull it off. If we could somehow perform the most complicated magic either of us had ever attempted.

Ending the enslavement of a race that my ancestor had begun over three millennia ago—I could do that. Me, the bookworm who'd been scared to learn magic.

But it would cost me Zylas. We couldn't do it without sending him through the portal first. He had to be in *Ahlēavah* to cast his portion of the spell.

I shook my head, water flying from my hair. No, it *wouldn't* cost me Zylas, because he'd never intended to stay. He didn't want to stay. He didn't want to be with me. I was just a human girl, a weak, silly *payilas*.

I bound myself to you. Only you, vayanin.

A tremor ran through me, and I shook my head again.

Because I promised.

Another more violent shake.

I want you to always be safe.

Why couldn't I stop his voice in my head?

Whenever you want me, amavrah.

Fresh tears mixed with the water running down my face. I bowed my head, hands pressed to the shower wall. He was a demon. Demons didn't care, didn't love. I repeated it. *Demons can't love.*

The words rang hollow in my mind.

I'd thought I could never learn to trust Zylas—but I had. I'd thought he could never feel empathy or compassion—but he did. I'd thought I could never love him.

But I did.

I loved him. I was *in* love with him, and I didn't even know for how long because I'd been denying it so vehemently.

I was in love with Zylas. I was in love with a curious, savage, playful, protective, deadly, gentle, cunning, and surprisingly sweet man who happened to be from another world. It didn't matter to me that he had glowing eyes, horns, claws, and a tail. It didn't matter that he could turn his body into crimson light and possess an infernus. It didn't matter that he was different from me in so many ways.

I loved him.

And I'd been rejecting my feelings—and rejecting him—over and over for weeks now. Even as I'd tried to convince Amalia that there was nothing wrong with me kissing him, I'd been denying the depth of my own feelings.

If I'd told her how I felt about him, would she have reacted differently? If I'd told her I hadn't listened to her warnings because I loved him, would she still have left?

If I told Zylas how I felt about him, would that change anything?

No. It couldn't. He'd always planned to go home and … and …

You are bad at telling me your thoughts.

I leaned my forehead against the shower wall. He'd always planned to go home—because I'd never given him a reason to stay. Maybe being with me wasn't a good reason. Maybe he would laugh and scoff and call me *zh'ūltis* for suggesting it.

But if I didn't tell him, I'd never know.

I shoved away from the wall and turned the taps, cutting off the water. Cold air hit me as I grabbed my towel and wrapped it around myself, then rushed toward the door. My courage wouldn't last. The shy, self-conscious, fearful part of me that couldn't handle rejection would overthink it and I'd go right back to convincing myself that nothing I said would change anything.

Rushing out of the bathroom, I veered into the living room. Socks was prowling across our papers, her green-eyed stare on my abandoned pen, but Zylas wasn't there.

I whirled around and sped down the hall, leaving a trail of water droplets in my wake. Across the kitchen. Through the open bedroom door.

Zylas sat on the bed, still in his human clothes. His photography book was open on his lap, displaying the image of a mountain in Oregon. The mountain he'd said he wanted to climb, and I'd thoughtlessly blurted that he could, then even more thoughtlessly dismissed his interest by reminding him that he wanted to go home, not travel the human world.

He blinked at my sudden appearance, then rolled off the bed, tossing the book onto the mattress.

Breathing hard, I stood a few steps past the doorway in a state of panic. I couldn't do this. I couldn't say it. I couldn't lay my heart bare. It was so much safer, so much easier, to reject him than risk his rejection.

Myrrine's words whispered in my ear. *Dare as I dared.*

"*Amavrah?*"

"I don't want you to leave."

The words rushed out. Blurted, stuttering, awkward.

His forehead scrunched, that familiar expression of confusion.

"I don't want you to go home, Zylas!" I didn't mean to shout, but it was the only way I could say it. Clutching my towel to my chest, I squeezed my eyes shut. "I want you to stay with me. I want to be together and stay here together and go see all the places in your book and not have to say goodbye for a long time."

Tears trickled down my cheeks as I finished in a whisper, "I don't want to say goodbye ever."

Silence.

I forced my eyes open. Zylas still stood in front of the bed, frozen with surprise, staring at me. Mysterious. Unreadable. No magical connection giving me insight into his thoughts and feelings.

So I had to share mine instead.

"I—I know you don't want to stay. This isn't your world and you'd always have to hide or pretend to be human or—or—and there's nothing for you here, but—but …" A shuddering breath escaped my lungs. "But I still want you to stay with me."

The selfishness of that declaration hit me hard, and I hunched my shoulders. I wanted him to sacrifice everything to stay with me? How cruel was I?

"Nothing?"

My gaze shot up to his.

"Nothing for me here?" He slowly tilted his head. "You are here."

My mouth went dry, my heart thudding as though expecting a killing blow.

His tail swished slowly, then he stepped toward me, gaze sliding over my face. "You are my *amavrah*, Robin."

"What does that mean?"

He stopped in front of me. "It means you are my chosen. It means I will risk everything to be with you."

I reached up and pressed my trembling hand to his chest, fingers closing around a fistful of his jacket. "Do you want to leave?"

Only a moment passed before he spoke, but the silence rang in my ears, a death knell for my vulnerable heart.

"I have to stop the summoning *vīsh*. Vh'alyir created it. I know how to stop it, so I have to."

A shudder shook me from head to toe. I exhaled roughly. "I understand. Our predecessors created the summoning magic. We have to stop it. We're the only ones who can."

If we didn't, who would? Would my daughter, if I ever had one, summon a Vh'alyir? Would that demon, younger than Zylas, weaker, less confident, lacking Zylas's unique skills, be able to form a bond of trust with a human? Would they have the ability or the motivation to end summoning?

It had to be us. Zylas and me. And that meant he had to go through the portal.

I drew in a deep breath. Another. Then another. Inhaling until I was steady again. Then I reached up, curled my fingers around the back of his neck, and drew his face down.

A slow kiss. Building. Intensifying. My lips parted, inviting his tongue, and his mouth fitted over mine.

I pressed against his chest, losing myself in the kiss. Losing myself in him, in this moment.

His light touch ran down my back, then he pulled my towel away. It dropped to the floor. His hands slid across my damp skin.

I unzipped his jacket and pushed it off his shoulders. He shrugged it off his arms and tossed it away. His hands returned to my body. As he touched and stroked me, I found the buckles on his chest plate. It came free in my hands. I let it fall to the floor with a thud.

Piece by piece, I removed his gear and clothing, all while his exploring touches grew more urgent. Finally, I loosened the laces on the sides of his shorts and pushed them down.

Now my hands were running over him. Exploring the dips and curves of his muscles. Sliding lower to take him shyly in my hands, my heart pounding and belly fluttering with heat.

This time, he didn't pin me down and take control. This time, he let me explore him. Let me push him to the bed so he was sitting on the mattress's edge. Let me climb onto his lap, press my hips into his, rock against him until I burned for more.

This time, his hands on my hips didn't grip hard or steer my movements. He held me, steadied me, as I slid myself down onto him, gasping as he filled me. A husky rumble vibrated his chest.

We moved together, holding each other, and we didn't need an infernus or a telepathic connection or a magical bond to be in perfect, breathtaking harmony.

We didn't need anything but each other.

26

I SAT ON THE LIVING ROOM FLOOR, surrounded by papers and notes. The Athanas grimoire, atop its case with my notebook, lay untouched on the sofa. The Vh'alyir Amulet lay beside the grimoire, its secrets revealed—over three thousand years later than intended.

Anthea and Myrrine had both called the amulet the "key," but it was more like a demonic grimoire than an artifact.

Its first spell: magic that could block demon contracts, likely to ensure Zh'rēil could never be enslaved. Its second spell: the vision of the past, created to show Anthea's descendant how summoning had come to exist. And its third spell: instructions for the magic that would end summoning.

Near-silent footsteps padded toward me, then Zylas appeared. He crouched at my side, and together we studied our work—our task. We knew what we needed to do. Accomplishing it was a whole other matter.

The two-part spell that needed to be performed from either side of the portal was reasonably straightforward. Zylas had already memorized his part: a complex array he could instantly cast in his glowing magic, to be accompanied by a long incantation in the demonic language.

My part was simpler but more difficult to pull off. I had an incantation to recite too—also in demonic, which I was working to memorize—and an Arcana array to add to the portal spell. Anthea had left a spot for it: a node near the center, the geometric lines already in place. All I had to do was add the correct runes in the right spots before reciting my incantation.

It wouldn't be easy, but it was doable. Our biggest obstacle was the portal itself. Arcana Fenestram required time, space, materials, and skill I didn't possess.

I looked down at the paper I held. The torn corner of Xever's map.

We didn't have the ability to open a portal—but Xever did. He'd already done most of the work. At dawn four nights from now, his portal would be ready—and we could use it to end summoning.

All Zylas and I had to do was find it.

I smoothed the crinkled paper, then rolled it up to pack into my suitcase. Everything needed to be packed.

Amalia and I had decided that three days was the maximum amount of time we could spend in one location while we were being hunted; lingering was too dangerous. This was now my fourth day in the safe house apartment, and I couldn't delay leaving any longer.

Quiet grief rolled over me. Once we left, the chance that Amalia would return shrank to zero.

"What is wrong, *amavrah?*"

I looked up, surprised to find Zylas watching me. "I wish Amalia were here. We started this together, the three of us, and … she should be with us."

But she'd left because my habit of hiding my feelings didn't apply only to Zylas. I hadn't told Amalia how I felt about him. I hadn't shown her Myrrine's journal entries. I hadn't confided in her.

I heaved a sigh. "I need to apologize, but I'll probably never see her again."

Zylas's tail swished. "I know where she is."

His words took a moment to sink in. "You … what?"

"The night she left." Another tail swish. "I followed her to a building. Last night I checked and she is still there."

"You went out by yourself?"

He frowned. "Not for very long. I do not like leaving you."

"Then why did you go?"

"Because Amalia is important to you."

I looked from the grimoire to the amulet then back to Zylas, my throat tight. I'd thought Amalia was gone for good, and the sudden revelation that Zylas had known where to find her all along left me mentally reeling.

"Let's get everything packed," I said, making up my mind.

We stuffed all our things into my suitcase except for the Vh'alyir Amulet, which went around my neck, hanging beside my *impello* artifact.

While Zylas dressed in his human disguise, I stood at the window, peering out at the street below. My thoughts drifted to Tori and Ezra. It'd been almost a week since we'd attempted the summoning ritual to separate Ezra and Eterran. Beyond the walls of this building, they were being hunted—or they'd been captured already.

And if I wasn't careful, I'd be captured or killed as well. If I was lucky, word had already gotten out that I'd fallen to my death, but that didn't mean the bounty-hunting guilds would just give up.

I slid the burner phone out of my pocket. Zora had tried to reach me for three days before giving up. My gut twisted guiltily, but I reminded myself I was much safer as an illegal contractor who was presumed dead.

As Zylas pulled on the hated shoes, I coaxed Socks into her carrier, then we ventured down the stairs and out onto the street. Cold rain fell from the dark sky, the air unpleasantly damp and chill in my lungs. I pulled my hood up, my suitcase rolling along behind me. Zylas carried Socks, the kitten's complaining meows loud and insistent.

We headed straight north, passing two blocks of small businesses in short, worn-down buildings. Crossing the street, we continued past a block of construction, then hurried through another intersection.

Zylas turned into the parking lot of a two-story motel painted a garish green, probably to distract from its rundown siding and disintegrating roof. He stopped at a door halfway down the strip, an empty parking lot across from it.

"This?" I muttered. "Amalia is here?"

He nodded.

Three blocks away. She'd been three blocks away this whole time.

I tightened my grip on my suitcase handle, then rapped my knuckles on the door. Nothing. I knocked louder. The door had a peephole, but it was so grimy maybe she couldn't see out of it. Or had she left? Had I missed my chance?

Hammering on the wood, I called, "Amalia? It's me!"

A clatter from inside, then the clack of the bolt. The door swung open. Amalia stood in the doorway, a dimly lit room with a single queen bed behind her. She glared at me.

Socks meowed more loudly at the sight of her missing human.

"I'm sorry!" I blurted before Amalia could say anything. "I'm so sorry for being a horrible friend and a horrible cousin and just for being horrible!"

She blinked.

"I didn't mean to ignore your advice. It was good advice and I tried to listen but there are things I haven't told you, and I should've been open with you about my feelings so you'd understand. I didn't listen because I—I—" I glanced at Zylas, hovering beside me, and panic spiked in my chest. I steeled my courage. "Because I'm in—"

"Wait!" she half yelled.

I broke off in confusion.

She shot me a warning look, then swung the door open wider, revealing more of the small room—and the man standing near a desk with a small TV bolted to it.

Stocky, bald, pot-bellied Uncle Jack offered a hesitant smile.

My jaw hung open in horror at what I'd almost said in front of my uncle. Snapping my mouth shut, I gave Amalia a painfully grateful look for stopping me.

"We'll talk later," she muttered, then added at a normal volume, "Dad arrived like fifteen minutes ago. We were just debating going over to see you."

"You ... you were? I thought you were done with me."

She huffed. "Yeah, well ... we can talk about that later too. Get your asses in here before someone notices you."

I scooted inside, dragging my suitcase, and Zylas followed. As soon as Amalia shut the door, he uncoiled his tail and pushed his sunglasses up onto his head, his cold crimson stare running over his summoner.

Uncle Jack gawked at the demon, then pulled himself together. "So that's how you've been managing without an infernus? Dressing like a human?"

"And it works pretty well," Amalia declared. "Especially with my special design."

"Well, that won't be necessary for much longer," he told me. "I have your new infernus."

Nervous excitement shot through me.

"It needs one more spell," Amalia added quickly. "If we start it right away, it'll be ready by Wednesday night."

"Wednesday? But that's—"

"Really freakin' close to Xever's portal opening at dawn on Thursday, yeah." She shifted her feet. "But maybe that doesn't really make a difference. Dad and I were talking, and we think ... we think it might be time to get out of here. That's what we were going to hash out before coming to see you."

I looked around the motel in confusion. "Get out of here?"

"Not *here*," Uncle Jack said impatiently. "Out of the country. I need to get you both off this continent—away from Xever and whatever he's planning to do with that portal. If you two are right and he wants to get his hands on one of these all-powerful female demons, then we don't want to be anywhere nearby when it happens."

"And we need to get away from the bounty hunters," Amalia added. "The MPD hopefully thinks you're dead, but that won't last if you're seen."

"Both scenarios are bad." Uncle Jack rubbed his hands together anxiously. "And I'm not letting you two be captured or killed."

Fleeing the country. We could. We could leave Xever to open his portal and use Zylas's blood to summon a female demon or whatever he intended to do. I could abandon my desire to avenge my parents and put my own safety ahead of righting the wrongs of my ancestors.

But I wouldn't. And neither would Zylas.

"I can't leave." I looked between them. "Not yet."

Amalia shook her head. "Robin, I get that you want to stop Xever, but—"

"We can stop *summoning*." I touched the Vh'alyir Amulet. "Zylas and I figured out how this works. It isn't a portal. It's the key to ending summoning forever and saving demonkind."

I looked up at Zylas, his eyes bright and fierce.

"And we're going to use Xever's portal to do it."

AMALIA PRESSED her palm to the Vh'alyir Amulet, her fingers curled over Zylas's hand as he held it with her.

"*Enpedēra vīsh nā*," he rumbled.

"*Enpedēra vīsh nā*," she repeated haltingly.

Crimson lit up the medallion, and a spell circle appeared beneath them, filled with jagged runes. Standing at the edge of the room with Uncle Jack, I watched them experience the vision of Anthea and Zh'rēil, Amalia's eyes wide with disbelief and Zylas's expression grim.

She gasped, then gasped again. As the magic swirled slowly around them, her astonishment darkened into bleakness.

The glow fizzled away, and Amalia yanked her hand off the hot amulet. "Holy *shit*."

Yeah, that about summed it up.

"That was … whoa." She gave herself a shake. "Anthea and her demon pal built summoning magic so that it could be deactivated? How does that work?"

"The King's Vow," Zylas said, dropping the amulet over his head to rest on his chest. "They created a … bridge … between their magic and the King's Vow magic. We will break the bridge."

"And sever the connection forever." I crossed the room to stand beside him. "Summoning circles will no longer connect to the magic of the demon world, preventing demons from being pulled through."

"*End* summoning," she murmured in disbelief. "End Demonica. Nullify an entire class of magic."

Uncle Jack rubbed a hand over his bald head. "Will this process affect existing demon contracts?"

"I don't think so," I said. "We're going to break summoning magic, not contract magic. Which, all things considered, isn't a bad thing. If thousands of demon contracts suddenly evaporated, at the least we'd have thousands of dead contractors."

"But probably a lot more death," Amalia mused. "Some demons wouldn't immediately kill their contractors to trigger the banishment clause."

I paced the short length of the room alongside the shabby bed. "Ending summoning requires an open portal. It'd take us years to master enough Arcana Fenestram to do it ourselves, but Xever's portal will open at dawn four days from now."

Amalia perched on the foot of the bed, watching me pace. "Okay, yes, but Xever has Nazhivēr and Saul backing him up, not to mention an unknown number of other demons *and* an entire cult. He won't have left his precious portal array unprotected."

I pressed my lips together.

"You and Zylas have never defeated Nazhivēr. You can't expect that to suddenly change just because we really, really need to win this time."

"I know, but …"

"You can't end summoning if you're dead," she said firmly. "How are you going to access his portal without him killing you?"

I halted my pacing, hands clenched with frustration.

"We will create *dh'ērrenith*."

My attention swung to Zylas. He stood eerily still, observing us with a predator's eyes.

"You cannot always wait for *dh'ērrenith*. Sometimes you have to make victory. We can do that now. We have time to prepare."

"Prepare … what?" I asked. "We don't even know where he made the portal."

"We can figure it out with that piece of map you stole," Uncle Jack said. "Shouldn't be that difficult."

I blinked at him. "You're going to help?"

He exhaled roughly. "I made a lot of selfish decisions, Robin. Decisions that got your parents killed and put you and Amalia in danger. I can't change that, but I can help you change this. The Athanas legacy is as much mine as yours."

Eyes narrowed, I pursed my lips. "You want to help us end summoning forever?"

"Yes—and I'd also like the chance to stick a knife in Xever's back."

I peeked at Zylas. The demon watched the summoner, then gave me a slight nod. My uncle was telling the truth.

As I smiled in relief, Uncle Jack dusted his hands together. "Get the piece of map and let's figure out where that bastard hid his hell portal."

27

AMALIA'S EYES moved across the page, a crease between her eyebrows as she read. I watched her with my hands twisted together, trying not to fidget too much.

Finally, she lowered the notebook—but she didn't look up at me, continuing to stare at my handwriting. "So Myrrine fell in love with her demon."

"Yes," I whispered.

"And you're in love with Zylas."

Heat flushed through my cheeks, and I wished I could sink through the floor and vanish—but we needed to have this conversation. Us *not* having this conversation was why she'd walked out.

"Yes," I choked.

At least we were alone for my confession—and somewhere much more comfortable than Amalia's hotel room.

Uncle Jack had chosen our new hideout: a furnished loft apartment in downtown with three bedrooms and a huge open living room with more than enough space for our preparations. He, with Zylas's help, was unfolding a huge stack of maps in the main room. His solution to our location dilemma had been surprisingly simple: there were only so many topographic maps of the province.

So he'd bought all of them. We simply needed to match the torn piece to an existing map.

While they'd gotten to work, I'd cornered Amalia in her room, where she'd just finished setting up a new sewing machine, and showed her my translations of Myrrine and Melitta's journal entries.

Amalia blew out a long breath, a lock of blond hair fluttering away from her face.

"I don't get it." She ran a finger down the page, passing across Myrrine's confession. "I mean, I get it a little bit, but ... he's a *demon*."

Instead of furious or disgusted, her declaration was simply bewildered.

"I don't know how to explain it," I said softly.

"I guess love is never all that logical, is it?" She flicked a glance up and down me. "So?"

"So ... what?"

"Did you do it?"

"Do what?"

She rolled her eyes. "Are you *sure* you're not a virgin?"

A blazing blush engulfed my cheeks as I belatedly clued in. "I'm not—that—that's private."

"No way! You *did?*" She goggled at me. "And you're still in one piece?"

"Of course I'm in one piece," I grumbled, mortified.

"Was it good?"

I clenched my jaw and stared at the floor, face flaming.

She let out a slightly giddy laugh. "Holy shit."

"Just—just drop it, all right?"

"Right, okay, but I'm curious now. How big is his—"

"*Amalia!*"

"Ugh, fine." She huffed, then leaned back, hands propped on the mattress. "So you're in love with Zylas—and banging him."

I glared.

"What about all your plans to send him home?"

Pain struck without warning, piercing my heart. I hunched forward. "He'll be going through Xever's portal."

A moment of silence.

"Does he feel the same way about you?" she asked quietly.

I raised my head, gazing toward the bedroom door. On the other side, Zylas was working to identify the portal location. He wouldn't rest until he'd ended what his predecessor had begun. Even if he hadn't promised a *payapis* that he'd change the world, he had to do this for Vh'alyir and for *Ahlēavah*.

Knowing that, I could only give one answer—the same one he'd given me.

"It doesn't matter."

WE WERE PREPARED for battle.

At one end of the spacious living room, a large topographic map lay across the floor, the matching piece of Xever's map taped to it. We'd extended the anchor lines to their point of intersection: the spot where he'd created the portal array.

My initial searches hadn't panned out because I'd been looking in the wrong direction. The landmass had resembled a peninsula or island, so I'd been looking for a matching shape along the coast. But Xever had gone in the opposite direction.

From the Pacific Ocean, the Burrard Inlet stretched fifteen miles inland, a swath of salt water that separated Vancouver from the North Shore Mountains. And ten miles into the inlet was a fat little peninsula called Admiralty Point. It was a forested foothill with a few hiking trails along the coast, but otherwise uninhabited.

The peak of the foothill was the spot Xever had chosen for his portal.

At the other end of the living room, our supplies were laid out. The biggest and possibly most useful items were hex-clothing outfits for me, Amalia, and Uncle Jack. Their inner linings were embroidered with hardening cantrips, allowing us to make our clothing nearly impenetrable for thirty seconds.

Amalia had made Zylas an outfit too, but since it couldn't go into the infernus with him, we'd decided to leave it behind.

Beside the clothes was a small stack of newly made artifacts for the three humans to divvy up. Two duplicates of my *impello* artifact, one each for Amalia and Uncle Jack, plus a few more options we thought would work well against Nazhivēr—and possibly cultists.

In the middle of the room was a six-foot-wide spell circle drawn directly on the floor. An infernus glinted under the overhead lights, positioned in the array's principal node. The center of the medallion was blank, waiting for a House sigil to appear.

I paced back and forth in front of the circle. Thirty more minutes, then we could gear up, collect our things, and head out.

Straight to Xever's portal.

Dawn was just under five hours away, and we intended to be at the portal well before then. As soon as the infernus was fully charged, Zylas and I would bind ourselves to it. Then we'd be ready to go.

Dizzy from pacing, I padded across the hardwood floor. As I passed the doorway to Amalia's bedroom, her and Uncle Jack's voices floated out, debating some facet of our plan. The only one missing from our new hideout was Socks. We'd checked her in to a cat condo yesterday … just in case we never came back.

I entered my room, closed the door, and turned to face the bed. Zylas sat on it, back against the headboard, a book across his lap.

My heart ached as I crawled onto the bed and sat beside him. The glossy page showing the mountain in Oregon stared back at me, the corner folded down.

I pressed against his side, his smoky scent filling my nose, and rested my head on his shoulder. His warmth soaked into me, his body solid against mine. The thought that in a few hours he would be gone … it didn't compute. It didn't make sense. How could I lose this?

How could I lose him?

"I wish we could've traveled together," I whispered, "and seen all the places in your book, even if it took a lifetime."

Especially if it took a lifetime.

"*Hnn.*" His head turned and I looked up. Our foreheads touched. "Would you have spent your lifetime with me, *amavrah?*"

His question sank through me, embedding itself in my crumbling heart. "Yes."

"Even though I am not *hh'ainun* and could not do all the *hh'ainun* things?"

Tears stung my eyes. "Yes."

"Even though it is more dangerous for you to be •a contractor?"

"That doesn't matter." I touched his cheek, then slid my hand up into his hair and pressed my fingertips to his small horns. "Would you have spent my lifetime with me, even though I'm not a *payashē* and you don't belong in my world?"

His crimson eyes moved across my face.

"Robin!"

I jolted at Amalia's shout, my hand pulling from his hair.

The bedroom door flew open and Amalia rushed in, Uncle Jack following right behind her. Her face was pale, a glowing cell phone clutched in her hand.

Instantly alarmed, I swung my legs off the bed. "What's wrong?"

"Dad and I were talking about the bounties on us, and he went to pull up my profile on the MPD site to see the charges, and look!"

She thrust the phone under my nose. A white webpage filled the screen with a mythic identification code across the top. Beneath that should've been her name, photo, and personal information. Instead, there was a single line of text:

```
Damnatio Memoriae
```

I stared at the two words. "What ... what does that mean?"

"I don't know, but it's on your profile too, see?" She tapped on the screen, then held it up again. "Same thing! What the hell?"

Like Amalia's page, "*Damnatio Memoriae*" had replaced my name and information on the MPD archive page. I looked questioningly at Uncle Jack, but he shook his head.

"I've never seen anything like that before. It could be a website error."

"No," I said with chilling certainty. "A website error wouldn't be in Latin. And *damnatio* means damnation, an adverse judgment."

Amalia recoiled. "You mean, like ... we've already been condemned?"

"*Damnatio memoriae*," I muttered. "Damnation of ... memory. As in ... erasing our memories?"

"Or erasing *us* from all memory? Removing us from the database is like telling the rest of the mythic world we don't exist."

A shiver ran through me. "Try searching for Ezra."

She typed on her phone for a moment. "All his info is gone too. Even the bounty and warnings about a demon mage."

"What about Tori, Aaron, and Kai?"

More tapping. "Same."

The cold in my veins deepened. "Look up the Crow and Hammer."

She shot me a frightened look, then typed the guild name into the search.

"*Damnatio Memoriae*," she whispered.

"Erased." I pressed my fingertips to my temples. "Someone erased us ... and not just you and me. The whole Crow and Hammer. Why would the MPD do that? They can disband guilds, but they don't erase them, not unless ..."

Unless a guild or group threatened the secrecy of magic. That was the MPD's ultimate mandate: to protect magic. But the Crow and Hammer hadn't tried to expose the existence of magic.

But they *had* tried to expose the existence of Xever's cult.

I closed my eyes, bringing up the image of the city map from the tower. The red circle around the Crow and Hammer, the paper creased from the pen being dragged forcefully across it. The other markings in different colors ... surrounding the guild.

Erasing the guild's listing from the MPD's database was a pointless move unless Xever also intended to erase the guild itself—and all its members.

I shot to my feet. "Xever is planning to destroy the Crow and Hammer."

Amalia and Uncle Jack started. Zylas, crouched on the bed, merely blinked at me.

"Where are you getting that from?" she asked dubiously.

"This is *him!*" I jabbed my finger at the phone. "He's behind it. I don't know how, but pulling strings from the shadows is his MO. He'll lose everything if the cult is exposed, and the only way to keep the cult a secret is to destroy the guild trying to expose it."

Amalia looked from her phone to me and back. "How do you just *destroy* a guild? It's not like he can drop a bomb on the building."

"He doesn't need a bomb. The vampires, Amalia, remember? He was trying to build up a force of demon-blood-addicted vampires. That wasn't just for fun."

"And the golems." Her throat moved with a swallow. "He traded them to that dark sorceress, but why did he have an army of golems in the first place?"

I nodded. "And demon mages. The cult worships demons, and stuffing them inside human bodies isn't what I'd call reverent. He wasn't making demon mages for the *cult*."

"He made them to *protect* the cult." She gripped the phone tightly. "We need to warn the guild."

I dove to the bedside table and grabbed the burner phone. I'd turned it off since we were all together, and I fidgeted anxiously as it powered up.

The screen flashed to life. No new messages from Zora. I tapped her number and started a call.

It clicked straight to voicemail.

"I mean, it's the middle of the night," Amalia mumbled.

"She answered in the middle of the night last time." I handed the phone to her. "Try Ezra and Tori and the others."

She dialed number after number. No one answered.

Taking the useless phone back, I dropped it on the bed. "If you were about to attempt rare, dangerous magic that you'd spent years preparing, and there was a guild poised to ruin everything for you, would you eliminate them before or after your all-important spell?"

"Before," Amalia and Uncle Jack answered in unison.

"He's going to destroy them tonight. Now. Before the portal spell is ready."

A long silence stretched between the four of us.

"We need to go to Admiralty Point," Amalia said. "We need time to figure out what Xever's protections are and how to get at the portal."

"If he's waging war on your guild," Uncle Jack added gruffly, "then he won't be at the portal. All the better for us to gain control of it before he arrives."

Their logic was solid, and I bit my lip as I turned toward Zylas. He gazed back at me, considering our options.

"Xever and Nazhivēr could be at the guild," he said. "That is a good place for *dh'ērrenith*. We can trap them between their enemies, and when they are dead, we can go to the portal." His wolfish grin appeared. "And I promised Darius I would protect his guild."

Adrenaline rushed through me. Pushing my shoulders back, I faced Amalia and Uncle Jack. "We're going to the Crow and Hammer first."

"Well, shit." Her eyes narrowed as they slid over Zylas. "If you're going to kick Nazhivēr's ass in public, then you'll need your hex gear after all."

His brow furrowed questioningly.

"A demon as recognizable as you can't go running around with all that glowy red magic on display. Everyone would know you're Robin's demon. But you know who *could* run around with demonic magic, and no one would be able to pin it on Robin?"

"Who?"

"A demon mage."

28

ALMOST EXACTLY FOUR MONTHS AGO, I'd thrust my hand across the silver line of the summoning circle, piercing the barrier that had separated Zylas and me from the moment we'd met. In the frigid darkness within the circle, he'd held me against his chest, squeezing my sliced arm to slow the bleeding, and asked what I wanted from him.

Protect me, I'd begged.

That day, his eyes had been dark with exhaustion, his life hanging by a thread.

Today, they glowed with power.

His fingers tightened over mine, pressing the infernus into my palm. The hard edges bit into my skin, but I squeezed it even tighter, staring up at him.

He stared back. Unblinking. Looking deep inside me in a way no one else could.

That day, we'd made our desperate promises to each other, driven to survive, and begun a partnership that had tested us both. Changed us both. Pushed us apart and brought us closer together. Then we'd lost that bond … only to discover an even stronger one that required no magic.

"Zylas," I whispered.

His gaze drifted over my face. He waited silently.

"Last time you asked for my soul."

He'd thought it was his only way to escape the human world, unaware that contract magic, and therefore the banishment clause, didn't work on Twelfth House demons. Just as Myrrine's death hadn't freed her demon from Earth, my death couldn't save Zylas.

I wrapped my other hand around his as he held the infernus. "This time, I promise you my heart. We won't be together, but I'll always think of you. I'll never forget you. You'll be in my heart forever."

His head slowly tilted, shadows dimming the glow of his eyes. He lifted his hand and curled it over mine, both our hands wrapped around the infernus.

"You are *amavrah* and *vayanin*. I will think of you every time I step into the sun."

A tremor ran through me. He pulled, drawing me closer until our hands were trapped between our bodies.

"*Enpedēra vīsh nā.*"

His husky voice whispered across me and I closed my eyes.

"*Enpedēra vīsh nā*," I breathed.

Red light flashed across the amulet and scorching pain erupted in my hand. The agonizing heat blasted up my arm and seared my chest, then faded.

In its place, a dark, fierce shadow with a crimson core had appeared in my mind. Zylas's thoughts rushed through me, too fast to follow—but I could *feel* so much.

His sadness. His regret. The hollow ache of desolation inside him.

My eyes flew open, and I reached for his face. My hand pressed against his cheek as I stretched onto my toes—bringing our faces closer as though that would bring his mind into clearer focus.

He pulled back, the infernus still caught between our hands.

"Done yet?" Amalia called from her room. "All infernused up again?"

"Yes," I said weakly, fighting for composure as I dropped my hand from his face.

She sauntered into the main room—and she had every right to add a little swagger to her walk. Dressed in her all-black outfit with a mixture of leather and spandex, she could've stepped off the pages of my favorite speculative fiction novel—the dangerous bounty huntress tracking cybercriminals.

Zylas released the infernus, and I uncurled my fingers from around it. The Vh'alyir emblem shone in its center. I lowered the chain over my head.

A few minutes later, the four of us were ready, including Zylas. Instead of traveling in the infernus, he was back in disguise—but he wouldn't be blending in with any crowds.

His finished outfit was as vaguely futuristic as Amalia's and even more intimidating, with a hooded jacket, pants that concealed the bulk of his greaves, and a pair of gloves with slits in the fingertips for his claws. Add the reflective sunglasses and he looked almost villainous.

We descended from the apartment building and loaded into Uncle Jack's black sedan while a light, cold rain pattered down on us. As the vehicle pulled away, Uncle Jack seeming rather uncomfortable in his simple but well-fitting outfit, I glanced across the back seat to Zylas.

We were leaving. We'd spent our last night together. We'd probably already shared our last kiss. This was it.

In my wildest dreams, I couldn't have imagined this. That I would be bound to a demon and how much it would change me. How much it would change him. The marks we had left on each other's souls would never fade.

The vehicle slowed to a crawl, the change in momentum pulling me from my thoughts. I leaned sideways to peer through the windshield, the wipers sweeping back and forth as rain speckled the glass.

The towering skyscrapers of downtown had been replaced with older four- and five-story buildings, their windows dark. The streetlamps illuminated empty roads—except for one vehicle dead ahead. A police car with its lights flashing blocked part of the road beside a temporary barrier.

I instantly recognized the sight—we'd seen the same thing when Tahēsh had escaped and the MPD had ordered the closure of most of the Eastside.

If they'd again ordered a civilian evacuation, that meant I was right. Whatever was happening to the Crow and Hammer, whether MPD-sanctioned or not, was happening *now*.

Barely slowing the vehicle, Uncle Jack drove up onto the sidewalk. The officer in the squad car threw his door open, but we were already speeding past the barricade. The vehicle bounced as Uncle Jack steered back onto the asphalt, and we zoomed along the eerily deserted street, drawing closer to the guild.

"Look," Amalia whispered.

I leaned over the center console, my seatbelt digging into my shoulder. A block or so ahead, rising above the rooftops, a column of orange-tinged smoke billowed into the sky.

"Stop here," Zylas ordered.

Uncle Jack pulled the car over and cut the engine. We got out of the vehicle, hoods drawn up against the rain, and gathered on the sidewalk, staring at the firelit sky a block away.

Outside of the car, I could hear it: faint bangs, bursts, crashes—and beneath the other noises, a chorus of shouts and screams.

"What the hell is happening?" Amalia whispered.

I clenched my hands into fists. "Let's go."

Zylas was already moving in a swift, smooth gait halfway between a prowl and a jog. I rushed after him, and Amalia and Uncle Jack followed. The dark, empty buildings loomed, the forsaken air of the deserted neighborhood underscored by the sounds of a desperate battle that grew louder and louder as we drew closer.

Cutting through a narrow alley, Zylas led us toward another street. He halted at the sidewalk's edge and peered around the corner. I leaned past to steal a glance.

Half a block away, beneath the innocent glow of streetlamps, mythics battled for their lives.

Fire blazed and flashes of colorful magic blinked and flared as sorcerers activated their artifacts in desperate defense against their attackers: monstrous wolves. With foaming mouths and bulging shoulders, they lunged among the mythics, jaws snapping and furious snarls drowning out the cries of the human combatants.

Fear plunged through me at the sight of the giant lupines. No animal should be able to move that fast, especially not ones that were a hundred pounds heavier than a mundane wolf.

They could only be werewolves—and I'd bet money that, like the vampires we'd fought, Xever had enhanced their strength and speed using demon blood.

Zylas watched them, his mind whirling. *Low—fast—four legs—like kanthav?—how strong—*

A wolf caught a man's arm in its jaws and wrenched, hurling its victim to the ground.

Very strong—only teeth to attack—soft hide—

His rapid assessments blurred as he analyzed the pitched battle in a matter of seconds, then he curled his fingers.

"We will go straight through," he said, his flashing thoughts quieting as he focused. "And search for Nazhivēr."

I'd barely begun to nod my agreement before he launched into the street. I burst out after him, Amalia on my heels, and we raced toward the fight. The darting silhouettes of mythics grew clearer.

Zylas's tail uncoiled from around his waist, whipping out behind him, then he dove.

He slid into the legs of the nearest wolf, bowling it over. As it tumbled, his claws raked across its belly—no glowing talons needed. The werewolf was still falling as he leaped into the next one, again taking out its legs before ripping it open.

I slowed my headlong charge, chilled by the brutal violence. The quadrupedal wolves were sturdy and agile—and by keeping low to the ground, Zylas was negating that advantage.

They couldn't knock him over because he was attacking on their level.

He kicked a wolf's jaw before it could bite him, then rammed his claw-tipped fingers through another's ribcage. I followed a dozen paces behind the lethal demon as he plowed through the wolves on the fringes of the battle.

A voice rang out in a hoarse cry, and I tore my eyes away from Zylas. A few yards away, a man had fallen and a wolf was on top of him, his forearm in its jaws.

"Drew!"

With a furious shout, Zora charged out of nowhere, her huge sword swinging. The werewolf tearing at Drew's arm lunged away with a snarl—but two more slunk in to join it. Standing over her fallen comrade, Zora brandished her weapon, unflinching despite the six hundred combined pounds of werewolf lined up to attack her.

I swerved toward them, grabbing for the artifacts hanging around my neck. The wolves advanced in a line, drool dripping from their jaws.

"*Ori impello cylindrate!*"

My new artifact flashed and a column of rippling air shot outward. It struck the nearest wolf, launching it into the other two and flinging all three beasts fifteen feet away. They slammed down in a yelping heap.

Zora's head snapped to me, her mouth gaping. "*Robin?* You're alive?"

I hesitated—we needed to keep moving, to find Xever and Nazhivēr as quickly as possible—but the three wolves were already untangling themselves and clambering up.

"We need to get Drew away," I said urgently, seizing his arm.

She grabbed the shoulder of his jacket with one hand, his torn arm bleeding everywhere, and together we dragged him across the pavement—but the wolves stalked forward, their eerily pale eyes fixed on us.

"Zora," Drew gasped. "Let go of your sword."

She released it—and it floated into the air. The long blade, smeared with blood and rain, shone under the streetlamps as it flew at the approaching wolves, slashing wildly at their faces.

Zora grabbed Drew with both hands—and Amalia appeared between us, snatching a double handful of the back of his jacket. The three of us hauled him across the street and into the shadows of a closed shop.

Snarling, the wolves darted past the free-flying sword and charged at us.

I scrambled for an artifact, but before I could figure out which was which, a roaring blast of fire engulfed the wolves. As the fire surged upward and the burning wolves yowled in agony, a sword appeared from the flames. It flashed down, its glowing blade slicing clean through one wolf after another.

For a second, I thought Drew had control of Zora's weapon again, but then I spotted the hand holding the sword's hilt—a hand coated in flickering orange-white flame.

And my brain belatedly picked out the man within the inferno.

Wreathed in dancing flames, Aaron dispatched the third wolf, then turned. Most of his shirt had burned away, the fire running across his bare arms and shoulders, mixing with his hair and dripping off his sword.

His blue eyes landed on me—and bulged in disbelief. "Robin?"

I gawked at him, eternally thankful the pyromage wasn't our enemy. "Aaron—"

He's here.

Zylas sharp warning cut through my thoughts, and I knew instantly whom he meant.

"I have to go. Amalia, come on!"

"Robin—"

Ignoring Aaron's and Zora's simultaneous shouts, I bolted away and Amalia caught up to me in a few strides.

"What is it?" she panted.

"Nazhivēr," I answered tersely. "Where's Uncle Jack?"

"He circled around to look for Xever."

We slipped past the outskirts of the werewolf battle. The intersection loomed ahead, and adrenaline saturated my veins as I scanned it.

If the skirmish we'd left behind was a battle, then this—this was the war.

Mythics everywhere—far more than the Crow and Hammer's membership. Blazes of magic, screams, blood, bodies, shattered walls, burning buildings. A shallow chasm split the intersection, and burst water lines flooded the street while the rain poured down, obscuring everything.

As my gaze sought the guild's three-story building, its windows lit with warm light, I lurched to a halt. Amalia skidded to a stop beside me.

Dark figures had gathered in front of the guild, and I didn't need to see their eyes to know what they were. I recognized the way they moved, the jerky swing of their limbs, the agile dart of their feet. Visceral memories of their fangs buried in Zylas's skin hit me like a punch to the gut.

Crimson power exploded, the concussion from the blast whipping rain and grit into my face. I flinched back, then tore my stare away from the horde of vampires to look across the intersection.

Ice plunged through me.

In an open spot on the southwest side of the intersection, Nazhivēr stood with his wings half unfurled, one arm extended. In his powerful hand, the demon held Darius by the throat, the guild master's feet dangling off the ground.

Zylas! I silently cried.

As though I'd shouted out loud, Nazhivēr's head turned, his glowing eyes searching.

And I realized I didn't need to call for Zylas. He was already there.

He stood thirty feet from Nazhivēr in silent challenge, anonymous in his black outfit. The only giveaway of his true identity was the flick of his tail behind him, nearly invisible in the rainy haze and shadows.

Nazhivēr released Darius and turned to face his new opponent. The demon's lips curved in a satisfied smile.

Zylas curled his fingers and crimson flashed up his wrists. His glowing talons appeared, the eerie light reflecting off the wet pavement.

I gulped at the sight of his magic in front of so many mythics. If his disguise worked, he would be mistaken for a human using demon magic—in other words, a demon mage. But if it failed ... I'd deal with the consequences after he was back in his own world.

Nazhivēr summoned his phantom talons as well. His wings stretched out, making him appear huge.

Zylas sank lower into his fighting stance, then charged. Nazhivēr lunged to meet him, and Zylas dove for the slick asphalt, sliding past the winged demon. He leaped up behind Nazhivēr—and slammed both sets of talons into Nazhivēr's back.

The winged demon roared in fury.

As Zylas darted clear, Nazhivēr whirled on him. Zylas leaped into the air, catching one of Nazhivēr's horns and wrenching his head to the side. Zylas's talons slashed, just missing Nazhivēr's throat as the larger demon hurled him away. Tail lashing, Zylas landed on his feet. The two demons faced each other.

I waved at Amalia to follow me, and together we sprinted into the intersection. We needed to be close enough to help. This wasn't a fight for Zylas alone—not anymore.

"*Robin?*"

My head jerked toward the shocked scream.

Her bright red hair unmistakable, Tori stood among the chaos in her leather combat gear, her pale face smudged with soot. Her wide eyes flashed from me to my companion.

"Amalia?" she added, her voice even higher with shock.

Before I could call back, red light blazed—Nazhivēr had created a writhing spell circle aimed at Zylas. I raced away from Tori, hoping I'd get a chance to find her again.

As I ran, I caught a glimpse of movement—Darius, back on his feet and not seriously harmed by Nazhivēr's attack. He held two silver daggers, light gleaming across the blades.

Then he vanished.

Gone, as though he'd never existed. And I remembered that he was a luminamage—a mage who could bend light to his will.

A booming explosion of magic shook the earth, and fear shot through me as I refocused on Zylas and Nazhivēr. A smoking crater had appeared in the pavement, Zylas on its far side. Nazhivēr leaped across it with wings spread.

The two demons slammed together as I grabbed my second new artifact—a one-inch metal cube—and stretched it out to the end of its chain. Taking aim, I pointed it at the two demons.

"Ori impello arcuate!"

The air boomed as a faint band of silvery light swept out from the artifact, expanding wider and wider as it rushed forward. Zylas broke away from Nazhivēr and vaulted straight into the air.

The spell swept beneath him and hit Nazhivēr at waist height, throwing him sideways. Zylas landed and sprang in the same motion, talons flashing.

Nazhivēr rolled, and Zylas's talons caught his wing, tearing through the membrane in almost the same spot Zora had sliced it last week. The Dh'irath demon shot to his feet, crimson blazing up his arms—and something flew out of the darkness and slammed into Nazhivēr's spine.

As the demon staggered, the object flew backward: a steel sphere the size of a softball, hovering in midair. Another object zoomed out of nowhere—a billiard-ball-sized glass sphere.

Nazhivēr ducked the glass sphere. It halted in midair, then whooshed toward him again like a persistent fly.

As the winged demon again dodged both the glass sphere and the steel one, Zylas called up a spell. It flared out beneath his palm, a pentagram filled with runes.

Evashvā vīsh!

Red power blasted toward Nazhivēr, but the instant before it struck, the demon called up a lightning-fast spell of his own. The two demonic forces collided—and exploded.

The blast catapulted Zylas away, simultaneously shattering the glass sphere. Zylas arched over backward, catching himself on his hands before flipping onto his feet. His tail snapped as he launched back toward Nazhivēr.

The demon flung his wings open, throwing off the pale dust that coated his skin. As his breath puffed white in the air, I realized what the glass sphere had been—an alchemic frost bomb. A thin layer of ice covered Nazhivēr.

Zylas rushed the demon head-on, then feinted right—and from behind Nazhivēr on his left, light flashed over a long blade.

Zora rushed in, sword swinging, and raked the blade across Nazhivēr's back.

The demon snarled furiously and leaped into the air. His wings pumped as he gained altitude, up and up, then he glided onto the rooftop of the nearest building. Glowing red eyes glared down at us from the demon's dark silhouette.

My heart skittered in my chest. Nazhivēr had fled from us.

"Robin!"

Zora rushed over, sword in hand, and with her came Drew, his wounded arm hastily bound in bloodstained fabric, and Venus, an X-shaped belt around her waist loaded with glass spheres, vials, and other small objects.

I opened my mouth, an apology on the tip of my tongue—only to almost bite my tongue off when Zora grabbed me in a brief, one-armed hug.

"I'm so glad you're alive! Tell me how you survived that fall out the window after we survive this." She spun to face Nazhivēr on the rooftop. "Okay, guys. Drew, can you fling something up there? And Venus, what've you got that can knock the demon down from his perch?"

The two mythics swept over to us, heads craned back as they studied their foe. I stared at them, then looked at Zylas, standing a few feet away in his human disguise, also calculating how best to attack Nazhivēr.

Did Drew and Venus not recognize Zylas as my demon? Did they not care?

"I told them," Zora said simply, noticing my anxious bewilderment. "They promised not to tell anyone else."

"But …"

Drew peered at Zylas. "Zora said he's not like other demons."

The demon in question watched Nazhivēr, tail lashing side to side. "I'm not. I am smarter."

Drew blinked—then laughed.

Venus bounced a glass sphere on her palm. "Hey Zee, will that demon hate my stink bomb as much as you did?"

He cast a glance across the alchemist. His sunglasses had fallen off during the fight, and his eyes glowed from within his hood.

"He will hate it."

"Then try this one, Drew."

She tossed her sphere into the air and Drew caught it with his telekinesis. As battles raged around us, he lobbed it at the rooftop three stories above. The sphere rushed upward—and crimson magic blazed over Nazhivēr's hands and feet. The demon's grin flashed, then his body dissolved into light and streaked off the roof.

I whirled, tracking the glow as it shot across the intersection—across writhing bodies and blazing magic—and disappeared among the pandemonium at the far end.

Xever had called Nazhivēr back to his infernus.

Xever was here.

And we were going to kill him.

"Amalia," I shouted as I reached for Zylas. "Find Jack and meet us a block to the south."

Nodding, she raced away, and I swung onto Zylas's back, legs around his waist and hands on his shoulders.

"Robin!" Zora yelled. "Wait—"

But Zylas had already leaped forward—racing toward the ferocious battle of mythics and monsters that had consumed everything in sight.

29

WEREWOLVES AND VAMPIRES. Demons and demon magic. Mythics battling for their lives—some familiar, some I'd never seen before. They all flashed past as Zylas ran on agile feet, ducking and weaving between combatants, chasing that elusive spot where Nazhivēr's telltale glow had disappeared.

Fire and smoke. Shouts and screams. Utter chaos as we charged through the thick of it, and thoughts jarred through my head—who were all these people? Xever's cohorts and cultists? Or, if Xever had somehow tricked or coerced the MPD, another guild?

I had no clue and no way to find out.

A final wall of combatants blocked our path, tangled in fierce battle, and I recognized faces from the Crow and Hammer. I also recognized the demon on the far side of the skirmish, standing alone as he faced several opponents.

Behind Nazhivēr's arched wings, Xever stood in a long black coat, his scarred mouth sneering.

Zylas sped up. I tightened my grip on him as he coiled his legs and sprang, vaulting over the battling mythics in front of us with so much force that the wind blew my hood off. We slammed down in the gap in front of Nazhivēr. Zylas straightened, breathing hard from his sprint through the urban battlefield.

Xever's gaze swept up and down us, as calm as though he were standing in his own home instead of a violent battle full of raging magic.

"Robin and Zylas," he drawled, flavoring our names with mocking contempt. "How kind of you to join us."

Smile sharpening, he pushed up his jacket sleeves. Silver bands, just like Saul's anti-demon artifacts, ran from his wrists to his elbows, each one engraved with miniscule abjuration arrays.

My jaw clenched. Killing Xever wouldn't be as simple as going through Nazhivēr first.

Xever glanced to the side, and I belatedly noticed a tall, willowy woman with dark hair standing with him, holding his arm.

"Xanthe?" he said.

She smiled, an expression as chilling as his. "Go play with your toys, then, Xever, and I'll deal with the important matters, as I always do."

Xever smirked. With a condescending tilt of his head, he retreated. Nazhivēr held his spot in front of his master, tail whipping side to side. Blood streaked his limbs, and the edges of the tear in his wing fluttered with each shift the demon made.

Nazhivēr wasn't defeated yet, but he wasn't in top shape anymore.

Zylas's thoughts darted across mine, and when I silently agreed, a low laugh rumbled through his chest. His arms tightened, gripping my legs, then he leaped in one powerful move.

As he landed in a crouch in front of Nazhivēr, I shouted, "*Ori eruptum impello!*"

The silvery dome of my original artifact blasted the demon backward, and Zylas sprang at the off-balance Dh'irath. Nazhivēr evaded, Zylas's talons just missing him, then grabbed Xever and shot down the street—away from the battle behind us.

Our enemies were on the run again.

Zylas followed, allowing them to keep ahead as they retreated farther from the intersection. When the shouts and explosions of magic from the battle grew dim, Nazhivēr stopped and released Xever.

Loosening his grip on my legs, Zylas let me slide off his back. I moved to stand beside him, my eyes fixed on Xever as I pushed everything else from my mind. This moment.

The moment I would defeat Xever and avenge my parents.

"Such a fierce look of determination, Robin," Xever remarked, smirking. "But you've forgotten something. Zylas belongs to me, remember? *Daimon hesychaze.*"

Red light flared over Zylas.

Daimon hesychaze!

His body melted into crimson light and flashed into *my* infernus, hidden beneath my jacket. The glow bounced out again and he reformed beside me, his armor on display and his human clothing in a heap on the ground.

Xever's mouth thinned angrily.

Zylas raised his arm, fingers spread and palm pointed at Nazhivēr. Bracing his other hand around his wrist, he summoned a spell, the arching circles and tangled lines spanning four feet.

I lifted my arm too. From deep in my chest, alien warmth rushed outward to race through my limbs. A red glow lit up my fingertips, then veined across my hand and up my wrist.

Xever's eyes widened in disbelieving astonishment as scarlet light washed across the wet pavement.

My own disbelief flickered through me. Nazhivēr had seen me use demonic magic before, so why was Xever so surprised? Had Nazhivēr not told his master what he had witnessed? Had he not told Xever why he'd destroyed my infernus?

The questions flitted through my head, but there was no time to consider the answers as Zylas's spell flared brighter. I visualized a cantrip—and a six-foot-tall glowing sigil appeared three paces in front of Xever.

His eyes widened further as he recognized the rune and realized what was coming.

With a blinding flash and a concussive boom, Zylas's spell exploded toward Nazhivēr—and at the same moment I screamed, "*Impello!*"

"*Ori unum!*" Xever roared.

A pale blue abjuration shield appeared in front of him—and it barely slowed my cantrip. The invisible force blasted Xever off his feet. He flew backward, arms flailing, and crashed down in a violent roll. Tumbling to a stop, he sprawled on the pavement.

Xever wasn't a demon. Unlike Nazhivēr, I didn't need to hit him over and over again to bring him down. Just like me, his flesh could bruise and his bones could break.

The quick flash of Zylas's thoughts darted through my mind, but I didn't glance his way as he charged toward Nazhivēr in the wake of his own spell.

I launched forward, racing for Xever as I summoned another rune in demonic magic. Xever shoved to his feet, raising his hand.

"*Ori ossa seco et ferrum!*" he barked.

Realizing instantly that the incantation wasn't an abjuration spell, I aborted my charge and dove to the side. A sizzling whip of purple light flashed past my head, barely missing me, and struck a lamppost. With a metallic shriek, the lamppost pitched sideways and smashed into the nearest building, windows shattering and glass raining down on the pavement.

I scrambled up, heart racing and adrenaline pumping. It looked like Xever's armbands weren't limited to abjuration spells.

Farther down the street, bright flares of crimson magic and ear-rupturing bursts of sound ricocheted off the buildings as Zylas and Nazhivēr battled for dominance.

I drew myself up, extended my hand, and summoned another rune.

Lips curling in a sneer, Xever mirrored me, the silver bands around his arms reflecting the bright flashes of crimson from the battling demons.

"*Igniaris!*"

A fireball erupted from my rune, but Xever's spell glimmered with pale yellow light and the flames of my cantrip crashed against the glowing barrier. I summoned another rune, and again, Xever countered with a spell. As my mind whirled for a cantrip he couldn't counter, he swung his left hand out, his shouted incantation lost in a booming explosion from the two demons.

I dove for the ground, and his spell whipped past me. Rolling, I pushed up again, but his next spell was already streaking toward me. I dove again, my palms scraping across the rough pavement.

Xever took aim for me again. "*Ori incidere—*"

My rune appeared beneath his feet. "*Surrige!*"

The levitation cantrip hurled him into the air, and he plunged back down, landing with a crunching thud.

Zylas's magic burned through me. "*Impello!*"

The rune threw Xever backward.

"*Ventos!*"

The wind cantrip blasted him, whipping rain and dirt into his face.

"*Igniaris!*"

This time, Xever didn't have a chance to counter my fire rune, and flames exploded over him. He vanished in the blaze.

I braced my feet, hardly daring to breathe.

The short-lived fire died away, and Xever reappeared, his clothing scorched and the skin on one side of his face an angry red. The rain had saved him.

I raised my hand to summon another rune. Mouth twisted, Xever reached for his chest—for his collection of infernus pendants. Crimson flared over his chest, then leaped toward the ground.

He was calling another demon to fight for him.

As the demon's glowing shape coalesced, I desperately drew on more of Zylas's magic—and felt a slash of sharp, wary surprise from him.

My gaze jerked away from Xever and his demon, seeking Zylas.

He clung to Nazhivēr's shoulders, one arm clamped around the winged demon's head to pull it back and the glowing talons of his other hand pressed to Nazhivēr's throat. He was an instant from the kill—but he hadn't delivered the final blow.

For a second, I had no idea why Zylas had hesitated. Then I saw it: Nazhivēr's mouth was moving. He was speaking to Zylas.

Motion rushed across my peripheral vision—and I remembered I was in battle right now. That I couldn't get distracted.

Except I had—at exactly the wrong moment.

I didn't see what sort of demon Xever had called out. All I saw was its arm swinging at me.

The blow struck my chest, the world spun, and I slammed into something. Brick, stone, concrete. I didn't know. Whatever it was, it was harder than my bones—so my bones broke.

Agony exploded through my entire body. I lost all awareness of my surroundings, trapped in a hellish nightmare of pain, so much pain, never-ending, all-consuming.

Robin.

Warmth and cold rushed through my limbs, then suddenly flashed to scorching hot. The agony quadrupled and my mind recoiled, thoughts spiraling.

Robin!

I jerked myself back from unconsciousness. My entire body throbbed, but it was bearable. I cracked my eyes open with effort.

A pair of crimson eyes, dimmed with fatigue, peered down at me—and I could feel Zylas in my mind, his presence steady and fierce. He'd been there all along, but the pain had consumed my attention.

I blinked—and noticed three more faces behind the demon, all pale and drawn. Amalia and Uncle Jack weren't a surprise, but ...

"Zora?" I croaked.

"That's me," she said, not quite managing a flippant tone. "Welcome back."

"Back ...?"

Zylas's hand brushed across my cheek. *Xever's Ash'amadē demon broke you.*

Broke me? I silently repeated, unable to remember which House was called Ash'amadē.

You were very hurt. An echo of his fear shivered through me. *I fixed you.*

I drew in a deep breath, an unpleasant ache in my lungs. Since I seemed to be fully repaired, I dug my elbows in the ground, attempting to sit up.

"Whoa!" Amalia exclaimed, kneeling on my other side. "Just stay put for a couple minutes, okay, Robin?"

"But what about Xever and Nazhivēr?" I asked, looking past them. The street, darker than before with a lamppost destroyed, was quiet and empty.

"Escaped," Amalia said. "Nazhivēr grabbed Xever and flew off with him, and the other demon flew after them."

The Ash'amadē House had wings too?

"Are they going to the portal?" I whispered, cold horror flushing through me.

"Probably." Amalia rose to her full height and glanced at her father. "Dad, go get the car. We don't have any time to waste."

He backed away, reaching for the pendant hanging on his chest. As he grasped it, red light flashed. I hadn't noticed his unmoving demon until it dissolved into a streak of power that rushed back into the infernus. He hurried away, disappearing in the darkness.

As his footsteps receded, I noticed how quiet it was. The rain had stopped—and so had the distant roar of the life and death battle. A bone-deep chill rolled over me. What had happened to the Crow and Hammer?

"Someone is coming," Zylas whispered.

I tensed. A moment later, a new sound reached us—two sets of footsteps crunching across the wet pavement. A pair of figures passed beneath a streetlamp, walking toward us.

Amalia turned sharply toward them, and Zora also pivoted. I gathered myself, but before I could sit up, Zylas slid his arms under me. He pulled me to his chest and stood.

The sudden movement set my head to spinning, and I buried my face in the side of his hood, eyes squeezed shut as I fought a wave of nausea. Only after I'd pressed my face to the fabric did I clue in that he was back in his human disguise; he must have redressed after healing me.

The footsteps drew closer.

"You're alive," Amalia remarked dryly to the newcomers.

"For the most part," a familiar voice answered. "Is she okay?"

I gingerly lifted my head from Zylas's shoulder and met Tori's exhausted hazel eyes.

Battered, bruised, blood-splattered. Exhausted with a weariness that hung around her like a miasma, as though this night—or perhaps the past week—had drained too much of her, dimming her vibrant spirit.

Aaron stood beside her, his fatigue just as prevalent. He'd acquired more bleeding wounds since I'd last seen him, his wet skin smudged with soot. Despite his sorry state, his gaze swept over me worriedly, searching for injuries.

"I'm fine," I told them. "Just … unsteady."

At my silent request, Zylas tipped my feet toward the ground. I straightened, but my knees wobbled weakly and I leaned against him, grateful for his arm around my waist.

Tori searched my face. "Xever and Nazhivēr?"

"Escaped," I admitted, wiping my wet hair away from my eyes. "Nazhivēr flew off with him."

They were on the run, and we knew exactly where they were heading.

"They are not the hunters any longer," Zylas growled, echoing my thoughts. "Now I will hunt them."

Together, I told him silently, my fingers gripping his shoulder. We hadn't yet defeated Xever and Nazhivēr, but we would make it happen somehow.

No matter the cost.

"*We* will hunt them," I said aloud, and Zylas answered with a sharp, eager smile. Determination steadied my legs, and I slid my hand down to his, curling our fingers together, then turned to Tori.

I had a hundred questions for her—if Ezra was alive, what had happened to the guild, if they needed help—but I couldn't ask them. The answers would only distract me.

How could I put the Crow and Hammer above thousands of demon lives—and their entire civilization? How could I worry about Ezra? Whether he was alive or not, whether he was still a demon mage or not, I couldn't help him right now.

Zylas and I had a mission that took priority over all else.

"Leave Xever to us."

Tori's eyes widened at my words, but I said nothing else. Gripping Zylas's hand, I turned. Amalia fell into step on my other side as we strode away, and with Zora trailing after us, we left Tori, Aaron, and the Crow and Hammer behind.

30

DAWN WASN'T HERE YET—but it was close. The black sky had softened to a deep, dark blue, and the rainclouds had broken up enough for the crescent moon to peek out, its faint light reflecting on the choppy water.

Half a mile ahead, Admiralty Point was a featureless silhouette jutting into the inlet.

The powerboat bounced across the waves, the roar of its outboard motor deafening me. I clutched my seat, pressed against Zylas's side on the sunken U-shaped bench in the boat's bow. Uncle Jack stood at the helm beneath a small canopy, a hand on the steering wheel as he squinted at the dark inlet.

On my other side, Amalia hunched her shoulders from the cold. And beside her, Zora sat with her feet set wide and not one but *two* swords braced against her shoulder with their sheathed points resting on the floor.

Noticing my attention, she flashed a grin.

I'd tried to talk her out of coming. I'd told her to go back to her guildmates—and she'd replied that I was her guildmate too. She was coming with us whether we wanted her to or not.

"Wondering about this?" she shouted over the icy wind, patting one of her swords. "I told you I'd be prepared to fight Nazhivēr."

I looked again at the weapon. The new sword was a two-handed bastard sword like her usual one—meaning it was *huge*—and though its hilt was plain, the pommel featured a smooth crystalline orb etched with an Arcana array. That weapon was more than mere steel.

Amalia frowned. "Is a *sword* really going to make a difference against a demon?"

"When it's this sword, yes." Zora quirked an eyebrow. "Especially since I mortgaged my house to buy it."

My eyes bulged. "You mortgaged your *house*?"

She caressed the inscription on the pommel. "Her name is Khione's Wrath."

"What kind of spell—" I began.

A stab of sharp chagrin from Zylas hit me and I broke off to follow his gaze. The landmass we were speeding toward was no longer dark. A pinkish glow emanated from the highest point on its crest.

"The portal," I whispered in horror, the wind whipping my voice away.

We'd taken too long. We'd gone to the Crow and Hammer to stop Xever and Nazhivēr, and though we'd saved all the lives Nazhivēr would've extinguished without us there to battle him, we'd failed—and we'd lost the one advantage we could've gained by beating Xever to the portal.

A flicker of unexpected emotion darted from Zylas to me. My gaze swung to him, my brow furrowed in confusion.

"We still have time," Amalia said bracingly, her ponytail blowing out behind her like a flag. "The portal takes a while to actually open. It won't happen until dawn breaks."

Uncle Jack slowed the boat as we closed in on the shore. The sky had lightened slightly, illuminating a short, rickety wooden dock extending into the water. Reducing speed even more, he guided the boat up to the dock.

We moored the boat and disembarked as quickly as possible, then we were rushing onto the grassy bank beyond the dock, where a rotting log cabin sat among overgrown shrubbery. Zylas took the lead, and I followed behind him as he angled onto a dirt track that led toward the hilltop. As towering spruces closed in around us, the pink glow of the portal disappeared from view.

Apprehension bordering on terror rolled through me. Over the past couple days, we'd set up access to a boat and located a spot to moor, but for all our preparation, we had no idea what to expect. We knew only that we would face Xever, Saul, Nazhivēr, and a number of other demons controlled by the two sorcerers.

I could feel Zylas's impatience as we trudged up the hillside, the humans tripping and stumbling on the uneven path in the darkness. My breath rasped in my chest, legs burning. How much farther? How close were we to cresting the hill?

Just when I thought I couldn't hike any farther, Zylas paused, his head tilted.

"Wait here," he told the others, then scooped me against his side and sprang for the nearest tree, an ancient spruce with a broad trunk. I wrapped my arms and legs around him, pressed against his chest as he rushed upward. As we cleared the forest canopy, he braced his feet on a thin branch.

Through a gap in the needle-covered boughs, we looked across the hilltop.

A space the size of a football field had been cleared of trees and the topsoil scraped away, revealing the granite foundation beneath. A large portion of the hard stone had been smoothed, creating a natural floor upon which Xever had laid out his arrays.

Shivering dread crawled through me as I took in the labyrinth of interconnecting rings, lines, and runes.

I recognized the portal array, set dead center on the flat granite. Two smaller circular arrays had been carved out nearby, forming a triangle of Arcana. Parts of the two smaller ones looked disconcertingly familiar.

Within one of the smaller circles, a human figure stood. Xever. I was certain of it.

Another human stood on the other side of the portal, his arms raised as though in supplication. Saul, I was betting. He'd completed the incantation needed for the portal and was waiting for it to open.

But they weren't alone on the rocky plateau.

Dark shapes, varying in size and appendages, stood in a silent, unmoving line near the arrays.

Demons.

Eleven of them.

A *Dīnen* from every House except the Twelfth, summoned and enslaved by Xever. How he could control them all, I didn't know. How he'd coerced them into contracts when he could only promise his soul to a single demon, I couldn't guess. But I knew that every one of those demons was at least semiautonomous and likely in control of his magic.

How could Zylas make it through *eleven* demons? With the exception of Tahēsh, who'd already been injured, Zylas had never killed a demon from the first rank of Houses.

And because demons could sense one another's power, all eleven already knew the Vh'alyir *Dīnen* was close.

It was impossible. If we went any farther, we would die. There was no way to win.

Zylas's arm tightened around my middle. "We will find a way, *amavrah*."

"What if we don't?" I whispered.

His crimson eyes turned to me, our faces inches apart. "*Vh'renith vē thāit.*"

A memory from months ago whispered in my mind.

"Are you afraid you'd lose in a fight?" I'd asked him.

"Vh'renith vē thāit," he'd growled in answer.

"What does that mean?"

"It means I never lose."

Among demons, losing meant death. Zylas might not always win, but he never lost. But tonight, we'd either succeed or we'd die. Victory or death.

Regardless of the outcome, I would lose him forever.

Gripping his shoulders, I stretched up and kissed him. His arm crushed me against his chest as his mouth moved with mine with matching intensity. Our final kiss. Our final farewell, because there would be no time for goodbyes after this.

I wanted this moment to last forever, but in mere seconds he was sliding down the trunk, and then his feet were back on the ground, and then his arm was slipping away from me.

A minute later, I stood ten feet from the granite plateau, hidden in the trees. The portal's glow competed with the brightening sky.

The line of waiting demons was positioned between us and the arrays, a mere thirty yards away. They'd already sensed Zylas. They knew which direction they needed to guard.

Gulping back my panic, I concentrated on the heat of Zylas's magic—and called it forth. Crimson lit my fingertips and spread across my hands and wrists, the glow bright to my eyes after so much time spent in darkness.

And a radiant beacon for the watching demons.

Eleven pairs of red eyes raked across the trees where I hid, searching for the source of the telltale magic.

The second demon—Nazhivēr—gestured toward the demons at the end. He said something in the guttural demonic language, and the last three demons started forward.

My hands still glowing, I spun on my heel and raced deeper into the trees. A shallow, narrow gully opened up, and I ran into it, following a dry creek bed. At a dense clump of bushes with dead leaves clinging to the branches, I ducked behind them and extinguished the glow on my hands.

The crunching footsteps of the demons turned to thuds as they reached the creek bed. As silently as possible, I stretched my head up to peer through the thinner top of the bush.

The first demon—nearly identical to Uncle Jack's eight-foot-tall demon with scaled patches on its limbs and an apelike face—passed the thick trunk of a spruce that leaned over the gully. The second demon—almost as tall with short tusks and a thin line of hair running all the way down its back to a lion-like tail—followed, its footfalls notably quieter than the first. The third demon—only six feet tall but twice the weight of the others, with an armored head as though it were wearing a bony helmet—stepped beneath the tree.

Now.

I summoned Zylas's magic again, created a small cantrip above my palm, and whispered, "*Igniaris.*"

A foot-tall flare of orange fire surged upward, the light bursting across the dark forest. The attention of all three demons shot straight for me.

And in that moment of distraction, Zylas dropped out of the tree above the third demon. He landed on the demon's broad back, grabbed his horns from behind, and swung over the demon's left side, feet braced against the demon's shoulder as he wrenched hard.

Bone crunched as the demon's neck broke.

As the demon fell, the other two whipped around to face Zylas—and that's when Zora leaped out from behind a boulder on one side of the gully. On the other side, crimson light erupted as Uncle Jack summoned his demon.

Against a faster, smarter, more loosely contracted demon like Nazhivēr, things might have gone differently. But these demons weren't smart enough to react to the ambush in time to save their lives.

One fell, bowled over by Uncle Jack's demon, and Zylas pounced, his claws tearing through the demon's throat. The other demon dropped to his knees, Zora's sword through his chest. Zylas ripped that one's throat out too.

Our quick and dirty ambush was done—but we had no time to set up another.

Zylas sprang away from the dead demons and landed beside me. Panic thudded in my chest as I looked at Zora, who'd just wrenched her sword free from the demon corpse.

"Are you ready?" I whispered.

Smiling tersely, she reached over her shoulder and grasped the hilt of her new sword. The crystalline pommel gleamed faintly as she drew the blade, revealing a jagged pattern of light and dark Damascus steel sweeping from hilt to point.

"Ready," she answered, a sword in each hand.

Zylas grabbed me around the waist and launched toward the plateau, but a moment before breaking through the tree line, he sprang at the enormous trunk of a spruce tree. I held on tightly as he climbed with agile leaps until we were a hundred feet above the ground.

Crimson flared over his arms and raced up to his shoulders. His power sizzled the air, tingling over my skin, and his eyes burned as he chanted in the demonic language.

Below, Zora appeared at the edge of the clearing. She stuck the points of her two swords into the ground, pulled something off her belt, and tipped her head back. A potion.

Strength enhancement, she'd said, so she could wield two weapons. It would last three minutes.

The power gathering at Zylas's shoulders flared brighter.

Zora grabbed her two swords and slid down a rough dirt bank to the granite plateau below. She charged toward the line of waiting demons—and four of them set out to meet her.

Four demons against one sorceress.

Zylas snarled the final words of his incantation, and the burning crimson flashed even brighter. Huge phantom wings spread wide on either side of him, magic writhing across them in webs of light. His arms clamped around me—and he leaped from the tree.

This time, he didn't merely glide. The wings swept down, propelling us out over the plateau.

Beneath us, Zora sprinted toward the demons. As they closed in on her, she launched into a spinning skid and swung her swords in a full arc around her.

"*Ori inimicos glacie ferio hiemis!*"

With her shouted incantation, a wave of white exploded outward in a violent ring. The blast swept into the oncoming demons, and she and her opponents vanished in a pale cloud.

His phantom wings beating, Zylas flew past them as the white swirled away, revealing a ring of jagged ice, six feet high, encircling a bare patch of rocky ground with Zora at its center. The four demons were frozen in the ice up to their chests.

Then we were past them, sweeping toward our waiting enemies.

The first rank. The four most powerful Houses.

And all of them had wings.

Lūsh'vēr, the First House—like Tahēsh, he was broad-shouldered, with a heavy, hairless head and a thick tail that ended in a bone-crushing plate. His horns were the longest, arching high above his head. An old, experienced demon.

Dh'irath, the Second House—beside the First House demon, Nazhivēr's six and a half feet seemed average, his build lighter and more agile.

Gh'reshēr, the Third House—taller even than the Lūsh'vēr demon, his chest was thick and his wings broader. His tail was extra long and heavy, maybe to compensate for his greater weight, and a messy mane of black hair framed his bony face.

Ash'amadē, the Fourth House—the demon I'd barely glimpsed before he'd thrown me into a wall with so much force he'd shattered my ribs and cracked my skull. He was closest in build to Nazhivēr, a bit shorter and leaner, with narrow wings for swift flight and a thin tail with barbs edging the entire bottom third.

All four demons—the Third and Fourth House in front, Nazhivēr and the First House demon behind—spread their wings, ready to leap skyward and intercept us.

Terror raced through me as Zylas folded his phantom wings and dove for the waiting demons.

They raised their arms, glowing talons forming as they prepared to rip Zylas apart. One small Twelfth House demon was no match for them. He was an ambush hunter attacking straight-on. He didn't stand a chance.

He hadn't even begun a spell. Holding the phantom wings was all he could manage. He was racing heedlessly into the claws of death, and I choked on a scream.

As we plunged toward our enemies, Nazhivēr drew his arm back to deliver the first strike—

—and drove his eight-inch talons into the back of the Gh'reshēr's skull.

THE MONSTROUS Third House demon pitched forward, dead before he hit the ground.

Zylas snapped his wings out, a pained breath rasping through his clenched teeth, and dropped down beside Nazhivēr.

For the briefest instant, he and the Dh'irath demon faced each other, cold appraisal in their stares, then Zylas released me, pushed me behind him, and turned toward the other two first-rank demons.

Nazhivēr turned as well, he and Zylas facing the others side by side.

For a moment, I just stared, as dumbfounded as the other demons by the sight of the Second House demon beside Zylas in his human gear—but it wasn't the first time they'd fought together. Faced with the bloodthirsty and indestructible fae Vasilii, they'd briefly allied once before.

But why now? What was Nazhivēr doing? Was it a trick?

As Nazhivēr squared off with the First House Lūsh'vēr and Zylas eyed the lighter-weight Ash'amadē demon, I shook off my shock and bolted away from the impending violence. My attention homed in on the spell circles—and Xever.

The summoner, standing in the smallest of the three circles, had turned toward the four demons, his stare locked on his most loyal servant.

"*Nazhivēr.*"

He didn't speak loudly, but his voice vibrated with blood-chilling rage.

Nazhivēr turned sideways to bring his summoner into view, his lips peeling back in a cruel smile. "Yes, master?"

"What are you doing?"

"Helping you."

"You just killed one of my demons," Xever snarled.

"For your own good," Nazhivēr crooned viciously. "That was the first clause you made me swear. To act only in your best interests."

Xever's hands curled into fists. "Betraying me isn't in my best interests."

"No? I believe it is." His wings unfurled. "It's also in mine. I have waited twenty years for you to open a portal so I can return home in the only way left to me."

And in mere minutes, maybe seconds, the portal would open. Nazhivēr had been waiting for his chance to escape Xever, his contract, and this world.

Xever bared his teeth furiously. "Kill them both!"

The First and Fourth House demons lunged at Nazhivēr and Zylas. Crimson magic exploded, a cold wind whipping across my back as I faced Xever, twenty-five feet between us.

His furious stare swept dismissively across me, then he focused on the portal, raised his arms, and began to chant.

The sky had turned cobalt. A purple tinge lightened the eastern horizon.

The portal spell was complete, the magic already in the process of opening a gateway between worlds. Whatever spell Xever just begun, it wasn't part of the portal.

I stretched my hand out, red sparking over my fingers as I tapped into Zylas's magic. Xever stood alone. This time I would defeat him. This time—

"*Ori astra feriant!*"

I spun toward the voice—and a hail of two-inch blades of golden light hit me. Pain tore through my limbs and I fell backward.

Saul strode across the plateau, his face contorted with murderous hatred and a silver dagger in his hand, the point aimed at me. "*Ori ignes—*"

Pain scrambled my brain and I couldn't picture a single cantrip.

"*—siderei urant!*"

"*Indura!*" I screamed, throwing my arms over my head.

Golden streaks like miniature falling stars with flaming tails blasted me, tearing through my leather jacket—but they didn't pierce the underlayer embroidered with Amalia's cantrips.

Though the magic barrage didn't slice me open, it hit with bruising force, the flaming tails scorching me through my clothing, and I gasped as I was thrown back into the rocky ground a second time.

Weight slammed down on my torso, driving the air from my lungs.

Saul clamped both hands around my throat and squeezed. "If I had the time, I would spend a week or two destroying you piece by piece while you begged for death."

I grabbed at his wrists, Zylas's magic glowing over my fingers, but I couldn't use a cantrip if I couldn't speak the incantation.

"Everything I dreamed of and worked toward for twenty years is about to happen," he spat, squeezing harder, "and my boys aren't here to see it. Because of you."

My lungs screamed for air. I scraped my fingernails over his hands, then dug my fingers under his pinky—and wrenched it backward.

His finger dislocated with a crunch, and his hands loosened enough for me to gasp out an incantation.

"*Ori eruptum impello!*"

A silver dome flashed out from my artifact, throwing Saul off me, but it hadn't fully recharged and the spell was weak. His feet scraped across the ground as he threw himself at me again.

My glowing rune appeared between us and his eyes bulged with disbelief as he recognized it—but he couldn't stop his momentum. He lunged right into it, the glowing magic disappearing inside him.

Terror flashed over his face, and for a split second, I wasn't sure I could do it—but then I remembered Yana and all the other women he'd killed. Had *their* fear ever inspired mercy in him?

"*Rumpas!*"

I couldn't see whether the rune inside him had activated, but I heard it: the sound of shattering bones.

The "break" cantrip.

Saul collapsed, his dead weight falling across my legs, his dagger lying beside him.

I dragged my legs from beneath him and shoved onto my feet, my knees trembling. Blood trickled from the slices covering my limbs—Saul's first attack—and bruises throbbed from his second spell.

As I spun, my gaze swept across the plateau—past Amalia, positioned protectively in front of her father, who held his infernus, controlling his demon as it grappled with one of Xever's demons; past Zora as she drove her sword into the chest of a different demon, another one trapped in ice while the fourth lunged at her; past Nazhivēr, magic swirling over his arms as he slashed his talons at the Lūsh'vēr *Dīnen*; past Zylas, his glowing wings gone, as he aimed a spell up at the airborne Ash'amadē.

I spun past all of them to face Xever, Ancient Greek flowing from his lips in smooth verses. The portal's pink glow was nearly blinding, light gathering in the central ring where the interdimensional doorway would appear. Whatever spell he was casting, he was aiming to unleash it at the same time the portal opened.

Orange light stained the horizon. The sun would breach the treetops at any moment.

Breathing hard, I stretched my hand out again. Zylas's hot magic flashed through my chest, and a ten-foot rune appeared a yard in front of my palm. I would blast Xever right out of the circle, interrupting his incantation and ruining his spell.

"*Impello!*" I yelled.

The air boomed from the rush of force—then boomed again as it struck an invisible barrier, ricocheting off. I staggered, eyes widening as a faint ripple danced through the air, revealing a familiar shape: a transparent dome.

Xever was inside a summoning circle barrier—and it had blocked my cantrip.

He continued to chant, lips curled in a smirk.

I rushed forward, hands outstretched—and slammed into the barrier. It didn't merely block magic but physical bodies as well.

Stumbling backward, I flung my arm up again, visualizing a glowing rune inside the circle with him—but nothing appeared. I couldn't reach him inside the barrier. I couldn't stop him.

Behind me, magic exploded over and over, but I didn't dare turn to look again—didn't want to see Zylas grounded and exhausted while battling the more powerful Ash'amadē demon. Didn't want to see Zora, Uncle Jack, and Amalia somehow holding off four demons on their own.

I had to stop Xever before he finished his spell—and before his demon slaves killed everyone I loved.

I pointed at the ground and called up the "break" cantrip again. The glowing rune appeared at the edge of the circle enclosing him.

"*Rumpas!*" I cried desperately.

The granite shattered beneath the rune, but not a single crack penetrated the outer ring. Xever's voice thickened with triumph.

The sky had softened to a pale blue. A yellow glow spread across the horizon.

Zylas!

I felt his focus shift as I fumbled through my artifacts for one that could penetrate the barrier and strike him.

A flash of motion—Zylas charging past me, magic blazing up his arms.

Nazhivēr sped past my other side, a spell glowing over his hand. Both demons unleashed their attacks—and the crimson magic exploded against the invisible dome. The barrier rippled, not a single spark entering the space within.

The Lūsh'vēr and Ash'amadē demons landed behind Xever's circle, but they didn't attack Zylas and Nazhivēr. They appeared to be waiting.

A blaze of golden light erupted above the trees, and long lines of light and shadows stretched across the granite plateau. In the same instant, the pink glow of the portal array burst into blinding radiance, then the center node went dark.

The portal was open.

Xever flung his arms skyward, his voice rising to an ecstatic shout. "*Daimonia panton te oikon kai oudenos, kore Ahleas, ne to ton kasigneton sou haima, se kalo!*"

I'd studied so much Ancient Greek in the past weeks, examined and studied so many facets of summoning magic, that I could translate his words with terrifying clarity.

"*Demon of all Houses and no House, daughter of Ahlēa, by the blood of your kin, I summon you!*"

In the empty third circle, red light ignited: twelve runes, surrounding the central node, shimmered with scarlet magic. Demon blood. Each rune was coated in blood from one of the Twelve Houses—including the blood taken from Zylas.

The red glow brightened.

Blazing ruby exploded from the dark portal. The streak of light shot straight up like a comet, ten times brighter than Zylas's glowing spirit when he entered or exited the infernus.

The power arched high above, then blasted downward and slammed into the center of the third circle. A boom rang out as the magic hit the transparent barrier of the summoning circle, turning the entire dome red. Even contained, the impact shook the plateau.

Zylas and Nazhivēr stepped backward, moving farther from the circle even though they were already thirty feet away.

The luminescent magic swirled, then faded. As the glow dimmed, a small, solid shape became visible: a body crouched in the circle, curled into a tight, protective ball.

No one moved. Not Zylas or Nazhivēr. Not Xever. Not the other demons. Not Zora, Amalia, and Uncle Jack, standing in a cluster on the rocky battlefield. We were all riveted by the vision before us.

The *payashē* raised her head.

She slowly unwrapped her arms from around herself, and just as slowly straightened her body, rising to her full height. Her large, softly glowing crimson eyes moved warily across the unfamiliar landscape.

I stared, not quite able to breathe.

She was petite, maybe even shorter than me, but her lean legs were firm with muscle. Her toffee-red skin was smooth, her waist-length black hair thick and wild, her clothes simple— and almost identical to Zylas's usual outfit, but without the armor. The only addition was a top that crossed over one shoulder, covering her slim chest but leaving her taut midriff bare.

A long, thin tail hovered behind her, ending in a single barb, and rising from her tangled hair were two pairs of six-inch-long horns that curved slightly inward.

Her head turned, her full lips tight with distress as her gaze moved across everyone in her immediate vicinity before settling on Nazhivēr, the demon closest to her.

"*Seminedh'nā?*"

Her voice was low and husky, only a few notes higher than Zylas's. Nazhivēr hesitated, uncertain how to answer her question.

"I summoned you!" Xever declared. His back was to me, so I couldn't see his expression—but smug satisfaction and eager glee saturated his words. "And you will submit to my command."

The *payashē* focused on the summoner. She couldn't know what he'd said, but she must've recognized his tone, because her uncertainty slid away. Her lips peeled back from her teeth, baring her sharp canines. The glow in her eyes brightened as rage transformed her delicate features.

Zylas and Nazhivēr stepped back again.

She lifted her thin arms, aiming both hands at Xever. Her palms lit with power—and glowing veins raced up her arms. The power flared brighter—and brighter—*and brighter*, until her hands were pure radiant energy.

Zylas whirled on his heel, grabbed me around the waist, and sprinted away.

I gasped, staring back over his shoulder as he fled. She was inside a summoning circle. It was impenetrable to demon magic.

Raw power exploded from the *payashē*'s hands and hit the barrier. The transparent surface rippled, and for a second time, the entire dome filled with blinding crimson light. The earth trembled. The glow brightened, beams of scarlet streaking skyward.

The dome rippled violently—then the world exploded into screaming red.

Zylas's arms clamped around me as the detonation catapulted us into the air. He landed in a roll, shielding me with his arms. The moment we tumbled to a halt, he launched up again, clutching me, fear sizzling along the connection between us.

A smoking crater the exact size of the summoning circle had replaced the arcane array. The *payashē* stood nonchalantly at the crumbling edge, her tail lashing and her hands and forearms alight with pure power.

My gaze shot across the plateau, frantically searching. I spotted Uncle Jack's demon first—crushed beneath a boulder hurled by the explosion of power. Amalia, Zora, and Uncle Jack were heaped among shattered hunks of ice.

Sudden movement yanked my attention back to the *payashē*—but she hadn't shifted. Instead, the Lūsh'vēr and Ash'amadē demons, scored with wounds from their fight with Nazhivēr and Zylas, had launched into the air—flying at the female demon. At the same time, the three surviving demons that Zora, Amalia, and Uncle Jack had fought charged in on foot.

And Nazhivēr, his limbs stiff as though fighting every step, moved cautiously toward the *payashē*.

Xever, inside his protective circle, must've commanded all his demons to attack her. The loophole in their contract that Nazhivēr had exploited to disobey his master no longer applied.

The *payashē* looked at the six *Dīnen* bearing down on her, then flung her arms out. Crimson blazed off her shoulders, taking the form of wings, and a spell circle appeared beneath her feet. The spell flashed, flinging her fifty feet into the air.

Her wings, identical to the ones Zylas had created, spread wide, catching the cold wind, and her glowing hands flared.

As the airborne Lūsh'vēr and Ash'amadē demons dove for her, her hands transformed into talons—but not the six- or eight-inch ones the males favored.

No, hers were three-foot-long *blades*.

She swept them up, catching the Lūsh'vēr demon across the torso. Dark blood sprayed, and the First House demon fell from the sky in pieces.

The lithe Ash'amadē demon veered away from her slashing blades with a desperate flail of his wings. As he shot past her, she turned, phantom wings beating.

A spell circle appeared in front of her. A second formed behind it. A third took form behind that one.

Red light flashed—once, twice, thrice.

The spells struck the fleeing demon one after the other, too fast for him to evade. He plummeted to the earth, leaving a bloody mist on the wind.

A shiver ran through Zylas, his arm clamping around me, then he dragged his attention away from the *payashē*—and to the portal. Its pink magic glowed brightly, that dark inner circle waiting.

But for how long? The portal's lifespan depended on how Xever and Saul had constructed it. It could last hours or minutes.

And if it closed, we'd lose our chance to end summoning forever.

"Zylas," I whispered.

He could sense what I was thinking. His emotions swirled, sharp and conflicted, then he swung me onto his back and sprinted toward the portal.

We could reach it. We could perform the spell while the *payashē* occupied Xever's demons. That wasn't why he'd hesitated.

He'd hesitated because ending summoning required him to pass through the portal—which would leave me alone on this plateau with Xever, his surviving demons, and an enraged *payashē*.

But we couldn't let that stop us.

He raced for the portal at top speed, the wind whipping at my hair. Red light burst behind us, but he kept running. Another flash, then a shockwave almost threw him off his feet. He stumbled and kept going.

The portal loomed, no longer pitch black but a deep shade of blue dotted with fading stars. He crossed the array's outer ring, and arcane magic sizzled through us.

Another flash of crimson—and my vision went red. The sky and ground spun, then Zylas crashed to the ground. The impact tore me from his hold, and I fell away from him, shielding my head with my arms as I tumbled across the granite. Sliding to a stop with my whole body throbbing, I scrambled to my feet, spinning in search of Zylas.

Sweeping red wings, and the *payashē* landed in front of me.

Ten feet away, blood dripping from a new wound across his back, Zylas rolled onto his hands and knees—then froze as the *payashē*'s gaze snapped to him. When he didn't move, staying submissively low to the ground, she turned her attention back to me.

To the human. An alien being of this alien world she'd been dragged into against her will.

Her gaze roved over me, eyes burning, magic glowing over her slim body. I panted for air, dizzy with terror, knees trembling. Without meaning to, I looked past her to the other end of the array.

Xever still stood in his circle, the faint sound of his voice rumbling—but he was the only one standing.

The demons ... they were all on the ground. None moved. Some were in pieces.

The most powerful males of the demon world, slaughtered in sixty seconds.

The *payashē*'s hand shot toward me, and I stumbled backward, far too slow to evade her. She grabbed me by the throat with one glowing hand—and her other thumped against my chest.

She dug her fingers into my breast through my jacket, then patted my hip as though to gauge how curvy I was.

"*Payilas hh'ainun?*"

Human girl. She was asking if I was a female human.

"Y-yes," I stammered weakly, then remembered she didn't speak English. "*Var.*"

She blinked in surprise, then her face hardened—and her fingers tightened around my bruised throat, threatening to cut off my air. "*Seminedh'thē nā?*"

Did you summon me?

The translation whispered in my mind, tinged with Zylas's fear.

"*Nul,*" I whispered, repeating the word he provided.

Her eyes narrowed. She pulled me closer, her lips curling up to flash her canines. "*Aidērathē sim Vh'alyirith. Kir gh'atanizh vēsis hh'ainun? Kir eshanā cun izh? Seminedh'thē izh?*"

"N-*nul,*" I stammered again, recognizing only "Vh'alyir" and "*seminedh,*" which seemed to mean "summoned."

I could see her patience dwindling. If I couldn't provide answers, then I was useless—and she had no reason to spare a loathsome human.

Her free hand rose, fingers curling and dark claws extending an inch from her fingertips.

"Vh'alyir," I blurted desperately. "He's my—my *amavrah*."

Her thin eyebrows scrunched. She glanced at Zylas, still crouched on the ground, then back to me. "*Esha Vh'alyirissā amavrahthēs?*"

This Vh'alyir is your chosen?

"*Var*," I answered as Zylas translated. "*Payashē* ... you can go home. *Ahlēavah*. It's right there. *Esha Ahlēavah illar*."

I added the last part at Zylas's prompting. Movements slow and unthreatening, I pointed at the portal only a few feet away.

She peered in the direction I was indicating—and her hand went slack around my throat. "*Ahlēavah?*"

"Yes."

Her nostrils flared as she searched for the scent of home. Relief softened her features—then her eyes widened with shock.

Red light engulfed her body. Her form dissolved, her hand disappearing from my neck. She transformed into glowing power and shot across the plateau.

Straight for Xever.

Her spirit passed through the barrier as though it wasn't there and slammed into Xever. He disappeared in a crimson blaze. The light flared even brighter, blinding me, then faded.

I blinked, my eyes watering.

Xever stood in the center of his circle, alone, his head bowed and shoulders hunched. The *payashē* and her magic had vanished.

With a deep breath that straightened his shoulders, Xever lifted his head. A crazed grin stretched his scarred mouth—and his eyes burned red with demonic power.

32

AS DAWN'S SOFT LIGHT washed across the plateau, Xever's laughter rang in the still air. It was a cackling laugh of triumph that bordered on madness, of eager conquest that verged on sadism.

I trembled where I stood, part of me insisting I keep looking for the *payashē*. Insisting she had to be here somewhere, because Xever couldn't have done this. It wasn't possible.

But she was nowhere to be seen, and his eyes glowed with power. *Her* power.

He'd turned himself into a demon mage using the most powerful type of demon in existence—a *payashē*.

That's why he'd needed blood from all twelve Houses—because *payashē* were related to all the Houses while remaining separate. And that's why his extra arrays had seemed familiar—because I'd seen parts of them while studying the demon mage ritual to save Ezra.

Four long steps away, Zylas stood hunched in pain from the slashing wound across his back that the *payashē* had inflicted. His eyes gleamed like hot coals instead of burning magma, most of his magic consumed.

Behind us, the portal waited—but we'd never be able to complete the ritual to end summoning before Xever killed us.

The demon mage's laughter trailed into silence. Mouth twisted wide with a maniacal grin, he looked across the bloody remains of his demon servants, slaughtered by the very *payashē* he'd summoned and trapped inside his human body.

"Nazhivēr!" he yelled.

Nothing moved—then a quiet rustle. From among the fallen *Dīnen*, a pair of torn wings unfurled. Nazhivēr pushed off the ground, blood streaking his limbs and dribbling from a piercing wound in his lower chest. Slowly, the Dh'irath demon straightened, lifted his chin, and sneered at his summoner.

Xever smirked as he strode out of his protective circle and stopped a few paces from the demon.

"How does it feel," he asked with quiet, vicious pleasure, "to have the open portal right there and not be able to reach it? After *twenty years*, you came so close."

Nazhivēr lifted his chin a little more, condescending disdain dripping from him.

"I could kill you," Xever mused, "but I would rather watch you suffer as my slave for another twenty years. Stand there. Do not move until I say so."

Unable to disobey, Nazhivēr held as still as a fully contracted demon. Not even his tail twitched.

Xever pivoted, turning those glowing eyes on me. "I think I'm actually pleased that you survived long enough to see what I accomplished using your family's grimoire." Magic blazed up his arm, burning so brightly that it completely engulfed his hand. He lifted his palm toward me. "And it's fitting that you'll be the first person I kill with the power you helped me gain."

He didn't create a spell circle—he simply unleashed the *payashē*'s power in a raw, uncontrolled blast.

The writhing crimson beam roared toward me, and Zylas slammed into my side. We hit the ground, rolled, and fell into the crater the *payashē* had blown into the solid granite to escape her summoning circle.

As we tumbled down the rough side, Xever's blast screamed past us, turning everything red. An ear-shattering noise erupted.

Zylas and I slid to a stop at the bottom of the crater, his arms clamped around my torso, shielding me. He raised his head, his dimly glowing eyes meeting mine.

Xever was now the most powerful demon mage to ever exist, and it was just us. Just me and Zylas against a *payashē*'s enormous power. Somehow, Xever had bypassed the magic of the King's Vow and enslaved her without her consent—without any restrictions on how much of her magic he could access.

Zylas leaned down, touching his forehead to mine. "There is no *vh'renith* here."

Despite his words, I didn't feel despair or hopelessness in his thoughts. He'd only fought battles he was certain he could win—but no more. This time, he had no intention of backing down, regardless of the odds against us.

"Yes," I agreed, pressing both hands to his cheeks. "But sometimes we have to fight even when we're certain we'll lose."

He swung to his feet, pulling me with him. My heart hammered as my hand closed around his, squeezing hard.

Beyond the crater that hid us, crunching footsteps approached. Xever was coming.

I lifted my other hand. Crimson sparked across my fingers, and I used Zylas's dwindling power to create a six-foot-wide cantrip in front of us.

The footfalls grew louder. Xever's head appeared above the crater's edge, his cruel smile tinged with insanity.

Zylas's hand crushed mine.

"*Igniaris!*" I yelled.

The cantrip erupted into a roaring orange inferno. Zylas pulled me against his side—and leaped into the flames.

Heat blasted me for an instant before cold swept in. As he soared through the fire, Zylas drew the heat inside himself—recharging his depleted magic.

He landed on the steep crater wall and leaped again. We shot up, right past Xever, and Zylas slammed down on the flat plateau. My feet hit the rock—and I sprinted away from him.

My legs pumped as I sped past the portal. Chains jangled, my hand fumbling through the artifacts hanging around my neck.

Crimson exploded behind me, the force so strong it knocked me off my feet. I fell, hands and knees scraping across the ground. Another blast shook the earth. Xever was hurling wild bursts of raw magic, the explosions almost drowning out his ringing laughter.

Scrambling up, I wrenched a chain off my neck. Not an item I'd thought I'd use. Not an item I'd imagined might save us.

I stumbled to a stop and looked up into Nazhivēr's glowing red eyes. He hadn't moved, trapped by Xever's command, blood running from his wounds and trickling from the corner of his mouth.

"Help Zylas," I gasped. "Kill Xever. Then go home. Do you agree?"

I touched the amulet to his chest, and his eyes went wide as he felt the amulet's power—its ability to interrupt contract magic.

"Yes," he rasped.

Rising onto my tiptoes, I looped the chain over his head and horns. It dropped around his neck, and the Vh'alyir Amulet thumped against his bare chest.

Wings sweeping open and his arm snapping up, he grasped the amulet tightly. For the first time in twenty years, he was free from Xever's subjugation.

He shoved me out of his way and launched forward. I fell painfully as the Dh'irath demon charged at the blaze of crimson power that was Xever. Zylas darted in front of the demon mage, his own magic pitiful in comparison.

As Nazhivēr closed in, Xever extended both hands toward Zylas. Crimson exploded from his palms into another twisting beam.

With a lightning-fast leap, Nazhivēr grabbed Zylas and shot into the air, his torn wings pumping. Xever's blast screamed across the plateau and hit the trees at the far end. A thunderous boom, then the beam of light died away.

A ten-yard-wide and thirty-yard-deep swath of forest had been obliterated, centuries-old spruce trees reduced to splinters.

Nazhivēr dropped Zylas, who landed in a crouch, and the two demons faced Xever. They lifted their arms, and arching spell circles appeared.

Xever flung his arms out, unleashing another wild blast.

The bright flash blinded me, and as I flinched, a glint of reflected light caught my eye. Fifteen feet away, Saul's body lay with one arm stretched out. Silver bands ran up his wrist and disappeared under his jacket sleeve, each one engraved with abjuration designed to counter demon magic.

As another explosion detonated behind me, I raced to the sorcerer's body. Dropping to my knees, I wrenched a band over his cold hand. Then another, and another, shoving them onto my much thinner arm.

One more—one more—then a blast of magic threw me on top of the body. The earth shook.

Xever's mad laughter echoed across the plateau.

I leaped up, pushing the fifth band onto my arm, and ran toward the demon mage.

Alight with power, Xever hurled blast after blast at the two demons desperately trying to land an attack on him. They needed an opening. They needed a chance.

I ran closer—close enough to make myself a target.

Xever's head turned to me. He swung his arm in my direction, a sizzling ball of crimson power expanding from his palm.

It blasted toward me.

"*Ori tres!*" I screamed, flinging my arm up.

A wave of sparkling green light appeared in front of me. The blast hit it—and fizzled away to nothing. The negation spell.

I flung my arm sideways. "*Ori quattuor!*"

Indigo spikes flew everywhere, but my aim was wrong. They missed.

Xever threw his arms up—and the air crackled, sizzled, burned. Zylas and Nazhivēr, who'd been rushing in behind him, drew up short—then backpedaled away. Zylas's dread pierced me.

Xever's entire body blazed with glowing veins—and howling magic exploded out of him in every direction, an expanding ring of death tearing toward me, Zylas, and Nazhivēr.

"*Ori duo!*"

At my desperate cry, the air in front of me rippled. The brunt of the oncoming tsunami rebounded—but the rest of the wave kept coming. Crimson power hit me, and everything turned to pain. I flew backward and crashed down, rolling, tumbling.

Vaguely, I realized I wasn't moving anymore. My eyes blinked slowly. A pale morning sky stretched overhead, streaked with white clouds.

Scuffing footsteps. Shimmering crimson.

Xever appeared, standing over me. He smiled. "Can you feel it, Robin? That he's gone?"

I stared up at him, my chest heaving with pained breaths.

"Compared to a *payashē*, male demons are weak." His red eyes glowed like bubbling magma, roiling with madness. "See for yourself."

He waved to my left. I rocked my head to the side and peered across the crumbling plateau.

Fissures zigzagged the granite, hunks of debris scattered over it. Among the rubble, an unmoving form was sprawled. Zylas, crumpled facedown. A short way beyond him, Nazhivēr lay in a heap, one wing twisted into a caricature of its normal elegance.

"Weak," Xever repeated, drawing my attention back to him. "Just like you."

I watched that strange roiling in his crimson eyes—and realized it wasn't madness. It was the *payashē* trapped inside him, raging desperately against her flesh-and-soul prison. Raging against the human who was stealing her power.

"I am the Red King," he whispered feverishly, lifting his hand toward me as power formed a crackling orb beneath his palm. "The most powerful mythic in history."

"You," I said hoarsely, "are a monster. *Ori novem!*"

Cool magic tingled against my palm, and I thrust my arm up. The long purple harpoon that Saul had used against Zylas flashed as I shoved it into Xever's gut.

He gasped, reeling back.

"*Daimon hesychaze!*"

My infernus vibrated against my chest. A streak of power hit it, then bounced out, solidifying.

Zylas's claws slashed, and Xever had no chance to unleash his magic. A swift strike, a spray of blood, a crunch of bone—and the most powerful mythic in history fell to the ground, limbs spasming.

I pushed up onto my elbows, forcing myself to watch as the summoner writhed. As his breaths gurgled from his torn throat. As his eyes bulged with terror and enraged denial. As his limbs stilled and the air wheezed from his lungs.

Sorrow for the slain *payashē* flickered through me. At least she'd died quickly instead of spending years as Xever's slave.

He was dead, and my parents were avenged. I expected to feel more than quiet, grief-tinged relief, but his death couldn't bring my parents back.

"Robin."

Zylas dropped to his knees and pulled me to his chest. A cool shiver of his magic ran over me as he checked my injuries—heedless of the blood dripping from his torn clothes.

Uneven footsteps plodded heavily over stone. Zylas tensed, then pushed to his feet, lifting me with him. Together, we turned to face Nazhivēr.

The Dh'irath demon halted a few long steps away. He lightly touched the Vh'alyir Amulet hanging around his neck, then lifted it off and held it out.

Zylas pulled it from the demon's grasp, his fist clenched tightly around the chain. Neither demon spoke.

A deep, thundering *crack* vibrated through the ground beneath our feet. All three of us looked across the plateau—at the fissures and fractures webbing the massive slab of granite that formed the hilltop.

Another *crack* rang out like a gunshot. A grinding sound as stone shifted.

Nazhivēr whirled on his heel, broken wings flaring, and charged away from us. Zylas snatched me around the waist and launched after the Dh'irath demon, and for a terrifying second, I wondered what we were fleeing.

Then I saw the pink glow ahead and realized we weren't running away from something. We were running *toward* the portal.

The plateau was damaged. The rock was shifting—and all it would take was one crack in the array to destroy the portal.

Power sizzled through us as Zylas ran onto the glowing array. The portal loomed ahead, a dark circle fifteen feet across. The alien sky on the other side had lightened to murky cobalt.

Nazhivēr didn't slow, didn't hesitate. He reached the edge and dove headfirst into the vision of a foreign sky. His body dropped through and disappeared.

Zylas skidded to a halt a step from the portal. I clutched his arm, anguish ripping through my chest.

His gaze swung from the portal to me. "Do you remember what to do?"

"Yes," I gasped, choking on the grief-stricken denials building in my throat. I scrabbled at my pocket, unzipping it, and pulled out an alchemic marker. The node of the array that I needed to alter was only a few feet away.

Another grinding crack shuddered through the plateau.

He looped the amulet chain over my head. "*Amavrah.*"

"Zylas." I pressed my trembling hands to his face. "I love you. I'll never forget you."

His warm hand caught the back of my neck, and he touched his forehead to mine.

Then he pulled away, his touch disappearing, and stepped to the circle's edge. His legs coiled, tail lashing.

He didn't look back as he plunged into *Ahlēavah*'s deep blue sky.

◆ ZYLAS ◆

HOME. Scents of sand. Recent rain. Night-cool rock.

Directions spin and reverse as I fall, then ground appears beneath me. My hands press into the red sand. Dig in my fingers, feel the rough grains. Inhale. Taste it. Home.

Look up, senses reaching out. Nazhivēr is close. Just ahead, on his knees, head bowed. Bleeding, wounded, wings shattered. Difficult to heal. Can he do it?

Doesn't matter. Don't care.

Push to my feet. Pain. Blood. Wounds are bad but won't kill me.

Clear sky above, dark blue that's growing lighter. Soft orange on the horizon, shining through the *Ahlēvīsh* that surround me, jutting high above my head. Their power calls to me. *Kish lēvh.* Become spirit. Can hide in them and recover.

Hide, fight, hide, fight. That is my world. That is my life in this world.

Turn around. The circle, the portal. Inside it, a soft sky and pale light. Like Zh'rēil's vision, the circle sits upon a destroyed *Ahlēvīsh*. Power stolen, transformed, turned into something new.

On the other side, she is there. Soft and warm. Beautiful, gentle, foolish, safe. She is there, alone.

She's begun the magic. Can feel it. Can feel her.

Drop to my knees in the cool sand. Call on my magic and create the spell from the Vh'alyir Amulet.

It appears. A circle around the portal, surrounded by webbed lines. Runes describe the bridge between worlds, between *Ahlēa* and human magic. More runes to unmake it.

Concentrate. Must be perfect. No mistakes. My House created this, and now I will break it. Time to change *Ahlēavah*. Time to end the magic so my world can heal.

The *payapis* would maybe be impressed. Should I find her again, tell her what I did? What I learned? What I lost?

Maybe.

Concentrate. Press hands into the sand. Jaw tight. Ignore pain. Ignore the others drawing near. They sensed us, and now they come to see who has returned. The new *Ivaknen*.

I am *Ivaknen*.

It is a strange thought.

On the other side, she has begun her chant. Her voice is distant. Quiet. Almost can't hear, even though she's so close. So far. Out of reach.

The sky brightens. Beyond the *Ahlēvīsh* where jagged rocks rise, orange stains the blue.

Footsteps coming closer. They stop. Nazhivēr watches me. "What are you doing?"

Hnn. Too used to human language. His words sound strange now.

"I am ending this."

"Ending what?"

Her voice rises, reaching my ears through the portal. Pain in each sound. The demonic words I helped her learn tremble, but she continues. The portal shimmers. Power builds, thickens.

"I learned how humans summon us. I will stop it now. Forever."

Nazhivēr is silent.

Breathe. Focus. It is time.

My voice joins hers, loud in my ears. Strong words. Steady. They flow out of me, memorized from the amulet. Do not understand them all. Zh'rēil was old, smart, experienced. He knew magic I don't. He created magic I will never learn.

Others are here now. Scents of many Houses. This place is close to the center of *Ahlēavah.* Close to the *Naventis.* Only there do Houses often cross paths.

Ignore them. Concentrate.

"Stay back!"

Nazhivēr's sharp command. The others halt. Questions. Demands. Anger. They have seen the portal. They want to destroy it.

"Stay back!" Nazhivēr snarls. "He is breaking the human magic that summons us!"

Quiet falls except for my voice. Not much longer now. Words rush from my lips. Almost there.

A shudder ripples across the portal, coming from the other side. Xever damaged the ground and it is breaking. No time left. On the human side, her voice rises as she calls out the final words.

Now it is mine to finish.

The sky brightens as I flood the spell beneath my hands with power. All my power. All I have left. Pour it into the spell. Everything. Crimson blazes, burns. The portal ripples.

"*Evashvā vīsh!*" I roar in triumph, in despair.

Red light blazes off the spell. The same light rushes across the blue sky within the portal. And the same light fills the *Ahlēvīsh* all around me. A deep boom of magic too low to hear thuds in my ears.

The red glow dies. Silence sweeps in.

And the sun appears.

Golden rays streak across the red sand and fall on my skin. Bright and gentle and warm. *Vayanin.*

The portal darkens. Shrinks. It is closing, the outer edge rushing inward, the circle of human sky turning to crystal.

Vayanin.

The scent of home. The sand under my feet. The life-bringing sun. *Ahlēavah.* My world.

I do not want it.

I want her.

The portal is shrinking. The magic is almost gone. Seconds. Less than seconds. No time to move, to jump, to dive into the vanishing circle of sky.

But I can feel it. Like an *Ahlēvīsh* but not.

The infernus.

We are still bound.

Kish lēvh. Become spirit.

In an instant, my body softens into heat and light, and I leap toward the fading call as the portal disappears.

The strange emptiness of the infernus meets me. I leap out again, finding the ground. My body reforms, hard stone under my feet. Bright. The sun in my eyes, too sharp. Squint. Inhale.

Scents of the human world. Their rocks, their dirt, their trees.

And *her* scent. Robin. Fills my nose, sweet and alluring and layered with pain.

Look down. She is there, kneeling, hunched, bent under her sorrow. Her face is turned up to mine, her eyes wide. Eyes the color of the sky. Wetness marks her cheeks. Tears. She is weeping.

Amalia is beside her, dirty and injured, holding Robin's shoulder. She stares too.

Sink to my knees, armor striking the ground with a sharp noise that echoes across the rocky terrain.

"*Amavrah.*"

My chosen.

She is trembling. Her hand reaches out but she does not touch me. "Zylas?"

She said my name wrong. Three sounds, not two. Sometimes she forgets.

Reach for her. Take her. Pull her to me, arms around her, her small, breakable body safe if I hold her. She trembles more.

"Zylas, you—you came back. You—" She looks past me at the portal.

Do not need to look to know it's gone. Scents of *Ahlēavah* have already faded.

Her small hands grip my shoulders. Tears shine in her eyes, her face contorted. "Zylas, how will you go home?"

Home. The place I have always known, always hated. Always the weakest, always hiding, always fighting. I wanted more than what I could see in front of me. The *payapis* realized that. She taught me how I could be more, how I could *have* more.

And I finally found it—here.

"It does not matter," I tell Robin, my fear of a future I never wanted slipping away. "Because I want to be with you."

EPILOGUE

MY PEN SCRIBBLED across the page, scrawling several quick lines before I closed the book. The leather cover shone under the yellow glow of the desk lamp, and I ran my fingers across it.

Last April, six weeks after Xever's death, Amalia and Uncle Jack had accompanied me to the cemetery where my parents were buried. On the first anniversary of their passing, we'd sat together at their graves and talked. Really talked—about the past, the present, and the future.

As we'd left, Amalia had presented me with this book: my first grimoire.

"You're a proper sorceress now," she'd said. "You can't uncreate an entire magic class and *not* have a grimoire."

Smiling at the memory, I leaned over and tucked the grimoire into the large backpack beside me, then rifled through its contents, ensuring I'd packed everything. My grimoire traveled with me, but the Athanas grimoire and its deadly secrets were safely stored at home, where I'd resume copying and translating it when I returned.

With a loud chime, my cell phone lit up with an incoming video call. I tapped the screen and Amalia's face filled it. Her hair was twisted into a messy bun, her fluffy housecoat wrapped around her.

"Morning," she said—then clapped her hand over her mouth to hide a yawn. "Ugh, sorry."

"It's okay," I replied with a laugh. "Thanks for staying up late for me."

"Didn't want to miss you." She rubbed her eyes. "It's super early for you, isn't it?"

"Five-thirty a.m., yeah, but I'm used to it."

She muttered something about torture, then said more loudly, "So you're heading out right away?"

"Yep, I'm all packed up." I leaned back in my wooden chair. "The big party is this afternoon, right?"

She nodded. "Should be a riot. Everyone at the guild's been whispering about it for weeks. I'm honestly surprised they haven't blown the surprise."

That sounded about right. The Crow and Hammer was terrible at keeping secrets, at least among its members.

"Tell everyone I say hi," I said. "And don't be late."

She rolled her eyes. "I won't be late."

"You were so late to the last guild meeting that it was over by the time you got there."

"I was focused on work! And Darius was completely unfair about it, too. He's the one who ordered ten full sets of hex gear for the guild. *And* he bragged about me to the Pandora Knights GM, who wants a new prototype."

I grinned. "So business is booming?"

"At this rate, I'll need to hire an assistant." She squinted at me. "Unless you're planning to stick around for more than a few weeks after this trip?"

"Nope," I said brightly.

She sighed. "You'll get tired of traveling eventually."

Not likely. I glanced at the open door behind me, then back at my phone. "How's Uncle Jack?"

Flopping back against the sofa behind her, she groaned. "He's gonna get himself killed."

My eyes widened. "What do you mean?"

"He went and—ah!"

The video spun wildly as she almost dropped her phone. She righted it, revealing Socks standing on her lap, ears perked toward the device.

"Hello, Socks," I cooed.

Her green eyes stared unblinkingly into the camera as though chiding me for being gone so long—or chiding me for taking her favorite demon away.

"What did Uncle Jack do?" I prompted anxiously.

"The MPD hired him."

"*What?*"

"Yeah, as a special consultant for all the new Demonica crap." Amalia rubbed Socks's ears. "It leaked out that no one can summon demons anymore, and shit's getting weird."

"They're only figuring it out *now*? It's been four months."

"Yeah, but summoners are cagey, you know? None of them wanted to admit they'd lost their touch. They were all feeling out their competitors and making excuses to their clients and stuff. It took a while for everyone to catch on that summoning was 'broken' for all of them."

"Hm. What's that got to do with Uncle Jack, though?"

"Summoners are getting desperate, so they've started experimenting and combining summoning rituals with other magic, that sort of thing. Dad is helping the MPD crack down on it before it gets out of control."

"Huh."

"Yeah. Who knew he'd ever put his shady talents to good use. He figures it'll all die down in a year or so. Just gotta wait for them to give up." She smirked. "We could speed up the process by telling MagiPol that summoning is done for good, but Darius says they'll figure it out on their own and he doesn't want to draw attention to you. Especially after … everything."

"Everything" being the charges of illegal Demonica activity and accusations of an illegal contract. But Zylas's disguise had paid off. In the battle for the Crow and Hammer, dozens of witnesses had seen me—but not my demon. Unable to confirm I'd done anything illegal, the MPD had dropped the charges against us.

"I'd rather not have any more MPD attention," I agreed. "Being responsible for the end of Demonica isn't something I want on my permanent record."

"Right? And speaking of the end of Demonica, Dad has this theory that once contractors realize they can't replace their demons, they'll be way more careful with them. Which means more demons will outlive their contractors and get to go home."

"That would be good. It's crazy to think that eventually there will be no more demon contractors."

"Yeah, I know what you mean." She ruffled Socks's fur as the near full-grown cat sprawled across her lap. "Good thing that's not the family business anymore, right?"

Chuckling, I glanced again at the door, gauging the level of light. "I should get going."

"Yeah, me too. I need some sleep before I pick up my new fabric order. It came in yesterday."

New fabric? That pretty much guaranteed Amalia would get absorbed in sewing and be late for the party.

"You'll call me next week?" she asked.

"As soon as I'm back in cell phone range."

She grimaced worriedly. "I can't believe you're just going to wander off into a jungle for a week. That's insane."

"We aren't *wandering*. We're going to see Angel Falls." I arched my eyebrows. "The tallest waterfall in the world, remember?"

"How impressive is a waterfall, really? Is it worth all that time picking leeches off your ankles?"

"I have anti-leech socks. And yes, it'll be worth it."

"You gonna climb one of those tipis?"

"Tepuis," I corrected.

"Yeah, those tabletop mountain things you were telling me about."

I rolled my eyes. "I'll let you know next week. Talk to you later."

"In a week," she agreed. "Oh, and don't forget to email Zora back. She said Drew and Venus are driving her crazy asking when you'll be home so you can all get together."

"I already emailed her. They just want me to bring Zylas over so they can interrogate him."

"Of course they do," she said airily. "Not every day you can have a conversation with a demon."

I snorted. "That wasn't your attitude when *you* first found out Zylas could talk."

She waved my remark off. "All right, get going. And say hi to the horned asshole for me."

I ended the call and tucked my phone in the waterproof pouch in my backpack. Then I swept the final item to be packed off the desk and hurried through the open door.

A covered lanai waited, thin log columns supporting the roof. Beyond the railing, a handful of trees with twisted trunks and broad canopies dotted the lush green grass before giving way to the wide, smooth surface of the Rio Carrao. On its far side, silhouetted against the rising sun, tepuis rose from the earth, wispy clouds clinging to their flat tops.

A woven hammock stretched between two columns, a figure reclined in it as golden beams of morning light fell across him. A long, thin tail hung over the hammock's side, the barbed end twitching lazily.

My bare feet padded across the stone tiles, a smile stretching my cheeks.

Zylas tipped his head back to bring me into view, his crimson eyes glowing faintly and the sunrise lighting one side of his face. My smile widened into a grin as I swept over—and swung into the hammock with him.

His arm came around me as I settled against his side and opened the large photography book. *His* photography book, each page featuring a different landscape.

And we were going to see them all.

We'd started with the mountain in Oregon, the one I'd promised he could climb. Taped to that page in the book was our photo of the same spot. I was the only one in it—demons, it turned out, were too magical to photograph properly—but Zylas had snapped the photo with my camera and he was just as present as I was, even if he wasn't visible.

A handful of other photos were taped to their respective pages, and I had piles of notes in my grimoire/journal about where we'd go next.

Uncle Jack had finally released my inheritance to me, and he'd taught me how to invest my money—*legally* invest it. I hadn't wanted to hear about his more "creative" ventures. Between my parents' life insurance, the sale of my childhood home, and the MPD bonus I'd gotten for slaying Tahēsh, I was set for a long time.

Which was good, because I didn't want to worry about employment. Zylas and I had far too many places to see—including today's destination.

I held up the landscape book. At the bottom of the page, small text read, "Salto Ángel, Venezuela."

"Are you ready for this one?"

"*Hnn.*" He canted his head. "It is tall. Will we climb it?"

I looked from him to the photo and back again. "It's thirty-two hundred feet, Zylas. I know we did some climbing in Oregon, but this is a sheer cliff. It's too high."

"Too high," he scoffed. "Why only look when you can climb, *na?*"

Squinting at him, I recognized the stubborn gleam in his eyes. Well, at least I had a twenty-mile walk through a jungle to talk him out of the idea.

I snapped the book closed. "Do you want to go over the map again?"

"I remember the map." He tugged the book out of my hands. "Do not worry, *amavrah*. It will be fun."

"Not if it involves climbing a three-thousand-foot cliff," I muttered.

He set the book on the tile floor beside the hammock. "You are packed?"

"Yep. We can head out whenever you're ready."

He turned his gaze toward the golden horizon and the drifting clouds. "Not yet."

I settled in beside him, watching shades of gold wash across the horizon. His arm was snug around me, the hammock swaying in a gentle breeze that held the humidity at bay.

Mornings like these were the reason I got up so early. No matter where we were, Zylas wanted to be outside to watch the sunrise—preferably with me beside him.

As the sun cleared the flat tepuis, he turned to me. He nuzzled my throat, and when I tilted my head to give him better access, his teeth grazed across the spot where my neck and shoulder joined.

Slow heat uncoiled inside me, anticipation tingling across my nerves.

He nipped and nuzzled up and down my throat, his other hand sliding over my side and teasing my breasts through my thin shirt. As my breathing quickened from his touches, he rolled off the hammock, sweeping me with him, and carried me back into our room.

Moments later, we were in bed and he was sliding my clothes off.

Sometimes it was like this—slow, leisurely, passionate. He explored every inch of me as though for the first time, his hands and mouth insatiable.

Other times it was completely different. It was like our first—hard, fast, aggressively dominating. He would pin my arms, hold my hips, drive deep inside me over and over until he sent me plunging over the edge.

And often, it was one immediately followed by the other, because it turned out that demons were a bit different from human males. Finishing didn't mean *finishing*. He was always ready for more, and I inevitably tired out before he did.

This morning, it was slow and breathtaking and head-spinning. Afterward, we quickly showered, redressed, and added the photography book to my backpack.

Alone, I stopped in the lobby to check out, then crossed the manicured lawn to a path near the riverbank.

Waiting for me with my backpack, Zylas stood in the sun, wearing black cargo pants and a loose long-sleeved shirt in a vibrant scarlet that dimmed the red tones in his skin. He'd given up his armor after our first trip, opting for comfort instead, and the clothes clung to his flawless physique in distracting ways.

A ballcap covered his horns and a pair of sunglasses hid his eyes. His tail was looped around his waist, and the only odd thing about his appearance was his bare feet. He hated shoes.

As I approached, he turned away from the river and grinned, flashing his pointed canines. Laughing, I broke into a run to join him.

The Venezuelan rainforest was dense and wild, with no roads to follow. Leaving the tiny town that was the last of civilization for hundreds of miles, we ventured into the jungle, using the wide river as our guide.

Trees towered around us, draped in vines, and rotting leaf litter and fallen trees covered the forest floor. I exclaimed over leaves the size of my torso, tiny bright flowers that looked like pursed lips, and a moth with giant fuzzy wings that spanned both my hands. Zylas rapped on the back of a very displeased giant armadillo, fascinated by its armored body, and spent over an hour watching an anteater, baffled by its long tongue. Whenever I got tired of walking, he carried me, the jungle heat providing him with endless endurance.

At night, we strung a hammock between the trees and I slept in his arms, a mosquito net draped over us—not that *he* needed it. Insects couldn't pierce his tough demon skin.

The next morning, we stalked a jaguar through the trees, climbed into the canopy to join a flock of bewildered toucans, and had a staring contest with a very large snake—though the last one hadn't been on purpose.

By nightfall, I could hear the distant roar of falling water. We slept again in the hammock, and I dined on the dry food I'd packed. I was a light eater and with only my mouth to feed, we didn't need much.

Sunrise filtered through the trees as we set out again, navigating by the roar of the falls. The forest was dense, hiding the view ahead—then, between one step and the next, we broke free of the rainforest.

And there it was.

Standing beside Zylas, I stared up at the most majestic sight I'd ever laid eyes upon.

The tepui rose over three thousand feet, its vertical sides a mixture of dull brown and bright sienna rock. Angel Falls spilled off the top, plunging so far that the water drifted away before reaching the bottom, a cloud of fog clinging to the mountain's base.

My fingers tightened around his. No photo could do this sight justice. No image could convey the size, the scale, the humid heat of the jungle, the roaring water, the buzz of birds and insects, the scent of life and rot, the tang of water caught on the faint breeze.

Words on a page or photos in a book—before Zylas, that was all I'd known. And, naïve as I was, I'd thought that was enough.

I could never have imagined a moment like this. A year ago, the idea that I would spend three days hiking through a jungle to see the world's tallest waterfall would've been preposterous. My timid, nonconfrontational, unambitious self would've laughed at the idea, then gone right back to the book she was reading.

I loved reading, loved knowledge, loved books. But books were complements to real life, not a replacement. And without Zylas, I might never have realized that.

Beside me, he stared wide-eyed at the towering mountain and rushing water. Was there anything remotely like this in his world? Were there majestic landscapes he'd never seen?

I faced him, my head tilted back. "Zylas?"

It took him a moment to wrench his stare off the waterfall. "*Hnn?*"

"Was it worth it?"

His stunned-by-the-beauty-of-nature expression sharpened with new focus, and his eyes skimmed across my face—then he smiled, that soft, pleased smile that made me melt inside.

"In my world, there is darkness and cold and fear. Maybe I will return someday, and I will be *Ivaknen* and raise sons and tell the *payapis* that I changed *Ahlēavah*."

My gaze dropped to his chest where, beneath his shirt, the Vh'alyir Amulet lay, imbued with instructions for creating a portal to his world.

"But before I return to those cold nights," he said, "I will spend every sunrise with you. There is nothing better than this. If I never return, it does not matter."

A strange, tight heat gripped my chest.

"You worry about what I lost?" His wolfish grin flashed. "*Amavrah*, I am getting everything I want."

Everything he wanted. A future he wanted. I'd offered him a lifetime with me—and he'd chosen it.

I stretched my arms up and he swept me into him, holding me tight.

"You're right," I said, breathless with amazement at the endless tomorrows awaiting us. "I worry too much."

"You do."

"I'm just *zh'ūltis*, I guess."

His husky laugh vibrated through me. "If you were *ahktallis*, you would not have come here."

My eyes narrowed. "What do you mean?"

Still holding me, he faced the waterfall. "We are going to climb it."

"No, we're not."

"We are. It will be fun."

"Whatever you think 'fun' means, you're wrong."

He grinned, scooped my feet off the ground, and launched toward the towering mountain, ignoring my protests the whole way.

Many hours later, sitting beside Zylas with the roar of the falls filling my ears, the frothing water plunging over the cliff right mere feet away and miles upon miles of rainforest stretching before us, bathed in the sunset's golden light, I had to admit he was right.

The climb had been fun—terrifying, but fun. And the terror had been well worth this indescribable view.

Leaning my head on his shoulder, I smiled into the darkening sky, ready for our next sunrise together and whatever it would bring.

ACKNOWLEDGEMENTS

The first person I must thank, without whom the Guild Codex world would be vastly different (and not nearly as awesome) is my husband, Jacob. He's been my sounding board from day one, a creative kickstart any time I got stuck, the voice of reason when I got crazy (bad) ideas, the first reader and then the final reader of every book before publication, and my rock whenever things got hard and the deadlines got bad and I got exhausted. Thank you.

Thank you to Elizabeth, my amazing editor, whose ability to keep on schedule simultaneously leaves me in awe and ensures I never screw up my own deadlines too badly (because I never want to release a book that hasn't passed through your hands first).

Thank you to Breanna, for dropping everything on far too many weekends to read each book and provide invaluable feedback.

Thank you to Amber, for also dropping everything when I needed you and for catching the little (and not so little) things.

Thank you to Jax, for your support, feedback, and fantastic character essays.

Thank you to Erich Merkel, master of Latin and Ancient Greek, who freely offered his time and expertise on every book and never got fed up with my "by the way, I need this tomorrow, I'm so sorry, thank you thank you thank you" emails. The Guild Codex world wouldn't be nearly as cool without your input.

Thank you to Cris Dukehart, who not only brought Tori, Robin, and the entire Guild Codex gang to life with her amazing narration, but also showed more passion and dedication for the series than I ever could've asked of a narrator.

Thank you to Kara and the team at Tantor, for bringing Cris on board and making the audiobooks happen, no matter the obstacles.

Thank you to Rob Jacobsen, for jumping onto the Guild Codex ship without a second thought, for unreservedly immersing yourself in my particular crazy, and for contributing your astonishing imagination to this world.

Thank you to Uma, for sharing so much to help bring Izzah to life and add such a fun, badass character to the series.

Thank you to Liz and Christina, for contributing your exceptional medical knowledge and experience so I could horribly wound my characters in the most realistic ways possible.

Thank you to Ashleigh, for allowing me to see my characters in a way I'd never imagined.

Thank you to Erich Orris of Fudo Forge, who enabled me to check a box on my author bucket list that I didn't know existed until his first email landed in my inbox. Sharpie is breathtaking!

Thank you to my author besties, for keeping me sane, commiserating, congratulating, and making me laugh when I most need it.

An extra special thank you to my ARC Team, for your enthusiasm, support, and dedication to making every release the best it can be. I don't know what I'd do without you.

And lastly, a huge thank you to my readers. Thank you for joining me on this wild ride, for reviewing and recommending the series, for cheering on each release, and for loving the Guild Codex crew as much as I do. I hope you'll join me for the next romp in their world.

ABOUT THE AUTHOR

Annette Marie is the author of YA urban fantasy series *Steel & Stone*, its prequel trilogy *Spell Weaver*, and romantic fantasy trilogy *Red Winter*.

Her first love is fantasy, but fast-paced adventures, bold heroines, and tantalizing forbidden romances are her guilty pleasures. She proudly admits she has a thing for dragons, and her editor has politely inquired as to whether she intends to include them in every book.

Annette lives in the frozen winter wasteland of Alberta, Canada (okay, it's not quite that bad) and shares her life with her husband and their furry minion of darkness—sorry, cat—Caesar. When not writing, she can be found elbow-deep in one art project or another while blissfully ignoring all adult responsibilities.

www.annettemarie.ca

THE
GUILD CODEX
SPELLBOUND

Meet Tori. She's feisty. She's broke. She has a bit of an issue with running her mouth off. And she just landed a job at the local magic guild. Problem is, she's also 100% human. Oops.

Welcome to the Crow and Hammer.

THE
GUILD CODEX
WARPED

The MPD has three roles: keep magic hidden, keep mythics under control, and don't screw up the first two.

Kit Morris is the wrong guy for the job on all counts—but for better or worse, this mind-warping psychic is the MPD's newest and most unlikely agent.

DISCOVER MORE BOOKS AT
www.guildcodex.ca

THE
GUILD CODEX
UNVEILED

Powerful druid.
Deadly alchemist.
Notorious rogue.

The Crystal Druid's identity has been unveiled—and
now his true story begins.

DISCOVER MORE BOOKS AT
www.guildcodex.ca

STEEL & STONE

When everyone wants you dead, good help is hard to find.

The first rule for an apprentice Consul is *don't trust daemons*. But when Piper is framed for the theft of the deadly Sahar Stone, she ends up with two troublesome daemons as her only allies: Lyre, a hotter-than-hell incubus who isn't as harmless as he seems, and Ash, a draconian mercenary with a seriously bad reputation. Trusting them might be her biggest mistake yet.

SPELL WEAVER

The only thing more dangerous than the denizens of the Underworld ... is stealing from them.

As a daemon living in exile among humans, Clio has picked up some unique skills. But pilfering magic from the Underworld's deadliest spell weavers? Not so much. Unfortunately, that's exactly what she has to do to earn a ticket home.

GET THE COMPLETE TRILOGY
www.annettemarie.ca/spellweaver

A destiny written by the gods. A fate forged by lies.

If Emi is sure of anything, it's that *kami*—the gods—are good, and *yokai*—the earth spirits—are evil. But when she saves the life of a fox shapeshifter, the truths of her world start to crumble. And the treachery of the gods runs deep.

This stunning trilogy features 30 full-page illustrations.

Made in the USA
Las Vegas, NV
20 September 2021